I0831528

Anywhere

Mayberry University Series

Kristina Welch

CONTENTS

Published by The Unbending Books, an imprint of The Unbending LLC.

Cover Design by Kristina Welch

With editorial contributions from Dori Harrell

 Created with Vellum

For Blair, my bold, brilliant, beautiful girl,
Remember who you are—daughter of the one true King. And keep living in technicolor, even when the world settles for grayscale.

And for Granny and Paps,
I carved The Farm into this story—gave it to another family—so I could hold onto it. But the magic was always because of y'all.

CONTENT NOTE

This story is clean and closed-door (no language, nothing explicit), but it's also real. Sparks and swoons? Yes. Redemption? Always. And also moments of depression and dating messiness that don't fit in a tidy box.

No eggshells here, friends. I've lived some of this. I know what it's like to love Jesus and still end up in a dark fog. Or the quicksand of my own choices. Whether or not that's familiar to you, I hope this story meets you with honesty, care, and hands pointing straight to the God who's too good to leave us in the lies—the One who calls us His.

Warmly,
Kristina

CHAPTER ONE

Sophie

Hugs haven't been a thing between us, but when I get there, I'm risking it. It's been two weeks, and I miss my friend.

Pasadena may be home on paper, but that penthouse with Mom is the exact opposite of campus with him. There, the yelling is over, but the oppressive quiet is permanent. She said exactly one positive thing to me over break—that the Chanel sweater she bought me for Christmas would look pretty on me. I won't be reliving that over spring break. I'd sooner subject myself to Kit's perfect little home sweet home.

His mini-smile comes into focus as I approach. It's not the same on FaceTime. I can almost smell his lumberjack scent from here. Hands in his pockets, back on his heels, waiting next to my favorite spot in my dorm's parking lot. I squeal into it, throw my Jeep into park, and nearly rip off the door. Jumping down, I ... screech to a halt. Some girl has stopped to chat with him. Red hair, delicate curves, short skirt. Right there on the sidewalk in front of my parking spot.

Already out of the Jeep, I 180 to the back to feign a fascination with my suitcase. Do the zippers work? Mm-hm. I can, in fact, access my belongings. I would trade every last one if she'd kindly remove her hand from his arm.

"What are you doing tonight?" she asks. Major eye contact, inching closer. Innocent eyes and a naughty mouth.

She could teach a master class on flirting with nonverbals. I have plenty to learn but no stomach for this lesson. I'm sure it would be great fun to watch her on a screen with my suitemates and a bag of tortilla chips. And—oh yeah—a different mark.

"Could you help me with my laptop?" she asks. "I know how smart you are. And handy."

Oh, verbals too. Cool, cool. He would have gone out with her anyway, but she phrased it like a favor, so now his plans tonight are set in stone.

"And helpful," she continues.

Suitcase, yep. Backpack. Some jackets I left in here a million years ago. Paper bowls, water bottles, more crumbs than make any sense ... I should really clean this out. Probably won't.

"I'll text you later, 'kay?" he says.

When I risk a glance around the passenger headrest to check on the happy couple through the windshield, she notices—yikes!—and sends me side-eye. I hop to pull my backpack out, like I'm way too busy to be spying, but I yank too hard and fall on my butt.

I let out a sigh as I wipe off my jeans. Wow. And the Klutz Award goes to ... me. I'd like to thank my parents, my severe inferiority to the girl in the skirt, and the Texas-sized guilt for my crush on the guy in plaid.

Shrug into one of the jackets, slide it off. It might be January, but my burning face is acting as a nice space heater at the moment.

I smooth my hair and straighten my shirt. In any other situation, I would prance over and make friends with Pretty Redhead. I bet she's fun when she's not hitting on this dude completely out of the blue on the first day back to campus. I wouldn't mind borrowing her boots either—boots that are standing obnoxiously close to the guy who was waiting for me. But I won't be going near her right now. I can only imagine us standing side by side for comparison, as if he has a rose in hand. *Which will he choose?* the narrator asks. Oof, the quickest choice in the history of reality romance shows. No rose for you, Blondie.

I'll stay back here with the luggage, thanks. I'm not a masochist.

Is Leo back yet? If he were, I'd know. He's learned to give me space, but he never leaves me guessing. No Open Dorms tonight, but we could do a field trip. Bowling? I'll text some friends, see who's in. Then suite movie night. Unless they'd be down to go to the lake again. I push the zipper around my suitcase, calculating the timing. Kit will be stocked up on sleep after break. The stars out there ...

A yelp escapes when my side is tickled, and I hit my head on Austin's hand. He had it braced along the edge of the Jeep, ready for my Tigger jump.

"Whatcha doin' back here?" That playful voice.

"Nothing! Something! Hi."

Redhead has vanished.

"Hey, Soph. C'mon." He tilts his head toward Saga. "Let's get you some dinner." He pauses with a hand on the tailgate. "Safe to say you're gonna leave your suitcase in here for a couple weeks?"

I grin. "You know ... in the event of a zombie apocalypse, I'll be really glad to have a few changes of clothes ready to go."

"Remind me to throw some things in there too. I don't wanna miss you fighting off a zombie."

"Don't blame you. Last semester I took—"

"Karate," he says with me, chuckling. "Oh, I remember. But I don't think you'll need it. Give you ten minutes and you'll have them committing to a vegetarian lifestyle and joining you for a nice night of laser tag." He throws my backpack over his shoulder and closes the door.

Ooh, laser tag. "Whatever. I'm super intimidating. Those zombies will turn vegetarian because of the terror I inflict."

I reach to tickle his side, and his giant hand gently grabs my wrist. "Nice try." Those blue-gray eyes smile at me as my blissful wrist calls a *bye, I'm going with him!*

I reach for a bear hug—just a friend hug—but he sidesteps with a practiced spin.

Right. Barely-there side hug it is.

"I missed you," he murmurs.

Yeah.

It's like this.

CHAPTER TWO

Sophie

That night Leo's jacket smells like popcorn. I pull it tighter to keep out the chill and find a box of Nerds in the pocket. He nods easily, so I tear them open. The night sky is celebrating our first night back on campus with a rare lack of clouds. Austin would want to plop down right here and watch the stars—

I bat the thought away.

Rather than meeting up, Leo left his scooter on Flooders so he could walk beside me on his own two legs. He stuffs his goose-bumped arms into his pockets, framing today's punny shirt: an orange staring at a glass of orange juice saying, *Mom?*

With a chuckle, I tug the hem of his shirt. "I like this one. It's too dark for your personality—oddly adorable."

His nervous smile draws me in like the first time I talked to him on Flooders. After like three months together, he still gets tongue tied. He still stares when he thinks I'm not looking.

I grin back. "So, I bet your Great Danes loved having you home."

His eyes soften, almost reverent, as he brushes the edge of my sleeve.

But a for-sale sign catches my eye outside Davidson Hall. Spin a slow 360. One outside Turner Hall too. A phone number is handwritten in Sharpie at the bottom of each. "Leo, look."

"Yeah, there's one at Albert too."

"Whose number is on there? We should text it."

"Uh, not sure."

For now, I snap a picture. I'll ask Austin. He'll know the extent of the prank and who's pulling it. He'll probably know whose number that is. I bet it's already in his phone—

I straighten. No Austin. I'm with Leo.

Okay. Yes. Dating a guy who barely scrapes into second place in my heart might be a crime against basic human decency. A war crime, even. But Leo is exactly the kind of guy I should like. What am I supposed to do? Sit back and watch Austin casually date his way through the entire campus? I refuse to live out the lyrics of a tragic Taylor Swift song. If I'm going to survive this pathetic, messy, unrequited crush on my best friend, I have to act. So I'm aiming toward liking a guy who's more realistic. This is healthy, right? If I just give it some more time, this could blossom into something good for both of us.

The problem is, moving on is like trying to untangle a knot that tightens the harder I pull. Austin is a walking paradox, and that's part of the problem. A boulder of muscles on the outside hiding a soft, gooey inside. The sweetest smile laced with an edge of mischief. Gentle eyes that smolder—

At this exact moment, Leo halts at the chapel and jerks all 100 percent into a chicken-peck kiss—not the 90 percent Hitch recommends. I freeze, wildly unprepared for our first kiss. My first instinct is to lean in and help him aim this time, but something stops me.

Is that you?

An involuntary montage plays in my head. Jeremiah, Peeta, Jacob, Lon, Prince Maxon. The Nice Boys Club—sweet, cautious, predictable, tame. I've yelled at them all, "What are you doing with your life? Find someone who actually appreciates you!" Stepping away, I bite my lips together as the pieces fall into place. He deserves so much better than my nonsense. I can't steal another kiss from this sweet, oblivious guy. Leo is a dream. Just not mine. Yes, he's everything that should make this work, exactly what I should want. But my heart keeps skipping school, and I can't keep pretending. I lift my eyes to his vulnerable, boyish face. He's not staring into my soul. Not expecting me to be something I'm not. He's just... here. Quiet, sweet, uncomplicated. I thought trying on commitment with the tags still on would keep me free. But now I've set off the alarm at the door.

One thing is certain—I can't act on this epiphany now. Guilt prickles my skin. Dumping someone after an awkward first kiss? Cruel.

My gaze drifts to Griffin Hall. I have no one to process this with. Kit would blame herself for Leo getting hurt, and I don't need her puppy-dog eyes. I mean, Sir Levi himself decided "Oh, actually, I do date" with one glance at her. What does she know about not settling? Mia has no patience for romance woes. Jenny, Izzy, and the G3-ers? No way would I offer this as gossip fodder. And Austin. He's already the best friend I've ever had. I'd tell him almost anything. But not about this. Not one flying chance.

Austin is selfless, compassionate, generous, gentle—but never "nice." There's a wildness to him. A spontaneity. A force of will. Still, I've never seen a better friend, a more sacrificial floormate and son. He cares so deeply, gives so wholly.

My chest constricts.

If Leo is a dressing room mirror of my medium-ness, Austin's goodness is the fluorescent lighting overhead. Some people weren't built for that kind of exposure. I'll never not flinch under that glare.

With a swivel back to Leo's searching eyes, I blurt out,

“Cool.” What? I have to get out of here. “Thanks for the ... walk. I’m headed to MSC, so I’ll see you tomorrow, yeah?” I fumble his jacket off my shoulders and hold it out to him.

He droops like a puppet whose strings were forgotten. “I’ll walk you over there.”

“Thanks, but I’m ... going to call someone on the way over. Adios y vaya con Dios!” I call, Zac Brown Band–style.

Not helping. *Tone it down, Sophie.*

That sad smile. I know. I’m horrible. But I don’t know how to fix anything right now, so all I can manage is to hightail it across campus. I’ll break up with him soon. I will.

But a familiar ache settles beneath my temples, and my pace slows. What am I thinking? I have no business dumping a quality guy like Leo. I’m a hot glue stick person—shiny in the package, a mess of strings once the pressure hits, raised by a family that could stick things together just long enough to fool the neighbors. Not exactly an appealing résumé to an Austin type—even if dating someone like that didn’t come with a side of slow emotional implosion.

I pull out my phone to call Mia.

“Hello?” She’s all business.

“Hi, roomie! Miss me?”

“Absolutely, but why are you calling?”

“Just wanted to see if we could do the lake tonight instead of a movie.”

“Kit’s with Levi, so let’s do tomorrow instead,” she says.

“Should’ve known,” I grumble. Behold the new normal.

“You sure there’s no emergency? You text. You’ve literally never called me before.”

“All good here! Oh—while I have you, is there a for-sale sign outside Griffin Hall?”

“Nope. Just the buildings with dude floors. I heard it’s A1’s prank and they covered their tracks with a sign outside their own building.”

"What's with the phone number?" I ask.

"Don't know yet. You're gonna text it, aren't you?"

"Duh. Unless Austin can clear it up for me."

"Figured. See you in the suite later."

"See you in a bit!"

A punch of the red button. Phone call, check.

Our student center, a.k.a MSC, is three stories of fun, including a coffee shop, movie rooms, and The Hive, home of greasy chicken goodness that's free with meal punches. Austin is their best late-night customer. He looks like a bear—broad shouldered, with a curly brown mess of hair—and he eats like one too. Always stocking up before hibernating in his dorm each night, lest he wake up hungry midsleep.

But by this time, he's usually gone, which means my trip here has maybe a 15 percent chance of seeing him. Even if I do, I'll avoid the topics of his computer tutorial with Pretty Redhead and my epiphany kiss. Yes, I'm great at making a mess of things.

I haul MSC's door open and pan around the mostly empty first floor. He's not here—probably into some kind of dude mayhem on his floor, Flooders. Leo will join in when he gets back. This kind of social overlap is unavoidable on the tiny Mayberry campus. I guess it's part of the charm.

Maybe I'll text Austin. Just in case.

Austin

At a *ding*, I check my phone.

SOPHIE

No chicken tonight?

I text back,

On my way there

There now!

Jackpot. Love me some chicken, but if Sophie's there, anything else is just gravy.

CHAPTER THREE

Austin

Through the MSC doors and into the three-story atrium. I pass Common Grounds and scan the square tables scattered around The Hive for the always-bouncing Sophie, the girl living in Technicolor in a grayscale world. We texted and even FaceTimed while she was home for break, but I missed her something awful.

There she is, dancing in her metal seat to the background music no one else notices. Guaranteed, she's singing along. Her voice is straight magic—when she sings something soulful, no one would be judged for crying.

I sneak up and tickle her neck. It works. She shoots up from her seat with a yelp and whips around so fast her golden braid smacks her in the face. Like a willowy fairy pretending to be mad.

"Twice in one day?" demands the fairy. "You're dead."

As long as she's the one to kill me, I can live with that. "I got you so bad."

She slides a basket of chicken across the table. "Here, I

ordered for you. They move at a glacial pace." Her voice signals a movie quote. "You know how that thrills me ... Oh, and extra sauce." She adds it to my basket. "Obvs."

I meet her gaze. "Thanks, Soph."

These latte-colored eyes. I've been without them for weeks. They warm me up when I'm cold and cool me down when I'm hot.

How much longer? I have to tell her.

But still that same feeling. Months now. A tension in my chest when I ask him. Not panic. Not peace. Just a weighty pause—like God pressing a hand to my sternum and saying, "Back up."

She snaps away and starts singing to the tune of "Need You Now." One of her legendary lyric swaps. "It's a quarter after ten, stomach's growlin' loud, and I need strips now. Said I'd do without, but I lost all control and I need strips now—"

Her song breaks into a laugh when I illustrate with a dramatic bite.

"Lady A would bring you on tour if they knew about you," I say.

She flits back an honored glance. "Yeah, right. Now dish about the sign prank. Is it A1?"

I tense. "Text the number."

"I knew it." She edges closer and folds her long, lean arms on the table between us, her thin gold bracelet catching light at her wrist. "Whose number is it? Can you tell me that?"

Don't push me, woman. I'd tell her anything with a single please, but this absolutely must stay a secret. "Just text it, Soph."

"You know I will. But during chapel"—she points—"when I can narrow down who it is."

I chuckle. "Narrow down to the ninety percent of the students on their phones during chapel?"

She holds up a finger. "Unless I come up with something hilarious. Can't be more than a couple people laughing at the exact same second."

"Clever. Lucky we sit behind you so I can watch this play out."

Chapel would be far more fun next to Sophie, but traditions are a way of life around here. Her floor, G1, sits on the back rows of the front section, and we Flooders sit in the front rows of the back section—the best seats in the house since we have railings for propping our feet—so we're separated by a horizontal aisle. Only the hardcore clingy couples break those rules. And the rare rebels who don't care about floor culture.

"Or ... maybe I'll forget all about it and have to find out with everyone else."

"Equally possible," I tease.

A thousand perfect freckles stretch across her cheeks into a grin. I try not to stare.

"Ideas for Saturday?" I ask.

She usually has an idea of what to do as well as the logistics, and my job is to check in with Levi and Haymitch. I'm a glorified messenger, but I'm not complaining. I'd do far more to see her almost every night.

"Hmm ... I'm feeling wild and different," she says.

"And that's new?" I dunk the last bite and pop it into my mouth.

Her eyes narrow playfully. "For our activity, obviously." She twirls a fry between her fingers. "Ooh, I got it. Line dancing."

My heart rate spikes. Line dancing is always found near two-stepping. Would I get to dance with her?

I'm already there. Laughing eyes, swishing hair. Energy bursting from her in waves and soaking into my skin. "Let's do it. Have a spot yet?"

I earn a going-along-with-her-crazy-ideas smile, a cousin of her sing-along smile. My nerves respond with an unhelpful hum.

"You must really like the idea," she says. "You're not even giving me a hard time."

Busted. "Do-over?"

She bends forward in challenge. "Too late. You tipped your hand. You're dying to go dancing with me."

The hum sharpens to a buzz. *Focus, man.* "Whatever. You just want an excuse to wear your new Justins."

A classic Sophie excited clap. "Doesn't hurt."

Sophie Appel in cowboy boots is lethal. She's California perfection with a newfound country streak. I'm six foot two inches and not small, but she could knock me over with a pinky when she wears those boots. Or casts a line. Or launches into a story around a campfire. Wish I could say I showed her the light, but it just took one too many hikes, one too many lakeside sunsets, and she was a goner for the forest. I didn't even get to be there for most of it. Girl has a million friends and more hours in the day than the rest of us—a result of her being secretly brilliant and an incredible multitasker.

"You don't wait for an excuse to wear your million plaid button-ups." She reaches across the table to pat my chest.

Buzz. Spark. But I force a teasing tone. "Hey now."

One shoulder lifts with mock innocence, and she grabs her phone. "Time to plan. Local expert?"

That's me. I grew up just thirty minutes from campus in the little town of Graham. East Texas has its faults— mosquitoes like a plague, six-month summers hot as Hades, noisy cicadas that all die at once and make a mess. But we get enough rain to keep those pine forests thick and endless, and our barbecue is the best there is. I'd live here forever if I could. I'm a simple drive-a-pickup-to-the-creek kind of guy. Throw in a fishing rod and Sophie in my Cowboys hat, and I couldn't possibly be happier. And that's an actual memory, unwise as it was.

Beside me, Sophie scrolls with purpose. I pull out my phone too, but my mind is firmly back in September. Her birthday. She'd been dying to jump into a creek "like in *The Notebook*," so I took her to my swimming hole in Graham—rope swing included. That day we were living a country song. The creek is dangerously close to my parents' house, but I held off on introducing her. Clutch move. She would've been so freaked out.

In college days, that was like four years ago. This hippie commune of a campus runs on a time warp—blink twice and suddenly you've got a second family. Eating every meal together and hanging out till late every night doesn't help. My roommate fell in love in three months, and he fell hard.

Without a glance, she moves from her seat to the bench beside me, tilting her screen my way. My body temperature jumps five degrees.

"Here?" Her arm brushes mine as she pinches to zoom in.

"Ah ..." Clearing my throat, I spin my phone on the table to busy my hands. "Lightning Cowboy is less than ideal."

She purses her lips and scrolls again. "Yeah?"

"Sort of a rager on college nights."

"Ugh. I couldn't find another place with under-twenty-one nights."

"Except—" Shoot. I said that out loud before I thought it through. "I know a place. Mostly two-stepping, but I know the owner. Might could convince him to clear some space for line dances if you wanna lead them." She will.

Her eyes gleam. "Austin, you're a genius. Please take us there?"

"Oh, a genius, huh?"

"Okay, no big heads allowed."

I sit back, arms crossed, and my shoulder grazes hers. "I have great ideas. I'm a genius."

She shoves my arm. "So you know how to two-step?"

"Since the sixth grade. Oh, Soph. I have a test." Over break, I heard the perfect song for her. With a gulp of air, I bravely launch into the chorus like she does—"Goldest" by Walker Hayes.

She lights up, already singing along. And now it's all her, singing her own anthem.

"You know every word," I say. "You showed me."

"It's Walker Hayes. Come on, Austin. Try harder." That smile is 100 percent contagious. “Fact is, ‘um’ and ‘platinum’ is the best rhyme ever.”

As I nod, I let out a content yawn. Our baskets are empty, but I’m in zero hurry.

Her expression fades to that sad look she never explains. She shifts in her seat, eyes flicking toward the door.

I know what this is. She takes “good vibes only” to an extreme.

“You don’t have to do that, you know,” I tell her gently.

She blinks. “Do what?”

“Leave just ’cause you’re sad.”

Her fingers curl around the edge of her sleeves. “Do not.”

I don’t push it. Just nudge her arm with mine.

And her eyes warm. Success.

CHAPTER FOUR

Sophie

"Bye, sweet girls! Miss you already!"

Dirty fingers jab at the screen, missing the End button again and again.

I grin and call out to their mom. "Bye, Miss Ayesha! Thanks for letting them call!"

Nannying these girls over break was the best decision I've ever made. Imani did my makeup every afternoon. Nyla is probably still convinced her princess wand holds magic power. The most precious little girls to love on. A cause to plan an adventure every day. And a reason to escape my own house. I miss those cuties. Their joy and giggles kept me afloat.

"Sure thing, Sophie. The girls haven't stopped talking about you since you went back to school."

When the call ends, my screen lands on the playlist I was building when the girls FaceTimed. Still smiling, I name it *Bops for Big Sisters in Withdrawal* just as Leo texts that he's outside. I adjust the song order and shoot the playlist to our suite text chain before heading for the hall. Kit will love it, but Mia especially has seemed off since we got back. With that, I stash my phone and push through the stairwell door.

"Hey," Leo says, jerking. "Uh. I think we should break up."

The door slips from my fingers to slam behind me. My mouth falls open. He pops his knuckles at his sides.

"Oh."

He rustles his hair and then finally grabs his scooter.

"You don't want to talk about it?" I ask.

"I'm guessing you really don't."

Guilty. I use every ounce of willpower to conceal my relief—at the breakup, at the brevity, at the hope of a quick escape.

But morbid curiosity wins out. "Is this about the kiss?"

He grips the handles, shifting his weight. "No. My buddies at home told me to have some self-respect. Threatened to dump you for me if I couldn't." He huffs. "I guess ... I guess I thought I could prove them wrong yesterday. I'm sorry I did that." He tries to smile.

When he meets my gaze, the relief freezes in an instant.

I'm a monster. This sweet guy deserved so much better than I gave him.

Music blares in my ears, drowning out my thoughts. My hands stay busy, touching up my "effortless" curls—Mom would call them messy—at a sink in our suite hallway. I watch like a hawk for Kit to glide around the corner, almost burning my fingers on the curling iron.

But my thoughts break through anyway. The guilt. Kind, gentle Leo. I could just let this quick-and-easy breakup be the end of it, chalk it up to another Sophie dumpster fire. But I can't let it go to waste. I have to shape up. It's one thing to be a one-woman disaster, but I can't rope in unsuspecting nice guys. No more collateral damage.

The second I see her, my curling iron clatters onto the counter and I rip out a headphone. "Kit! Do you know how to two-step?"

She flinches, eyes clamping shut as she yanks her books to her chest.

"Ah!" I whisper. "Sorry!"

I know better than to surprise her like that. More guilt tightens in my fists.

She counts under her breath, grounding herself, then looks up with an apologetic smile.

I grimace. "You okay? Sorry."

"You're good, Sophs. Don't worry."

I scared her out of her skin, and she's the one comforting me.

"Two-step?" Her Megan Fox eyes squint into slits as she kicks her flats off into her room. "That's a country dance, right?"

"Yeah. You're all huggy snuggy with Levi now, so dancing should be a go?"

Her dimples deepen. There it is. She's picturing herself dancing with Levi, the guy she's majorly gushy over and finally dating.

Clapping, I nearly squeal. But then I remember Leo. And I hate myself more than ever. I should feel sad. Some sadness is just respectable.

But my feet take off in a grapevine to the left. "I found some YouTube tutorials. And also some line dances." Grapevine to the right. Clap. Selling both of us on this. I need it.

And air. And space. And a notable lack of further damage.

Kit's books land on her desk with a satisfying clunk. Ayumi's not in the room they share. Weird—she always is.

"I'm sure Austin's already mentioned it." Kit pulls out her phone. "But let me text Levi really quick."

I shift my weight from foot to foot. "It's our standing Saturday time. I'm sure he's free."

It's obvious the second he texts back because she emits

sunbeams. Someone roll over a solar panel and we'll cancel fossil fuels here and now.

"Mamma Mia!" I call.

No answer. Not in the suite. We'll loop her in later—this can't wait. I will not miss out on couples dancing with Austin. For the first time in months, I won't even have to feel guilty for not inviting Leo. Except, the same day as—

No. I wave my thoughts away.

"Where's Ayumi been?" I ask.

"Um, she's been making some new friends ..."

Weird. Except not. She never liked me. Barely said a word when I was in the room. Pretty sure I'm too loud. Too ... much.

But dancing. It will be the best possible distraction ... unless Austin brings a date. My nails pause mid-tap on the counter. Torture, though nothing undeserved. But no—he never brings dates to our friend stuff. I let out a breath and continue tapping.

"You okay?" Kit asks from her doorway. "You seem off."

Relentlessly insightful Kit. Only-child life did not prepare me for someone to be so deep in my business without permission. Or ever.

"Fine," I say with another wave of my hand.

She's always bummed when I don't spill, but not everyone gets to grow up with Lorelai Gilmore for a mom. In my house, feelings weren't just unwelcome. They were a liability. Besides, Kit has zero place to talk. It took her months to fess up about her secrets. And more importantly, she couldn't possibly understand what it's like to be me. Perfect Little Kit. The perfect relationship. The perfect curves I would kill for. The perfect blend of meek yet conversational. Disciplined and focused, with plans for the future. The polished, effortless presence Mom always tried—and failed—to instill in my restless body.

My eyes flutter closed. I know Kit deserves better. She does. And I hate this train of thought—she wouldn't dream of thinking this way about someone else. But the unfairness sticks like gum to my shoe.

Shake it off. "Lounge?"

"I have an entire dance studio, Sophs. Let's make use of it."

"Ooh yesss. Magic boyfriend present."

She nods dreamily.

With a flourish, I lyric-swap some *Golden Hour* by JVKE, "It was just two lovers—fixin' up the barre, she was seein' stars, crushin' on each other ..."

She bends over in a laugh. And then belts out the rest of "Golden Hour" with me while she toes back into her flats and I tie my high tops. Kit's super fun. It's not her fault she's everything my parents wished I was.

And she's been a really amazing friend. Like when she got Levi to coach Leo. Well. At first I hated that she felt the need to help me catch a guy's attention when Sir Levi himself was all about her on Day One. But it turned out that Leo just liked me to the point of speechlessness. He always felt so outmatched being with me. And now even he's gone.

I wasted my sweet relationship with Leo wishing for something I shouldn't even want. Something that would destroy me. Falling for Austin wouldn't be dating—it'd be jumping out of a plane with a bedsheet. A beautiful thrill... until I crash-land in the middle of nowhere, stranded with nothing but the echo of my mother saying she told me so.

Best-case scenario? He'd move on after two dates and add me to the slew of gorgeous girls he immediately forgets. A compliment, sure—but it would still pummel my heart with the force of an industrial meat tenderizer.

Worst case? He wouldn't. And I'd end up stuck. In his small town. In his picture-perfect life. The mistake he'd spend his life trying to justify.

So I'll just go ahead and add my feelings for him to my list of aimless screwups. Mom could add a hundred more without blinking.

Tears threaten at my throat, but I clear them away with a swig from my water bottle and grab my tripod. Two-stepping. Line dancing. Video while we're at it.

"Song choices?" Kit pushes open the suite door.

"Austin's dancing spot is super authentic, so I was thinking old school. 'Check Yes or No'?"

"Awww. My dad loves nineties country. I've been properly indoctrinated."

"Aca-believe it."

We exit Griffin Hall and aim for the gym at the southwest corner of campus.

Kit jumps when a tailgate is slammed shut. My heart cracks for her. I don't give her enough credit for everything she's been through lately.

"How's the counseling going?" I ask. "If you don't mind me asking."

"Oh. I don't mind. I'm kind of ... conflicted about it."

"Conflicted?"

The truck rolls forward as a pack of guys in purple holler from the back. Must be some Club floor thing. They have even more weird traditions than Flooders.

"I mean, I had to see someone. I needed a professional opinion about my trauma stuff and strategies for fighting my freakouts. But she kind of ... I dunno." Her eyebrows press together. "When you were talking to her, did she ever talk about her past?"

"Her past ... I think it came up sometimes. Like, what about it?"

Jenny and some friends wave across the street. I blow a dramatic kiss instead of stopping. Jenny and Kit are not worlds I want to blend. Let's just say their Venn diagram would have a very small middle.

"She's been talking about her divorce. And now she works with women who have been emotionally abused. It really doesn't have to do with my symptoms or experiences, so at first I thought we were just getting to know each other. But then she started asking about Levi. And yeah, he was the catalyst for more than his fair share of flashbacks, but it wasn't his fault. She kind of ... Anyway, it's clear she doesn't like him. She expects the worst from him when I tell her a story."

"Huh. Yeah, I remember she said she was married before. I never had a serious boyfriend, so maybe that's why that stuff didn't come up. We mostly talked about my parents and depression stuff." This is a great pregame for line dancing. Nothing lifts the mood like my unresolved family issues and history of mental health concerns.

We cross campus under a grayish January sky, shoes scuffing against the sidewalk. The grass is winter worn but still stretches from path to path like the school's version of wall-to-wall carpet. Redbrick buildings flank us like a Hallmark movie set, and students zigzag in every direction—hammocking between oak trees, tossing frisbees, sprinting in superhero capes for some floor tradition I'll never understand. The whole place feels like it's seconds away from bursting into a town-wide musical number. So chipper. Almost choreographed. I love every square inch of it.

"I've never seen so much grass. How are they allowed to have this much grass?"

A pause as she recalibrates. "You don't have grass back home?"

"No one does. Droughts and water restrictions, ya know—until it floods." I flick my wrist to explain. "Meanwhile in East Texas, a college campus is built like a golf course."

Silence. Probably stuck in her head again.

No exotic flowers or sculpted succulents here—just dozens of oaks and pines and quiet, earnest flowerbeds. Compared to Pasadena, where the sidewalks were just swarmed with people watching the parade, this place feels practically deserted. Like I've stumbled into Stars Hollow or Virgin River or some other magical town where the locals are quirky and know your breakfast order.

Maybe Mayberry offers summer classes. I could stay on campus and avoid a summer like Christmas break. I'd miss the beach and nannying the girls, but that's a price I'd have to pay.

And the Gulf is just a few hours south—definitely road trip-able. I wonder if Austin will be around.

"Can I ask you something?" Kit says.

"Yeah, shoot."

"Do you think Levi is bad for me?"

I eye her like she grew a second nose. "Come again?"

"I mean, I've asked my mom, but she's only ever heard about him from me. But you see us together every day. What do you think?" She blinks up at me, so trusting.

I can't believe Perfect Little Kit wants my opinion. "You and Levi are nothing less than relationship goals. Like Flynn Rider and Rapunzel—post haircut. You're sorta overly clingy and ooey gooey, but I didn't even think a relationship could be so ... sweet. It's weird that you're doubting it."

"Okay," she says quietly. "So ... Levi isn't domineering or demanding or abusive? From your view?"

"Seriously? No. He's a little pleased with himself. Kinda bossy sometimes, but not to you. He bends over backward to make you happy, doesn't he? Am I missing something?"

"That's what I keep wondering. He's not perfect, but he's amazing."

"What did Dr. Shannon say? She must really not like him to have you all tangled up like this."

"Well, she's said lots of things, but this last time I happened to mention that I didn't leave lunch early enough on Wednesday to get across campus in time. She asked what Levi would say if I insisted on leaving earlier. Implied I should test him on it."

The truck previously full of Club guys is now parked along the campus loop by the pond. We can't see much from here, but loud chanting signals some crazy ritual.

"Sounds like they're channeling Betty White and Sandra Bullock over there," I say.

Kit's serious expression melts into a laugh. "I can only hope they're dancing *Proposal*-style."

She holds the gym door open for me, and we swipe our cards

on our way to her studio. The smell of lemon and sanitizer hits, and I compulsively check the weight area for Austin.

"Do you think testing Levi is bad?" she asks.

"It'd be more of a test for her than for him, wouldn't it? Tell him you have to leave lunch early and just see what happens. It'll give you a quick answer on whether she's seeing something you're missing."

"Huh. Okay."

What am I doing giving relationship advice? I know less than nothing about that subject. And she's got her forever guy wrapped around her finger. The familiar sludge slides into my stomach.

The dance. Just figure out the dance, and I'll be on to the next thing.

CHAPTER FIVE

Austin

"Takin' care o' yourself, Samwise?" Haymitch claps me on the shoulder as I pass him in the hall. "Findin' some downtime?"

"Course."

His head shake is interrupted by a buzz from his phone.

"Bet I know who that is," I tease.

He grins and saunters off, eyes glued to the screen like never before.

I greet Levi with an arm whack as he types on his couch, and I catch my reflection in the mirrored closet doors on the way to my desk. My hair is getting gnarly. I always put off haircuts because I hate asking favors, but at this point I might have to suck it up, get someone to take clippers to this mess.

I rake a hand through it. "Dude, my hair's too long, right?"

Maybe that's a weird question to ask my roommate, but he helps me with this stuff. Levi grew up in New England old money world and knows how to look good in any situation.

The last two and a half years I've asked him about everything from sneaker colors to how not to regret my life choices at a wedding.

"Not if you love the seventies."

I chuckle. "Well played. But seriously."

His hesitation is concerning. My gaze slides to him. "What?"

"You get what you pay for, bro," he says lightly.

He's been sitting on this? Embarrassing. Dude rarely gives advice unless directly asked.

I plop onto my couch and grab a ball. "Okay, Jeeves. Lay it on me."

He closes the laptop. "The haircuts you get on the floor are atrocious. Never do that again. Your hair is wicked cool if you'd just pay for a real cut and buy some product."

I snort.

"You could have Nick Jonas hair—better—if you'd do something about it."

"Dude."

"Really." He pulls his phone out, already on a mission. "Not everyone can do curly hair, but I know my barber can. Maybe he'll have a last-minute cancellation."

"You know too much about this."

"Genevieve." He barely glances up. His last high-school girlfriend. The one who messed him up. "Curly hair, very chatty."

"Ah."

"Sent you the link." A sly look appears. "Wait till Sophie sees. Mark my words—her face will justify the price tag." He stands and sets his laptop on his desk.

I throw some side-eye. I'd trust Levi with my life—and to read the mind of a girl—but I don't talk to him about her. He'd never spill, but I know he must hate that I'm hiding my feelings from her. He had to wait so long before Kit was honest with him, and it nearly sucked out his soul.

He holds out a hand to catch the ball, settles into his desk chair, and throws it back. It's bro time.

"Playing in Dontrell Wayne's league again?" he asks. "When does that start up?"

"March. And yeah ... If I'm still here." Ball to him, ball to me.

"What's the latest?"

"Coach says he can seal the deal. I dunno."

"You don't know if he can, or you don't know if you want him to?"

"If I want him to. I mean, if it was any other school, I wouldn't even consider it. But this was always the dream—mine and my dad's." I try to shrug. "I have another month to decide." Pressure builds in my chest every time I think about leaving this place. I bet Levi hasn't even had to think about next year. He's with Kit now.

"How's KitKat?"

He lets out a breathy laugh and scrubs his face. Lovestruck.

"That bad, huh? Tell me about the meet-the-parents over break."

"I only dragged her out there so she could meet Granny before—" He squeezes the ball, swallowing hard. "She and Kit are so much alike. But with everyone else ... Kit fit right in, in the best ways, and she was appalled in the best ways."

I can see it. Like Levi, Kit has the good posture and intelligent gleam in her eye. They could walk around with Harry and Meghan and no one would blink.

"We got out alive." He sends the ball back in motion.

"She still nervous about all the money everywhere?"

I watch his face, hoping I didn't step on his toes. He doesn't talk about his trust fund or the castle he grew up in on the ocean. But nope, we're good.

"Yes. But concern is warranted. She and I are on the same page about how we want to live moving forward, and she's keeping me honest."

"Moving forward? You think she's The One?"

A quiet nod.

Man. I knew he was crazy about Kit, but I didn't think he'd be this sure already.

"That's big, buddy." I step over to slap him on the shoulder.

He grins like he won the lottery. He's not wrong. Kit's crazy about him and even crazier about Jesus. I couldn't pick a better lady for him.

"Want to hear a secret?" A rare privilege.

"Out with it."

"Granny gave me her wedding ring. After she met Kit, she apparently moved things around in her will. Didn't even tell me, but she called Kit out in the estate documents."

"Dude, that's epic. Tell that story to the grandkids someday." I lower to my own desk chair. "Wait, where are you hiding it?"

"It's at home. I'll fly back for it when it's time."

I'm terrible, but my head goes swirly. I shake it, snap myself out of the jealousy spiral.

Levi is Mario cheering at the end of the track, while I'm Donkey Kong, driving like a maniac, about to hit a string of Item Boxes—except I dunno if they're the good kind or the upside-down kind.

I'm trying not to rush it, but I can't wait forever. Should I have Coach send in the game tape and be done with it? Should I bail on The Game?

"You'll get there too," he says. "God's got this."

Like he read my mind. He does that. "Yeah. So is Haymitch running soccer practices this year?"

"I'm pushing for that. He killed it last year."

And we're out of the touchy-feely zone.

CHAPTER SIX

Sophie

My pen flies across the paper as I finish outlining the Bible paper that was just assigned for Monday. The faster I knock this out, the less time wasted on schoolwork later.

My watch buzzes with a text.

KIT

Meet up in the lounge after class?

I swipe back to the time. Seven minutes until the beautiful freedom that is Friday afternoon.

Izzy leans in. "Is our adopted G3-er busy tonight? We're dressing up and going out for Mongolian food."

Mongolian. A night out. Sounds like what I'd be doing at home. Some stellar planners live on G3. FOMO hits every time I miss one of their floor events. Luckily, they've grafted me in whenever I need an escape from my own floor, but Izzy doesn't know I keep my weekend nights open. Because I'm pathetic.

I imitate Ryan Gosling in *Barbie.* "So cool."

She laughs out loud. The professor raises a brow, and we drop our heads. I need a run and a shower before dinner, but I can squeeze in a hangout before that.

I lower my voice. "Can't tonight. But I'm free after class?"

"Oh, right. Boyfriend life. Must be nice."

About that.

"Yeah, I'm done after this," she says.

"I've got some crazy plans to pick up books at the library." I wiggle my fingers like I'm luring her into a heist. "Wanna join?"

Can't compete with Mongolian food. Not this time, at least.

"Ooh, the guy who does work-study in there is so cute," Izzy says.

"Oh, Arjun?" I grin and elbow her. "Let's see if he'll flirt with you in front of the crotchety librarian."

"Girl. Say less."

I could invite Kit along, but I don't have it in me to be in close proximity to her any more than I already am.

No, just wait—before you judge me, hear me out. Perfect people on red carpets and social media? Not real. I know this firsthand. I've actually been to an A-lister red-carpet event. And some of my friends back home are successful influencers. Trust me, those people don't look like their pictures. Just regular people. It's all angles, lighting, and stylists. But Kit? Kit is actually that perfect. Looking at her is like staring straight into the reality of my own inadequacy.

While I was home, one of my friends asked all about Mayberry, swiping through my camera roll and squealing over Austin—a proper response to the man. But then she pointed at a picture of Kit and me, toggling her finger between us. "That's your friend? She's so pretty. I mean, you're pretty too, but, like, whoa."

That comment has been stuck in my head on a loop.

What she said was true. It shouldn't bother me. But it does. And it bothers me even more that it bothers me. But lately, it's worse. Because girls like Kit get their dream guy and ride off into the sunset. Of course they do.

I slide out my phone and type two words—*Sorry can't*—and stare at them, like they're aimed at more than just her.

CHAPTER SEVEN

Austin

At Saga I shovel chicken and rice into my mouth like I'm competing for prize money. Ethan begged for calc help as I was on my way out this morning. At least he gave me a granola bar, but it didn't do the trick.

Across the gleaming wood table—Saga's a cafeteria with country-club delusions—Kit leans toward Levi. "Who's playing goalie for Flooders?" She sounds all girlfriend-y asking about his floor stuff, but she's always been like that. She's good to him.

"No one volunteered, and that was our weakness last year." Levi looks across the table. "Ideas, Haymitch?"

Out of nowhere, rain pounds the roof like someone dumped a bucket. Kit freezes. Levi catches her eyes and reassures her silently. I won't forget her reaction on that drive last fall, when I saw a PTSD flashback tear her apart. It's a testament to Levi's commitment to Jesus that he's kept from finding—and destroying—the guy who messed her up like that.

Haymitch collects his napkins and water cup onto the Saga tray as he ponders.

"I'll play goalie if y'all need me to," I say between bites. Goalie sounds awful—no scoring, stuck at the goal the whole game. But I can take one for the team.

Levi sends a silent no, confident as a senator. "You're too good of a runner to waste you at goalie."

"He's right," Haymitch says in his Alabama drawl. "Let's think on it. And we need a couple guys to help ref the girls' football season." He flicks a finger at me. "Not you, Samwise. You don't have the time."

I close my open mouth around the fork. He knows me well. I might do it anyway—I don't want them left hanging. Although, I'm coaching the G1 team this year. Might be a conflict of interest to ref the others.

His chair scuffs back on the carpet as he stands. "Got some senior design stuff I gotta do. See y'all tomorrow."

"Bye, Haymitch!" Kit chimes.

His senior project is complex and terrifying. I've got a bad feeling he'll be pulling a disappearing act this last semester we have him. The engineering program here is no joke. Haymitch is mechanical and I'm electrical, but watching him has been a good indicator of what's coming. I've never been the smartest guy in the room like Levi here, but I work hard enough to make up for it. Just gotta survive three semesters and then I'll have a job that pays all the bills. And feeds the kids I wanna have someday.

Finally, I swallow my last bite and draw in a huge breath. Just a few minutes and I'll feel better. I down my cup of water.

"So how's my favorite freshman liking Linear Algebra and Discrete Math?" Levi asks Kit.

"Ooh, Discrete was so fun today. We made truth tables to determine logical equivalence and ..."

My eyes—and all mental capacity—are drawn to the double doors. I had the luck to sit on the side of our table that faces the entrance to Saga, and guess who's here for dinner? Sophie and

Mia drip all over the tile and curl over laughing. I follow Sophie's path as she shakes off like a puppy, picks up a tray, chooses her food—

I bounce my gaze away when she's about to walk this direction. And pretend not to notice Levi's shaking head.

"Hey, Soph." I feign surprise. "Ever heard of an umbrella?"

"Never. Want to mansplain it to me?"

I chuckle.

"Sophs! Mamma Mia!" Kit says. "We need a rain-scene movie. Tomorrow after lunch?"

"I'm down. We could do *Sweet Home Alabama* again," Mia says. "Speaking of, I saw Haymitch left already?"

"Senior design strikes again," Levi says.

Sophie sits next to me and scooches in her chair. Static skitters under my skin at her proximity. The table lights up in her glow.

"Not sure if I'll be there for the movie," she says. "I'm going on a G3 field trip tomorrow. You guys can join if you want."

I don't get why she spreads herself thin with random people when her real friends care about her so much. At least she's never done that with me.

Her thick blond hair drips down her back onto her soaked sweatshirt. Impulsively, I grab it all into a handful, fingers grazing her neck, and squeeze it into my empty cup. It works. She bursts out laughing, covering her full mouth with her hand.

"Like in *Princess Diaries*!" Kit says.

"Rain scene!" All three of them shout.

I've seen that one, but I don't remember a rain scene. My sister makes me watch all her chick flicks with her when I'm home, but it comes in handy because sometimes I have a partial clue what these girls are talking about.

Sophie's face softens as a question fills her eyes.

Oh. I'm still holding her hair. I drop it and play it off.

"I'm gonna look like a wet dog," she says.

I frown. Her self-deprecating jokes are never funny.

Kit turns to Mia. "You and Haymitch have poker tonight, right?"

"Yeah, girl. High stakes tonight. Rules are we can bring cookies of any kind as our chips."

She's a killer poker player. Only a fool would bet against her.

"What's your cookie of choice?" I ask Mia.

She shoots me a look when I drape my arm on the back of Sophie's chair. It's not the first time. I heard on the floor this morning that Sophie finally dumped Leo, but I drop my arm anyway.

Still waiting down here. Please, can I tell her?

"Abuela's butter cookies." Mia tips her head back. "Ahh, so good. But it's Famous Amos tonight."

"See if you can finagle another care package," I say. "Just have her send it to me and I'll make sure it gets to you."

She waggles a finger at me as she swallows. "Like you need to steal my care packages. You can go home and have fresh-baked goods any time you want."

False. I learned freshman year that going home means being trapped there until my next class. I've had to bring friends along who will convince them I have to get back. Last year I brought the guys along several times on Sunday nights ("Sorry, class in the morning!"), but I couldn't manage it last fall with all the football games.

But I talk to my parents and sister every week. They're good. I'd drop everything if I heard otherwise.

"Sophs?" Kit asks. "Favorite cookie?"

Her eyes dart from table to table like it's an important question. "Mmm. Cookie cake. With tons of icing. You have to be strategic about which piece you take, you know?"

I wanna bolt out of here right now and buy her a whole cookie cake.

Levi and Kit melt into matching smiles.

"Should I ask?" I raise an eyebrow.

"Macarons," Kit says, fixed on Levi.

"Agreed," Levi murmurs.

"Uh-huh ..." Those two. I tell you what.

Pretty sure there's a Mrs. Fields at the mall here in Pinecrest. If Mia and Haymitch are playing poker, Levi and Kit'll pair off, and I'll have Sophie to myself. Might oughta cook up a reason to go shopping. Surprise her.

Oof. Sophie elbows me in the ribs. "What?"

"Favorite cookie! You're in la-la land. What are you thinking about?"

"Ahh ... what we're doin' tonight."

She perks up. "Have an idea?"

"Yeah."

"What? What?"

"It's a surprise."

She claps.

Another spark at that freckled smile.

Maybe I can whisk her off. You know, as a friend. Wait. I don't have anything, do I? I check my phone calendar. Nope, all good. I'd feel bad if I had to cancel on a girl, but I'd do it.

I turn to Levi. "Doing your own thing?"

He confirms with a dopey grin. I whack him. He whacks me back.

"But, Austin."

"Yeah, Soph?"

"What's your favorite cookie?"

Sweet of her to keep asking. Oh, her fork is down.

"Mama's snickerdoodles. Ready to get out of here?"

She nods eagerly.

I just have to get her in the Jeep before the G3-ers beat me to it.

CHAPTER EIGHT

Sophie

As we approach Davidson Hall from Saga, the newest puzzle on campus is impossible to miss. White poster boards in the windows, most of which now have two-foot-tall letters scrawled in Sharpie. The message is almost finished—only one letter left to make it true. Two letters are chosen each night by popular demand, and we've only gotten three wrong so far. A stick figure with a head, body, and one arm has taken over the Mayberry Hangman profile picture to mark our mistakes.

MAYBERRY
W_NS
B_G

We'll get the last letter easy tonight. But the mystery I'd like to solve is this—who is making this magic happen?

My eyes are yanked from the hangman game when Austin

pushes his plaid flannel sleeves higher over his elbows. I never need a reminder to look at those distracting forearms—wide and sculpted, wrapped in warm, tan skin from his Mexican grandma's side. The muscle? I bet he's been in a committed relationship with the gym since kindergarten. The undersides are paler, veins pumping. Like a peek at the bear while it's sleeping—muscles relaxed, claws tucked in, still dangerous but completely cuddly. I've been friends with this guy for months, and I still can't shake the desire to touch those arms.

Forcing my eyes away, I tell him about the library earlier. "Izzy came with me, and we tried to get a rise out of the librarian. You know, Arjun works in there—" I stop to steer him away from my Jeep. "I need to go back and change."

"How come?"

"Because I look like this?"

He frowns in this gentle way that makes my heart skip a beat.

"I don't have my keys anyway."

"Oh." He pats his leg, antsy.

"In a hurry?" I ask.

"Li'l bit. So I assume y'all succeeded in your mission to horrify Mrs. Casey?"

"Totally. How'd you know?"

He sends me a knowing look. "Please. Arjun didn't stand a chance."

I didn't think he knew Izzy. Apparently he does. And he's noticed she's pretty. My chest tightens, but I redirect hard and check his shoes—the laced leather boots he always wears when he's not in sneakers. As if Levi helped him pick out work boots. Which is probably exactly what happened.

"Do you know all these G3-ers from volleyball last semester?" he asks.

"Some of them, yeah." I jab him in the side.

He reaches for mine, but I've already taken off.

"Hey!"

Now he's chasing me, and I have to flat out sprint. He's

impossibly fast. I wish I could watch him running behind me, all champion-running-back speed and agility. Football season is over, and it's a terrible shame.

My major head start barely gets me to my building first. I manage to badge in, but his hand meets my side as I pull the door open.

Fully giggling, I hold on to the door for dear life as he squeezes my ticklish spot.

"Don't start what you can't finish," he teases.

When I push him away, he pretends I'm actually strong enough to move his bear body.

Still gripping the door handle, I grin. "Well, Austin, I think …" I lunge to jab at his side and then jump through the doorway. "I won this round!"

"Cheater!"

The door slams.

He's allowed in my building on Friday nights, but he's too much of a gentleman to barge into a girls' dorm without an invitation, even as a joke.

I sprint to my suite's lounge, round the corner, and stop at the mirror.

Wow, what a sight. My wavy hair has frizzed into a full-blown disaster. But Austin's in a hurry. With a sigh, I finger comb and French-braid the sides, trying not to flinch. As Mia Thermopolis said, "This is as good as it's going to get." I'll never compare with the girls he'd normally be on a date with. Still, I wish I had longer to try.

But no time to think. I grab my cutest pair of jeans off the floor and scan for a top from the closet. Something that makes me look like I have a waist. Clothes on, makeup touched up, phone in pocket. Grab my keys, run down the hall. I can't miss my chance at a not-date with Austin.

Austin

She looks beautiful, but I hate that she fixed herself up. I wish I could tell her how much I liked how she looked five minutes ago. I wish I could tell her that her hair wild and free sends a chill up my spine. I wish I could kiss her until she believed me. But I can't. I'm not the boss.

"Hey, you. All dry?"

"You okay?"

She caught me. Nerves churn in my stomach. An almost date with Sophie feels like the NFL Scouting Combine. When it's finally time to ask her for a relationship, I hope I've done enough to make the cut.

"Yeah." I nudge her arm. "I'm great."

"Samwise," Ethan calls down the sidewalk. "Can you help me out again tomorrow? You were money before my last test."

I turn to his voice and hold out a fist bump. "Finn, my man."

Sophie steps in. "How were the Bahamas, Ethan? I'm so jealous!"

He flashes a smile, teeth bright against his dark skin.

Don't get any ideas, buddy.

"Oh, it was the best," he says. "Super fun."

"I bet. The water is so clear, right? Amazing snorkeling."

"Yeah, for sure. So—"

"See you at the first soccer game of the season! Exciting!" Sophie grabs my arm and beelines across the grass for the Jeep.

Trying to take care of me again. And touching me while she does it. I want to love it, but Ethan asked me because he knows I'll come through. If I don't make time, who else will?

Dad never let things slip. Even before his surgery, when his back had him in pain every day. He never slacked. Work? Covered. Chores? Done. Football fees, travel, gear? Somehow, he always made it work. We never had to wonder. Never even had to ask. He made sure we had everything we needed—most of what we wanted too. Reliable, steady, the kind of man people don't have to second-guess. The kind of helpful only one-upped on the pages of the Gospels. Does Sophie really think I need help getting out of things?

"Are you aware that no is a multiple-choice option?" she asks, voice low.

"Finn's my buddy," I say. "I wanna help if I can swing it."

"Everyone's your buddy. You're the nicest guy on campus. The nicest guy in the world."

"He's your friend too."

"True, but you don't see me killing myself to tutor him. I wish I could tell everyone no for you."

My arm clunks cold to my side when she drops it. "I'm really good at it." She eyes me. "Maybe you're the one who needs tutoring."

She's not wrong. My sister, Janie, likes to imitate Miranda's *that's all* wave in *The Devil Wears Prada* as a joke, but Sophie does it naturally.

What she doesn't know is that Levi already heads people off on my behalf. He thinks he's subtle, but I've seen him run interference for years—redirecting people, convincing someone to go in my place. I know he means well, but it grates that he thinks I need the help.

In some ways Sophie and I know each other so well already, but she doesn't live on my floor, so there's a lot she doesn't really get. Plus, she's never met my family. She doesn't know about the walk-on thing at UT yet. And honestly? I don't always understand her either. I want to though. I wanna know every golden detail. We're in such a weird spot.

"You don't tell me no." I nudge her arm, baiting her. She does.

She sends a look over her shoulder. "Prove it."

That sassy, flirty spark in her eye. I almost pull her close. *No. Can't.*

"Drive your Jeep into the pond."

She gasps, horrified. "My baby? That was too easy of a no."

"Tell me a secret."

"No."

I almost push her on it, but I've gotta stay in bounds. "Well, you showed me."

"Yes I did. Learn from the master. Now, your turn to practice."

"Shoot."

"What do you say if a guy on your floor asks for help with his homework?"

"Soph, I wanna help if I can. They're—"

"Your buddies. I know, I know. Come on, Austin." This started as a game, but suddenly she's serious. "You can tell them no if you can tell me no. Do it as a personal favor to me."

I would sell all my possessions and join the circus as a personal favor to her. If she said my name while making the request, I'd really do something nuts like ... become a vegetarian. A vegetarian zombie.

"Okay. I'll try to tell them no."

"Somehow that sounds more like a yes," she teases.

"It was a no. To them."

She pushes me, her affectionate gaze pulling me like a magnet. "Tutor me, Austin."

"Yes."

"Help me shower someone, Austin."

"Yes."

She keeps saying my name. It's physically impossible to refuse.

"You're supposed to practice saying no!"

We've arrived at the parking lot. So close. "Okay, no."

"No to me?" She spins to a stop in front of her Sophie-yellow Jeep, bends toward me playfully, pokes my chest.

Am I screwing up? She's so flirty tonight. I love it. I want more.

"No no no no no no no." I swivel my head for emphasis.

"So proud of you. I think. That was confusing." She laughs, but the air between us shifts—grows heavier. Another step closer.

It's not time. Snap out of it. "Soph." My body got the memo, but my voice didn't. "I know you're just playing, but my dad would make the time. Jesus even more so. He was so interruptible. I want to be like that."

She studies me. "That's why?"

"Saying no also just feels gross. But that's part of it, yeah. When God brings someone along who needs help, I wanna be the guy who drops everything. That's what love looks like."

Latte eyes stare up at me with ... what is that? Admiration? She props against the front of her Jeep, too beautiful to be real. "Jesus was interruptible, huh? And when he helped people, he did it with flair." She gestures dramatically. "Here, I'm just gonna put this mud on your eyes."

I chuckle. "Yeah, no kidding." My voice is still too quiet. Traitor.

Sophie. I almost touch her hair, grab her hand, drag her close, kiss her, tell her what she means to me. I shove my hands in my pockets before I lose my grip. She has no idea how many times I tell myself no.

I clear my throat. "You wanna drive?"

"I have an urge to yell no right now," she jokes. "But yes."

Please, can I have the go-ahead? I'm trying to wait for your timing, but this sucks. She loves you. She's ready, right? And anything else we can learn together. Please?

As I move toward the passenger seat, I release my detained hands and try to flick the tension from my arms.

She's driving, so it's my job to play DJ, a game she made up long before Mayberry. I know the rules—impress Sophie with songs she forgot about or hasn't heard yet. It's a great setup. If I nail it, the thrill of making her happy. If I miss, a quick redo. And bonus points if I earn her perfect-song-for-the-moment sigh.

I type in her code and scan through what might fit tonight. Prime storytelling. Upbeat country with sentimental lyrics is a safe bet—Sam Hunt maybe. Or optimistic hip-hop, like Forrest Frank.

She rolls the windows down. Rolls her shoulders back. But her fingers keep tapping a frenetic beat on the wheel. "Something slow."

A slow song? I risk another sidelong glance. That's weird. She never wants those. Ever.

CHAPTER NINE

Austin

How accurately should I capture the current vibe? I tap the song before I weasel out.

"Hello Beautiful" by Noah Schnacky—pop country, sappy narrator. Sophie's half obsessed with his sister, so that should count for something. The first notes trickle through the speakers.

A lack of clapping is never promising with Sophie. She gulps.

When she turns to me, I raise my brow. She nods, so I queue up a few more like it. I swap her phone with a water bottle in the cupholder and offer her a swig. She passes it back, so I toss it to the back seat. That's what she'd do.

A slow song? What's that about? I clear my throat. I need a topic. No telling what's going on over there, but I'm too high strung.

"How do you like your classes this semester?"

She squeezes the wheel. "I don't know what I'm doing."

"The pedal on the right is the gas. The one in the middle—"

"Ha-ha."

"It's okay to not know your major freshman year, Soph. God'll get you to the right spot."

She attempts a smile. "I'm trying to believe that. You're lucky you're just great at something."

What she means is that I always liked math and science, so engineering made sense. But I'm not great at it. And I don't like how she's talking about herself.

"No, I was great at football. I've just been winging it since I got hurt."

With a quiet sigh, I avert my eyes to the trees passing by. I hate keeping secrets from her. But telling her I might be leaving? That would force the issue on my other secret. If she asked me to stay, that's it. All I'd need. But if she didn't ... I don't know how I'd come back from that. Anyway, I can't tell her about football until she has all the facts.

"Pity this school doesn't have life-of-the-party or singer-from-heaven majors," I say.

Show her what you have for her, God. Show her how much you love her. How much you like her.

My thumb brushes her shoulder until I realize—and yank back the offending arm. With her hair pulled back like this, I can see her tiny ear. I wanna kiss it.

I rub my eyes to reset. Maybe a green light with Sophie was never coming. Maybe what I've been praying for isn't mine to hope for. Maybe I was meant for something else.

You get to pick. You're the boss.

I clear my throat and force my voice into something normal. "Where ya drivin', Soph?"

"Oh! Where am I going?"

"You're on the right track."

Using her phone, I check the hours—we're good. I tell her the turns as they come. We pull into the mall, and she blinks at me.

I slide out of the Jeep and head inside. "Wait for it."

Past Dillard's, Mrs. Fields is almost in sight. I reach around to cover her eyes with my hands. Bad idea—too much touching—but I'm already pushing my luck tonight. She stops in the middle of the mall corridor, and I nudge her along, soaking in her shampoo of the day. She smells like berries today—raspberries.

"C'mon," I tell her. "Almost there."

Every inch of me aches this close to her. She's pure voltage, and I'm a breath from closing the gap. My lips hover inches from her neck. The air between us fizzes. I want to get this right ... if there's ever a right time. But I'm only making it messier. I let my hands fall—before we're all the way there—and tip my head instead.

"Oh! Cookie cake! Austin!"

Bouncing. Clapping. Just the reaction I was hoping for.

"Instant gratification!" she says with a squeal.

I wish. Waiting sucks.

Sophie

We continue our wandering loop around the mall after finishing the last bites of cookie cake slices. Austin's quiet tonight, but I'll take time with him in any mood.

He pushes up his sleeves for the millionth time, sending his comforting scent into the air. Like pine trees and dryer sheets. "Ready for the next thing?"

"I thought you were in a hurry. How long do you have?"

He tilts his head in question. "I just wanted to get going. I have all night."

I barely suppress an embarrassing grin. "Next thing."

"You drive or me?"

"You."

As soon as he starts the Jeep, I have "Chicken Fried" by Zac Brown Band waiting and add a couple more to the queue.

"How are things at home?" I ask. "Miss it already?"

He half-smiles. "My dad gets to help Uncle Drew do a controlled burn on their property. They had to wait for a good rain, so I missed it. Janie's looking at colleges. It's always good to be back." His eyes gentle. "Was break okay for you?"

"So quiet." I grimace. "My dad has his own life now, and Mom just works all the time. Anyhoo ..."

"The New Year's parade was a lot more interesting this year," he says. "I had the coolest tour guide."

I bump him with my elbow. My place is walkable to the Rose Parade. I always go with a group of friends with a connection—someone who can get us into a building on Colorado Boulevard, where we can watch from high above. The masses have to peek around heads or pack onto metal bleachers. This year I FaceTimed with Austin so he could watch with me.

"Maybe someday you can come see it in person," I say.

He'll deflect. Flying all the way to Pasadena isn't really a friend thing.

"Let's do it."

My breath catches. That wasn't his agreeable yes. He wants to. I could actually book the trip when the time comes. Which means ... he plans on being friends in a year. Close enough friends to travel with. Is he thinking of staying at my house? Under the same roof as my mother? That's not happening. I'll find a way out of that part when we get there. But sharing the parade with him would be everything. Seeing the floats—completely made out of flowers and plants—being built from scratch and then lined up along Orange Grove. I barely refrain from clapping and sneak a glance at him.

He clears his throat. Been doing that a lot tonight.

"You said you made it to the beach a couple times?" he asks.

That was a shift.

"Yep. Wouldn't miss my beach time. The waves crashing, the sand in my toes, the wind flapping everywhere." I mime a chef's kiss.

"You don't seem like a lay-in-the-sun person. I bet you play in the water."

"It's too cold to swim without a wetsuit this time of year. This last time I got to play beach volleyball." The closest I get to my club volleyball days. "That's my favorite."

His eyes slide over, wide and unblinking. "Right. Of course. Beach volleyball," he emphasizes, "and field trips with your mini-mes."

I chuckle. He's loved hearing about my girls' antics.

He lets out a breathy laugh.

"You're being weird tonight." I tap his arm.

He swallows, then nudges mine. "Just missed my bestie."

My heart squeezes. He makes this so hard.

CHAPTER TEN

Sophie

The sky darkens out the windshield, the last of the sunset draining away.

I play with my seat belt as Austin drives, his arm draped over the steering wheel.

"Hey, do you ever pray while you run?" I ask.

"Yeah, definitely. Do you?"

"I've been trying it. I hate running without music though, and I can't really pray when I keep singing lyrics to myself."

His lips quirk. "I have an idea, but you're gonna laugh at me."

"Ooh, what is it?"

"Some of the songs on the *Wonder Woman* soundtrack would be so good for that. Instrumental and epic."

"That's amazing."

"Bet you'll feel like a million bucks too. Super Sophie. Some of the songs are too dynamic for good pacing though. You'll have to check 'em out first."

It should be illegal to be that cute. "'Too dynamic for good pacing'? Where did that come from?"

"Oh, I dunno. Just researched good music for running a couple times. You know I love a good run. What have you been praying about?"

I shrug. "My parents. My major. You." No idea why I'm being so honest. He doesn't know the details, so it should be fine.

"Thanks, Soph." So quiet.

Shoot. Maybe I freaked him out.

Just in time, the first words of "Country Stuff" by Walker Hayes fill the Jeep. Hunting. Dirt roads. Tractors. I can tell from his smirk that he follows the queue's theme. I send a goofy smile to confirm I'm messing with him.

He pokes my shoulder gently.

"What, country boy?" I tease. "What is it?"

Pokes on my arm and stomach and leg.

I squirm and laugh. "Hey, no fair. I can't get you back while you're driving."

"Ohh. You mean I'm cheating?" He tilts to me with meaning.

"Yes, you're a naughty cheater!"

"Takes one to know one." He pokes me again.

I grab his finger but drop it just as fast. My hand stretches out like Mr. Darcy's.

"Is that your dream life?" I ask him, only half joking. "Driving a truck and fishing in the dark?"

His expression turns serious. "I like those things, but they're not my dreams."

"Well?"

His mouth opens. Shuts. "I want a family, a home ... a wife I'm crazy about."

And just like that I could crawl out of my skin. I have to get out of this conversation. Now.

"I wanna feel like God used me ..." he continues.

I let my breath out.

"... that I helped people."

That's Austin.

Please give him all the things he wants, Jesus.

I try to picture her, even as my insides revolt. Sweet and content, like honey dripping off a biscuit. Gorgeous, obviously. A goodness that matches his. The type who owns an apron and actually uses it, pie cooling on the windowsill.

"Tell me your dreams, Soph." Gentle. Locked in. He sees people in a way others don't. Maybe that's why he's never wanted more with me—he can see that I'll never be her.

"My dreams? I want to do things, see things. New things." I snort. "I sound like Dr. Seuss. I just want to feel ... free."

My throat grows thick. What's the opposite of my room in Pasadena? I want that.

A softened smile takes over his face as he drives. I have no idea what goes through his head, but I know it's good. Selfless. Thrilling. He always is.

Why couldn't I just like Leo? Or literally anyone else? How do I stop this madness?

I twist my bracelet around my wrist.

Should I quit this dysfunction with Austin? Cut ties?

I know he doesn't want anything more with me. I know I couldn't handle it even if he did. I know my heart gets more tangled every day with him. So what am I doing?

He pulls up to a giant, wooden, castle-themed playground. I've been here once before, but this time it's quiet. Faded red light spills across the bridges and climbing walls. My heart skips. I've always been called exhausting. Too much. *Calm down*, they say. *Chill out. Take a seat.* But Austin never makes me feel like I need to tone it down or grow up. He brought me somewhere I get to be loud. Unpolished. Fully myself.

The second we're parked, he pockets my keys and takes off, like a little kid cooped up too long. We play hide and seek through towers and tunnels, climb a pine tree, race down the tallest slide. No one's more fun than Austin. He's all open sky and motion, contagious joy. Every second with him, my soul can breathe.

Eventually he drifts toward a painted railing and pulls out his phone. That heart-stopping smile, but quieter now. He taps a few words, pauses, taps again—flicking the back of his hand like he does when he's thinking too hard. I hang back, give him a second. Whatever it is, it's got him somewhere else for a beat.

"Who is it?" I try to squeeze down the undeserved jealousy.

"Huh? Oh, nobody. I'm working on something."

Okay ...

"Here, sit for a minute?"

"No." I wander off to find something to occupy my mind.

"Hey, come back here."

My pulse doubles. Flirty Austin. *Down, girl—leave it,* my mind tells me, but I'm already turning.

"Make me."

His eyes light up—pure mischief. My favorite. For half a second, neither of us moves.

Then I take off running in the opposite direction, scrambling up steps. Two seconds and he's right behind me. With no warning, he wraps a huge arm firmly around my middle and leaps off the playground through a gap. Leaps. Off. The biggest rush. A happy scream. We land on the wood chips, the world vibrating, and he gently sets me on my feet. I don't even know what happened to me until I see the fireman pole he—we—apparently slid down.

"What was that?" I push his chest with both hands, huge smile overtaking my face.

He lets me push him around the playground, up the steps, onto the wiggly bridge.

"That was pretty cool, wasn't it?" He shrugs a shoulder. "I'm basically Tom Cruise doing my own stunts. No, Keanu Reeves."

"Ohh-kay," I say over a laugh, dropping my hands. "No big heads."

But then he pulls out his phone again. My shoulders droop. I can't keep his attention tonight. My feet drag me down the steps, across the wood chips, toward the car. I have to learn to quit him, but how? He's ... Austin.

"I know you like your chicken late—" The Zac Brown Band song from earlier but with a wrong word. His eyes follow something on his phone while he sings.

"Somewhere new on a Saturday night. A movie quote that hits just right. And so much queso"—laughing eyes flit to me—"you sleep in, no sunrise. Bring tears of laughter to your friends' eyes. You make us all feel more alive." He pockets his phone but keeps singing. "We wish you'd si-i-i-i-ing more." His shoulder twitches. "A couple lines need to be reworked, but you got impatient."

That? That's what he was doing? I toe the wood chips and risk a glance at him. He sits on the wiggly bridge, facing me, legs dangling off the edge like a kid. No one has ever lyric-swapped for me before. Not like that. "A lyric swap, Austin?" I try to hide the awe with a teasing voice. "Trying to beat me at my own game?"

He shrugs.

"You make some solid competition." Too quietly, I add, "I love it."

A grin crawls across his face, and mine grows hot. I hope it's too dark for him to see me blushing. Wow, this is so embarrassing. Subtlety? Never heard of her. Where do I go?

He ducks his head to shimmy off the bridge.

I don't know what I'm going to do when I find him next to me, so I plop down in the middle of the park and wave my arms and legs into wood chip angels. I don't know what to talk about. I don't know what to think about. La-ti-da, this is normal behavior!

I boxed myself in on this field trip with him. Can't escape like I could on campus. Not even my phone can distract me. The elephant isn't just in the proverbial room—it's sitting on my chest. A soft crunch, then that disarming mix of pine and soap hits as he drops beside me. But I stare at the sky and try to breathe. My heart competes with my brain for most erratic.

Stars and a bright moon peek around the wispy clouds. He'll want to see them. But he lowers to his side, head on his hand, and looks straight at me. His breath tickles my cheek. What are we doing here? Why doesn't he have a date like usual? Did someone bail on him, or did he never make plans? Why would anyone bail on Austin? I cover my face, trying to clear my head. It's so quiet between us. I desperately hope he can't read my mind. Am I freaking him out? Am I ruining my very favorite friendship? How am I going to get through the next year and a half until he graduates without losing my mind? What am I going to do when he leaves?

"You okay, Soph?" His pensive voice. Deep and gravelly.

I nod behind my hands.

When I finally drop them and turn to him, his eyes are sad. Silence hangs between us.

Finally he speaks. "I love hanging out with you." Then he lets out a sudden breath, climbs to standing, and offers a hand to help me up.

The last thing I need is to remember how good it feels to touch his enormous, rough hand. Forget that—I grab it.

"Race you to the Jeep," he says.

And we're off.

Austin

That's not what you meant when you told me "She's not ready," is it? I botched it. I'm sorry. Help me do better. And if I have to ... help me let go.

CHAPTER ELEVEN

Sophie

Jenny invited me to a party at some off-campus apartment tonight. I had said no, but after the chaos of that not-date with Austin and the ever-present, niggling Leo guilt, I shoot her a text.

You still going? Can you pick me up?

I park the Jeep, wave goodbye to Austin, and badge into Griffin Hall like I'm heading inside for the night. Then I slip out the back, where he couldn't see on his way to Flooders. Shady, I know, but Austin doesn't do parties like this, and I don't need him questioning why I suddenly feel like going. I just need to do something. Anything but sit alone in my room, overthinking.

Jenny pulls up in her bright-red beater car, music thumping, headlights bouncing off the pavement. The decision is made.

With a sigh I plop into the passenger seat.

"You okay, girlie?" Jenny asks.

"Yeah. Just a weird night. I don't want to talk about it."

"Aww. Well, everything's gonna be better soon!" She cranks the music up, and I let it swallow up whatever's still buzzing in my brain.

The second we step inside, the smell hits—stale beer, sweat, and something sour. Not a great start, but Jenny links her arm through mine to tug me deeper inside and I let her. The dim lighting and pulsing music offer exactly what I came for—something else to think about.

She introduces me to her friends, and I do my part—smile, nod, play along when I'm supposed to. Let it all blur. But it's been a long time since I was the only sober one at a party. Their jokes deteriorate fast, and I can only exaggerate a laugh so many times. The girls start making dares, and I dart another glance at the kitchen. I don't drink anymore—not since I started following Jesus—but a lot of these people are Christians too, and they don't feel the need to be holier-than-thou about it. And I didn't drive here, so there's no risk of me being dangerous on the road.

The image of Austin staring at me in the wood chips jumps to mind for the millionth time since. I've rattled the Magic 8 Ball one too many times to clear it. I try bouncing in place. *Just loosen up.* Swallowing the last sip of Cherry Coke, I let go and aim for the kitchen.

A firmer nudge. **This isn't freedom.**

My bracelet slides down my wrist—a reminder of the life I chose. I waver but continue on my path. Just some more soda. I snag some chips, open the fridge, grab the two-liter.

A guy swaggers in, smiling, looking me up and down appreciatively. "Hey, beautiful." He twists the cap off a bottle of vodka. "Can I buy you a drink?"

"Hey." I eye the bottle but shake my head, lifting the bottle of Coke in response.

As I pour the Coke into my cup of ice, he splashes some in anyway.

"Who are you here with?" he asks.

"Jenny." I point back at the living room. "We're—"

At her name, she skips in and hooks an arm through mine. "I know, I know, my friend is pretty, but it's time to dance." She drags me into the living room.

Party Guy follows and holds out a hand in invitation. "Just following orders."

No one is sitting anymore. It's just a dance, right? Nothing weird.

He sways and bobs, pulling me closer. I sip my drink for an excuse to step back, but he closes the distance.

"I'm just here to have fun," I say over the music. "I have a boyfriend." Outdated information or blatant lie? Don't care right now.

"I can do fun." His eyes skim down me, shoulders to toes. His hand grazes my arm.

I'm pathetic, but it's nice to be touched, wanted. In the hours I spent with Austin tonight, he barely touched me at all, with his hands or his eyes. But when Party Guy's hands find my hips, I twist away.

"Fine, fine." He checks my drink. "Here, I'll get you some more."

When he returns, I can tell from the smell of the cup that I can't drink much of it. This is not my first rodeo, and I have a list of regrets I don't want to add to, so I thank him and weave through the group to Jenny.

"You caught Chase's eye, huh?" Jenny says. "Want me to play wingwoman?"

"I'm good."

"Of course. A girl like you doesn't need my help." She flips my hair.

My chest warms, and I don't know if it's her compliment or my drink.

Chase's eyes follow me.

Leo never looked at me like that. Austin's always flicking his gaze away from me, like I'm not enough to hold his attention.

With a last sip, I set my cup down. It's been so long that even those few sips have my head fuzzy. It's fine. I'm good. Kinda slow, but not stupid. Already my laugh is easier, my dance moves looser. It's such a relief to be away from the judgment, the high expectations, the Christian-y talk. I needed to get out of my head.

Half an hour later, skipping down the short hallway to the bathroom, a shadow stops me.

"Having fun?" Chase asks.

"Always."

His grin is back, but something's different. "Come on. I want to show you something."

My gut says *no, no, no* and I jerk back.

"Don't be a prude. This is my apartment. I just want to show you something in my room."

I step toward the bathroom instead. "Can't. Sorry."

When his eyes darken, my stomach drops. He reaches for me, and I lurch inside—and barely get the door locked behind me. My hands tremble. This was stupid. What am I doing here?

Help?

Mia. I fumble for my phone. My thumb stalls over her name. Here come the high expectations.

"Hey, boo," she answers. "What's up? What's that music? Where are you?"

I hate this. "Hi. Sorry. It's just that a ... a guy ... I said no, but he ..."

"Where are you?" Her voice is deadly.

"The bathroom."

"Stay there. Lock the door. Send me a pin."

I swallow my tears. What if I'm making this up? Maybe I'm being dramatic.

A rattle of the doorknob sends me into a jolt of a flinch. "Hurry up," a girl whines. "Gotta pee!"

"Hang on," I call.

Sitting on the toilet lid, I squeeze my phone between my

hands. I pace, play with the shower curtain. How long can I really stay in here?

"Hello-o-o, frenny," Jenny slurs at the door. "How are you sick already? Lemme in so I can hold your hair back."

"No, I'm good. Be right out, okay?"

Desperate, I request Mia's location. Even wash my hands to give me something to do. No hand towel, so I dry them on my jeans. I almost reach to twist the doorknob, but that *no, no, no* buzzes in my gut. Minutes crawl by. I pace, follow Mia's bobbing blue dot. Twenty minutes feels like an hour. I jump at a loud knock on the door.

"Sophie."

I'd know that voice anywhere. I trip over myself to unlock the door.

Austin, with Mia beside him.

I nearly run into his arms but stop just before I embarrass myself. He never hugs me. His face is stone, and he motions for me to follow. Is he angry? As he guides me, his right arm curls around my waist. Possessive. Protective. Fulfilling and shattering my dreams at once.

"Which one?" he growls.

My throat locks.

"Which one?" he asks, more gently this time.

"Tell him, Sophs," Mia presses.

I bite my cheek and nod toward Chase by the door. The music beats around us. We weave around people dancing. Necks turn. Eyes flit between Austin and me. *I know it's absurd. Don't worry, it's fake.*

"Did he touch you?" he asks into my hair.

Even here, my eyes flutter closed. I must be broken.

"Um, no. I mean, barely, earlier."

A rumble vibrates inside his chest until he halts mid–living room, drops his arm. "Was that okay?" It's so loud in here that I have to read his lips. He gestures with his arm. "To make a point?"

To make a point. One hundred percent explicit that he's only touching me for my benefit. Humiliation threatens to flatten me.

"Yeah," I answer.

He replaces his warm bear arm and beelines for Chase.

I shouldn't, but Austin will assume I'm following his charade —I wrap my arm around his back and lean into him. He's so good, so safe. A bomb could go off in here and I'd be fine. He'd make it fine. My stomach clenches.

His hand comes up to gently scratch my upper arm. An "I'm here" scratch.

Three more Austin steps to the front of the apartment, where Chase stands. Austin looks down on him. In all the ways, since he's at least four inches taller and a different species of man. I drop my gaze to the dirty tile.

"Sophie's no will be respected." I've never heard his voice so stern, so threatening. The grizzly bear has been provoked. "Do you understand me?"

"You're giving King Kong right now."

I glance up, and Chase's gaze of contempt lands on me.

"Does that make you Ann Darrow?"

Mia eyes him warily. I've never seen her make that face before.

Chase searches the room before meeting Austin's blue-gray laser beams. "Might wanna do a trade. Doubt you'll get much out of that one."

Austin drops the arm around me to point at him. "Look at her again and see what happens."

Chase sneers. "Samwise, the gentle giant. We both know you're not going to risk getting kicked out of school—"

With a shove, Austin slams him against the wall. I feel the thump through the music.

I yank his arm and beg. "Take me back?"

"Logan." Chase's voice cracks as he calls over the music. "Jaxon."

Arm around my shoulders, Austin nearly snaps off the doorknob to slam the front door open. Without waiting for his friends, Chase bolts away, eyes wide.

Then, Jenny's muted voice. "Sophie? What's going on?"

But I don't look back.

CHAPTER TWELVE

Sophie

Mia glances between Austin and me before badging herself into Griffin Hall. The stairwell light spills out of the doorway and vanishes with a clap.

"What was that, Soph?" Austin asks softly. "You could have gotten hurt."

"I didn't ask Mia to bring you, I swear—"

"You can always call me."

"I just thought I could use some backup. I went with Jenny, but she was ..."

"Drinking," he finishes. "She can't look out for you like that. You could have gotten hurt."

"It was just a party. I didn't know."

He levels a look at me. He went to parties in high school. I'm not fooling him. "Are you ... Never mind. See you tomorrow." With a smile that doesn't meet his eyes, he turns toward Albert Hall.

"What?" I demand.

"None of my business."

I shuffle to catch up, wrapping my jacket around me. "I barely drank anything. I haven't in over a year. It was just one time."

He stops to study me. "I thought we had a really good time tonight. It wasn't enough for you?"

I sputter. "What?"

Spinning around, he shakes his head, as if it's an iPhone with an Undo feature.

I can't let him leave. Not like this. "Isn't it time for my lecture from Mr. Role Model? 'I'm really disappointed in you,'" I taunt in a low voice.

It works. He turns back. "I don't talk like that to anyone." His soft eyes gut me. "Least of all you."

Dropping my eyes to my feet, I notice his. No socks. Sneakers, athletic shorts. Was he going to bed when Mia called?

"How come you're partying again, Soph?"

"It was one party," I snap.

Why am I like this? I should thank him. He deserves groveling gratitude. And apologizing for making a mess he came to clean up. But my throat closes. Like I'm allergic to genuine kindness. And then I'm assaulted with the memory of when Kit planned that amazing projected movie night for my birthday—and I proceeded to ignore her the entire night.

As if he hears my thoughts, Austin sends me a gentle nod. "See you at lunch tomorrow?"

"Yeah," I manage.

"Night." And off he goes.

Back in the suite, Mia's in her favorite oversized KB shirt that says "God's Feelings Matter." "You did the right thing, calling me. Wanna talk?"

I shrug.

"I go to parties too sometimes. You know that."

She never drinks a drop of alcohol, brings her own water bottle. She only goes to play DD when she's worried about her friends driving drunk. The blubbering drunk people open up to her, and she shares the gospel with them. It's laughably different from what I was doing.

Avoiding her eyes, I busy myself by changing into pajamas.

"You don't drink," she says, and watches me for an explanation.

The nudgy feeling says something like **Be honest**. Like that time I was supposed to tell Kit about my counselor.

My gut pulls. I've been ignoring Jesus, but he hasn't been ignoring me.

You kept me safe tonight. Thank you.

"I ... really don't think about drinking anymore, but at the party I was sort of ... drawn to it again. I kept wanting to. So when that guy poured some in my cup, I let him."

Still standing, Mia leans on her bed, tilts her head. "Mira, Sophs."

Uh-oh. Spanish is leaking out. Her Dominican side shows when she's in the zone.

"Mami has a soft spot for donuts. She'll have one at church, but she won't buy them. She never goes through the Krispy Kreme drive-thru, gives the grocery store bakery a wide berth. She knows if she brings home a box, she'll finish them off."

I blink. What?

But Mia walks out and turns on the sink.

Crawling into bed, I untag myself from the party pictures and grumble to myself. This Christian campus is stifling. Everyone's in my business. There was less gossip at my high school. People here have opinions on the length of my crop tops, my workout shorts, how I let off steam, who I'm friends with.

But the words sit wrong in my head. This? Tonight? It wasn't me. Not the new me.

"I'm not judging you." Mia stands in the doorway, toothbrush in her mouth, scarf around her hair.

"I am," I mumble.

"There is now no condemnation for those who are in Christ Jesus."

I drink in the words. "Is that a Bible verse?"

"Yeah." She spits into the sink. "Don't let this pull you away from Jesus, okay? Let it push you toward him. He wants you close."

A lump forms at my throat.

She unwraps a single-use shot, pinches her belly skin, and shoots it in like it ain't no thang. No grimace. No hesitation. Just the click of plastic snapping closed, and a toss into the trash. As simple as brushing her teeth.

Most people don't even know she has a blood-clotting disorder that could kill her—and a hormone cocktail that makes it even riskier. What would it be like to wonder whether you'll live past twenty? To need a nightly reminder that you're living on borrowed time? It doesn't seem to faze her at all. But that's Mia for you.

Wrapping an arm around me, she kisses me on the cheek before climbing into bed.

"Thank you, Mia."

"Duh."

Wiped but wired, I plug in my phone and curl up with my blanket, like it's a makeshift teddy bear.

I'm sorry I let you down.

There is now no condemnation for those who are in Christ Jesus.

I squeeze my blanket.

Thank you.

I want to do better. No more parties. How do I make it up to my friends?

Mia and I are good. But Austin.

I reach to unplug my phone.

Thank you for helping me tonight.

And then,

I had the best time with you earlier.

Blue dots. He's still awake.

AUSTIN

You're welcome. You can call me anywhere

Like if Kim Possible had a hulking older brother. Call him, beep him if you want to reach him.

We good?

So good

Good

The next morning I wake to a bright, empty room. My stomach twists, equal parts queasy and hollow. But I can't just prance to Saga. No.

Must. Avoid. Kit.

Of course, she was asleep the whole time, but I can't bear knowing I put myself in the position I did after everything she's gone through. And I can't look her in the eye knowing she'd never make mistakes like I make. Perky Perfection Kit is just so far from Sophie the Cautionary Tale.

In record speed, I throw my hair into a clip, get dressed, and pull socks on. I channel Charlize Theron as I open the door—like it's an *Italian Job* safe. Coast is clear in the hall. Sneakers in hand, I creep past the sinks and peer around the corner. No luck. Kit is studying in the lounge—headphones in, feet on the coffee table, pointing and flexing in absentminded rhythm. A perfect little picture of discipline and order. So I tiptoe back to my room. My ground-floor window ... perk of living on G1.

"What in the blazes are you doin'?"

At Haymitch's voice, I drop my shoes—and almost my balance on the windowsill's ledge. He veers off the sidewalk, laughing.

Busted.

A quick line of the song "Should've Been a Cowboy" is the only response that comes to me, still straddling the window frame uncomfortably. I wield an imaginary lasso above my head, all Jessie from *Toy Story*, before falling (with style) into the landscaping mulch outside my window.

Grinning, he lends me a hand.

"Headed to lunch?" I ask.

"Yup. Were you by chance in a pickle last night?"

I toe into my high tops and start tying. "Who tattled on me?"

"Nobody. Samwise got a call from Mia and ripped outta there. And now you're slippin' out a window like you're on a jailbreak."

"Just keeping life interesting!"

"Avoidin' Kit again?"

I snap my mouth shut.

He pockets his hands. A beat. And then, "Ya know, I got a feelin'. Could be wrong. But I think Kit's gonna be the friend who sticks like glue. That you're the Samwise to her Jeeves."

I frown.

"Might be nice to skip to the good part."

"How?" I blurt.

He pauses, looking around the campus. A minute crawls by. Then two. Guess he's thinking it over.

My mind drifts. Line dancing tonight. What should I wear? My new cowboy boots, obviously. I used to have some fake ones, but I pestered Austin about what makes boots legit and then ordered the cutest pair of tan Justins with tiny pink embroidery.

He showed me how to break them in, and they're finally ready for action.

A dress? I have a red one that might work, but I can't look like I'm trying too hard. Maybe a denim skirt.

"I didn't get details," Haymitch says, heading toward Saga. "For starters, figure out why you're escapin' out windows and do som'n about it."

"Okay."

"And maybe ask yourself—why Kit and not Mia?"

Why not Mia? He has a point. Mia is gorgeous and strong and capable, but I've certainly never jumped out a window to avoid her.

"God loves you. He ain't mad. He wants ya close."

My breath catches. That's what Mia said.

Was that you?

Pushing through the Saga doors, we're hit by the dull roar of laughing and chatting and forks clinking against plates.

Haymitch hands me a tray with his trademark smile, and I know I don't have to say anything else.

CHAPTER THIRTEEN

Sophie

That night, my pristine Justins crunch against the grass as I cross the field with Mia and Kit, humming "First Time in Forever." *I don't know if I'm nervous or hungry, but I'm somewhere in that zone!* I haven't seen Austin much since last night, so I'm not sure what to expect from him. He may never look at me the same way. No use trying to guess until we get to the parking lot. *Quick, something else to think about.*

"You guys vote yet for the next hangman letters?" I half yell.

"What's all this about hangman?" Kit asks.

"See the poster boards in the windows at Turner Hall yesterday?"

"Yeah."

"They're blanks for a campus-wide hangman game. If you texted the number on those for-sale signs, you got an Insta handle back. That account posts the rules and drops a comment for every letter."

"So you vote by liking the comments?"

"Exactly. The girl running it picks the top two. If they're right, the letters show up on the posters. If not, the hangman gets another limb. If you can't tell, I'm fully invested."

"Count me in," Kit says. "Send me the handle."

"Brilliant to involve everyone like that," Mia says. "I wonder what the angle is."

Kit nods. "You said it's a girl?"

"Oh, no," I say. "Just a girl in my head."

"Probably a self-aggrandizing floor," Mia says.

"Not a bad guess," Kit says.

"Hey." I tap her arm. "Did you leave early from lunch yesterday? Test Dr. Shannon on her theory?"

"Yes." She gnaws on her lip.

"Aaaand?"

She glances toward Levi's Range Rover. "He jumped up and walked me to class, happy as ever."

"Checks out."

"So ... the exact opposite of what Dr. Shannon predicted." Kit looks to Mia. "My counselor doesn't like Levi."

"About time that happens," Mia says.

We snap to her.

"I'm joking. 'Cause everyone likes him. What?"

"You mean, besides Mateo," Kit says.

"Eh, he barely likes anyone."

"Isn't it super concerning that my counselor doesn't like my boyfriend? I'm literally paying for her advice."

"Are you though?" I say. "You're paying her for advice about PTSD. How's that going, by the way?"

"That part is so helpful. Now I have strategies in place that have already been game changing. And Dr. Shannon and I get along well. She's just been venturing off into other areas of my life. Way past the one event and its consequences."

"I never look back, darling," I quote. "It distracts from the now."

But my *Incredibles* distraction flops.

"Sorta the MO of a therapist, no?" Mia says.

I straighten my skirt and move my hair behind my shoulders. Almost there.

"I wouldn't know," Kit says. "Everyone acts like counseling is exactly what a person needs to live a good life, but ..." As if she caught herself, Kit looks to Mia to save her.

"What?" I press, too sharply.

"I'm not ... I'm just saying that if you have a thing you need to work through, then yeah, but then once that's getting better ... She just goes on and on about me and what I need and what I deserve, and it just feels kind of ... self-centered?"

Chest tightening, I raise my eyes to heaven. But that reminds me—I should pray.

Her mom literally whispered kind things in her ear every night as she went to bed. Of course she doesn't need to be told what's normal and what isn't. My hands clench into fists. *How dare she.*

But also ... She doesn't get me, which means I probably don't get her either. And Haymitch was right that I should work on things with her.

Help me do that?

I don't know what to say that's friendship promoting, so I do the next best thing—clamp my big mouth shut.

"Say more about that," Mia says unhelpfully.

"Um? Well, Dr. Shannon is so defensive of me, and that's nice, but I don't think demanding respect from everyone and everything sounds like what I should be doing."

"You *are* too agreeable," Mia says.

"Right. And I've been trying to pay attention to my motivations. But Jesus wasn't prancing around demanding things. He served humbly and selflessly. I just think the time with my counselor is sort of unproductive now because not everything is about me. Like, when I ask my mom about something, she wants to know what the other people need and say. She makes me see their perspective. It's really annoying at the time, but it's what I need."

See? Her perfect little mom and her perfect little life.

Except, I know better. Her life hasn't been perfect at all the last year.

"Might be onto something with that," Mia says. "I'm sure not every counselor has that bent though."

Kit peers over at me, but the best I can do is pretend not to notice.

Besides, that's not my focus right now. The guys are joking about something by the Rover. I can see the back of Austin's head. Looks like he got a haircut.

"Sorry, Sophs, I shouldn't criticize something that's helped you. I only have a few weeks of data, and—"

I wave it away. No awkwardness allowed tonight. "Let's just have fun."

Austin's sleeves are rolled down and buttoned—his version of fancy. Pearl buttons. Bootcut Wranglers. Those beloved cowboy boots he only wears for special occasions. He takes such good care of them that they may as well be a live animal instead of a dead one.

I give Austin's arm a push from behind. "Oh good, you found a plaid button-up. I was worried."

He spins around. "Hey, y'all." His eyes drop to the cowboy boots below my skirt. My eyes, on the other hand, are firmly on his hair. *Oh, heyyy.*

"Austin, your haircut is fire," Mia says. "Good change."

"'Preciate that," he says.

I turn to Kit, holding in the schoolgirl giggle about to escape and accidentally puff out my cheeks, all chipmunk. She pops them like we're kids, and we both dissolve into immaturity. He always looks incredible, but this hair thing is doing me in.

Austin shoots Levi a look, eyebrows doing the talking. Levi answers with a smug little nope of a smile—whatever that means in bromance language. Then they both turn for the car like the conversation never happened.

Stepping beside me, Mia kicks my butt from behind. "Vámonos."

I return the favor. "I sent you a country playlist, Levi."

"A Sophie playlist. I have high expectations."

Levi's a sweetie.

Up front, Haymitch feels his way to the front passenger door. Oddly, it's the seat we all avoid. Kit still won't sit there because of her car issues, and Mia and I don't need to chat with Levi the whole way while Kit stares at us. Mia and Kit crawl into the back, leaving the seat next to Austin for me. I could kiss them for that.

He glances over as I buckle in. "Hey, you." There's still a lilt in the "you" from being home. "Excited?"

My jaw stills. I get another chance. He's not holding last night over my head. How? I instinctively touch his arm.

He's so forgiving, so fun, so adventurous. I'm his biggest fan on a normal day, so on a thrilling day like today, I have to work hard to cool it.

"Completely. Thanks to you." Yeah. Cool as a furnace. "How do you know the owner?"

"He goes to my church. The place is called Mabel's Dance Hall after his mom, who opened it."

"Aww."

He smirks. "Wanna tell me I'm a genius again?"

"Nope." Almost worth it to see his beaming smile.

"I'll be around if you change your mind." As he buckles, I have a split second to fully take him in. Those magnificent plaid-wrapped shoulders.

"You look really good, Soph," he says, voice low and rough.

My greedy eyes flick to his face. My heart hammers. "Thanks ..." What was that? He never talks about how I look.

But he jerks toward the back. "Hey, Kit."

If he compliments her too, I might actually shed a tear.

"Ground rules on dancing? You gonna stick with Levi or ..."

"Yeah, I don't think I'll risk it. Sophie will be way more fun to dance with anyway."

I take back every negative thought I ever had about you, Kit.

"Yeah? You up for a dance or two with me?" he asks me. As if it hadn't occurred to him.

I study his face. Still no judgment. Just normal Austin.

"I might be convincible," I say.

He breaks into a sly grin. "Okay."

"Oh-kay!" Mia says too loudly. "Sophs, you have some line dances ready? I'm amped."

"You're gonna slay, Mia. And you know I'm on it. Kit and I added the *Step Up* line dance to our repertoire today."

It's true. After lunch we made use of her dance studio and actually had the best time. Kit's years as a dancer made her weirdly good at memorizing steps in order. She picked them all up in thirty seconds flat. Also, she loves *Step Up* and will actually watch it again now that she and Levi are finally together.

"Ah-ah, ah-ah," I start.

Right on cue, Mia rolls her shoulders to the imaginary beat.

"Levi, turn the music down for a minute," Kit calls, and then joins in so I can do the next part. She starts a miniature version of the steps right there in her seat.

Austin watches us, amused.

I suck in some air for the long "yeah," "ohs," and "nos" that start the song.

Mia lifts her hands, fully invested, and belts the ridiculous high note from the movie: "O-on the weekend!"

And just like that, we're laughing too hard to finish the song.

CHAPTER FOURTEEN

Austin

It's official—I'm a goner.

As I lead Sophie back from a turn, she grins up at me, and the rest of the world takes a polite step back. Every freckle tempts. Every touch buzzes with electricity. The look of shame last night is gone. Now, she glows. For the moment, one hand is in mine and the other clutches my shoulder, warm and at ease. She trusts me to lead with no hesitation and no looking back—completely sure I've got her. Her eyes shine with thrill like this is exactly where she wants to be. Maybe she's as done holding back as I am.

Frank was chill about letting Sophie take the far side of the dance floor while the rest of the patrons carried on with the usual. She was gut-punch gorgeous while she line danced, sliding on the beat-up floorboards, throwing her head back in laughter. You bet I joined in, and I couldn't wait to change direction when I faced away from her. She curled her hair for tonight, and it bounces around her back, pointing down to that skirt that shows off her long, toned legs. Takes all my self-control to keep my eyes up. And those boots. She looks so good it hurts. I can hardly believe I'm holding her hand, leading her around, catching these latte-colored eyes. I'm burning up, but tonight they're only making me warmer. I wish we were dancing to "Free Bird" so I could have nine minutes instead of three.

Please let me shoot my shot with her. Before it's too late. I know she's going through some stuff, but I can go through it with her. Please. Just let me have this.

Mabel's still smells like wood polish, Dr Pepper, and brisket leftovers. Boots scuff in rhythm. Ceiling fans whirl overhead, and strings of warm bulbs hum above the dance floor. I grew up here —watched my grandparents spin and laugh under these same dim lights. Now my parents' friends are watching from the rail as I spin Sophie back. Mama will hear about this by tomorrow.

Maybe Sophie'd be horrified to hear it, but she belongs here. First time and she's already been joking with half the room like she's a local. All spark. All glimmer. Fading paint, low ceiling, but she's got the place switched on. Laugh loud. Ideas wild. She makes life bigger. Fuller. Every day's a thrill just waiting to see what she does next. I know she likes city lights and crowds, and I could do that. I'd move to Timbuktu to keep her in my life. But watching her tonight—free, unguarded—I can't shake the thought she might be happiest right here in Graham.

Keeping things platonic-ish requires every ounce of my willpower, so when her face turns serious, my chest constricts. I wish I could keep her here all night, but the song is ending and I'm not gonna screw this up. *One last spin, Sparky.* I'm not gonna hurt her if I'm leaving. I won't. I allow myself a brush down her forearm as I let her go.

"Thanks for the dance, Soph. Can't believe you just learned. You killed it." And I have to walk away.

Sophie

It's official—I'm out of my mind. Why would I dance with the guy I desperately want but can't have? That incredible three minutes made just-friends life fully unbearable. And now he's asking Mia to dance like it meant nothing.

Since our dance, Austin's kept his distance—like someone dimmed the lights on us. I've gotta fix this. Bring back the color. Normal Us. He sees me coming and pivots, pretending he's on his way somewhere.

Not so fast, mister. I grab his shirt from behind. "Austin, hold on."

He spins around with a gulp.

With splayed arms, I pretend to tap dance—no idea why—and answer for him. "Of course, Sophie. I'd love to talk to you for two minutes." And I throw in an exaggerated smile.

He agrees with a smirk, so I lead him to a wall where we can talk semi-privately.

"Did I make you mad or something?" I ask.

His eyes shift. "Hey there, Mrs. Turner. How are you?" His accent is thicker than it was an hour ago.

I spin to see an elderly woman melting at the sight of him. I get it, but *Get in line, lady.*

"I'm just splendid, Austin. So nice to see you. And lookin' so spiffy."

"Thank you. This is my friend Sophie, from school."

"Oh, I've met Sophie already. Fine as frog hair, idn't she?"

"Hi again!" I say. "I saw you out there cutting up the dance floor."

"Oh, I'm just an old fogie gettin' some exercise." She chuckles, then gestures at Austin. "Get to dance with this one yet? He's the best we've got." She lowers her voice. "By a mile, bless their hearts."

Best what? Dancer? Eligible bachelor? Human being? I bet she means D, all of the above.

"I only ranked one dance," I say sweetly. "Did you get a turn yet?" I look up at Austin, all innocence.

He suppresses a grin.

"Don't want my date gettin' jealous now, do I?" she teases. "Y'all have fun now." She pats Austin's cheek. "Tell your mama hello."

"Yes, ma'am."

When the coast is clear, I spin back to him and poke his chest. "You've been avoiding me all night."

"Oh."

"Is this about last night?"

"What? No."

"Then the dance was weird."

"Ah—" He shuts his mouth when I look at him levelly.

I want past this ASAP. I am not losing my best friend because of a perfect three-minute dance.

"No more dancing and we're back to normal," I demand.

He kicks my boot and leans against the wall, looking out at the dance floor.

"Careful. You might scuff your themed footwear." I join him on the wall. "Think of the alligator that gave its life."

He just kicks my boot again. I bump him with my shoulder, and he nudges me with his hip.

I let out a breath. Back to normal.

Pajamas on and hair in a messy bun, I curl up in bed late that night.

Oh. Hi. I didn't pray very much today. I'm sorry.

Mia shuts the door behind her, scarf wrapped around her hair and nosy expression firmly in place. "What's this about Leo?" And she sings a line of "I Forgot That You Existed."

I grin. "I could never." But my smile dies. "I dunno. He broke up with me a few days ago."

"*He* did it?"

"He mentioned self-respect." I grimace.

"Diache. Poor kid." She flicks her fingers. "You wonder why I want none of that mess."

"You would never be Leo."

"No. I'd be you."

That sits heavy in the room.

"You really think you'll never get married?" I ask.

"Nunca. Marriage is supposed to be special—one of those rare times two people can be more good for the kingdom than they could be apart. Like a force multiplier. Paul said single people can have undivided devotion to God because we don't have to worry about taking care of a spouse. But everybody got it backward, and now that's the rare thing."

"What if God brings someone to you anyway? For real this time."

"I guess it's possible. I kind of hope he doesn't. I'm not slowing down for someone unless God makes me."

As she pulls out her blood thinner shot, a thought spills in.

I've been treating you like I treated Leo. You could never be Leo to me. You're everything. I've been looking at it all wrong. Teach me to see you the right way.

CHAPTER FIFTEEN

Sophie

When Leo-breakup-guilt creeps in again, I slump in the suite lounge and reinstall my social apps. I never last long without them. Especially when I need something to do.

Feet on the coffee table, I scroll, not really seeing. Just moving my thumb, letting the videos blur past. My brain fills in the blanks anyway—how to edit my posts, what wardrobe pieces I need, which trends are already dead. The same pointless noise.

I don't care. I just need to not think. I double tap and scroll, double tap and scroll.

This isn't helping.

With a sharp exhale, I lock my phone and slide it onto the table. I almost pick it back up, but then ... a quiet pull. A whisper of a thought that isn't mine. I try to lean in.

Hi.

But whispering back just cracks open the door I'm holding

shut. Like my bedroom door. It had to stay closed if I needed to cry. Rules are rules.

I jerk a glance at my phone.

Sophie.

Like he's right here. Doesn't he know the mess is about to leak out? Doesn't he know people leave when I need too much?

But my chest eases. Like my body knows something my mind doesn't.

I'm sorry about Leo.

A shaky breath lets out more tension.

Give him good things, someone who appreciates him.

A thought bounces around my head. "Teach me to see you the right way." My prayer last night. My back straightens, legs cross under me.

I'm ready. Teach me.

Rifling through the bookshelf next to me, I snag a notebook and borrow one of Kit's erasable purple pens—she said all her stuff was up for grabs. The only child in me was disturbed, but I won't say no.

Twirling the pen, I glance around the lounge. It's gotten snazzier lately. I used to have all these lantern lights and posters and things in my room, but Mia and I are rarely in there except to sleep. Kit and I scavenged a hilarious stash of ancient posters from a thrift store before break. My favorite is a kitten dangling from a rope, with pink script that reads "Hang in There." As I trace the rope with my eyes, a tune pops into my head. I grab my phone and send the song to the speaker. "More Like Falling in Love" by Jason Gray.

That's it.

I flip open my notebook and write *L* on one side of the page and *A* on the other.

On Leo's side, I write,

Duty

Forgetful
Obligatory
Trying
Nice
Too safe
Bare minimum

On Austin's side, I write,

Delight
Thrill
Laughing
Playing
Fun
Edge of my seat
Blown away
Safely dangerous
Always wanting more

Duty versus delight. If the difference between me-with-Leo and me-with-Austin is this startling, how much more should it be for me-with-my-Savior? I clutch my bracelet. Delight.

Okay, Jesus. I'm so in. Let's make this fun.

I've always wanted to try hand-lettering, and this is the perfect opportunity, so I pop on Amazon and order myself a journaling Bible—spiral-bound with huge empty margins. And the pens the reviews recommend. Cool.

Next, I open my Bible app.

Where should we start? I half-think, half-pray.

Esther. Why not?

"Now in the days of Ahasuerus." There's a name.

Kit materializes and taps my foot like she does. "You broke up with Leo?"

I fling the notebook closed before she reads between the lines. "What?"

"Leo. I've been waiting for you to bring it up. You don't want to talk about it?"

I purse my lips. Not to her.

And ... the puppy-dog eyes.

My exasperated sigh escapes.

Just as I'm going to relent, her face hardens. "I'm not gonna beg," she mutters, and continues to her room.

I stand to gape down the hall. She never used to be like this. She'd cling tighter—apologize, roll over. It always made me flinch. It was too much. I'm not used to people staying when I push. Not used to anyone wanting more from me than I know how to give. Like Mia. She doesn't need much. Easy peasy. But with Kit, I hold a firm line—keep a healthy distance.

But my hand drops to my notebook.

Have I made this a Leo-style friendship?

I have. One-sided. One person does all the work. All the apologizing. All the chasing. My head jerks up. I never heard the door close. She should've shut it on me by now. Locked it, even. But no.

I don't get it. I pick at my nails as Haymitch's voice flickers through my head. *Might be nice to skip to the good part.*

"Kit?" I call, shifting my weight, not quite ready to walk down the hall. "Wanna go on a field trip?"

I expect her to call out a reply, but she steps—hesitantly—around the corner.

I don't know what to do with that.

"Sure ... I have a couple hours before Praise and Prayer."

I pat my pockets, pan around for my keys. When I track the AirTag with my watch, they ding from a pair of jeans on the floor in my room.

Field trip ... Groceries for the suite, maybe. Kind of lame, but the cold, dreary drizzle rules out anything outdoors. And indoor stuff gets tricky—Kit has zero money, and I hate dragging her places she can't really enjoy. I could pay, but it makes her all twitchy.

As we push out the building doors and head for the parking lot, I don't even know where to start. I've been hiding the whole Leo-Austin mess for so long. What if I just spilled it all?

Her shiny brown hair glides around her back, and her magazine-worthy hips sway as she walks. She's beauty incarnate. It's hard not to hate her.

Help me love her?

Her expressive eyes ask the same question as her delicate eyebrows. She's a Disney character come to life. It's why we gave her the floor name Belle. Plus, she's all bookish and quirky. She doesn't even try—does nothing to her hair, rarely wears makeup, never paints her nails. She used to, but her high school friends were awful to her, and now she avoids the popularity game like the plague. But the joke's on her. The second she hard-launched a relationship with one of the most well-liked guys on campus, she became the accidental queen of Mayberry. Freshman queen at that.

She's still waiting.

"I feel really bad," I finally say. "I think I was mean to Leo."

"Because you actually just want to be with Austin?"

My head snaps over without my consent.

She blinks innocently.

How does she know that? Does everyone? Does ... he know?

Her face scrunches up. "Whoa. I'm sorry, Sophs. I should have eased into that. I've just been avoiding asking while you were with Leo because I didn't want to make you defensive. So now that you're not with him, I thought I could finally be forthright."

"Umm." Too high-pitched.

She bites her lip, then starts singing "Low Key" by Forrest Frank.

A shocked laugh bursts from me. I couldn't have done that better myself.

"Maybe it's your thing to answer with a song line? Sorry."

I open my mouth, but nothing comes out. Again. This is not how convos go with Kit. She usually tracks me down, and I chatter away. She says like seven supportive words, zones out sometimes, and smiles a lot. Right now, we're in some kind of role-reversal *Twilight Zone* episode.

I force my brain into gear. "Nope, perfect line. Just catching up over here."

Pretty Redhead passes, looking a little too happy. The one I watched from the parking lot that first day back. Maybe she was awarded a second date.

"Just the one hangout, to my knowledge." Kit glances over compassionately and motions to me. "Yeah, I know that too."

I close my gaping mouth like a fish.

"You're beautiful but compare yourself all the time and don't value what you have. Is that why you stayed with Leo so long? Because he was so in awe of you?"

My brain goes haywire with all my secrets filling the air. "Okay, okay, Patrick Jane. No more *Mentalist* tricks for today. You're freaking me out."

After climbing into my Jeep, I heave a sigh. I love this bright yellow beauty. She's been with me for so many adventures. My transportation to adventure, to new and different, to a better place. Maybe she can make this bizarre and tragic conversation bearable.

As I reverse out of the parking spot, I gather some words. There is one pressing question. "Is it, like, a publicly known fact that I'm"—I drop my voice needlessly—"into Austin?"

Into doesn't begin to cover it. When he's close, someone could hook me up to an electrical grid and power a small town with the voltage running through my body. It's ... a lot. Dancing with him last night? Even the memory sends a shock through me.

Her no is a tiny movement, but I feel it. "It's not like that. But also, it wouldn't surprise anyone if your friendship turned into more in an instant. There's chemistry, you know?"

Chemistry? I mean, I'm a walking lab fire around him, but he doesn't flirt with me any more than with other girls, does he? He's Austin. Gorgeous and present and always smiling and teasing. He's Austin.

"Does ..." I can't get it out. It's too mortifying.

"I'm not sure if he knows that you like him as more than a friend," she says carefully.

She knows something.

CHAPTER SIXTEEN

Sophie

I'm driving, but barely. Emotionally speaking, I'm nearly fetal, as the reigning fairy princess rides shotgun. Kit. The fairest of them all. The sugary sweetest. The very smartest. No surprise she got her dream guy, even while slamming the door in his face. Me? I've got a soul-crushing, unrequited crush and a breakup-shaped boulder of guilt. What's worse, I've let myself fall for Austin when we could never be happy long term. I can't even fantasize about a future with him because he'll settle down in that small town with wheat fields or whatever, and my imagination always pops a *Little House on the Prairie* bonnet on my head. I'd be in there trying to bake apple pie, trapped in a gossiping small town, stressing about the mending I need to do. For Kit to imagine her future, she just needs to add a castle and a designer bag. How do I not hate her for that?

Okay, hate isn't the right word. But still. It's complicated. I want to be happy for her—and I am—but I want that against-all-odds fairy-tale ending too. And it's not going to happen. Not for medium, lanky, over-the-top me. And definitely not with Austin.

I'm so bad at this, Jesus. Help me just be her friend right now?

She attentively watches me.

"It's bleak, Kit. Like ... I'm a mess." Just spit it out. "Remember when school had just started? That Flooders movie night that Mia and I dragged you to? And then Austin sat by me at Saga and invited us to play games in the lobby?"

She confirms.

"And then that first time we went to B-Dubs for wings?" My heart can't decide whether to flutter or collapse at the memory. "He fought with me about country music with that smile of his, and I fully lost my mind." Okay, my heart. I lost my heart.

Me with Austin? Unlike Levi with Kit, mine was a master class in delusion. I tried everything in the flirting handbook—from answering his texts right away to curling up next to him during a movie. At first he'd reciprocated. Then something shifted. He pulled back—not a full wall, just a half wall I could still see over. And when I tried steering our conversations toward longer-term relationships, he shut it down every time.

And honestly? Good thing. It's not okay how strongly I feel about him. It's not safe. It's not wise. It's just, no. Still, it sucks to be rejected any way you look at it.

I let out a breath. Can Kit handle any of this? Maybe she already knows.

"He ... never implied he liked me as more than a friend. Even at my birthday adventure, he kept saying it was a 'friend thing.'" I risk a glance. She's listening. "He's asked out every other girl instead. Like, *every* other girl. You know. He kept things strictly friend-like between us, just like he did with you and Mia. Except, that's what you guys wanted." Grimacing, I continue. "I wondered if he might respond to jealousy, which is why I tried to talk to Leo."

Kit pivots to her window.

"Gretchen, is that you?" I try. "Your hair is full of secrets."

"So fetch!" She turns back to attempt a smile.

I brace for judgment.

"Leo ... It was always about Austin?" she asks. "I guess I made a mess."

"Well, at first it was, yeah. But then I was embarrassed that Leo wouldn't talk to me at all, and I dug in my heels. And then ... he was actually so sweet. In the words of Elaine, 'yada yada yada,' and here we are."

Kit sits silent.

I grasp for something more to say. "Have you watched *Seinfeld*? It's basically *Friends* before *Friends* was *Friends*. So ancient. But funny. Inappropriate though. Maybe you wouldn't like it. We could try it in the lounge. But we don't have that much time for binging anymore ..." I run out of oxygen.

Her half smile. Yep—she's blaming herself. "I remember Austin at B-Dubs that first time," she says. "Flirting hard with you." She bites her lip and considers me. "Can I ask you something?"

"Yeah, shoot."

"How are you and Jesus?"

I snort. All that about Austin and my enormous, not-actually-secret crush and she slams on the brakes for a Jesus interrogation? Leave it to Kit. But also, it's cool that he's her favorite topic—she gets it in a way other people don't.

"I've actually had sort of a major breakthrough recently."

But I don't share the Leo versus Austin concept. It's too fresh right now, too personal. "And I feel like he actually answers when I pray. Not the big ones really, but the little ones."

Like how I'm already feeling way nicer toward Kit.

Thanks for that.

"Do you still ask your *What would Jesus do if Jesus were me* question?" she asks.

How does she know about that? I can't and don't talk to her about Jesus-y things. When it comes to our faith, she's in calculus and I'm in preschool. I don't go there.

"Remember when I asked you to convince Austin to take me on the experimental car ride?" she continues. "You said it then."

Am I ready to actually cannonball into Jesus Land with the local expert?

Do I have to?

I cringe. Can't do it.

She pulls a leg up to face me. "But then our lives exploded a little, huh? Levi and finals and Alabama, and then we all split up for break."

"Okay, KitKat ..."

Oops. Austin called her that to mess with Levi the other day. It just slipped out of my mouth.

She grins. "Yay, a nickname."

Aw. She's a cute little thing. Lovable, if you give her a chance. Like a bunny on the side of the road that you hope won't become roadkill because of her innocence. I'll just own the nickname like it was my idea. Austin can tease me later. I wonder if she'll drop the topic if I just continue—

"So do you?" she presses.

So much for that. I grab my phone from the cup holder.

"Hey, can I type for you?" Her voice is high and breathy.

I frown.

"I have enough car issues without getting in a wreck," she says quietly.

Oh. Guess that makes sense. I check the previous couple messages from Austin before handing it over. Nothing she could judge too hard.

I drum my fingers on the wheel. "Ummm, just say, 'Need anything while I'm at the supermarket?'"

Bloop.

Ding.

She reads aloud. "'A few more plaid shirts since you like them so much. Want a shopping buddy?'"

Kit types on my phone without my consent. Not a fan.

"Wait, what are you saying?" I ask.

"'This is Kit. Back off, buster. I'm the shopping buddy today.' Can I send it?"

"Love." I hope he fights her on that.

Bloop.

Ding.

She types again without reading aloud.

"Hello-o?"

"This is my phone," she says.

What could those riveted eyes mean?

Bloop.

"What?" I ask. "Is it Sir Levi?"

She shakes her head. "So what are we getting at the store? Snacks?"

"Uh—"

Ding.

I need a neck brace for this whiplash.

"Austin says, 'No fair. I call dibs for next time.' And a Jimmy Fallon GIF saying 'Pick me!'"

I whimper and start a *Hamilton* song I know she'll recognize —"Helpless."

"Aw, Sophs! This must be so hard."

"You have no idea."

What's missing here? Oh, I'm being lame. This is not how friends have fun together. "Girl. Time to play DJ. We need some tunes."

She types on my phone, and a song plays in seconds—"Fake It." Points for Kit. This is the perfect driving bop.

"Excellent work, Iago. When Tauren Wells went all Bruno Mars."

And we're dancing in our seats, rolling down the windows, singing.

Thank you. I needed this.

I'll get to the honesty part, okay? I'll get there.

Fifteen minutes later we wander down the candle aisle of the grocery store. Overhead, Barry Manilow is vibing. Below, I'm wrangling a cart the size of a U-Haul.

"Favorite smell?" Kit asks.

"This one." I sniff another. "Nope, this one. No, *this* one is so good. Your favorite?" I ask. "No, wait. It's the cookie one, isn't it?"

"For sure."

"Crushed it," I say, like Fat Amy.

She giggles. "I don't actually buy candles with scents though. It's too much to think about or something."

I snort. "Calc III? No problem. It's those floral scents that'll get ya."

A full laugh.

"Chip aisle next."

"Favorite chips?" Kit asks. "Anything with queso, right?"

She gets me. "Girl, yes. The worst day can be improved with queso. And the right queso is a complete meal—protein, carbs, fiber, fat." I grab a bag of tortilla chips. "Same for trail mix. But that's not chips. You like barbecue, right?" I toss that one in too.

"Yep. And kettle corn. Does that count as a chip?"

"Totally counts." I point for her to grab a bag. "Way more than trail mix."

She hands it to me, and I throw it in the cart, avoiding her eyes. She's probably tallying what she can afford. She'll fuss when I pay for all of it, but the poor thing has zero funds. Pretty sure she's at Mayberry on scholarship.

Something tells me I should talk to Kit about Levi. No idea why. They seem perfectly nauseating to me, and she already talks about him all the time.

Is that you?

Not sure, but I do it anyway. "How are things with Sir Nods a Lot?"

Her shoulders shoot up in pleasure. "He's amazing. I mean, when I'm not doubting everything because of my counselor, it's the best thing ever. I still can't believe it's like this now. I really didn't think it ever could be." She slows. "The no-kissing thing is new for me."

"How's that going?"

"You know, it's helpful in more ways than I realized ... I wanted to do it this way for a few reasons, but partly because I thought avoiding the physical boundary quandary would save us some heartache. Kissing isn't actually a line at all, and things get so complicated so fast. But I'm also finding that having a more obvious line in the sand makes us freer to show affection in other ways."

I wouldn't know. I've never had a boyfriend I wanted to keep kissing.

"I'm so thankful that Levi was willing to do this with me. It was so not his idea of a good time. He's—"

"Amazing," I tease her, fanning my face.

Is that what you wanted us to talk about? Seems random.

She smirks. "Yeah. I think ... I love him."

Love.

"Aw, Kit. Wow."

I've never fallen in love. Unless this Austin fiasco counts as one-sided falling in love. Yikes. And yet, peak Sophie.

"How was dancing with Austin last night?" As if she can read my thoughts.

"It was rough. I mean, incredible in the worst way. Terrible in the best way. I've been thinking about something you said to me a while ago."

Look, I'm confiding in her. Help me out, okay?

"You said that God really cares about every little thing that happens to us," I continue.

She bobs her head with enthusiasm.

"Something is telling me that if Jesus wanted Austin and me to be together, then things would be different, a lot of things. If the Austin thing can't happen, God has his reasons. He has something better."

Kit grabs my hand from the cart and flaps it in victory. "Sophie, yes. This."

She's a one-woman pep rally. Spirit fingers heavily implied.

And then I feel a whisper-y nudge—**Praise and Prayer.**

You want me to go? Tonight?

But ... I don't want to.

Church is not for me. Too much pressure, too many expectations, and way too many people ready to tell you what's wrong with your life. Pass.

But Jesus? He's different. I want all the Jesus. At that, I grip the cart and sigh.

I will not treat you like Leo. Not for one more day. Whatever it takes to dive in with you on this.

"So ... you're still super into Praise and Prayer, right?"

Her face lights up. "Absolutely. Come with me tonight?"

Okay. Let's do this.

"If you can play bodyguard. I'm not trying to get pounced on by churchiness."

"Yes, yes, yes." Then she points at dozens of bouquets. "Hey, favorite flowers?"

I scan the options and point to the brightest tropical bunch. "This one."

Beautiful. Loud. The only one of its kind.

I see you. Thanks for this.

It's just Praise and Prayer. Just one time. But something about it feels like a before and after.

CHAPTER SEVENTEEN

Austin

It started like every other morning.

Bible studied. Real-life application considered. Prayers sent up. Same desk, same routine, same mug of that fancy coffee Levi bought me.

But then—

The brakes-screeching, gut-check feeling I always get when I pray about Sophie? Gone. I prayed the whole walk to breakfast and back, just to be sure. And every time it was the same. I got the green light. *The* green light. I get to go for it.

Finally! I'm amped!

And no more Leo—another confirmation.

Levi strides into our room as I'm pacing like a loon.

"Yo, Jeeves."

Maybe Kit told him about my text. No—she's still guarding my not-secret.

"Samwise. You're peppy."

"Sophie. Saturday's the day." Almost there. No more holding back. No more second-guessing.

"The day for ... Oh." He points toward me in focus, dropping his stuff on his desk without looking.

Lucky he read my mind, so I don't have to get all sappy.

"Have some time to help me talk it out?"

"Absolutely. Now?"

"Now. I'm fixin' to bounce off the walls, man."

He lets out a laugh. He gets it more than anybody. "What's different?"

"I got the green light. I prayed and prayed and ... I just know."

He pumps a controlled fist. "Why Saturday and not today?"

"I know—another six days is brutal, but I need time to plan something worthy. Our group field trip is the time. And also, I need to set myself up for success, lay a little groundwork." I motion, as if he doesn't know what groundwork is.

He lowers to his desk chair and grabs a new box of Tic Tacs out of his drawer, never taking his eyes off me. "And UT?"

"Now? Just a tragic backup plan."

Clarity. Like a gift floating down with a parachute.

He studies me. "Alright. So this is it." He rests his forearms on his knees, serious as a heart attack. "Let's make sure she says yes."

That flicker of relief in his eyes means more than he knows. Classic Levi—wants what God wants, but he'd rather have his friend than some football star.

I rub my palms together. Let's go. Falling back into my pacing, I point at my desk, where a vase sits, borrowed from G2. "I'm gonna have flowers smuggled into her room Levi-dessert style, so when she wakes up after our first date, she already has a present from me."

"Classy. And finally using The Game to send her a message?"

"That was always the plan. But now ... I can't do it. What if she needs to say no?" My gut clenches. "It's too much pressure on her. I'll get to that after. I gotta do this live. In person."

"Great call, Samwise. Way to think about her side of it."

"Thanks, buddy. So for Saturday, I need something adventurous." I pause my pacing. "It's Sophie, you know? She doesn't want traditional. Something big. A surprise. Trouble is, she's already done everything around Pinecrest."

He nods thoughtfully. "We haven't taken the crew to Portside yet. You know, Kit and I could go down with you another night if you don't want to wait until Saturday. We could ward off suspicions and then get lost."

"You would like to get lost with KitKat, wouldn't you?"

"Without a doubt." Levi always grins when he's teased now. So freakishly happy.

"I'll think on that. Thanks."

"I recommend you decide specifics based on details only you know. Seal the deal with the more-than-friends thing." He slaps his armrests, almost as jacked about this as I am. "She's gonna cheer and clap like the monkey with cymbals, dude."

"Oh man, I hope so. Okay, what does she like to eat?"

"Everything? She's always up for eating. Why are you asking me?"

"I dunno what other people know about her."

"Got it. Shoot."

"Does she like to be fancy or casual?"

"Don't know."

"Does she like day or night better?"

"She hates mornings. Otherwise, no idea. You're the Sophie expert. You're gonna kill it."

"'Preciate that, buddy. Oh, and, uh, does she know I like her?"

"Beyond oblivious."

Oblivious, Sparky? Seriously? I hesitate before the next question. Whatever Levi says, I'll have to live with it. "And ... what are my odds?"

He exhales, slow and steady. "I like your chances."

My chest tightens. I can't let him be wrong.

"Okay, God," I pray aloud, "if this is your thing, just keep me from messing it up."

He chuckles. "Yes. That. And help him trust you with this." To me, "Let me know if I should plan something for Kit and me as supporting roles."

He wants in. What a sap. *You and me both, buddy.*

I text Sophie.

Saturday. Got an idea

Wanna come up with group costumes for us?

I know you were bummed about missing out on Halloween

SOPHIE

Are Levi and Haymitch actually down to dress up?

Yup

My friends are real ones to give Sophie carte blanche on this. Especially when they know her so well.

Yessssssssssssss

I might go a little overboard.

I expect nothing less

You're the best!!!!!

Let's do CLUE!

Five more days.

Sophie

"Does it fit? Come on, come on."

"Hold your horses," Kit says over a laugh. "I'm trying the other one."

"Why is no one ready?" I say in my Miranda Priestly voice.

"By all means, move at a glacial pace." She doesn't miss a beat.

I stare at the dressing room door. Something's different lately. Maybe, once you hear someone's voice singing to Jesus, you hear their laugh better too. Or maybe it was my own singing. Maybe promising commitment to him in song makes it come true sooner. Either way, I'll be at Praise and Prayer again next week.

"Going to jewelry," I call. "Still need some pearls for Mia's costume." I weave my way through the store to a table packed full of necklaces.

"Costume party?" A dude voice comes from behind me.

When I spin around, I'm greeted with a crooked smile. Cute stranger. My age maybe. Open face, easy confidence. A whiff of cologne drifts off him, and I'm not mad about it.

I lift the hanger to my shoulders and curtsy with the dress. "What gave me away? The bright-red velvet or the hilarious silver embellishments?"

He chuckles. "I heard you yelling about Miss Scarlett."

"Mm. You're a detective too."

"As long as I'm not Mr. Boddy. I might oughta keep quiet about the candlesticks back there." He points with his thumb.

Chuckling, I motion to his armful. "Find a treasure yourself?"

"Check this out." He unfolds a vintage denim jacket.

I gasp. "Like the guy in *The Breakfast Club*. Or Marty McFly ... but you'd need a vest. Or—wait, wait—Bruce Springsteen."

"Oh, let's go with the Boss."

Ding.

It's Kit.

"Miss Peacock is looking for me. Enjoy your jacket, Bruce!"

"Enjoy your party, Scarlett."

I stride back toward the dressing room and flick a glance at the ceiling. Maybe when you smile at God, his world smiles back.

As if to confirm it, Kit rounds the corner in a feathered hat and a grin you could see from space.

CHAPTER EIGHTEEN

Sophie

I'm sure Austin heard already, but I won't advertise my breakup with Leo. I can't have him thinking he's the reason. Things might get weird. But if Kit invited—

In an instant she's at my doorway, tugging her shiny brown hair out of a tight ballerina bun. "You should come hang out with me in Levi's room tonight."

In addition to the weekends, we're granted a few hours of Open Dorms on Thursday evenings. For months those nights were reserved for Flooders football games, but when the season ended, Kit and I filled the time doing homework with our boyfriends in Leo's room or the Flooders "light lounge." Flooders on a Thursday might have been weird since I'm no longer going there for Leo, but now I have a personal invitation.

"Great!" I nearly yell. A valid reason to be in Austin's room, his couch maybe. Sadly, I doubt Austin himself will be there. I never see him on his floor on Thursdays. I should just ask what he's doing at that time every week, but he doesn't talk about things that veer into the Leo topic, so neither do I. I start humming. *We don't talk about Leo, no, no, no.*

Kit's legendary in those yoga shorts over opaque tan ankle tights—strong and feminine, like she walked out of *Step Up*. And she fills out that fitted workout tank in a way I never could.

But then she looks at me—bright red and sweaty, physically spent and glowing. Just Kit. A person, not a body.

Is that you answering my prayer?

"Hey, Kit?" I follow her to her room, where she kicks off her shoes.

"Yeah?"

"You sure that's okay with Levi?"

"Yep."

"I mean, he was clearly resistant to us doing homework in his room before, so ..."

"I talked to him." She grabs her shower caddy and pauses, a secret dancing on her features.

"Thanks, girl. So ballerina Kit has entered the chat."

She glances up, like *Uh oh*.

"Gorgeous. Dinner after your shower?"

Her brows rise and her voice softens. "Thank you. Leave in twenty?"

After dinner, I hover in Austin's doorway, laptop clutched to my chest. As suspected, he's not here. Levi lowers his propped-up feet to greet Kit, but she beats him to it, running to curl up with him on the couch. He gently wraps an arm around her shoulders, like he's bubble wrap. She pulls in a deep breath, and her Disney eyes blink up at me. Is she taking that risk for me? I send her a thankful smile. She nods almost imperceptibly and unzips her backpack.

Levi addresses me with a knowing hello. It's annoying how well he can read people, but he doesn't know exactly what I'm thinking right now. I glance at him again. Fine, he does. I'm lucky he doesn't blab the results of his Edward Cullen telepathy to his roommate.

With a stilted wave, I cross the room to Austin's side. Couldn't miss a chance to sit on his blissful rust-colored couch. Soft but firm—the perfect place for a nap. But when I lower, I end up perched on the edge like a *Pride and Prejudice* character, back straight, hands folded. I should be embroidering or writing in calligraphy like this. Maybe someone will suggest we take a "turn about the room." I open my laptop and force myself to slouch—casual, normal. Being in here just feels so ... loaded.

Austin left a hoodie and some shirts on the back of his couch —his stuff is draped everywhere on this side, not unlike my room —and it smells deliciously like him. Like a freshly laundered lumberjack. Levi's side is perfect of course, as if Marie Kondo is hiding in the closet. Both beds hide way up near the high ceilings, lofted above their old, passed-down sofas. Austin's desk faces the window, and Levi's sits next to the doorway. Something about this room ... Even with Levi reading my mind, it feels more like home than anywhere that was supposed to be. Not the sterile Pasadena penthouse. Not my dad's new apartment with that woman. Not the places I've stayed, but the feeling I've wanted. Safe and thrilling. Like Austin.

"Hey, Soph."

My heart bounces like a Labrador spotting its favorite playmate.

Austin. Here. He's never here on Thursdays.

He flicks a glance to the lovebirds, sends a head tilt. Back to me. "Pretending to study?"

"Pretending?" Leaning into my regency impression, I place a dainty hand on my chest in horror.

His giant frame plops next to me, arm on the back of the sofa, body angled toward me. That knee brushes mine, but he doesn't move it. His voice dips, easy and warm. "I like walking in here and finding you on my couch."

Heat creeps up my neck, threatening to give me away.

Levi twists around to peek at us.

I lower my voice. "I think we're disturbing your roommate."

Austin glances behind him, then matches my volume. "KitKat's right next to him. He's not thinking about his work right now."

Sure enough, Levi brushes her hair behind her ear and trails a knuckle down her jaw.

Leaning into his touch, Kit says, "Let's go see what's happening in the light lounge."

Friend of the year.

"After you." Levi makes eye contact with Austin as he leaves.

And we're alone.

"Play a game with me?" Austin asks.

I banish my laptop to the floor.

He shifts to face me completely. Always upbeat and positive —some of my favorite things about him—but tonight, mischief in his eyes is the cherry on top. This is Austin at his best.

"Truth or dare?" That playful voice surprises me with an edge of seriousness.

My mouth hangs open, but I snap it shut. There he goes again. Safe yet thrilling.

"You sure about that?" I send a coy smile. "I won't hold back."

A grin grows. "I'll go first."

I edge forward. I'll have to keep myself in check. Just because he's in a great mood doesn't mean I won't freak him out with too much flirting.

"Okay," I start. "Truth or dare?"

"Dare."

Figured. "Run down the hall and back like a gorilla."

At least a dozen guys are milling about the floor, any of whom would tease him for far less. It's hard to embarrass Austin though, another of his many wonderful traits.

He jumps up and I follow, hiding in the doorway so it's not obvious that I'm behind this. I don't want to be a jerk to Leo.

Austin flies down the hall, waving his arms around wildly and shouting the most ridiculous gorilla noises I've ever heard.

My laugh curls me over against the doorframe. He went big. But that means he'll have high expectations for my turn. Nerves swirl in my belly.

"How'd I do?" He pauses in the doorway with me, closer than we usually stand.

My laugh calms, and I try to speak seriously. "Austin, you've found your calling. That was an inspiring performance."

Unashamed, he steps into the room and leans his hip on Levi's desk next to me.

"Why, thank you. Try not to feel intimidated." His face is flushed—couldn't be from the run. He unbuttons a few buttons, then grips the back of the plaid shirt and slides it off in one motion. "Gorilla-ing is hard work."

I chuckle. "Is that how you take your shirt off every time?"

He smirks and steps to drape it on the arm of his sofa. "Yeah."

And now it's T-shirt time. He has plenty of printed shirts from over the years—the ones that haven't been made into a quilt—but this one is plain, with more stretch than usual. I suppress a sigh, keep my face straight. "Unbuttoning it all the way is so tedious?"

"Exactly." He kicks a football under his desk and lifts his backpack onto the chair. Hesitant eyes finally meet mine across the room.

"Dare," I say, without being asked.

As he meets me at Levi's desk, he pats the back of his phone, presses his lips together. Like he's working up to something.

Then sets his phone down. Deliberate. His eyes find mine. And hold.

Vulnerable. Intense.

He rubs a thumb over his knuckles. Then—

"Dance with me again?"

CHAPTER NINETEEN

Sophie

My face falls. Dance with him? I thought we were being funny.

Luke Combs starts singing from his phone—"Beautiful Crazy." My feet shuffle backward toward the door, but when he holds a rough hand out to me, I instinctively accept it. Shocks of pleasure run through my palm and fingers. I try to stop my gulp mid-swallow and choke instead, cough into my elbow, try to clear my throat. Could Austin ... no. That's impossible. So what does it mean? When I regain lung function, I demand—more confidently than I feel—"You're not going to avoid me again, are you?"

A quiet no. A sweet smile. And then he tugs me closer, and I let my other hand land on his enormous shoulder. At first he positions his other hand on my shoulder blade, but then he slides it to my lower back to pull me a step closer. My back blazes along its trail. His foot guides between mine since we're too close to be toe to toe. The YouTube tutorial couple would not be happy.

No spinning and twirling and happy chaos like last time. He

leads me in a curve between the desks, the tiniest steps and the gentlest touch. Although my lungs may not inflate, oxygen is still flowing. Is that how it goes? I know nothing right now.

His chin drifts to my temple as we glide around. My eyes flutter closed—he can't see me like this, okay? I soak in the closeness with no regard for Future Sophie, who will be confused and crushed. She's dead to me. Muscles slide under my palm as he nudges me into a dainty spin. Turn and a half out, turn and a half in. When he pulls me back, Levi appears in the doorway. I open my mouth to say something, but I don't get a chance. He grabs Kit's bag, biting his lips together, and steps silently back out.

I know Austin spots him, because he straightens, and those blue-gray eyes turn sheepish. But he pulls me even closer until we're nearly hugging. I've never been anywhere near here. This isn't remotely friend-like. I can't turn my head or I'd—

Nope. Can't even go there.

My nerves are haywire. Too much to process—his hand steady around mine, the warmth of his palm on my back, the easy pressure guiding me closer. The way his shoulder shifts under my fingers. The space between us—barely there. His weird and wonderful behavior. His smell—clean, woodsy, like a campfire without the smoke. The way he's watching me, relaxing under my hands like ... like he wants this.

The end of the song, and I lose any chill that remained. What's gotten into him? Why did he avoid me half the night at the dance hall but dance with me in his room? Is this non-friend stuff a onetime thing, or is there hope for the impossible? Should I lock that dangerous thought in the closet, like the Dursleys with Harry Potter?

I yank my hands away and stumble back—too far, too fast. My leg shoots out to catch my balance, landing me in a reverse lunge.

"What?" He steps to the desk to stop the music. "You're a good dancer. It was fun the first time."

"Right. Sure. Yeah. Okay." Wow, could I stutter any more? I

grab a piece of hair. Stop, no hair twirling. Spontaneous combustion is a thing, right? Pretty sure that's happening to me right now. I try to stand like a human but shift my weight. I don't know how to be normal right now. This is so far from our usual.

Austin, on the other hand, has fully transitioned to cool with a side of naughty. Like Ferris Bueller meets Jughead. He saunters back and drops onto his couch, tilting his head for me to join him.

His arm drapes over the back again when I sit down. I love it when he does that. His hairy bear arm can protect me.

"Truth or dare?" I ask.

"Truth."

Okay, I can handle this part. We can talk about anything. Except that. Anything but that. "What's your love language?"

"Wait, my love language?" His eyes flick between mine, as if he can read something there. "What are my options again?"

"Words of affirmation, acts of service"—I count on my fingers—"gifts, quality time, physical touch."

"Quality time." Intense face, pensive voice. "Truth or dare?"

"Hold on. Is that what you give or receive?"

His face relaxes again, and his brows raise teasingly. "You're trying to cheat. It's one question, Spar..." He trails off.

"You were just unclear." I shrug my shoulders innocently, smile playing on my cheeks.

"Quality time for both, I think." His knee nudges mine. "Maybe some service or words of affirmation. You're already a good friend."

I graze his arm. "Back at ya."

Are we closer now? I don't know who moved. He smiles back at me with the most kissable lips I've ever seen. I know I shouldn't look at them, but my boundaries are slipping in this alternate reality. They're so full and ... juicy. The lips are talking, but I don't know what they're saying. My head shake does little to clear it. "Sorry, what?"

So cool. So naughty. "Can I guess yours? It's not your truth for the game, so either way."

Just gotta reboot my brain really quick. I squeeze my eyes shut and open them. Helps a little. It's just Austin. But tonight he's Wildly Confusing Austin—a guy who dances with me like I'm precious. Who stands too close and doesn't say words and looks into my soul.

I reset with a breath. No. It's just Austin. Like Just Ken. This is fine.

"Sure," I manage.

"You seem to really like when someone plans something fun for you, like Kit's birthday movie. So that would be service."

And his incredible creek adventure. Big yes. Massive yes. All the times he's washed my Jeep. How he snags a plate of what I'll want if it's running low at Saga. Collects everything I lose and returns it to me—hair ties, phone, keys. My breaths go shallow.

"And do you give quality time too?" he asks. "And maybe a side of physical touch?"

He knows. He knows me.

He knows how I feel about him?

I spend as much time as I can with him. He's one of the few people I touch, and I touch him a lot. He's the most important person in the world to me. And to make matters worse, this game of truth or dare has been a string of fun things. It's going to ruin me, but I can't manage to stop. Future Sophie's problem.

"Nailed it," I squeak. "Very impressive there, pal. So what's my real truth?"

His eyes drill into mine, his body perfectly still but for his chest moving with his breaths.

I poke his leg. "What is it?" His arm, his shoulder. "What's your question? What are you gonna ask?" I have to poke lightly lest I hurt my finger on his rock-hard muscles.

A girl voice carries down the hall. Maybe Mia.

Breaking into a grin, he pokes me back with every word. "So - impatient - I'm - thinking." Leg - arm - stomach - leg.

Curling in laughter, I reach to grab his side, where he's most ticklish.

He catches my hand gently. "Nice try."

My hand is so happy in his. It will disown me if I dare pull it away. I bravely try harder to reach his side as he squirms and laughs. He tugs my hips onto his lap and tickles my sides. I've never been here before. Big no-no. I love it too much. He curls around me, his laughing breath warm against my neck. That deep voice fills my ear. Sorry, Future Sophie. He effortlessly scoops me out of his lap, stands up, turns around, and drops me onto the couch.

My laughter dies in my throat. Pretty Redhead stands in the doorway, loose curls tumbling over the shoulder of a short winter dress. My stomach lurches. What is she doing here? No.

The doorframe stands like a picture frame to exaggerate her beauty. It says, *Here she is! Pay attention!*

I need to get out. Now. What was I thinking?

Her arms cross, eyebrows high, tongue going to her teeth in annoyance. "Are you coming to study group or ..."

"Hey, Lily. No, I—"

"Okay! Bye! It was fun!" My best imitation of a peppy voice won't fool Austin, but it might fool her.

He grabs my hand, silently asking me to stay, but I jerk it free. I have to outrun Future Sophie. So I bolt out of the room—Lily steps aside—and down the stairwell nearest this end of the hall. It's a longer distance to my building this way, but anything to get out of this place.

Sprinting full force across the grass, I'm an Olympian. No, Julia Roberts in *Runaway Bride*. Someone get me a horse.

A reel runs behind my eyes as I careen like a madwoman. Grin, gorilla, dance, surprise, tickling, Lily. I swipe at my forehead. Can't compute.

What can I do tonight? Something to keep my mind engaged. What could possibly distract me from the last half hour?

My heart nears a reasonable beat as I badge into my building and plow through the stairwell. I pull my phone out to see what's going on around campus. I'm sure I can join whatever Mia's doing, especially if I send her an SOS text—

Ding. It's Austin.

Oh no.

My brain slams the door.

But my heart sends a fruit basket.

CHAPTER TWENTY

Sophie

AUSTIN

You left your laptop speedy Gonzales

Shoot.

Can I bring it to you?

I cover my face. Future Sophie is flying toward me at warp speed, but I do need my computer back.

Sure

Thanks

And then I climb onto my bed to finish the message to Mia, but I don't get to it.

Austin is already leaning on my doorframe with high, teasing brows and my laptop at his side.

Wow, that was fast. Did he run too?

"What was that, Sparky?" Then his eyes widen, like the nickname jumped out without permission. Like a secret he didn't mean to share.

I will my face not to beam. "Nothing. You just seemed busy. Didn't want to interrupt."

He settles against the doorframe and waits for the real answer.

"We don't usually hang out on Thursday nights, so ..." I squirm.

Dude looks unreal smirking at me in his gray T-shirt. What brand is that shirt? Someone should let them know that his modeling is gold. Slap a picture of this man on an ad and they'll never keep up with the demand.

No, Future Sophie! I'm not ready!

Where is Lily? I never finished my text. I need my phone. Where did I put it?

"You're usually with Leo."

I jerk. We don't talk about Bruno. I mean Leo.

"Yeah," I say, as casually as my high-pitched, frantic voice can manage. "You do a study group on Thursdays?"

Leaving his perch at the doorframe, he crosses the room to drop my laptop on the desk. "Not tonight."

"Oh. Seems like Lily—"

"I'd pick hanging out with you over Lily any day." His eyebrows gather to say *duh*. And then he gives a theatrical sigh. "You tried to cheat again. This is becoming a problem."

"Oh." I half laugh. "I ran out mid-game, huh?"

Walking farther into the room, he stops right in front of me. I've always been aware of his proximity, but now my skin remembers his vividly. It screams "touch him again!"

I shrug off the impulse. Gotta pull myself together. That was a once-and-done thing.

"Okay, shoot," I say. "I picked truth."

We're eye to eye as my legs dangle from the bed. His blue-gray gaze drills into mine, like he's trying to read my mind. I glance away.

We always hang out on Flooders during Open Dorms. He's only ever been in here waiting for me while I finish getting ready. I don't have a couch in my room like he does, and my desk chair is covered in stuff.

I smooth the blanket and pat the bed next to me, trying to be as un-weird as physically possible. It's just a sofa equivalent.

He eyes it like it's off limits. Or gross.

Of course. Right. Back to business as usual.

Great. Good. I have no idea what to do with flirty, dancing Austin anyway. I like the status quo. He's my closest friend. I like this. *I do.*

So I hop down and push him out the doorway, too aware of his strong chest under my hands. He walks backward down the hallway, pretending I'm strong enough to make him—until he sidesteps. I stumble forward with a gasp, and he catches me with embarrassing ease. His laugh is infuriating.

Half enamored, half panicked, I smack his arm.

He bumps me gently with his shoulder as those full lips curve into a little smile again. An Austin smile.

When we plunk to the concrete love seat and chair in my suite lounge, his mouth falls in disgust. "Every time, I forget how bad it is."

I let out a breath. "Right? Like torture devices. But Zoe says we're not allowed to move them out of the suite lounge." So relieved to be freed from the horribly magical last hour, I continue on needlessly. "A thrift store love seat could wedge in here with this one on its side, but we have four girls who need seating. Well, three, since Ayumi—"

"Soph?"

At his gravelly voice, I snap to him.

"You and Leo broke up." Just a casually outdated newsflash.

I twirl a piece of hair and drop it. "Sorry. Should I have told you?" I dart around to look at each poster. Cat. Sunset. Hawaii. "We talk about everything else. But we don't really talk about that. I didn't know if—"

"Nah, it doesn't matter. I heard on the floor. Sophie."

I blink. He never calls me that anymore.

"Are you sad?"

My brain swirls. *Don't make me answer that. Don't make me think about this. I can do the status-quo thing with you. I can't do two-stepping and tickle wars and discuss it!* What if I bolted out of here? But I can't—he'd just show up in the doorway again.

"It's your truth question. Are you sad about the breakup? Do you need some time to feel yourself again?"

My head tilts, despite myself. "Oh. I'm not sad about that at all." It's official—I'm awful. After months with Leo, I feel nothing but relief ... and that healthy dollop of guilt. "That's messed up, huh?"

He shakes his head.

What happens now? I'm too scared to ask.

"B-Dubs?" he asks. "Wanna get a group together?"

I perk up like a cartoon character catching a whiff of pie. An escape from this disaster waiting to happen, offered on a silver platter.

"Yes!" I almost yell. "I do like my chicken 'late,' after all."

His eyes ignite, and my skin catches fire like a trail of gas connects us. He couldn't know that's exactly what I lacked with Leo.

But instead of standing, he slaps one hand against the back of the other—his nervous tell. He does that before a big game, walking into a hard test. Never with me.

His gaze traces every feature on my face. Like he might paint me soon. He edges closer. Is he going to confess something—

But he jerks up. And strides out the doorway.

Guess I imagined it. I scramble up. Shake out my limbs. Suck in a fluttery breath. Must recover my composure. Must be a person. I get a Thursday night with Austin. He's choosing wings with me over studying with Lily. I'll take it.

And I stuff Future Sophie into the closet, along with all the hope trying to sabotage me. *You two can stay in there.*

CHAPTER TWENTY-ONE

Sophie

When Marketing ends, I check for notifications.

Your Amazon order has been delivered.

I clap around my books and weave through the people funneling out of classes. Escaping through the door, I aim for MSC. The smell of fried food from The Hive hits me the second I open the door. It's already packed in here, but I snag my package, ask a friend in line to order me a quesadilla and bolt out the second I have it in hand. The grease burns my hands, but I inhale lunch on my way to the lounge. When it comes to lunch, I'm not a Hive-and-hide kind of person. That's Ayumi's MO. I crave Saga's chaos and possibility. But today, this package is heralding Christmas morning. I'm not waiting another two hours.

Running into the suite, I almost flatten Ayumi herself. "Oh. Hey. Where have you been? You're, like, nowhere lately."

"Oh," she says, quiet as ever. "Um, G2?" She points up.

I open my mouth to ask more, but she escapes out the door without another word.

Okay, then.

Tossing the last of my quesadilla on the lounge coffee table, I rip open the cardboard. A brand-new Bible. Hardcover, crisp pages, spiral-bound. The wide margins beg to be filled with the ink of these pretty, aesthetic pens.

I flip to Esther again and melt into the pages.

She's the Katniss Everdeen of the Bible—brave because she has to be, risks everything for her people, and clever too. She stays in the danger. She sacrifices.

I write, underline, highlight in every pen. With every flip of a page, life flows from the words into color. It's alive. I don't realize how much time has passed until the clunk of the stairwell door jolts me to reality. I check my watch.

I'm late!

My pile of books bounces in my arms as I sprint to class. The whole way, I wish I had covered up my Bible. It's not really a secret, but it's private. Precious. Just for me and Jesus.

Snagging the seat next to Izzy, I dodge a questioning glance from our Bible professor. I only missed a couple minutes. And now after running full speed, sitting still feels impossible. He drones on about expectations for our exegesis paper. It's all in the syllabus, so I tune it out and busy myself with calc problems.

Izzy edges in. "Free tonight to be our adopted G3-er? Now that you're a free woman."

I'd normally save tonight to see Austin, but ... Future Sophie rattles the door of the closet. A no-Austin night would really be for the best.

"Yeah, I think so. What's the adventure tonight?"

"Glow-in-the-dark putt-putt after dinner."

I should be thrilled. I think I am. But my mind is still tangled in Esther's story, in the way I couldn't stop reading. Something magnetic is in those pages. I just want to slip back there. But what if Austin asks to hang out tonight? I can't survive that again. I need a solid plan.

"I'm in."

At her room after my run, Izzy digs through her bursting closet.

"So, Miss Recently Single. You don't seem bummed."

My stomach twists. Not this topic. "Not really."

"Cruel." She says it like a compliment, pulling out a pair of maroon pants. "Tell me more."

"I just shouldn't have dated Leo." I busy myself by running a hand over the pants. "This color is so fun."

"Why not?"

"Kinda knew it wouldn't work out." I hold them up to her waist. "Are you gonna go tone on tone or pair it with a neutral?"

"Why was it not going to work out?"

I suppress a sigh. "Eh, a vibe thing. This is such a good cut too. You could go crop top or bodysuit or oversized."

"Fine, don't tell me."

I bite my lips together. I have to give her something. "I ... like someone else. It's a major secret, okay?"

"How juicy."

"Have your eye on anyone?" I ask too quickly. "I hear A2 is full of snacks."

"Wait, Austin Scott?" She twists around. "He's in your little crew, isn't he?" A dangerous smirk. "I bet you could snag a date."

Izzy isn't known for her discretion. I eye the door.

"Oh, you want him, like, long-term?" She huffs a laugh. "You might have noticed he's, like, Mayberry famous."

I shrug and stand. Can't afford to spill anything else.

"You aim high, girl. So what's your plan?" She whips through shirt after shirt.

I mess with the hair on the back of my neck, ooching toward the doorway. "No plan. He doesn't know, and he can't."

Unimpressed, she rips a shirt off the hanger and changes clothes like we're in a locker room. "Do you, boo. Now down to your room. Can I pick your fit?"

Passing Turner Hall, I look for a blank set of poster boards in the windows. Yesterday, the second message was completed:

NO
SPOILERS
YET

The hangman game has been the talk of campus. Whoever is orchestrating this is brilliant. Only sending the social handle to those who texted the for-sale signs number made it feel like a big secret. So of course it spread like wildfire. On our tiny campus, hundreds of votes stream in every night for which letters should be next. But today, not one poster is left in a window. As if it never happened. Someone went to so much trouble to get permission from dozens of residents in Turner Hall to leave blanks and letters in their windows, but without a whisper of who's behind it. I can't wait to figure out who made that happen. And why. I ask the gaggle of G3-ers as we walk, but no one has more than guesses and hearsay.

"The post said a new one should be up tonight, right?" I ask.

"Yeah," Jenny says. "I saw posters in the Albert Hall windows today. Just Flooders and A1."

"No way. Albert now?"

"Yep," Izzy says. "I thought for sure it was a girl."

"Me too. But it still could be. If she knows the right people."

They look at me, but I wave them off. "I wish I came up with this. I have no idea who's doing it."

"Ask your boy Austin," Izzy says. "If the letters are on Flooders now, he'll know something."

"Ask Davis Powell," I deflect. "You say he knows everyone." I still have no idea who that is, but the G3-ers dissect his life like he's a celebrity.

"Jenny?" Izzy kicks her.

She laughs. "I'll ask. But the letters aren't even on his floor."

We arrive at dinner in a pack. Saga may be at the far corner of campus, but it's the town square of Mayberry. There's Austin, leaning back, unfairly resting his hands behind his head. *Not okay in short sleeves, buddy.* He's oblivious to his manly perfection, chatting with Ethan, Zoe, Levi, and Mateo. Judging by all the plates on his tray, he had seconds—at least. And then he spots me mid-chuckle. The second our eyes meet, his grin deepens, slow and easy. His arms drop.

I'm dying to go over there, but that dangerous hope threatens. I tear my gaze away and steel myself—for what, I don't even know.

Izzy raises an eyebrow. "He really is yummy."

I burst into "Backseat Driver" to avoid answering. I mean, I'm living this song.

To her credit, Izzy jumps in like it's karaoke night. She even knows my TobyMac songs. We fill our trays, and I follow the others to the G3 table.

"No way." Izzy pulls my arm. "I'm coming to your table."

"But—"

Something about her face reminds me of Tom Tom in *13 Going on 30.* Dread courses through my veins. What if she says something? What if, with a misplaced word, she blows up my suddenly tenuous friendship with Austin? "Izzy. Wait."

"Good, Kit's not here," she says. "She's, like, too pretty to be friends with us. It weirds me out."

I frown and try to keep up. "Izzy."

Ethan stands from his spot next to Austin, and she plows straight for it.

Someone taps my shoulder from behind. "Hey, Scarlett."

I spin around. Denim jacket guy? From the thrift store? He smells just as good.

My mouth opens before my brain catches up. "Bruce Springsteen goes to Mayberry?"

He rocks back on his heels, enjoying the recognition. "Sure do. You going to mini-golf tonight?"

"Yeah, actually." How does he know about that?

He shifts. "Can I … be your date? Might be nice to have someone fetch your balls and your drinks. From what I know of Miss Scarlett, she's accustomed to luxury."

My brain stutters. *This* guy? A date?

"Oh, nothing but the best," I manage.

His brow rises into his messy brown hair, as if to plead. Dark-brown eyes. He really is cute.

My head spins. My thoughts scramble for footing. I'm ten feet from Austin and dying to see what havoc Izzy is wreaking in my life. But I can't spin around and look at him while this guy asks me out. Not if I want to protect my secret. Bruce here can see him, but he's watching me.

I force a breezy tone. "All I know about you is you have great taste in denim jackets."

Ready smile. Spirited eyes. I wonder if he likes adventures.

Not him.

Was that you?

"Fair enough," he says. "I'm a native Texan, I love fried ice cream, and I can ski—water and snow. Does that help?" He reaches a hand out, like an afterthought. "Oh, and my name is Davis Powell." I try to shift my tray, but he can only jiggle my hand.

My fingers tingle. They actually tingle.

"You're Davis Powell, huh?" A2. G3's brother floor. We know the same people.

He smirks. "You've heard of me."

"A little." A lot.

He crosses his arms like he's got all day to stand here and play. "What have you heard?"

That he's a good guy. That he plans huge volunteering events off campus. That he's not really a Christian anymore but still goes here because the international business program is top notch. That he and Austin are childhood bros.

I just broke up with Leo, but I dunno. This guy could actually be an Austin remedy. Enough to get my mind off him for good. And it's a compliment that Davis is even talking to me.

"This and that," I tease. I readjust my grip on the tray between us.

"Not like this, Samwise." Levi's voice. "Trust me."

At that, I twist to peek at our table. Austin is standing, apparently livid, and Levi presses him back down to his seat. What is that about? I need to get over there. At least Izzy is busy chatting up Mateo.

"Are you with Scott now?" Davis sends a wary glance that direction.

"Who? Oh." No one calls him that. "We're just friends."

"People say you two are tight, so I kinda wondered."

I gape.

He chuckles. "Sophie Appel, right? I've heard of you too."

"What have you heard?" I hear myself ask.

"That you're fun. And you can sing." He nudges me. "But the girls didn't mention how pretty you are."

I try to laugh, but it sounds like a squeak.

"I'll be at mini-golf tonight," he says. "Offer's open if you change your mind. Or after, just the two of us?" With a tempting grin, he turns to go. But he slows at Austin. Stops for a beat. "Didn't think you'd mind, man," he says.

"Didn't ask either," Austin says, clipped.

Davis studies him. And then he saunters toward the door, turning back to send another smile.

A concoction of unknown feelings stirs in my belly. What if this whole time, Austin was just an obstacle to finding Davis?

CHAPTER TWENTY-TWO

Sophie

I jump when Austin appears beside me. My plate clatters on my tray.

"Powell asked you out?" he asks.

"Huh?"

"For when?"

"Uh. Tonight. Why?"

"Are you going?"

His jaw is tight, his body rigid. What happened? I turn to the table. Levi looks fine. Did something happen with his family?

Even like this, Austin gently takes my tray and sets it on the table for me.

I search his hard eyes. "I thought you liked Davis."

He rolls his shoulders, as if begging for calm. "Not right now, I don't."

"Hey." I start to reach for his arm but stop myself. "What's wrong? Is everything okay?"

His voice dips lower. "Just, please don't go out with him. And especially not tonight."

Dread settles in my gut as I flash back to Chase. "Why?"

He turns imploring. "Because ... we're gonna be out late tomorrow night."

My spine stiffens. "Seriously?"

"No. Please, Soph. Come out with us." He gestures to Levi. "We can do whatever you want. We'll bring along anyone you want. Except Mia and Haymitch are busy. But anyone else. And you'll understand tomorrow." He pulls gently on my forearm, the please heavy in his eyes, like a neglected puppy.

The nerve endings in my arm won't shut up. They're throwing a party down there. I rip it away. It's not enough that I pathetically follow him around like a shadow, but now he thinks he can tell me who *else* I'm not allowed to date? "Look, I appreciate your help at the party last weekend, but I don't need your help with this."

"Right, but—"

"So I'll understand what tomorrow?" I spit. "That you can go on twenty dates a month and keep up appearances, but I need to wait longer after Leo?"

"What? No." He looks desperately to Levi, who sends him compassionate bro vibes.

"What's happening over here?" Izzy skips over. "You know Davis? Did you convince Austin to come tonight?"

I gape. She invited Austin? And the pieces fall together.

"Mini-golf is a joint-floor thing?" I ask her. "G3 and A2?"

"Yep. Why?"

Austin rubs his eyes with one hand.

"Come with us, Austin." She flips her hair. Flips. Her. Hair. "I'll make sure you're never bored."

Austin vaguely shakes his head at Izzy and stares at me like I'm going to concede the date any second.

Chill, she mouths to me. *You need two dates?*

A long grunt escapes as he spins on his heel and aims for the door—until he huffs, pivots, and jerks his tray off the table to take it to the dish return.

Kit glides through the doors and beams at Levi from the line. When she waves to me, her smile dims. Abandoning her empty tray, she beelines for me. "What's wrong?"

I'm the problem. Me. Kit's only ever wanted to be a good friend. Gratitude slams into me, and I mash her into a hug like a crazed fan. She hugs me back, rubbing circles on my back.

"Um, hi?" Izzy says. "Coming, Sophie?"

I want nothing to do with Izzy's casual wrecking-ball energy, but if I'm going to mini-golf tonight, I'll have to be friendly-ish. "I'll come find you later."

"Fine." She plucks up her tray and saunters to her usual table.

A few minutes later, I get a text.

AUSTIN

I was out of line. I have a good reason for what I asked but you don't need anyone bossing you around. I want to hang tonight but no pressure

Ugh. I slide my phone to Kit.

"You might want to show that to ..." *Levi*, she mouths, as he listens to Calvin next to him.

I frown. "Why would I do that?"

She grimaces. "I promise I didn't say a word to him. But he ... already guessed. And he's the best problem-solver in the world."

I groan and scrub my hands down my cheeks. "Sure, whatever. Pass the phone." Now that Izzy knows, it's only a matter of time before the whole school does. All the more reason to go out with Davis tonight. It'll soften the awkward blow when word leaks to Austin.

Kit achieves Levi's attention with a simple turn of her head and pushes the phone to him.

He reads the text and looks to me, poker face in place. "How can I help?"

"You're kinda biased. You love the guy."

I'm not the only one, he mouths.

I purse my lips. "I've heard good things about Davis. And Austin shouldn't be telling me who to go out with."

"True." Levi leans back, cocky as ever. "But I have a much better track record." He hesitates. "At Mayberry."

Kit was Levi's first date here, and they'll probably go on to have three perfect babies.

"You're not wrong," I concede.

He remains quiet.

Fine, mind Jedi. "What do you say, Mr. Perfect College Dating Record?"

"I say not Davis."

That's what you said.

Kit squeezes Levi's arm, like all that was a personal favor to her. Why is everyone so interested in this random turn of events?

I let out a breath. "When you can unpeel your hands from your boyfriend, let's head to Flooders. I have a grizzly bear to make up with before I head out."

Levi's poker face melts as Kit stands from her seat. "Something for you is on my desk." Like, *Pat me on the head and tell me I'm a good boy!* How the mighty are brought low by puppy love.

And then her shoulders launch to her ears, as if she hasn't received dozens of similar dessert gifts from him.

"You two are disgusting," I mutter.

They both snap to me, and Levi's hand finds Kit's.

CHAPTER TWENTY-THREE

Sophie

I chuckle to myself, smoothing my bejeweled red velvet dress. This thing is perfectly ridiculous. Group photo, posted. Davis, tagged in a comment. So he can witness the Goodwill masterpiece in all its glory.

Yes, I declined the ball fetching and after-date with him last night—mostly to appease my weirdly invested friends—but I flirted as much as I wanted. He's fun and sweet. And actually straightforward.

When he DMs me, I jump at the opportunity. The perfect distraction from Colonel Mustard. More like Colonel Spicy Mustard because Austin looks so good in his costume. The yellow ascot I bought him is nestled into his white button-up and tied to perfection. Levi can be thanked for that, I'm sure. Austin's sleeves are notably rolled down. Khaki chinos. I didn't even know he owned those. Close-and-Touchy Austin was indeed a Thursday-only event. In fact, he's been distant and off tonight, still hasn't told me what got him all wound up yesterday. But I refuse to dwell—Future Sophie is still safely locked in the closet, and I will not allow his confusing behavior to ruin my perfect night.

Kit and Levi prance behind me like it's just another evening in rich-person land. She can't help but look unnecessarily elegant in her thrift-store dress, navy trench coat, and peacock feather, and he's no worse for wear in a purple tie and glasses. I couldn't find a purple suit, so I didn't even get to embarrass him. Mia is killing it in the black jumpsuit I bought her, pearls and all. Over the top? Maybe. Do I regret it? Absolutely not. I had tickets to a Hulvey concert on Halloween—unskippable. Missing out on a chance to dress up was a bummer, so Austin is the best for this second chance at a night of costumes. Haymitch searched high and low and found a green blazer to borrow. He's a sweetheart to go to such efforts for a random night out that I care about more than anyone else. I sent a pic to his girl because that jacket and his red hair are worthy of commemoration. And because a few hours without his baseball cap is straight historic. I can't believe we pulled this off in just five days. Our crew is the absolute best.

Levi drove us an hour across the Louisiana border to stroll down the boardwalk in Portside. I guess Austin kept it a surprise for me because he knows I love that kind of thing, but it's odd that everyone else knew the plan. At least he warned me we'd be walking a bunch so I could wear my sneakers. Only a hill and a railing separate this sidewalk from the inky black river below, and the danger of probable alligators adds a thrill. For dinner we ate finger foods from the kiosks lining the street. Austin treated me, which was random and sweet, and I got to try everything—always my favorite.

Stars shine in the clear sky. Enthusiasm and anticipation buzzes. I love nothing more than a new place and a new experience. So much possibility. I can't stop singing "Good to Be Alive" by Jason Gray, lyric swapping what I see around me. And the one by Andy Grammer too.

Kit and Levi murmur behind me, probably holding hands like

it's the most magical thing in all the world. Mia and Haymitch bring up the rear. I bet Mia is twitching at playing caboose back there. We usually switch positions as we walk, but tonight no one has budged.

Austin starts hitting the back of his hand against the other palm. Not that again. I pull out my phone, but before I even unlock it—silence.

When I glance back, I expect to see the lovebirds gazing into each other's eyes, but they're gone. All four of them. I stash my phone and nudge Austin. The little ninjas—where did they go?

Austin stops to face me. One of his fidgeting hands reaches for mine. My entire focus lasers to my fingers and palm, singing with electricity. His huge, rough hand engulfs mine. It's even sweeter felt and seen. He holds my hand like it's dainty and must be protected. Then he adds his other hand over the top, so mine is completely sandwiched away. All safe and warm inside. Forbidden contact—Thursday again. Weird and wonderful Thursday. I'm all longing and terror. Doesn't he get it? I can't handle this.

"Sophie."

Dread floods in as I lift my head. This is a new voice from Austin. I know his playful voice, pensive voice, football voice, stern voice. What is this? A deeper version of his affectionate voice?

"You're so much more than a friend to me." His eyes lock onto mine. "I can't help it. You're so beautiful. So curious and creative and playful. So golden and ... *alive*."

My lungs have stopped inflating, and the oxygen is not flowing. My mouth dries. Ambient sounds cease.

Strangers silently edge around us. He guides me to the side.

"I've been waiting to tell you because this—*us*—is a big deal to me. You're a big deal to me. I had to wait for the right time. So I ... I kinda freaked yesterday 'cause I've been planning this. It killed me to think of losing my chance with you."

CHAPTER TWENTY-FOUR

Sophie

Breathe. I forgot how to breathe.

Austin drops a sandwich hand and pulls me closer. "Soph? You okay?"

Look at him. His curly hair all McDreamy-like on his huge head on his massive shoulders. His eyes—soft, steady, good—like a teddy bear turned human. He's the most perfect person I know, inside and out.

This doesn't make any sense. This cannot happen.

The line of girls before me. Savannah, Camila, Lily, Faith, Fatima, Mikayla. And those are just the ones I know about. Every last one, stunning. Some smart, some funny, some sweet, some fierce. Most of those girls never even got a second date. The world tilts. I need one of those oxygen masks.

Protecting my freedom means keeping my heart out of the crosshairs. Half-miserable, maybe, but at least endurable. Even if I somehow didn't screw this up—and, oh, I would—we don't make any sense together. Best case, he'd follow me around and never be content. Worst case, we'd grow to hate each other. I ...

Have to get out of here. I snatch my hand away. I'll figure out how to play this off. We'll find the others and have a normal night. By tomorrow we'll be back to Normal Us.

"Sophie." His voice is strained. "Say something."

This will blow over in no time. I'll go out with Davis to make things really clear, and Austin will have moved on to the next girl by Tuesday.

I jerk my head to pan like a caged animal. The others are MIA. What do I do? How do I survive this?

Help?

So if you sinful people know how to give good gifts to your children, how much more will your heavenly Father give good gifts to those who ask him?

My panning slows to a stop. I hand-lettered that this morning. Wrote it like six times until I got it just right.

So if you sinful people know how to give good gifts ...

This is a gift?

But how? Why? I don't know what I'm doing. I barely know how to follow you yet.

My eyes fill.

A gift. For me?

Austin steps back. His jaw tightens. His gaze flickers everywhere but me. He presses his fingers into his eyes, like this is physically painful.

What if it's true? If this is a gift, I can't waste it.

I couldn't waste it.

Impulse wins, and I take the step back toward him, answering with a kiss. Just a peck. A *No more panicking* peck.

And then I suck in an audible breath.

I. Just. Kissed. Austin. My face lights on fire.

His hand drops. Wide, relieved eyes. Relaxing shoulders. I almost laugh at his reaction.

He wraps an arm around me and pulls until our hips touch.

Oh. I like this.

His hand on my back is at just the right height, like Hitch taught Albert, like when we were dancing. The other hand finds my chin, tilts it up to his.

"You scared me," he murmurs, lips so close they almost brush mine.

"Sure about this?" I whisper.

His answer is the most glorious kiss, his lips pressing into mine with slow, deliberate certainty. My nerves erupt, my mind fogs, my lips buzz with energy. I can't believe this is happening to *me*.

Wait, is this real? What happens when it doesn't last?

Another kiss. Shorter. Firmer.

He pulls back, and I blink up at him.

Back to full height, his face splits into an impossibly attractive, mischievous grin. "Ready for the next adventure?" But he makes no move to go anywhere.

I need an out-of-office reply. *Thank you for your inquiry. I'll respond just as soon as my brain completes a factory reset.* Instead, my mouth goes rogue. "Oh, kissing me is an adventure?"

His grin deepens. "The best kind."

That kiss-smile combo. How many girls have seen it before me? How many times will I see it? How long until it's gone forever?

I swallow, begging my brain to take a break, and somehow manage, "Lead the way."

His eyes go gentle. He doesn't budge. Instead, he brushes hair from my face, the pads on his fingers sliding across my skin. My eyes almost roll into my head.

"Talk to me, Soph."

Should I bother with the truth? It comes tumbling out anyway. "I didn't think you liked me like that."

His face crumples like I told him something absurd, like I'm transferring to Texas A&M.

"You've already dated half the girls on campus." Part question, part accusation.

He rolls his eyes. "Half? Really?"

What am I doing? My best friend just declared impossible feelings for me, and I'm picking a fight.

"I wasn't kissing those girls. It wasn't the same at all."

He wasn't? Process. Can't process.

My feet ease me backward. What have I done? That was the stupidest, most impulsive decision of my life. Three kisses—

"Hey," he says softly. "You didn't like it? Me dating?"

I half laugh, pitifully. He's gently pulling my cards down one by one.

"I hated when you were with Leo," he admits quietly.

Too much honesty. All at once.

When he reaches for me, I cave—fall into his bear body. I spent an embarrassing amount of time imagining this.

It's better.

Warmth. Safety. Trust. Electricity. I could live here. Goodbye, world.

"I'm sorry," he says softly, pressing a slow kiss to my forehead. "I'm sorry," he whispers into my hair.

The best apology of my life.

"I didn't think any of that through," he says. "Since I met you, I've just been biding my time. Distracting myself."

More kisses around my face. Bliss.

Biding his time? Distracting himself? Cannot compute.

"A song," he says. "I need a relevant song, Soph."

It comes in an instant. I mumble the title, still half drugged from the apology kisses. "'Life with You.' Walker Hayes."

Austin starts murmur-singing it, exactly the part I mean—about commitment issues and being done flying solo. His thumb runs down my arm. "Let's listen to it where we're going."

What a perfect, infeasible dream. He smells like fresh air and firewood. Like a lumberjack. How do I keep him this close? How do I keep reality from hitting me like a brick?

"C'mon." One more kiss on the bridge of my nose. "You're gonna like this."

"Mm. Surprises."

He catches my hand and takes off jogging down the boardwalk. The best hand. The best night. The best guy. And yet, my eyes sting with unwanted tears. Because this relationship will destroy me.

But I'm still following. Running to my doom. I blink the tears away and steel my heart. I can't say no to this. Dating the dream guy is the experience of a lifetime—I refuse to refuse it. I'll enjoy every bit of Austin for every minute I have him.

Future Sophie will just have to rot in the closet ... until she haunts me for the rest of my life.

CHAPTER TWENTY-FIVE

Austin

The Portside water tower is so high that vertigo swirls in my head when I look down, but the view is spectacular. The girl beside me, though—she's even more terrifying ... and far more beautiful.

Kit had brought her a change of clothes, but she's Sophie and did her own thing—leggings under her dress, a quick rip up the slit so she could climb. It's enough to make a guy lose his mind. She looks like a Cirque du Soleil performer in the best way.

I bump her shoulder, and her grin peeks through.

What a can of worms I've been begging to open. Help me do this right. I'm all yours. All of this is yours.

She's uncharacteristically quiet, my fingers laced around hers. These are the hands that have been poking and pushing me for months. Finally holding them is deeply satisfying.

"We're good after yesterday, yeah?" I ask. "Powell has terrible timing."

"Oh, come on." Voice dripping with sarcasm. "One guy asked me out. Meanwhile, Izzy wants next on deck."

I send her a look. "Cut it out. If this goes the way I want it to, there is no 'next on deck'—" I wince. Too late, too unfiltered. My adrenaline is running out, and my mouth is running ahead of me.

She stares at our hands, avoiding my eyes. "Your hands are huge. I love them. They're like bear paws."

I chuckle, trying to brush off the nerves. "So what's your assessment? Was the climb worth it?"

"Beyond worth it. It's crazy how well you know me." She glances up from under her lashes, vulnerable. "This whole night has been ... perfect. You're just the best." Then she furrows her brow, relaxing into her playful usual. "If I keep telling you that, are you gonna get a big head?"

"That's a real risk, Sparky."

A perfect grin. "Oh well. You're the best."

When I kiss the back of her hand, I linger a second longer than I should. I didn't know it could be this good. We made it past the friend zone. The girl I love kissed me. Yeah—pretty sure this is the real deal love. And now we're on top of the world. Kind of literally.

Then she pulls her hand away. "I'm an idiot for saying this right now, but I really don't know how this can work."

My body goes still.

"I'm not saying we don't try, but we aren't really ... compatible." She darts a glance at me. "Surely you've thought about this already. I mean, I want to see the world, and you want to drink sweet tea and watch the sun go down."

All this time, that's what's been bouncing around her head?

"Why not both?"

She smiles, but it doesn't reach her eyes.

On one hand, she's thinking long term on our first night together. That means she's serious about this. But on the other hand, she's already penciled out the reasons we won't make it.

"Can we take a picture?" she asks suddenly.

Whiplash much? "'Kay ..."

She expertly angles her phone, snaps a few shots before settling on one where I'm watching her instead of the camera. A hard launch? That means something. And Powell will see it. Her fingers fly across the screen, typing a caption I don't catch, and then the phone disappears into the pocket of her leggings.

"Are you gonna wreck me?" I blurt.

Her face droops into something apologetic.

My stomach falls off the water tower. Nope—that was my heart, and I'm waiting to hear it splatter below.

I can't bring myself to ask what her face meant. It couldn't be the sweet-tea thing, right? Surely not.

She's always responded to me so effortlessly. I tease her, she teases back. I smile, she smiles back. I tap her arm, she pushes mine. I kiss her, and boy did she kiss me back. But now the game's changed. I've fallen for her, and she's ... what? Hovering in midair?

The play isn't going well, but it's not a total emergency. I'm in the pocket, still got a second to scramble. I'll win her over. I'll take care of everything for her, in every part of her life. I'll be her hero, her friend, her confidant, her partner, her admirer, her planner, her biggest fan. I'll make sure she gets all the new and different she can stomach. I'll captivate her like she's captivated me from day one. Levi waited months with barely any encouragement. I've already got three kisses to fuel me. I can do this.

So I lean in, lips brushing her ear. "We'll see about that."

Her shoulders rise, her eyelashes flutter. Success. I made it back to the line of scrimmage and gained at least a couple yards. For good measure, I press a kiss under her ear.

"You'd better quit that," she says, hushed and wobbly. "I'm gonna fall off this thing." And she inches her hand back into mine.

Yeah, I'm not mad about this. She's already making it a thrill for me.

I need this to work. I want it so bad. Please help me.

When we meet up with the others to drive back, they shove us into the back row like the ride-or-die friends they are. Sophie doesn't argue—just fakes a yawn, as if she's Kit, then drops her head onto my lap as natural as can be. I'm only a man, so I slide Haymitch's ridiculous green jacket under her head while she pretends to sleep. *Yeah, right, Soph.*

I love that she wants to be close to me. Love that she decided to try a New Us despite her reservations. Love that she's giving me a shot to prove that I can be what she needs.

Levi's got Switchfoot blaring up front to stay awake, so I can't sing to her. Instead I run my fingers through her hair. She exhales long—content, I hope. My heart presses against my ribs.

I love her more every minute.

Sophie

Okay, no, I'm not sleeping. How could I, when Austin is this close, his hands in my hair like some kind of dream? How could I after a night like this? I'll never process it all.

Pre–water tower, he wadded up his ascot and button-up—three buttons and over the head—so it's just me and his T-shirt. One of his hairy arms rests on my side like a weighted blanket. I've never felt safer.

Levi announces he'll pull up to Griffin Hall to save us a walk. The Rover's interior lights flick on, too bright. I drag myself out of the most magical position on earth to climb out of the car, rub my eyes.

Oh—Austin swoops me up, his arms warm beneath my knees and back. Not even an exhale from him, as if he just picked up a backpack or a football. I curl into his chest.

"I'll at least carry you to the door."

He's not even allowed in the lobby this late—school rules—but I kind of get it now. If he carried me to my room, I'd have a hard time letting him leave. I want to do things God's way and wait till I'm married for, well, a lot of things. That commitment suddenly feels incredibly confining, but I reject the thought. I'm not bailing on this. That stuff isn't freedom.

Kit's a champ for staying out till four in the morning for me. Campus is silent except for the sound of my friends' footsteps on the pavement.

When we reach the side door, he sets me down gently. I tug on his shoulder, but he shakes his head. "I'm fresh out of discipline. Night, Soph." But he does kiss the top of my head before he makes for Albert.

"Good night," I call. "Thanks for tonight."

Move over, Cinderella. Tonight my prince was also my fairy godmother and my carriage.

In the blindingly bright stairwell, Mia and Kit suffocate me in a squealing, delirious hug.

And then a song link arrives, just as I land in my bed.

AUSTIN

Song of the day

"In Case You Didn't Know" by Brett Young

CHAPTER TWENTY-SIX

Sophie

Based on the sun blazing in, it's late. And yet not late enough. I groan and bury my face into my pillow.

"Morning, sunshine," Mia says, writing at her desk.

"I had the craziest dream that I kissed Austin," I mutter. "And he climbed with me up a water tower." I mash on my achy eyes. Why did I tell her that?

"Girl." A laugh hovers in her voice.

I huff.

With I-told-you-so eyes, she points. She told me what? A glass vase of flowers waits on my desk, flowers like the ones I saw at the grocery store with Kit. What? ...

"Ki-it," Mia calls. "Freakout on aisle one."

Kit swings through the doorway and studies me, eyes rimmed with exhaustion.

I jolt up in my tangle of blankets.

"Do you regret it?" She studies me, then turns to Mia. "Maybe we should have stayed so she could bail if she wanted."

Mia holds a hand up. "Let it cook."

I scramble off the bed and snatch the note from the bouquet. No one's ever bought me flowers before. Austin's scraggly handwriting stares back at me.

something pretty to look at since you don't look in the mirror all day

My head spins. I collapse onto my desk chair, squashing four days of clothes.

"He thinks you're gorgeous," Mia croons, channeling *Miss Congeniality*. "He wants to kiss you."

Kit giggles. I gape.

"This is good, right?" Kit asks me.

It's too good.

He's too good.

It's only a matter of time before I screw this up or he moves on.

This is crazy. Help?

I got myself into this. Is this something I should even be asking Jesus for help with? I flit between amused Mia and hopeful Kit.

Leo and Austin ...

I wouldn't bother Leo with it, but I can talk to Austin about anything. And Jesus is way more "Austin" than Austin. I want his help.

Okay. You care, right? About all the things? I have no idea what I'm doing. I have no idea what's happening or how long it's going to happen.

Just another step and another step.

I sit up straighter and comb hair out of my face.

"Have you checked your phone?" Kit asks. "I bet they're at lunch if you want to—"

I leap up and dig through the clothes under me. "Ready in five! No, fifteen! Ah! Thirty." Check my hair in the mirror. "Fifteen!"

More than fifteen minutes later, I plow through Saga's doors. There he is, wedged between some Flooders, chowing away. He jerks up like he senses my gaze.

I wave, like *Hey, whatever. This is cool and super-duper normal. I think we're together now, but I dunno, it was late and maybe you changed your mind.* My limp wrist is weird. What am I doing? I head for the trays. I should have a salad after all that fried food last night. Probably won't. Is that Pad Thai? Odd. Maybe it's a previewers' weekend.

Without warning, blurry flannel buries me in a bear hug. Whoever this is smells like Austin, but actual Austin would never do this.

"Get some sleep?" Almost Austin murmurs against my hair, fingers threading through it.

Not almost. Real-life Austin.

My jaw is gone. Floor, probably. I blink, too stunned to answer.

He frowns. "Do—"

I cut him off with another hug, nearly tackling him. With a rumbly laugh I feel more than hear, he squeezes me tighter. I'm in a blender with a pine tree and a bar of soap. A hug for the record books.

Mia shoves us out of the food line.

"And you thought Levi and I were bad," Kit says.

"Like he just returned from war," Mia says. "Get a room, you two. Or ... don't, on second thought."

People stream past us, grabbing trays.

Austin pulls back but doesn't let go. "Soph. No other girls for me. I hope that was obvious. And, I wanna be your boyfriend. The only guy taking you out. Can I?"

My heart flips. "Yes, please."

He presses his lips to my forehead. "Thank you. I won't let you down."

No one pinch me. No one talk any sense into him. Everyone remain calm and leave me be. This is the best dream of my life.

That night, I get a text. Another song link.

AUSTIN

Song of the day

"Goldest" by Walker Hayes

CHAPTER TWENTY-SEVEN

Austin

Sophie's walk between classes should take her right by here, so I'm hovering outside the math building, creepily waiting for her to materialize. Four days into the relationship that I'll do anything to make work. This is Mission: Captivate. My fingers drum against my palm. The plan will work best during the short period between classes because I'm my own biggest risk. All these people around are going to keep me in line.

It's crisp and wintry today, but I'm overheating. She's not even here yet. I yank off my button-down, ball it up, and drop it.

I should not be this nervous. It's not like she's my first girlfriend. Or the first girl I've kissed. But it's so different with her. With her I crave more. I scare myself. What if I lose my resolve and screw it all up? I know how much is at stake, so I've been holding a hard line.

I still my hands, but it only lasts two seconds before I start up again. I'm as fidgety as Levi.

Is this shady? It's so hard to know.

There she is, walking with a friend I don't recognize, but that should be fine. I step over and grab Sophie's hand.

A startled jump precedes her signature smile.

With a wave to Random Friend, I lead Sophie to the wall. Protecting her head with my hand, I press her hip against the bricks. Okay, one slow and firm kiss. Passionate but classy. Captivating but careful.

Kissing her feels incredible. Like stepping inside a volcano without getting burned. My entire body leans in, demands more.

Breathe ... Remember the plan. "Hey, Soph." My shaky voice gives me away. "I'm so lucky to be your boyfriend. Have a good class."

Her sweet mouth falls open.

With that, I lead her back to the now-gawking friend, turn her body to her previous position, and take off without another word.

Success ...

Shoot—

My shirt.

Sophie

Austin's already inhaling his lunch when I arrive at Saga. An hour and a half ago, that surprise kiss sent my pulse clear to the moon. No idea what he's up to, but I'm not mad about it. Tray in hand, I head toward our tables and scope out the seating situation. Levi and Kit just left, and Austin is surrounded by other Flooders. I'm almost to a seat by Zoe and Rosemary when Austin bends forward to drop a comment to Noah. Noah smirks, glances at me, and—without a word—stands and moves down the table. The guys around Austin trade knowing looks, shaking their heads and shoving him like they're in on some joke.

"Yeah, yeah. Hey, you," Austin says to me, all Nick Wilde

from *Zootopia*—that effortless, sly confidence that makes my pulse misfire.

"Hey, everyone." I sheepishly take Noah's seat. "How's it going?"

They greet me and continue their conversation about a football game.

I edge forward. *What was that?* I ask Austin with my eyes.

"Look at you," he says. "He gets it. Also, I'm gonna do him a favor."

I can't decide if I'm embarrassed or honored, so I dig into my mac 'n' cheese. "How was your morning? Any surprises?"

His cheek twitches. "Funny you should ask. There was a surprise. But I want to hear about your morning."

"I couldn't concentrate in Marketing. It's a good class, but today I felt ... strange."

"Oh no." He pushes his tray forward to lean those magnificent forearms on the table. "What were your symptoms?"

"Elevated heart rate," I report, raising a clinical brow. "Shortness of breath. Mild dizziness."

He tries to hold back a grin. It only half works. "Are you okay?"

"Yeah, I'm fine now, but those symptoms might return, you know?"

"Maybe I should walk you to your next class, just to make sure you're okay."

I give him my best coy smile. "Do you think that will help? Or hurt?"

"You never know."

Sultry. The new voice is sultry.

"Hm, well, completely unrelatedly, a friend I walk to Marketing with has been telling everyone that she wants to steal my boyfriend. Not cool, you know?"

His full grin sneaks through. I can't help but reciprocate.

"He's yours as long as you'll have him."

I wave my fork, feigning nonchalance. "I'm pretty happy with the arrangement."

His expression fades to serious. "Good to hear."

AUSTIN

Song of the day

"The Hill" by Thomas Rhett

CHAPTER TWENTY-EIGHT

Sophie

The next day I wake up ... off. A pit carved into my stomach overnight. The defiance I rely on for survival has all seeped out. I know why—I've lived with this off and on for years. But also, I don't know why. I never do.

Since middle school I've been calling these Dark and Twisty days. Thanks to Meredith Grey and Cristina Yang for the helpful terminology. I wake up or I wind up—it just depends—with a weight on my mind and heart and body. Sometimes it's just one day, out of nowhere. Or a few days. Or months, and they call it a depressive episode. I can't control it. I can't predict it, except that it seems to latch on to overwhelm. I'm just along for the sickening ride.

Sometimes, Dark and Twisty is the emotional equivalent of wearing sunglasses inside.

Sometimes, it's an IV drip of apathy and exhaustion.

Sometimes, it's a black hole.

Today I manage classes with minimal interaction. I almost skip lunch, but a muffin from Common Grounds is my attempt at self-care. Carefully avoid Kit, mirrors, Saga.

I start typing an excuse to our suite group chat so Kit and Mia don't track me down, but—

Ding.

I flinch. It's Austin.

AUSTIN

Lab is canceled

You free? I'm outside

I can't let him see me like this, but I won't lie to him. Won't leave him on read. Wiping under my eyes, I push out of bed. Sneakers, joggers, hair in a clip. I check my reflection—ouch. Should not have done that.

Maybe he can distract me from myself. If anyone can, it's Austin. It's a slog into the stairwell, but the second I remember the life-giving hug within reach, my legs take over. I blast through the stairwell door and slam full force into Austin's brick-wall body. A bear hug from my immovable grizzly. His bulky, hairy arms wrap around me, and I melt into his chest. A T-shirt day. Warmth seeps through his shirt, grounding me. He tucks his face into the hair at my neck. For three fleeting seconds, I feel good. Like my brain flickers on after hours in the dark.

Maybe a kiss would hit harder than the hug. Maybe it would drown out my thoughts. I reach up to steal one.

"Hey," he murmurs against my lips.

I huff. That was not a kiss. My insides ache with the almost, the not enough.

"What's wrong?" His giant hand brushes my hair out of my face clumsily.

I shrug.

"Is it a Dark and Twisty day?"

I nod.

He knows about these, but he's never seen one. I've felt so light in the alternate reality of Mayberry, like maybe this part of me wouldn't find me here.

A sinister voice cuts through. *"Of course it did."*

"Worst day ever," I mumble.

My brain interjects that nothing bad has happened all day, but my heart shrugs, rolls its eyes. The world is dark, and I've never been so out of place, so lonely, so out of my league. What am I thinking trying to make a relationship work with Austin Scott? If he's the prince, I'm just a stepsister.

"C'mon."

I'm not getting the kiss I need, but his hand is warm, his confidence a relief. He leads me toward the pine grove next to Griffin Hall, all the way to the fence. Only thirty or forty steps from the edge to the fence, but it may as well be the Hundred Acre Wood. Strong pine smell. Crunching under every step. No grass, just fallen needles and scattered pinecones. Going outside is on the list of tasks Dr. Shannon gave me for these days. This is good.

Austin slides to the ground against the chain-link fence, facing the campus way out there. When I join him, he takes my hand in both of his and kisses it. "Wanna talk?"

I shrug again. I don't have words.

"You said the hard things feel harder on these days. What feels hard today?"

My chest warms at his affection, his attention, his memory. "Maybe I like you too much," I blurt—and cringe.

His eyes widen. Both paws fold around mine. "By all means, please keep talking," he jokes.

I stare at his hands.

"What can I do to help?" He smirks at my expression. "No, Soph. You're too important to me to let this become just physical. We have to work through what's bothering you."

"You're the one guerrilla kissing me."

"Gorilla kissing? What in the blazes is that?"

I almost smile. I needed this. "Like guerrilla warfare."

He chuckles, deep and warm. "Guerrilla. Got it." But then his face softens. "Maybe I shouldn't have done that? I'm new at this too."

No he's not, and I shouldn't have mentioned it, and I'm ruining the one good thing I have. Despair washes over me again.

His bushy eyebrows furrow. "We can just sit here if you want. But something tells me you need to talk."

"I'll talk if you agree to a kiss." Anything to get a hit of that stuff that lifted the fog for a second.

With no apparent intention of kissing me, his giant hand encases the side of my face, his expression all care and acceptance. My eyelids droop.

I think ... I love him.

Why this moment? On one of the bad days? Those realizations are supposed to hit during fireworks or running through a field of sunflowers. Not for me apparently, because mine just knocked the wind out of me like a volleyball to the chest. I love his enormous hands and his otherworldly patience. I love his loyalty, his positivity, his cleverness. I love that he's up for anything—my wacky plans and his floor's pranks. He never makes me feel like I'm too much or not enough.

I want the love to fill me with joy and warmth and contentedness—it's supposed to, right? But no. My breath turns shallow and fast. I've always been so fiercely independent. I had to be. I've never needed a single soul. But now? What happens when he leaves? I squeeze Austin's fingers and crumple over my knees. There's only one thing I can do ...

Pray a prayer I've been too scared to pray.

Please make this work. Only you can. It doesn't make any sense, but I want it so much it hurts. Please.

Kit could do this. She is doing it—one day at a time, locking it down with Levi. But I'm no Kit. I wish I could be happy for her. I should. I would if I were a good friend. But all I can think is, why does she get to be Kit?

Did Austin notice her first? I remember the first time I saw him at Saga, talking to Levi, when we caught Kit staring. I remember him walking over. I remember him on his floor at movie night. He talked to Kit first. He invited her to game night the next night. Levi must have called dibs.

They would have made beautiful brunette babies. Their parents would have become instant best friends. An explosion of perfection with so many functional people in one family tree.

Austin elbows me gently. "Soph?"

"Huh? Yeah."

"What are you thinking about so hard? You look like you're getting mad."

"Just Kit." I shudder.

"Kit?"

"She's so perfect. And perky. She's just"—my voice turns into a shaky whimper—"the worst."

"She's our friend," he says quietly. "I'm not gonna talk about her like that."

With a jerk up, I stare him down. My worst nightmare. "Did you ... do you ..." I don't want to know, but I have to. "Kit is ... attractive, right?"

He eyes me suspiciously. "She's practically my sister-in-law. And I want to be with you."

"But she is, isn't she?"

"Is Jeeves?"

"Huh?"

"You're mad at Kit because you think she's pretty?"

I press on my eyes. This is probably irrational. I'll hate myself for this tomorrow. But the screaming thoughts are no quieter than five seconds ago.

"Just ... did you notice her? In August. I need to know."

Please help. I know I'm breaking this.

"You still don't get it," he mutters.

When I peek at him, his eyes are scanning my face. Then they close. Is he praying?

"Okay, Sparky." He bumps my shoulder. "Here's what happened."

CHAPTER TWENTY-NINE

Sophie

"Once upon a time," Austin starts, settling into the chain-link fence. "I heard you singing at Saga. I was almost to our table when your voice yanked my head over so fast I almost pulled a muscle in my neck. What were you singing? Shakira, maybe?" His lips tug up at the memory. "You were motioning along, your hair bouncing all around. One glance, and I was sold. So into you. You're more ... alive than other girls."

My eyebrows have shot up to Mars. I will miss them.

"I smiled at you," he says. "Do you remember that?"

My jerky nod gives me away.

"I didn't wanna be a creep and hit on the brand-new freshman—those first couple months of college life are a lot—so I left you alone that day. But my resolve didn't last long."

Wind flits through his hair as I study him. All those times I'd bump into him on campus or he'd end up sitting by me at Saga. Was that ... on purpose?

"Lucky for me, you showed up on my floor for Jeeves's strategic movie night. He wasn't concerned about hitting on a different brand-new freshman." He chuckles. "Kit freaked him out on their walk back, and I had to intervene with a game night the next day. But yeah, the more I got to know you, the more of a goner I was. You're not just beautiful—" He stops when I grimace. His gray-blue eyes shrink to slits. "Seriously?"

His fingers come up to push my eyebrows back to their usual place, then his thumb nudges my mouth into a smile that starts to set.

"Listen up, little lady. I get to decide if I think you're beautiful. They're my eyes taking you in, my hands touching you, my stomach dropping when you come into view."

My lungs make a fool of me with a sudden breath.

"Your smile is beautiful." His thumb brushes tingles across my bottom lip. "Your eyes are beautiful. Your freckles. Your hair." It arcs to my cheek and then my hairline.

Sparks everywhere.

But then he pulls his arms in, as if to keep them to himself, and edges back against the fence. "Your body is beautiful."

When his eyes drift shut, I gulp.

"You're ... a dream. Strong. Delicate. Wild. Capable. Inviting. Golden. Blinding ... Legs for days." His voice drops, and my face heats. "I couldn't make you up." He turns. "I wish you'd agree with me, but I can't help that. And *you* can't help how I feel about you. Got that straight?"

His stern voice is so attractive that I bob my head without thinking.

"Since that movie night, you were always the one to beat, the one I was begging God for a chance with. Bounced around so the other girls wouldn't get the wrong impression. No one ever measured up to you." He pulls a face. "I sound like a jerk. Maybe Jeeves had it right with the dating boycott."

His words are a little curled-up hedgehog. Adorable. Precious. But too sharp. I can't hold them no matter how hard I try.

"About Kit," he says. "She was in my Calc III class. We barely talked until we were friends through you. She's so good to Jeeves —now—and of course I love her for that." A pause. "I kinda wanna be mad that you're making a thing about her, but also I can relate to you."

"You can?"

"When I showed up here, my roommate was Levi Whitaker, of all people, and I was too big for my britches after my success with football. It took him two seconds to do his homework. People respected him before they even met him. He got whatever he wanted." He shakes his head, amused. "He was even faster than me for a short time."

I search his face. "But that stuff is ... Who cares? You're you. Why would you ever want to be him?"

He half-smiles. "But you're you, Soph. Why would you ever wanna be Kit?"

My heart does a weird dip.

Could it be real? Everybody is Tad Hamilton to somebody?

I grab his hand and kiss his palm. "What changed? You don't think that way now, do you?"

"Nah. It didn't happen overnight. Or 'cause I tried. I guess God just made me see him different. Now that feels like a million years ago. The world needs one Jeeves—no more and certainly no less."

I curl up close to him, hands on his chest. "You're incredible. I want you exactly like this."

He plants a kiss on my head. "I'm trying to help you, and you're making it about me." And then a string of kisses from my forehead to my neck. "Stop that."

"I don't think you understand how incentive works," I murmur. "Maybe come with me to my Marketing class sometime."

His arm wraps around my waist as he retraces the line of kisses. "Can I sit next to you? The professor wouldn't mind if I do this, would she?"

"Mmm."

He pulls away, and I grunt.

"I have literally no idea what I'm doing," I say. "I learned my dating advice from *Gilmore Girls* and *Gossip Girl*. And *New Girl*. All the 'Girl' shows. Pretty sure those couples are neither realistic nor functional."

With a chuckle, he runs a thumb down my jaw. "I don't know what I'm doing either, Soph. We'll figure it out together. We're not doing this on our own, right?"

Frustration rises in my throat. He doesn't get it. He can't see what his happy parents gave him.

"What's helped you before? On your Dark and Twisty days."

When he stretches his legs out, he cringes in pain. I almost drown in a flood of self-consciousness. This isn't fun or exciting for him. I'm draining him instead of filling him up. I'm too much and yet not near enough.

I reach for his knee, rub on it the way I've seen him do. "Is it hurting?"

He smooths hair from my face. "Kinda stiff today. What helped?" He presses.

"Um, running makes me feel halfway normal. Counseling. Hibiscus tea. My list of tasks. But this is the first day like this in a while."

His attentive gaze—so kind, so patient. How am I here with him right now?

Even still, the weight is still here. The dimness. The cliff I could fall off any moment. He's so good, and I'm still just ... sad. I don't know what it's like for other people. Maybe they're always cool and chill, so these days bounce off a little better. For me, it couldn't be further from my usual self, from the real me. People around me easily notice the change, and it's hard to sit in my skin this way. I just want to feel normal. To bounce and skip and sing and experience life. Except today, I don't even really *want* those things. Like an alien inhabited my body. Like that book *The Host*.

I turn to Austin. I need his help. I need a reprieve. A hit.

"I was honest," I try. "We worked through stuff. Did I earn a kiss?"

The chain-link fence jingles as he leans back against it, leaving me even colder. "Affection isn't earned, Soph." His voice is low, firm. The man-bear is protective, but there's something unsteady underneath. "I kiss you because I like you, not because you were compliant."

I grab a fistful of his shirt, tug tighter than I mean to. "Please, Austin."

His breathing stutters. His eyes go desperate. "Look, I'm trying to leave some space between us so I don't get too close to trying everything else." His head droops to the side, just in front of mine. "That's a real risk, you know. I have to stick with my convictions on this. Anything past kissing is a no for me."

Something twitches in my gut. *Kissing isn't a line at all.* That's what Kit said.

But my leg bounces. The craving grows.

He's overthinking this. It's just a kiss. More than just a kiss—more of Austin. More closeness. More of his goodness.

"I'm not gonna defy God's orders on that," he says. "And anyway, if you rub against the grain of the universe, you get brutal splinters. I don't want that for you. Or for me."

That voice while he tells me no—low, warm, threadbare. It has the opposite effect. I know that kiss is what I need. The only thing to lift the fog.

I trace his lips with a finger. "I respect that. And I'm on the same page. But you shouldn't get to pick every time."

His gaze drops to my lips, his voice dips with it. "I love it when you're feisty."

Finally I weave my fingers into his thick hair and press my lips to his. The world blurs. It's as distracting as I'd hoped. Slow and deep and reassuring—enough to convince me I'm okay. I kiss him again. And again. My legs slide across his, half in his lap.

When a small, guttural moan escapes from his throat, I pull

back to look at him. Every bit of focus and comfort drops in a breath.

He droops back to the fence, gently moving my legs to the ground. "You." The painful edge to his voice stabs me with guilt. His eyes lock onto mine. "Soph? I can ... trust you?"

"Yeah. Yes."

"Okay. So. Ready for your run?"

I turn his hand over, running my thumb over his calluses. So rough. So much weight lifting. So much tingly goodness. He watches me like I'm something rare and valuable. When he squeezes my hand, the buzz of his touch just reminds me I need more of it.

"In a minute," I finally respond.

"Oh." He flits his gaze out to the pines. "Hi, God."

I eye him. He's praying out loud? With his eyes open?

"I thought you told me to pray that verse over Sophie today. It must have been for now, huh? Let's see ... 'And this is my prayer: that her love may abound more and more in,' um"—he pulls out his phone and skims the screen—"'in knowledge and depth of insight.'"

Yes, Jesus, I pray involuntarily. *Yes.*

"I read that this morning," he says to me. "Kinda random, I know."

My squeeze on his hand says what I can't. "Where is that?"

"Philippians. I started it this week."

Love? Abound?

I have no words. Or reasonable thoughts. But somehow, right now, I have Austin. Arm around me, hand in my hair, he sits with me in the dirt. Like it's enough for him.

Please let me keep him. Please.

AUSTIN

Song of the day

"Banks" by Jordan Davis & NEEDTOBREATHE

Be prepared. I'm coming for your mirrors.

CHAPTER THIRTY

Sophie

"Excuse me, gorgeous."

That deep, playful voice, a light Texan drawl. We were just together at lunch, but my mind, body, and heart light up at the sound of it. I spin around with a grin. My rabbit hole of darkness yesterday appears to be gone. For how long I don't know.

Austin saunters toward me, workout shorts tight on his hips, hair damp from a recent shower. "I think you dropped something."

I scan the ground. "What?"

"My jaw."

A laugh bursts out of me. Before I know it, my arms are around his neck. I am officially one of those obnoxiously blissful people—the kind who used to make me gag. Days when my mind is finally better again are always great days. Having my life back, myself back? What a gift. And then compound that with the too-good-to-be-true Austin. An absolute dream come true.

His hands wrap around me, and he presses a kiss to my head, like I'm precious to him.

My fingers wander to his damp curls. This touchable mess of hair.

"Midday shower?" I ask. "Or did Levi talk you into swimming laps?"

"Shower. A Flooders thing."

My stomach flips.

When a Flooder wins over a girl who's a big deal to him, he gets thrown—fully clothed—into the communal shower. He must think I don't know about that. As the story goes, those guys always end up marrying her. Levi got showered last semester when Kit finally came to her senses.

"Oh really?" I keep my voice light. "Did you get the girl?"

His smile fades. "I dunno. Did I?"

My mouth dries. I scrunch my nose, like it's a silly question, like I'm not still an anxious wreck about our relationship. Like of course I just believed what he said to me in the Hundred Acre Wood and that's that.

"Up for a walk?"

"Hm." I stretch dramatically. "I'm feeling lazy." I love a good walk, but I'd much rather finagle a kiss out of him.

He narrows his eyes, like he knows exactly what I'm up to. Then with zero warning, he pivots around and drops to his knees. The movement is careful—still mindful of the left knee he injured in high school—but the way he motions to his shoulders is not careful. It's spontaneous and confident and Austin.

"Wait. Really?" I'm already grinning.

"Really. Climb up."

I clap in delight as he hikes up his sleeves.

Arranging my legs over his broad shoulders, my hands rest lightly on his head for balance. He stands easily, like I weigh nothing. No big deal—just carrying an entire person. This guy is my boyfriend. I am the queen of the world in all the ways.

"You're the best," I gush for the millionth time.

From up here, I can see his grin return.

"You're not getting a big head, are you?" I pat his curls.

"I'm well on my way." He heads straight for the field across from Flooders. "Have you seen the latest?"

Two more letters today. T and ... G.

YOU ARE
THE
GOL_EST

My gasp is so big, I have to steady myself on his shoulders.

"Any guesses?" he asks playfully. A light squeeze on my calves.

"Austin ... it was you?" My voice is barely audible. "All this time?"

"I don't know what would cause you to think that," he deflects. "What'll be your vote for the last letter?"

But I can't speak. I gape at the campus-wide message. The secret message. For me. Thrill and wonder course through me.

I can't keep it all to myself. I curl down to his ear, punctuating with kisses. "I can't believe it's you. I can't believe you did this. Thank you. I can't believe it."

"You'd better quit that." He tugs on my ankle. "You might fall off this thing."

A laugh shudders out in recognition, but my head is still spinning. "Let me down?"

"Already? I can—"

"Let me down."

He kneels again, and I scramble to get off ... and knee him in the side of the head! Like Hitch on a Jet Ski.

He winces. Clutches his ear.

"Ah! I'm so sorry. Are you okay?"

He's still on his knees, chuckling, and lowers his hand. No blood.

I kiss all over his ear and face.

"I'm fine. I'm fine. You're good, Soph."

"Austin ..." I motion to hangman, but no more words come out. I press on his shoulders and search his eyes, like he can telepathically explain.

"It's your theme song."

"I ... But ... Hangman. Is it the Flooders?"

His mouth opens. Shuts.

"Please, Austin. Just tell me."

"No. But I have help." He meets my eyes vulnerably. "It was always just for you."

Just for me. All that? A storm brews in my head. It's too much. It doesn't make sense. It can't be right.

"I meant to use it to ask you out, but then I decided it was too much pressure." He scratches his neck. "In case you didn't want that ... I mean ... us."

I lower my forehead to his. "Why did you do this? I don't ..."

He slowly lifts to standing, wraps me up in his arms. Gently. Firmly. His head nuzzles into my neck as he murmurs. "Because you deserve it. Because you need to know. Because nothing is big enough to show you."

AUSTIN

Song of the day

"Done" by Chris Janson

Austin

Praying for Sophie on the way to the gym, I let out a jaw-cracking yawn. I never used to be up this early, but it's the only way to fit in a workout and Jesus time without slicing into my afternoons with her. I huff a laugh when I catch Levi at the Albert doors—hair wet, post-swim. He's always been like this. Up before the sun. Swims like he was born in the water.

I hold out a fist bump as I pass him.

"Morning, buddy," he says. "You're up early again."

"Must be done. Hey, can I run a grand gesture idea by you real quick?"

"For The Game?" Our code name, in case someone's around.

"No, a new one."

I 180 to follow him through the lobby, but he jerks his head toward the gym, already moving.

"Another grand gesture," he says.

"I can head up with—"

"No."

He doesn't slow, doesn't ask. Just expects me to keep up. I feel bad cutting into his morning routine for this, but he's already on a mission.

"Walk, Samwise. Grand gesture?"

"What do you think about taking the gang up to Kit's parents' house for spring break?"

A worried line settles between his brows, but it disappears just as fast. "That'd be her Christmas morning. All her people in one place? You'd never hear the end of it."

"Okay, sit back down on the couch, Tom Cruise."

He laughs. "There's a throwback reference. Does that make you Oprah?"

"I'll take it."

"I can ask Kit. Do you prefer it stay a surprise? You know she'll take a secret to her grave, but her face is far from neutral."

"Right. I want it to stay a surprise."

He squints at me as we walk. He's reading my mind. Dude's super smart and cares a lot, so I can't get out of it. "Just ask, Samwise. You know I want to help out."

Nope. I hate asking favors. Hate it. I'll figure out another way. "I need to talk to Haymitch about some more footwork drills at soccer practice," I say, avoiding the subject. "I keep getting ahead of the ball."

Levi's brows rise in growing determination.

Shoot, he's onto me.

"I'm barely helping with The Game," he says.

"Finn's on it. He's been all in since you told him he could put 'project manager' on his résumé."

Ethan—floor name Finn—turned my pie-in-the-sky idea into a full-blown thing. Freshman, but he's got more hustle than a kid at an Easter egg hunt. I outlined it, and he ran with it—handling the socials, hauling poster boards, carrying the whole deal like it actually matters to him. Grateful doesn't begin to cover it. His anonymity made it possible, but he doesn't seem to value that. After this, it's gone.

"I wasn't just saying that," Levi says. "If Flooders were a fraternity, he'd get an official title for his prank involvement alone. Now stop changing the subject."

"I still hate that he's doing so much of the work for my thing. I need to let him pick a message. But I know he'll pick something Flooders-related, and then it'll be over." Cue the campus-wide eye roll. They'll see it all as just another Flooders prank. And that's fine—my guys would eat it up. But this was never about them, and I need all the credit I can get with Sophie. "Maybe two more for Sophie, and then I let Finn have the last hurrah and take the credit for the Flooders message. Does that seem fair?"

"Samwise. Focus."

The runaround never works with him. Haymitch coined it—Levi is a dog with a bone.

"Should we talk about when I showed up at this crazy place with a single bag and had literally never done a load of laundry?" he demands.

I roll my eyes.

"You taught me everything, man. Not just vacuuming and epic sandwich making and how to function without a staff, but how to be down to earth. How to be like Jesus. I owe you. Now start talking."

"You paid me back and then some. The only reason I had a shot with Sophie was because of what you taught me."

"False. Now speak."

"Fine. I don't know how to get us up there. To Colorado."

It'd be messed up to leave Haymitch and Mia out. And neither of them can afford a plane ticket. I could cover theirs, but that'd clean me out until summer. My painting job won't start up again till then, and I really should be applying for summer internships instead. But those pay nothing. I rub a hand over my face. Money sucks.

"Oh, that's it?" Levi says. "You don't need a kidney?"

"Cute."

"Let's see. Assuming Mia and Haymitch want to join, we can drive the Rover or I can buy us all flights—"

I lift my hands. "Whoa. Buy all our plane tickets? No. I'd pay you back for the other four of us. I just know it will drain me until the summer, and Sophie's love of adventure isn't exactly cheap." It all spills out. "But I'd pay you back. Maybe by mid-June?"

"No."

I exhale. Here we go.

"The problem with driving," he says, "is Kit will be nervous that we'll run into rain. Especially that time of year."

"Yeah, I thought of that."

"She's managed some road trips, but the Rover's also pretty tight for six on a—what?—twenty-hour car trip?"

"Fifteen, but—"

"Problem with flying is Kit gets nervous when I spend money."

"Huh?"

"She wants me to be happy."

I glance over. He's dead serious, but I have no idea what he's talking about.

"Letting the money flow is a great way to destroy a life. She knows, and I know, and she keeps me honest. For you I'd do it without hesitation. You haven't asked me to spot you a dollar in two and a half years. But it feels like her money too ..."

Whoa. He is sure she's The One.

"... So I'd like to find a way to run it by her."

"Except I—"

"No. I want to cover the tickets, Samwise. Cut it out."

"Dude. I couldn't accept that. You're not listening—"

"I'm calling it now—Sophie's it for you. And when I'm right, I want wedding-toast rights. Or at least a permanent spot in the group text."

I chuckle. "Eh. You can come as Kit's plus-one. That's all I'm promising."

He pushes me off the sidewalk.

Bro wants to bankroll my grand gesture. Fly all six of us to Colorado. What does a guy even say?

"But really. That's so cool of you, Jeeves. You're a real one. But I don't want you to think—"

"No, you are. And I don't."

CHAPTER THIRTY-ONE

Austin

Since Sophie's been back from break, I've had her out experiencing something new on both Saturdays. Two-stepping and water-tower climbing. Third Saturday in a row—gotta keep it up. Sophie lives for this stuff, and I want her happy. She *will* have everything. I've been working on a list of bucket-list-worthy experiences that won't cost me an arm and a leg. Can't be buying yachts or flying to Tahiti. But I've got a buddy lined up to lend me his motorboat when it's warm enough to swim, and I know a place to cliff-jump safely. With some research I found an escape room that's supposed to be wild and a zip-lining spot in Dallas. There's also a cool under-twenty-one karaoke bar in Austin, but we'll see if my cousin Caleb is up for that visit. And if I can convince my guys on the floor, I'm gonna see if we can't make a masquerade party happen for Valentine's here in a few weeks.

Tonight's adventure is just minutes from becoming reality. I'm driving back to campus with a meal from a Levi-recommended fancy-pants restaurant that Sophie and I are gonna eat in the pitch dark. It's called dark dining, and I'm pretty sure she'll get a big kick out of it. A dark bedroom won't work for obvious reasons, so I borrowed the Dark Lounge. While the other Flooders were super cool about sharing it for a couple hours, the trick was clearing it with Calvin—a.k.a. Abu, our resident adviser. He's the one who has to walk around during Open Dorms and make sure we're behaving ourselves. This school's strict rules include that doors must stay open if a girl is in the room, but an open door during a pitch-dark dinner would ruin the effect. I swore up and down to Calvin about no funny business during Open Dorms—this time or ever—and he was kind enough to talk to his boss, Albert Hall's resident director, into bending the rules this once. All the favor asking has me woozy. I've been pulling strings left and right for Sophie reasons lately.

Speaking of which, I asked Levi and Haymitch to help me cover the windows of the Dark Lounge earlier. Black trash bags and duct tape did the trick. The walls are already black. With a strip below the door, absolutely nothing is visible in there. We won't even need blindfolds. I won't be able to have a waiter since no one can come in or out, so Haymitch and Levi are in the lounge right now filling our water glasses and setting the table like a couple of champs. Here in a minute, Levi's gotta run—hot date with his own girl.

At a stoplight I text Sophie another clue.

Black is the theme of the night

SOPHIE

I have no idea what you're talking about!!!!

See? She loves surprises.

I've been texting hints all day like "Be hungry when I pick you up" and "Can't wait to 'see' you."

But really ...

What do I wear??

My girl is all about the last-minute rush.

Anything

Just be comfortable

There's something about Sophie that makes me feel alive. Her larger-than-life energy is contagious, a defibrillator that zaps my heart into a better beat. Another guy might wear a snazzy suit tonight, but I'm—wait for it—dressed like Zorro. Black tee with black jeans. When I get back, I'm gonna loop a red tie like a belt. I even cut eyeholes into a black strip of fabric. It's in my pocket, so I gotta remember to throw that on too. I know, it's barely related to a dinner in the dark. But she loves Zorro, and he wears black. She brings this out in me—this playful, reckless side I forgot I had. A side that feels a lot more like me than anything has in years. It's an addictive cycle. Sophie grins and draws closer, and suddenly I'm free. Free to be wild, to let loose, to have fun. And the more I lean in, the happier she is.

I'll never forget that first trip to B-Dubs, before our crew was even a thing. Sophie argued with me about country music, and a flash of brazen, cocky, and reckless ignited in me after lying dormant for years. The part of me that used to mastermind middle school pranks and organize all-out Capture the Flag battles. The part that peeked out when I first moved to Flooders but got buried under homework and football.

I had let it go when Dad's back went out. When I saw him covering everything and stepped up to help. When I realized that football made him happier than anything else, and I threw myself into it. Wouldn't change a second of it. He was proud of me. It all mattered to him. But those two years before his surgery were long. Irreversible. After, I kept pushing—more explosive, more elusive, more relentless. Every extra sprint, every brutal drill, every ounce of exhaustion was worth it when I looked up and saw him in the stands. The tall, quiet guy, pumping his fist and screaming like a lunatic. I lived for that.

Hot food in hand, I thank my overachieving buddies about seven zillion times. All the favors.

Then, jogging to Griffin Hall, I text Sophie that I'm outside.

She's yours first, God. Keep me in check.

When she flies out, I nearly fall over, and it's not because she slams into me with a Sophie tackle-hug. She's dangerous—jaw-dropping—in a stretchy black thing that bounces up when she runs. I'm the Luckiest Dude Alive. Except, I planned a dinner where I can't even look at her? Make that World's Biggest Idiot. Someone start printing plaques.

"Soph, just wow. What is this thing?"

She glances down. "I know. It's just a—like a workout dress. It's not even real clothes ..."

Like she's about to play a vicious game of tennis. And then do a backflip off a building. All angles and elegance, power and precision, like someone designed this little dress to showcase her perfectly ... and to ruin me slowly.

She turns to badge in. "Sorry, I just don't have much black, and you said comfortable. I'll change—"

I grab her hand and tug her back to me. "Don't you dare." With a kiss on her temple, her ear, my hands sneak around her back, to her waist. Drop to her hips. And stay there. It's safer here. "I've never seen you in this."

"Yeah." She studies her sneakers. "I don't really ... fill it out."

"What?" It comes out a growl.

A blush creeps across her cheeks.

"If you heard the thoughts I'm trying to get rid of," I murmur in her ear, "you'd need to dump me. And you'd never think that again."

Her eyes widen before she tucks her face into my chest.

Oh—I dig the mask out of my pocket and pull it over my head.

She gasps. "Are you Zorro??" She curls around my neck,

bouncing again. "I'm dying. Tell me, tell me. Where are we going?"

"We're gonna have to go out after, Sparky. I can't waste this dress."

"Waste it? What does that even mean? Austin, you're torturing me with suspense!"

Her voice wraps around my name. I wish she'd say it again.

"You'll see." With a nod, I direct her toward Flooders.

Those gorgeous long legs speed over the field in record time. Halfway across, she halts, pulls my face close, her hands gripping my jaw. "New letters?" she whispers.

No time to reply about The Game before she presses a heart-stopping kiss to my lips. And then continues dragging me across the field.

Luckiest. Dude. Alive.

We've barely stepped onto the floor when the guys pounce, throwing jabs and peppering Sophie with questions. She's laughing, eating it up, and I can't stop staring—only making it worse for myself. I deserve the merciless teasing ... I'm so gone for her. And she deserves this full Flooders welcome. It's standard trash talk, but there's an undercurrent of awe. I'm not just settling down. I'm settling down with *her*. Flashing them my cockiest grin, I pull her closer.

Leo's door stays closed.

I dip down. "See what I put up with, dating someone out of my league?"

Her laugh stills for a second, and I wonder if she's thinking that this is the same floor that watched her try to make it work with Leo. But then she plants a noisy, over-the-top kiss on my cheek. The guys lose it, and I about melt into the ancient carpet. She backed me up. Claimed me right back. Hiding it, I turn to the guys and spread my arms wide, like *Let's go.*

Their laughter fades behind us as I steer her toward the Dark Lounge. But when I open the door, her shoulders droop. *Give me a chance, woman. It's not just a movie.*

Levi strolls by in his fancy pants, looking like a million bucks, sort of literally.

"Attaboy," I call.

"Attaboy yourself. Keep your hands to yourself, Sophie!"

She laughs.

And then he sends me a look that says *Careful, bro*. He's not wrong. This is dangerous territory.

We step into the Dark Lounge, and I click the door shut behind us. Pitch. Black.

"Uhh." She's confused, but not scared.

"Okay, Soph. We're gonna try out dark dining. Apparently eating in the dark makes you more aware of your other senses."

She gasps.

"We get exactly twenty minutes. It's picnic-style. Everything's on the floor, so watch out, okay?"

A beautiful smile must accompany the clapping I hear. As I guide her in roughly the right direction, she starts singing "Into the Unknown." *Frozen,* maybe?

I toe the blanket on the floor. "Here."

Sitting across from her was the plan, but why would I want to be farther from her than absolutely necessary? Instead, the second plate lands beside hers as I lower next to her.

"This. Is. Amazing. What are we eating?"

"Italian. I got us the sampler platter so you can try everything."

"Austin."

Chills run up my spine. My name. That tone.

"Yeah?"

"Thank you," she whispers.

Breathe.

Can't ditch the dinner and kiss her all twenty minutes. Just breathe.

"At least try the food before you gas me up like that," I say.

"Or maybe it'll be gross and we'll need a backup plan."

My heart misfires. I guess we'll be having that talk now. "I was thinking, maybe no kissing until after we eat? You know, to keep things PG in here."

"Mm. I don't love that plan. I'll make you a deal, mister."

She's so adorable I can hardly stand it. I sit on my hands.

"No kisses on the mouth, but I can't promise I won't kiss your cheek or your hand or something."

Her lips on me. "Okay." Like I'm being strangled.

"Okay," she says, a smile in her voice.

Her hand finds my shoulder. It follows the line of my arm and pulls my hand from under me. Her perfect lips kiss my palm. Ecstasy. Ridiculous that something so small could send me there.

My kissed hand follows her face to her neck to her shoulder to her arm all the way down, and I do the same to her hand.

A tiny moan escapes her mouth, and I'm living one second at a time. Good thing the lights are off. Who knows what crazy expression is on my face.

Gotta tone this down. The dark setup is working too well. "Hungry?"

"Starving."

I position her hand on her plate. She must figure it out, because I hear the slide of her fork and "mmm" and chewing. It's not just dark in here—it's quiet. I hear every sound she makes, every time she readjusts her weight. I'm hyperaware and loving every minute. The food's good I think, but I'm pretty distracted.

"You eating it up?" I joke.

She giggles at my pun. Only for Sophie.

We chat a little, but I'm nervous and my banter isn't the best.

Finally I hear, "All done. That was incredible, Austin."

Look, I love to eat, but I can't drop my fork fast enough. I move my hand cautiously until I catch her shoulder. Rise up on my knees, edge closer. A kiss to her shoulder. Her neck. Her cheek. Her ear.

"Say my name again," I whisper. Hope she doesn't think I'm a weirdo.

Her hands find my face in the dark. She goes straight for a kiss on my lips.

Oh wow.

"Austin."

Oh. Wow.

Her hands skim lower, and she kisses my ear. "Austin." Down to my neck. "Austin." She trails back up, finds my face again. Another kiss.

Heart. Slamming.

Million degrees in here. Need to breathe. Need to think.

I scoot back an inch and run a hand through my hair.

Help. Did I foul this up? How do I get out of this one?

"Soph?" Hoarse voice. Great. "I, uh. No more kisses for a sec, 'kay?"

I did it. Said something. Hardest part's over. She's got me.

"Okay."

Why does her voice have to sound so beautiful? I can't even see her, and I'm dying over here.

She slides her hands from my face to my shoulder and lays her head there. I kiss it and move my hand chastely across her upper back as I try to recover.

A knock on the door. "Time's up, Samwise."

There's no way it's been twenty minutes. No way.

"Got it, Abu," I call. "Out in a sec." I pull my phone out of my pocket. "Get ready for some light."

I turn on the flashlight and check Sophie. She's squinting. Glowing.

And the way she's staring at me? Guaranteed that'll be the last thing I see before I die.

CHAPTER THIRTY-TWO

Sophie

I rip my heels off and take off in a horror-movie sprint for my life across the cold, crunchy field. I told Austin we need to cool off, but the pitiful truth is I have to get to my room before anyone sees me cry. Something about that perfectly planned perfect dinner by my perfect date sent me over the edge. All the edges. My rational thought must have flown out, crashed, and burned somewhere on campus.

As I grab the corner of the wall to propel me through the suite, I've never been more relieved to find it empty. Barely reaching my room in time, I sob into my pillowcase like a modern artist whose medium is mascara.

What is wrong with me?

The second my eyes start to dry, my gut tells me to move. To find my happy face and skip back to Austin. Or to make my excuses and throw on a movie. To run up to G3 and see if anyone's around. Even to start some music and drown this silence. Anything to replace these scary and confusing feelings. But that little nudge —the one I desperately want, but sometimes don't—is at it again.

Something like, **I want you close. Slow down and talk to me.**

Slow down?

Scary. Foreign. And grates against every instinct of survival.

But I try.

Okay?

Trust me.

My real Bible is in the lounge, so I snatch up my phone, a relief in itself, and try to obey by typing "trust God" into the search bar.

It's Saturday night, the hottest of hot dates is waiting, and I have makeup smears all over my face, but I'm sitting here looking up Bible verses.

There's the one. "Trust in the Lord with all your heart and lean not on your own understanding; in all your ways submit to him, and he will make your paths straight."

Straight paths. What would that even look like?

My parents were a mess. Are a mess. I want none of it. I don't want to scream at Austin, hate him, make him hate me. The only sure thing about relationships is that they burn in horrific flames, right?

Trust me.

I'm trying. I don't know how to submit to you in this. I don't know what I'm doing at all.

Unable to still my limbs a second longer, I lock my phone and jump down from bed. The only thing I really know is that this thing with Austin is too fairy-tale like to walk away from. I'll soak up the time we have and try to end it before it goes the way of a Greek tragedy.

Bat my hair away. Adjust my dress. Wash my face. No more weeping like a psycho or I'll scare him off before it's time.

AUSTIN

Song of the day

"Speechless" by Dan + Shay

Austin

The next morning, Levi clicks his laptop shut and pulls out his Tic Tacs. "Samwise, can I ask you something?"

I have my phone out to text Sophie, but I slide it back into my pocket. Time with Levi, just the two of us, is getting rarer. Gotta make sure we stay bros. "Yeah, what's up?"

He bends forward, forearms on his knees. "Why did you hold your thing for Sophie so close to the vest? And for so long?"

"Oh. It kinda freaked me out that I liked her so much. And then, once I had more answers … Well, it sucked that Kit was holding off on telling you the truth, and I knew you wouldn't love me doing the same to Sophie."

"Were you afraid I'd talk you out of your secrecy?"

"Maybe." Hadn't fully pieced that together. Bro's superpower is persuasion, and I don't always want to subject myself to it. "I mean, I'd been praying about it, and I knew it wasn't time yet."

"How did you know when it was?"

I shrug. "I just did. I dunno how to explain it. I'd been praying about it every day for months and could feel God saying to hold off. Until one day, it was different. I didn't fully do my part on the hold-off, but I tried."

He relaxes in his seat. "It didn't occur to me to ask God about timing. I only ever prayed about dating Kit as a binary thing. You're the real deal, Samwise. Good call waiting on him for the details." His heel starts bouncing. "I wish I had talked to you more about Kit. I thought she needed convincing, but really, she needed time."

I glance at him, a little stunned. Levi may be new to the faith, but he's locked in with God in a way I'm still learning. He's usually the one teaching me. For once, I got there first. "Thanks, man. Means a lot. Pretty sure you did plenty of patient waiting for Kit though."

He huffs a laugh, raking a hand through his hair with an easy grin. "Minus the patient part." But he falls serious. "Do you pray about everything like you did with Sophie?"

Sure, I pray every morning, and about random things. But since I got a green light for Sophie, I'm usually praying for her. Or my family. Somebody else. Before I can answer, he follows up.

"Did you pray about going out with the random girls? I mean, I'm not trying to act like I'm a saint." He swallows, eyes sad. "Far from it. But I worried you were getting into a habit. Date her, drop her. Like you're always looking for a reason to bail."

I gape.

"Just think about it, okay? I want you in a solid place for where you're headed with Sophie."

I clear my throat, readjust on my couch. "Course. How does Kit like her studio?"

His grin turns goofy—the kind I never saw on him until Kit jumped in. "She's obsessed, dude. Trains in there every day."

"Can't blame her. That place is fire."

We remodeled a storage room into a legit dance studio, with Levi's suave handling of the school admin, Haymitch's reno knowledge, and our bare hands. Okay, and a mess of rented power tools.

"I couldn't have done it without you guys. How was week one with Sophie?"

"So good. Better than I hoped, even. But it's already a lot."

He knows what I mean. "You have a plan?"

"Yeah. I hate it though." I rub my face. "So, Caleb.

Remember how he and Cora were attached at the hip?" I hate to spill this kind of personal detail about my cousin-nearly-brother, especially since he and Levi got to know each other last year. But I need Levi to understand this if he's gonna help keep me in line. I can trust him with it.

"Yeah, of course. Are they still going strong?"

"No, he blew it. To smithereens. We talk a bunch, you know, so I heard the play-by-play." The weight settles. "It ... made an impact."

"You're kidding. What happened?"

"Ah ... They ditched their boundaries. Couldn't seem to go backward. Wrecked their relationship. He lost her."

Levi winces.

"Yeah. She's long gone now, with some other guy. It all happened so fast." I falter. "Sorry, bro, I feel bad talking about this stuff when you and Kit don't even ..."

"No, you're good. Not kissing is Kit's thing, but she really might be on to something. Truth is, I'm more on board all the time."

"Y'all are kind of cheating the system."

He half laughs. "You're not wrong, but it's not simple, like I expected. There are still plenty of question marks we have to decide on. It's a work in progress."

"Checks out. So how does that process look?"

Levi's so private. I'll be shocked if he gives a straight answer.

"With kissing off-limits, we've found it's more about intent and result. We all have our ... things, you know?"

Boy, do I.

"We have to be honest about what leads us down a dangerous path. There are plenty of non-kissing things that wipe my resolve off the map. And her too."

"No doubt."

"Think you can stick to your plan? Is Sophie with you?"

"Yeah, she is. It's a huge relief. I've always wanted to do things God's way, but the Caleb mess made me pull my line even more.

He can't get that back, you know? And he can't get Cora back. He loved her hard—still does. Now he's at UT, kind of blowing up his life with partying and stuff, trying to get over her."

"Ouch. Does that impact your decision about UT?"

I let out a breath. "It really sucks that I can't be there for him right now, but I won't leave Sophie. I'm gonna tell Coach to call the whole thing off."

"Alright. So you said you pulled your line more?"

"Yeah. It helps that I'd do anything to protect her. I just didn't expect that would mean protecting her from me." I pause. "I'd never pressure her. Obviously. But I want to push her toward God—not away. You know?"

He gives a slow nod. "Absolutely. You're killing it, dude." Then he shifts. "Help him do this," he prays out loud. "Help him lead the effort and obey you radically." Then to me, "And keep up the honesty. Doesn't matter that Kit and I are doing it differently. Keep it all in the light."

"Thanks, buddy. Back atcha."

I will not wreck what I have with Sophie. I won't.

Sophie

This morning, I found my verse. Tattoo-worthy. While scrolling, of all things. "For we are God's handiwork, created in Christ Jesus to do good works, which God prepared in advance for us to do." Every time I reread it, goose bumps. So I'm going all out—poster board, sketched outline. I tear open a package to fill it in with colorful marker magic. Hand-lettering handiwork about being God's handiwork. Every stroke on the poster fills me with resolve, with peace, with confidence. I really can choose what I think about. I can choose what I believe.

You're so good, Jesus. You made me to be close to you. You want to know me. You planned good things for us to do together way before I even believed you were real. Back when I mocked you, waved you off, rolled my eyes at your people. You still wanted me, chased me down. You had already planned a whole life of adventure for me. You're so good. I'm so in. Let's make up for lost time.

I'm belting out "The Great Adventure" and working on finishing touches when Kit walks in, gnawing away at her lip.

"Hey, Sophs. Mind if I borrow your curling iron again?"

"Anytime." I cap my marker. "What's the occasion?"

She wavers. Shrugs.

Intriguing.

"Can I do your hair for you?" I offer, trying not to spook her.

"Are you kidding? Yes. You're the hairstyling queen."

With a grin, I flick my hair for dramatic effect.

She runs a hand down hers, sleek and straight. "Wait—when you sing, will my hair glow or just yours?"

I burst into a laugh. Theatrically singing Rapunzel's hair song, we head to the sinks, and I notice half of Kit's room is empty. My finger demands before my mouth can get to it.

"Ayumi went ahead and moved up to G2. They had an extra spot."

"And *left* you?" Knowing about her nightmares?

"No, it's okay. She's really happy up there. We're good."

"But—"

"Really, she and I are great," she says. "We still hang out. But you should talk to her."

"Leave your door open at night. We'll listen for you, okay?"

Her eyes go glossy. "Thank you."

I can't believe Ayumi would up and leave her alone like that. With a shake of my head, I detangle my curling iron cord from the other tools I've left on the counter. "Okay, what vibe are we going for?"

She hesitates. "Not sure. Levi wants to take me somewhere tonight. He's acting all nervous, so it must be a big deal to him."

"That's amazing. Why do I hear a 'but' coming?"

She weaves her fingers together. "The whole getting dressed-up thing was ruined for me last year. I still feel twitchy about it. As if somehow that's what led to every other bad thing. But I think I'm ready. To try again."

I let out a breath and lower my voice. "I've had the same kind of feeling." I nearly change course, but no. "That year my parents were fighting, I used to braid my hair every night before bed. I know it sounds dumb, but every time I start to braid my hair now, I feel like I'm bracing for something awful."

She squeezes my arm. "Not dumb. Thanks for making me feel less crazy."

"Just simultaneously crazy," I tease.

She shrugs a slender shoulder. "That's what friendship is, after all."

"Hey. Can I do your makeup too?"

"Super natural?" She shoots me a knowing smile.

"Natural with a smoky eye? Come on, KitKat, Levi will love it. Grant my wish!"

Kit chuckles. "Fine. Wish granted. Thanks, Sophs."

I grab my makeup bag and start toward the lounge—then stop in my tracks.

Six Months Ago Sophie would have sooner stabbed herself in the eye with an eyelash curler than helped Perfect Little Kit get ready for a date. Maybe even Six Days Ago Sophie.

But today? I want this for her. Not tolerating. Not pretending. I want all the good things for her.

I'm not sure what's happening to me, but it feels past due.

I'm here for it.

CHAPTER THIRTY-THREE

Austin

It's game day. I'm rounding up the Flooders who forgot where their loyalty lies.

"Come on, boys. G1 supported us at every single game. See y'all there—no excuses."

They don't hear me bossing them around much, which is probably why they hop to attention. "Yeah, okay, Samwise."

Haymitch and some of the guys scrounged up about a thousand camping chairs so the Flooders can go full soccer mom on the sidelines. Let's go. The more hoopla, the better. These girls have shown up in a big way—Sophie the drill sergeant had them practicing before Christmas break, weeks before any other floor even thought about their intramural football team. Truth is, I actually expect some points on the proverbial board.

G1 was pretty terrible last year, but Sophie took the reins and recruited me as their coach. That was months ago—back in just-friends life—and I couldn't be happier I agreed. I've actually loved working with them at practice. Not to mention Sophie's thousand-watt smiles would be enough to motivate the greatest of men.

My favorite game and my favorite girl. It's a beautiful thing.

They've put in the work, and if I call out the right corrections, make the right substitutions, keep everyone focused, maybe I can make sure they get the outcome they deserve.

It's just some casual flag football, but standing on the sideline while the offense plays sends me straight back to senior year. I had signed to play football at the University of Texas—a lifelong dream—until I destroyed my ACL at the end of the season. Very few 4A players get recruited, so to have it ripped away? Dad and I were devastated. Took me a year to get back to full speed, and by then making the pros was pretty much out of the question. Besides, by that point I had fully embraced this school's awesome weirdness. Levi and I lucked out getting each other as roommates—God's provision to us both.

He showed up like the richest, suavest runaway in history, and I was trying to figure out who I was without football. I had spent my whole life with the same kids in our town, never really learned to make friends. Plus, Varsity had rolled out the red carpet for me, and when my team won the Texas State Championship—4A, but still—it made us town royalty. Girls flocked to me. Guys respected my skill. Then I showed up at Mayberry with a bum knee and no idea how to navigate life without football. Levi taught me everything he knew, and I became someone again. But now? Seeing myself through Sophie's eyes? It's not so simple. If all of that made me someone she liked, maybe it was worth something. But knowing how much my serial dating hurt her, I'd take it down about a hundred notches.

When I'm with her, even over here running the sideline, that reckless side she brings out crackles beneath my skin. The commitment, the focus, the loyalty that drove me in football—it's all still there, but it's different with her. Healed, somehow. Whole.

It's too easy to lose the joy of it when everything hinges on performance, but Sophie reminds me why I loved it in the first place.

She's not my first girlfriend or my first kiss, but she's the first to hit me like a lightning bolt. She's been different in every single department.

I wish she'd believe that, but it's my fault she doesn't.

Sophie

As if I weren't already smitten, Coach Austin is enough to knock me off my cleat-clad feet. His football voice is all business, but paired with a constant stream of encouragement, Austin-style. His patience is unreal. He's taught us so much, and even the less-than-coordinated girls are making real contributions.

Rocking his new "Coach Taylor" G1 shirt and sleek black running shorts, his strong legs are on display. It's chilly out here, but he'll keep his heart rate up clapping and pacing.

I love playing his game. Spending more time with him wasn't a deterrent, but I didn't ask him to be our coach because we were friends. Or because I was hopelessly into him. He's by far the most qualified. Not to mention the kindest, most understanding, most fun ... I could go on.

His intense coaching face keeps slipping, softening into an affectionate smile when our eyes meet. I didn't expect that.

This is nothing like competitive volleyball. My teammates in high school were my girls, but they were also fierce. Cutthroat. This team is singing "We're All in This Together," all "sorry!" and giggles. Club volleyball was focus and drive, proving myself every second. Flag football is me trying to tone down my competitive nature enough to actually have fun. I mean, I had to play volleyball with G3 last semester since G1 didn't even compete. At least everyone's showing up for this one.

And get this—Kit is a stellar kicker. She was decent in practice, but something about game day has *kicked*—ha!—her into overdrive. That charming grin from the blond dude on the sidelines isn't hurting. I've still never seen her dance for real, but apparently she was a straight-up child ballerina for over a decade. She's got the legs, the power, the focus. We're putting them to good use. She's been graceful, powerful, deadly accurate.

I got her and a few of the others to agree to war paint for our first game. Kit ditched her signature knot and the shorts she wears to the dance studio. Tonight? Ponytail. Joggers. A teammate. An equal. And it's ... good.

We won. We actually won!

"Who are we?"

"G1!"

Victory buzzes. My girls are jumping and cheering, acting like a team in a big way. An immediate celebration field trip is in order. Austin's running around, delivering high fives and specific compliments to every girl on the team. And for a second, I almost want to be the girl who stays back with her guy. Almost. In large part this win belongs to him, and I don't want him to think I don't appreciate him. Levi always missed the start of floor celebrations to wander off with Kit, and that's not the kind of relationship I want.

"Soph."

He saved me for last. His eyes are on fire. His mouth tilts mischievously.

My breath catches.

"Tryin' to beat me at my own game?" He draws closer.

"Maybe. Wanna make it official?"

"Tackle?"

I push his arm at his roguish grin.

He pulls me out of the chaos, hands gripping my upper arms, turning his back to everyone. "As your coach, I have to say, it's not fair that you were MVP *and* the total knockout. Try to share with the other girls, okay?"

Can a face split open from smiling too hard?

One hand low on my back, pulling my hips to his. The other holds my jaw.

Behind me my teammates are singing like second graders. "Sophie and Austin sittin' in a tree."

His herculean body shifts to shield us from everyone else. "You are absolute fire." That glinting smile grows as I'm left waiting.

Then finally his full lips meet mine—slow and loaded with meaning. And another. Before my vision can focus again, he spins me around and nudges me toward the girls.

I twist back to look at him. *What did you do to me?* I'm dizzy enough to swing at a piñata.

AUSTIN

Song of the day

"No L's" by Forrest Frank

CHAPTER THIRTY-FOUR

Austin

SOPHIE

Are you going to study group tonight?

Nope

Truth is, I can't fit any more friend groups in my life right now. I'm already past capacity. Besides, Sophie lost her marbles about Lily that one time. I don't need her reading into anything.

You can go if you want?

Can I come talk to you for a minute?

Yeah but I have to leave soon. Come with?

This is the trickiest thing with Sophie. If I had it my way, I'd narrow my life down to our six, keep things simple. It's like she needs me to have a life of my own so she feels free to live hers. Tonight I just want to watch basketball. Melt into my couch and eat my bodyweight in beef jerky. Do nothing for once.

My life was already full before Sophie. Bible time every day—no skipping. Engineering classes that are no joke. Floor activities running nearly around the clock: soccer twice a week, late-night hangs, campus events, pranks. Bro time with Levi and Haymitch whenever we can. Gym every day or I feel like a slug, especially with no football pushing me. Two nights a week locked in for coaching G1's football team. Not complaining—my heart gets rebooted every five minutes when Sophie grins at me from the field. Problem is, it's all adding up. No time left to recover. I want to be with her as much as I can. I want her obnoxiously happy. Every spare minute I can find goes to making her laugh, planning over-the-top adventures, turning her world into a perfect dream.

Time to cross the field and avoid texting weirdness, but when I get to Griffin, she's already outside, clutching her bag. She waves me over—all bounce and affection. Sophie.

"Hey, Soph. When are you leaving?"

"Any minute. Wanna come?"

"Nah, you go have fun."

Her shoulders slump.

I suppress a sigh. *Bye, basketball.* "Do you want me to come?"

"I mean, not if you don't want to."

That's the thing—of course I don't, but I can't have her disappointed. Steeling myself, I tug her hair, sing a line from "Anywhere with You" by Jake Owens. She grins, and I can breathe again.

"Where are we headed?" I ask.

"Bowling. Here they come."

An old minivan pulls up. Sophie calls to the driver, "Have room for one more?"

"Uh, no, but the car behind us does."

She grimaces.

I'm home free. "No worries, Soph. You go have fun. I'm gonna hang on the floor tonight."

"What? I thought you were coming. You've been on the floor the last two nights."

That's not fair. I was just feverishly catching up on homework.

But … those brown eyes I love watch me expectantly, hopefully. Her freckled cheeks are poised to stretch into a dazzling smile if I give the right answer. Nos are an impossible match for that smile.

"Okay."

Sure enough, she grins. Beautiful. Too beautiful.

I flag down the car behind—full of girls. The driver rolls down the window.

"Hey, are y'all going the same place as that van?"

"We are. Want to come?"

"Yeah, if you don't mind."

"I'm Abbie."

"Austin. Nice to meet you."

She smiles. Oh. That kind of smile.

"'Preciate the ride. My girlfriend wants me to tag along."

"And she didn't even sit with you?" Abbie says. "Hmm."

Wait, what now?

By the time we reach the bowling alley, I've been patted, nudged, and fawned over for twenty minutes. When we arrive, there's no van carrying Sophie.

SOPHIE

I'm bringing you two bacon cheeseburgers and a chocolate milkshake unless you tell me differently.

Girlfriend of the year. Maybe I'm just hungry.

You read my mind

Thank you

I focus on my game, trying to ignore the conversation behind me climbing in pitch. Their friends must be here. When I finally bowl a strike, the girls erupt, touching me, squealing, like they've been doing the whole time.

Sophie watches from across the room, too still.

I jog over to make a show of greeting her—lifting her off the ground, kissing her full on the mouth. *Notebook*-style, minus the rain. Yeah, Janie indoctrinated me. When I set her down, her hands trail to my stomach, the Whataburger bag crumpling between us.

"Hi," she says, dazed. "You made some friends?"

"Mind coming over? They wanna meet the illustrious girlfriend." An exaggeration of their intent, I'll grant.

Her eyes shine, and I forget I haven't eaten in hours. Who needs food when she looks at me like that? This is it, why I'm here. I'm hooked. Can't rest till that smile's back.

We barely escape my first lane, and then I'm stuck entertaining her classmates for an hour and a half, ensuring no one feels left out. But at least I have cheeseburgers to sustain me. And watching Sophie bounce around pulls at my heart.

A happy Sophie is enough.

Sophie

Mia's still out when I curl up in bed. I usually avoid going to bed this early—partly because I overthink my whole day if I'm not tired enough to fall immediately asleep. But I'm not on my own. I'm not fighting my own battles, so I don't need to be afraid of my own thoughts.

Right?

I take a steadying breath and let the memory tornado loose.

Those girls all over him. Just like they always have been. I mean, look at him. And once he starts talking, they see how fun and sweet and funny he is. He's impossible to resist. The squealing fan club dragged me straight back to the pining-for-Austin period of my life. Major ick. But I had the mental fortitude to run through my verse: *For we are God's handiwork, created in Christ Jesus to do good works, which God prepared in advance for us to do.*

And then, standing in that grimy bowling alley, something new bloomed in me. A breakthrough.

What I've been told my whole life is wrong. Celebrate yourself. Love what you have. Own your power. None of it ever helped. The affirmations in the mirror, the desperate attempt to summon pride in my own attributes, the compliments that never sank in deep enough. None of it eased the pain of comparison, because all it did was keep my focus on myself.

I need my eyes on Jesus. He's the beautiful one. He's the one who wants me close, who makes me enough. He loves those girls —sees them, made them—and he has bigger plans for me than competing with his other creations.

CHAPTER THIRTY-FIVE

Austin

A few days later, the six of us pile into Levi's Rover to bring my grand Dallas zip-lining plan to life. I should be amped, but I'm wiped.

I finally talked to Dontrell Wayne this morning. It stings to give up the semipro league this spring—Dad's gonna take it hard. But I'm not chasing my spot at UT anymore. And even before Sophie, squeezing in the practices and travel was a stretch. Now with my life packed to the seams, it's not even on the table.

Being with Sophie makes me feel like myself. Like I can curl up with her and just be. So I don't get it—how being with her is a deep breath but somehow I'm still gasping for air everywhere else. Maybe that's just what happens when you care about someone this much. When losing them isn't an option.

Jesus time and workouts are staying priorities—in that order—so I've been skipping sleep, skipping meals, barely scraping by on homework. You won't find a bigger fan of food, but Saga's all the way across campus and The Hive's always got a line a mile long. Either way a real meal costs me an hour. Lately I wash down spoonfuls of peanut butter with coffee between Electromagnetics problems and pretend that counts.

Levi noticed and started sneaking me five slices of meat-lovers pizza at a time. He's such a good dude, but he's got a full life too. I don't want him worrying about me. One time he brought me a plate full of salad because he's weirdly obsessed with nutrition and felt guilty about all the pizza. I had to eat the whole thing just to pacify him. I hate salad.

And then, get this. Sophie asked why I haven't been at Saga for lunch, and my subject dodging got me nowhere. The next day she DoorDashed a medium-rare steak to my building at lunch. Sure wasn't mad at it, but it's far too much to accept. At least not again.

Obviously it's getting complicated around here. Something's got to give. Except, nothing seems like it can. Or should.

Okay, what do you say?

I tune out the road-trip chaos to listen for an answer and start thinking about Jesus's life on earth. How he kept ditching people —the ones who needed him—to go up on a mountain and pray for ages.

How did you do that, Jesus? Weren't people mad when you ran off?

I squeeze my eyes shut, trying to focus. God often brings things to mind when I stop and really listen.

And then it hits me. Jesus's Father was the one calling the shots. Not obligations.

Aw man, so disappointing people was just part of the job?

I beat against the headrest. I don't do disappointing people.

But you're the boss, not me. And you take care of everybody, not me. Teach me to run off and rest like you did.

Next to me, Haymitch is enjoying the relative quiet of the

back row. He's an introspective guy, and we can sit in silence without it being weird.

He clasps my shoulder. "Praying for you, Samwise."

You told him, huh? Thanks for that.

And he's back to staring out the window. Love that guy.

What if I just close my eyes for a hot minute? Maybe no one would notice.

Sophie

Austin's back there trying to sleep while Mia and I belt out some KB rhymes. I haven't had girl time with her in too long.

Levi let me drive his car—the one that costs as much as a college degree—so he could claim a middle-row seat next to Kit, as if they're not already surgically attached. This is not the time for whispering sweet nothings. It's time for dancing and laughing and pure, chaotic road-trip energy.

Austin's nap isn't eye-rolly though. Actually it scrapes my conscience. I'm worried about him. He burns the candle at both ends, playing Superman absolutely always, and I know his exhaustion is largely my fault. I've tried insisting—drop coaching, cut down on friend hangouts, give up our Tuesday afternoons, even quit soccer if he doesn't love it. But not the incredible dates he keeps planning ... I love those too much.

I would force him to slow down if it were just one thing. But, hi, yes, it's me. I am absolutely the problem.

He grew up in a small town where life moves slower. Where stores close on Sundays and people sip homemade lemonade on front porches. The kind of world country songs romanticize. Of course my pace is too fast for him. Of course I'm too much. That front-porch life is what he wants. And I want it for him.

But I, frankly, wouldn't survive it.

I can't be stuck in some tiny town where you run out of

things to do in two weeks and people gossip about you just to pass the time. The whole thing just screams *trapped.* I need freedom. I need new places, new things. I don't want to rest—I need to go.

I knew that for sure at sixteen. My parents were still together, but barely. The screaming never stopped. I got grounded for a party gone wrong—just two weeks, but it might as well have been a twenty-year prison sentence. No Jeep. No escape. Just me, pacing like a caged animal, forced to listen as the walls shook. Forced to pretend I didn't hear my dad say the words that finally made Mom kick him out. Forced to watch Mom continue her normal life, frizz-free and emotionless, as if her life weren't exploding before her eyes.

Music should have saved me. I blasted it in my room, in my headphones, let it fill the silence between fights. But it didn't work. Not when I couldn't drive, couldn't roll the windows down, couldn't put miles between me and the mess. It just became background noise to the walls closing in.

So I counted down the days, the minutes, the seconds until I could run again. Until I could press my foot to the gas, feel the air rush through my Jeep—gone. I promised myself I'd never set myself up like that again. Never be trapped.

And certainly not with a bonnet and a goat.

This tornado of love I have for Austin is bigger, stronger, more all-consuming than I thought it could be, but the future beyond his graduation—just over a year away—is a gaping void I can't see past. Only one part is clear. We don't make sense together. He'd spend his whole life appeasing me—until one day he'd snap. He'd want to nap on a Sunday afternoon, and I'd want to try jet-skiing. Or get Indian food. Or meet up with new friends. And I wouldn't slow down for him.

I can't.

Even for him.

He's a door and a deadbolt, all at once.

But I squeeze the wheel, try to shove the thought away. Not now. Not today. I'll wring every last second out of this fairy tale, even if it ruins me for anyone who'd come after him. But when I glance in the rearview mirror at my man-bear dozing fitfully, my eyes fill and my throat grows tight.

You're all up in our business, in the best way. You know and care about everything that happens to us. So ... I don't get it. Back in Portside, I was going to say no. I was going to save both of us all the heartache of it ending. But in that moment, I really thought this was your thing. A gift, right? And now I care about him even more, but us *doesn't make any more sense than it did then.*

Did I fall in love with the wrong guy?

Am I missing something?

Show me what to do and how not to break our hearts in the process. Please. I have no idea what I'm doing.

My thumb taps a frenetic beat against the steering wheel. This is why I read my Bible before my afternoon runs. I'll never hear back from him like this.

I turn down the music and speak just above it. "Hey, Mia."

She doesn't miss a beat, dark-brown eyes drilling into mine.

"I'm kind of stressed about Austin. Mind giving me some advice?"

"Yeah, girl. Shoot."

"We're so ... different, right?"

"Yep."

"He's all chill and likes to fish, and I'm like 'let's try bungee jumping.'"

"Yep."

"So?"

"So you compromise. He breaks his back doing your stuff, so take something off his load. Do something for him."

Compromise sounds nice and all, but is it enough? Is it just a Band-Aid?

"Got it. Thanks, girl."

"Yep."

And we're back to jams.

But as I sing along, something stirs in my chest.

Is that you?

It says that it's time to stop doubting this relationship—this *gift*. That it's time to dive fully in. To go big. Despite my brain's terror of heartbreak and warnings of small-town-shaped prison cells, it's time for my heart to take charge. To invest in what I'm dying to keep.

CHAPTER THIRTY-SIX

Austin

"Yahoooooo!"

Mia and I are doubled over at Haymitch's accidental Fred Flintstone impression as he zips from point to point. The gang is loving this adventure place. Missing my favorite team live in the NFC Championship Game is a major bummer, but it's worth it to see everybody happy. Mia's birthday yesterday took precedence, so I planned around her celebrations. No regrets. But I'll ask Sophie to check my messages during the game so nobody ruins the surprise.

A ticklish jab from behind makes me jump. "Hey!" Only one person would dare use my ticklishness against me. "Sophie ..." I swivel around with my best fake glare.

She's all innocence—until she cracks. I reach for her, but she's off. I actually have to try to catch her.

When I do, I throw her hips over my shoulder like a rag doll. "Nice try!" And I spin her around in circles.

"Aus-tin! Okay, okay, put me down."

She's still laughing and breathless as I slide her to her feet, and she smacks into my chest—oh, on purpose.

Snaking my arms around her, I push my luck on the PDA. "Hey, you."

That glowing grin … I wanna buy her a cookie cake. And something sparkly. And this whole adventure park.

"Pretty sure I won that round," I taunt.

She scoffs and reaches up to kiss me—not a peck. My nerves come alive.

"Okay, sure, you won," I concede.

"Hey, Austin?"

Mm. My name. I will be eighty-five and still love hearing it in her voice. "Yeah, Soph?"

"I'm worried about you. How can I help?"

My heart swells and grows Grinch-style, but I shake my head. I have no idea.

"Safe to say you have a plan to ditch these clowns and take me somewhere tonight before we head back?"

"Am I so predictable?"

"That's not predictable. It's romantic. Your planning is one of the very best things in my life."

And appreciation is my catnip.

"I hate to ask," she says, "but would you be up for adjusting the plan somewhat?"

"Course."

"I want to do something for you for once."

"Hey. You do tons for me."

"Not taking no for an answer, mister."

She's the feistiest little thing, and when she turns that spark on someone else's behalf? Game over.

"Yes, ma'am."

She draws up straight, like I've answered appropriately. "Can I tell you?"

"Yes, please."

"Apparently in Korea there are these places where you can rent a room with a couch and watch a movie." She steps away, painting a picture with her gestures. "My friend studied abroad there and had the best time. Anyhoo, there's one here in Dallas. I checked, and you can watch the championship game live."

Oh ... I tap Sophie's watch to check the time. Game starts at three. There's still time.

"It's not that different from the Dark Lounge, except for three important features."

"I'm listening."

One finger. "You won't be taunted about your Cowboys love affair."

My team hasn't been in the NFC Championship since I've been alive, and the guys do love to mock me.

Two fingers. "And the opposite of Flooders—it's private."

Uh-oh.

"I mean, the waiter comes in all the time, so it's not like that. But that's the third feature. You can order wings or whatever while you watch."

Wings.

My voice drops too low. "Sophie. You're speaking my language."

She beams. "Just us. I'm hoping you'll take a nap, during part of the game at least."

I stare, head tilting forward. She has never uttered such words.

"What?" she says. "You need it. It's a room with a couch, remember?"

I bob my head dumbly. Sophie, football, wings, nap. Some of my favorite things. I'm bone-tired, but I won't be missing that game, even if I figured out how to sleep in a private room with this beautiful girl.

Thank you for her, for us.

Help me keep the balls in the air.

Oh right. I mean, help me find times to sneak away and get the rest I need.

Sophie

"Uggghhh. I was going to let you make ground rules, and now we don't even need any."

Austin insisted on the room with two recliners instead of the sectional sofa. Now we can't even cuddle. And it's a T-shirt day.

"Oh, we still need ground rules, little lady."

I roll my eyes with drama and curl up in the recliner—annoyingly comfortable—and lean toward him. "Yes?"

"No kissing until the last twenty minutes." He smiles at my coy expression. "And you sit in your own chair."

"Fine. If I can have a kiss now to hold me over."

His eyes turn wary.

A hop-step later I'm at his chair, leaning on the armrests. He's right—this setup isn't deterring me. If this is the last kiss for hours, I'll have to make it a good one. I barely resist the urge to crawl into his lap, but my fingers twitch upward, brushing the biceps poking out of his sleeves. "Do you by chance have a cowboy hat? Asking for a friend. Not picturing anything."

He grins. "At home. Should I bring it to campus?"

"For my friend? That'd be weird."

He laughs.

"But really, Austin—"

Oh.

His hands are suddenly in my hair, tugging me toward him. Lips crash into mine in the most intoxicating kiss.

A sound escapes me—half moan, half question. No words, so I just nod dreamily as he releases me, my hands still gripping his armrests.

His reaction to his name sends a chill up my spine. Blue-gray eyes gaze into mine, full of longing, but then—click—his jaw locks with determination. He pulls his head back.

In the shuffle back to my seat, I throw in an overdramatic shiver of pleasure and a smile over my shoulder.

Humming "Cowboy Take Me Away," I press a button to lift the footrest. This chair really is comfy. And really, whatever it takes today for Austin to live his best old-man life. Is this what a relationship looks like? I never saw my parents do this give-and-take stuff. It's maybe a tiny bummer at first, but then it feels ... good. Great, even. I'm obsessed with that lazy grin on his face, and I got to put it there. What a thrill. A terrifying thrill.

He assures me he'd rather skip the nap, even orders a huge coffee, but the second his wings are demolished, he's out. I'm torn, but I can't bear to wake him up.

As I scroll through my treasured Songs of the Day playlist, I pop in an earbud. "Banks" hits hard. I want this for him. I creep over, click his phone to silent, slip back into my chair, and send him a text.

Remember when you sent me Banks by NEEDTOBREATHE?

Now it's from me to you.

You don't have to handle it all alone.

Austin

I wake to Sophie's warm voice in my ear. "Austin. It's a close game. Do you want to watch the end? Or wait and see it all in a row?" She's holding the remote, aimed and ready to switch it off at a moment's notice.

Where did she learn the importance of not ruining a game? Did I mention that at some point? This all feels like a fantasy, but that's Sophie for you.

"You're better than a dream," I slur, rubbing my eyes. I won't have time to watch more than the highlights later, so I'm thrilled to have the last quarter. "Watch the end."

Then I catch her signing the bill, and I about pitch a fit. She brushes it off, telling me she should get to treat me sometimes and to get over it. Her feistiness wins out. This woman is a riptide, pulling me into deeper water. It's scary, but I'm here for it. I want this with her. I want all of it.

A glance at the time says we're almost to the twenty-minute mark.

How does a guy scrounge up superhuman self-control on the regular like this? To my right, temptation pulls hard. I'm dying to go over there ... yet dreading my own animalistic instincts. How do I take care of her—protect her—when I can't even trust myself? How do people do this?

No wonder Caleb didn't. Zero judgment now.

Help?

This feels impossible. How am I supposed to act right?

Levi doesn't have to do this. Their crazy commitment to no kissing makes more sense all the time. Not that I'm signing up for that. No way.

"Kissing you is my favorite." Sophie's voice jolts me out of my thoughts. "But I only want to if it makes you happy too." Her brows gather in concern.

I jerk up. "What? No, it definitely does."

"You look terrified over there."

"Oh. Maybe I like you too much?"

She half-smiles, tilting her head. "Ice cream before the others pick us up?"

My breath out is almost a whimper. Giving up those twenty private minutes is a gut punch.

The second we step from the building into the fresh air, I haul her into my arms and sink into her lips. My affection and appreciation bubbles out into a manic, desperate kiss. I have to rip myself away.

She slow blinks, floating.

Someone walks by on the sidewalk, but who even cares.

"Soph, I gotta tell you something."

A groggy noise.

I squeeze her arms. "Thank you—for seeing me. For taking care of me today. In all the ways. And also ..." Buck up. She needs to know. "I love you."

And then she's wrapped around my neck, her lips back on mine. Kiss after kiss, all over my mouth.

Staggering, I get my arms around her small frame just as she slows.

"I love you too," she says against my lips. Her hands slide up my neck and into my hair.

When she pulls back, I peel open my eyelids.

Those latte eyes smile into mine with wonder, thawing me out and heating me up—straight to boiling.

She loves me.

Wow.

It's time for some ice cream. Pronto.

Song of the day

"Love Your Love the Most" by Eric Church

CHAPTER THIRTY-SEVEN

Austin

Things with Sophie are off the charts. Insanely good. Next level. Somehow I already love her more than two weeks ago, when I told her for the first time. But everything else? Well, my shirt is scratchy, the protein bar I ate for breakfast was dissatisfying, and it doesn't feel like a Sunday. Sundays never feel right anymore. I should drive back to Graham, go to church with my family. I never do. Never even go visit on Sunday nights like I used to. Sunday is always a mad dash to get my work done since I'm escorting Sophie all over the place on Saturdays.

All the stuff I plan isn't on her. I want Sophie to love her life and have all the new she can stomach. But it feels like nothing quite satisfies her. Like yesterday. I gave her two options of escape rooms. She picked one, the crew came, and we had a blast. But ... then she talked them into doing the second one, which was as unnecessary as *Avatar*'s water sequel. Same plot, just soggier. And after that she convinced Levi and Kit that they were dying to go on a double-date dinner I hadn't planned on. So, zero homework done.

She was so thrilled with me after the full day of excitement that she dragged me to the fence deep in the pines that night. We huddled in our spot, where she kept snuggling into me, singing "Happy Anywhere," whispering in my ear, kissing all over my face and neck and ear. It was incredible—how's a guy supposed to leave? But safe to say I didn't get nearly enough sleep last night. What else is new?

It's Super Bowl Sunday today, one of the best days on the calendar. A1, A2, and Flooders band together every year, turning Albert Hall's shared public lobby into a full-blown football fiesta. Lofts from every lounge. Couches hauled in by the dozen. A potluck spread for days. It's an all-day ordeal. Usually I'd be pumped, but this year ... no energy left. No time left. I don't get to enjoy my own stuff anymore, and I hate that.

As I carry loft after loft, couch after couch with the other Flooders, I'm mentally calculating how long my homework will take and whether I can knock out a big enough chunk before kickoff. Electromagnetics is a cool class, but it's tough. Advanced Electronics is no breeze either. And no sneaking upstairs to work during halftime, because the guys do a talent show I need to support. So ... a late night. Again. At least there'll be plenty of food, even if it is a hundred different kinds of chips. I'm the worst for not pitching in this year. I used to bring chili.

Midway through the Great Couch Migration, I spot Sophie in the lobby, setting up tables. She knows girls aren't really invited to the Super Bowl event. There's barely enough room for all the guys. But there she is, knocking out our tasks, humming to herself, looking like a dream come true. It's the first shorts day in months, and she's taking full advantage in her favorite teal workout shorts. Her hair is full and wavy, like she let it air dry. My favorite.

Oops, I'm leading the guys astray, veering toward her instead of the lofts.

The second we get it situated, I beeline for her.

"Soph, hey." I rub a thumb across her upper arm, happier than I should be to see someone I spent every minute with yesterday. A hint of vanilla floats in the air between us. I'm dying to pull her close and breathe her in.

Like she heard my thoughts, she droops her whole body against mine with that perfect smile. Her iced-latte eyes cool the heat in my chest. I squeeze her close and bury my nose in her neck. Yep. Vanilla. Her fingers sneak just under my T-shirt sleeves. Hitches my breath every time. Grade A flirting from my drop-dead gorgeous girl.

"Austin," she says low, "you looked so good carrying that like it was nothing."

I inch back and play it off like I'm not a bowl of Jell-O when she talks to me like that. "Whatcha doin'?"

She steps back into motion. "Tables and whatever else Calvin gives me. I just called in reinforcements. They'll be here soon to pitch in. Lots of girls are already in the Griffin kitchen whipping up a feast too. It's the least we can do for our sensational football coach." Her fingers find mine. Her eyes sparkle.

I deteriorate from Jell-O to oatmeal.

"I know this isn't supposed to be a G1 thing, so maybe you could say the food is your contribution?"

Speechless, I bob my head like an idiot. I wish I could pick her up and carry her around instead of another stupid couch. Almost lifting her off her feet, I turn our bodies to give us the slightest bit of privacy. The guys will have a field day with this, but who cares. Hand behind her head, I plant an intense kiss on her lips. Like I need it.

That woman will be the end of me, but one look at her smile and I'm not even mad about it.

She slow-blinks—like every kiss matters, like it carries weight—and pushes me toward the stairwell with two hands. "No more distractions, mister. Off you go."

The game is over now, and Sophie and I have a few minutes to hang in my room before Open Dorms end.

"I'm sorry." I flip open my textbook. "I hate that I barely saw you today. But I have to get this done before tomorrow."

"For sure, Hiro Hamada. Lock in." Producing a nail-filer thing out of nowhere, she settles against the armrest, legs draped across my couch. Singing "In Christ Alone" absentmindedly, completely content. A soft smile rests on my favorite human's face. Obviously I'm getting nothing done. Couldn't be happier my sofa isn't one we carried down to the lobby.

"It's cold in here," she says.

Yep, goose bumps on those beautiful legs. I half reach for the T-shirt quilt hanging off my bed—until I catch the look she's shooting me. That sly smile?

Pencil down. Book irrelevant. I'm all hers.

And then she grabs my button-down off the arm of the couch and starts unbuttoning it.

"Hey now. I'm gonna have to button alllll those buttons next time."

But that's not the troublemaking she had in mind. She slips it on, buttons it up, rolls the sleeves three more times.

When she stands up, I can't see her shorts beneath it. I gulp.

"Do I look like you?" She poses, exaggerates the way I push my sleeves up.

I'm not laughing. My heart is racing.

Wild waves. Bright eyes. Big smile. My shirt. Bare legs.

She's breathtaking.

My brain? Gone.

I try to reboot. To form words. "Soph. Keep it."

Calvin calls down the hall for the girls to head out.

She leans on my shoulders, presses a kiss to my lips. With a wave, she walks out, grinning at my paralysis.

And now I'm supposed to concentrate on homework?

The. End. Of. Me.

Haymitch slows to a stop at my doorway. "Okay, up ya go. Time for a cold shower."

I rub the back of my neck. Avoid his gaze.

"No, none o' that. It happens. Gettin' married doesn't magically flip a switch—it's there all along. C'mon."

I stand and shuffle off obediently.

Sophie

Halfway back to Griffin, something makes me stop and twist back. New hangman letters I noticed earlier, on my way to help set up the Super Bowl party. I pull his shirt tighter around me, still laced with that clean, woodsy scent that's tangled itself around my heart.

_ETTER
THAN A
REA

He said those words to me half asleep in Dallas. And now they're on display—a message for the world, written in a language only I fully understand. He knows people will figure out who's behind these hangman games. And still, he doesn't try to cover it up or tone it down. He's not hiding how he loves me. He's letting the world see it. But not yet. It's still just for us.

I cross the field with a smile that's starting to ache in my cheeks.

When I skip out of Griffin's stairwell into the hallway, Zoe stops me in my tracks.

"Sophie," she accuses.

"What?"

"You look like you just crawled out of someone's bed."

I recoil.

"Did you?"

"No. Not that it's any of your business."

"Actually, it is. But separate from being the RA, you're not being fair to Austin."

I sputter. "What is that supposed to mean?"

She shifts her bag. "We used to hang out. He's one of the most quality guys at this school." Her eyes drag down my legs, then back up. "You're either going to change that or you're going to lose him."

My blood goes cold. "Slut-shaming much?"

Her expression falters. The edge slips. "Sorry. Just ... think about it, okay?"

AUSTIN

Song of the day

"More Than I Know" by Jordan Davis

More than he knows what to do with. He doesn't know what he's gotten into.

I tap out a reply before I can talk myself out of it.

Compliment or complaint?

Compliment for sure. What's up

Nothing

CHAPTER THIRTY-EIGHT

Sophie

For once I'm on time to Bible, and the spot next to Izzy is open.

I slide in. "Hey, girl!"

She presses her lips together. "Sorry, I was saving this seat."

"Oh. No worries. I'll catch you later?"

She watches the door.

I brush it off and find another seat, but that afternoon I bound up the stairs to G3. Guess I've been neglecting my borrowed floor.

"Chicas!" I call to a group walking down the hallway. "What are you up to?"

Jenny breaks the awkward silence. "Hey, Sophie. I have to get some homework done. I'll see you around."

"No worries, girlie." I smile, but it doesn't land right on my face. "You okay?"

She sends a little nod and continues with her group, who send knowing looks.

Izzy's daisy-embroidered backpack is in the floor lounge, but she's not in there. I find her in her suite.

"Izzy! Up for a hang? Sorry it's been a minute."

She purses her lips.

"What? Why are you being weird?"

"Name-calling isn't nice, Sophie."

"I'm not name-calling. You're mad at me? Why?"

"Seriously?"

"Seriously. Please just tell me why everyone is acting all"—not weird—"different."

"I mean, you made your bed. Maybe literally. You've kinda been a homewrecker."

"A *what*?" I choke out.

"You wanna do this? Fine." One hand on her hip, another to count with. "First it was Leo who you stole from your own poor floormate. Well, ex-floormate."

"*Leo*? Who could I have *stolen* him from?"

"Whoa. Let's try to be civil, yeah?"

I look around. I don't think I'm dreaming. It looks like normal G3.

"Then it was Chase and whatever happened there. Then you stole Davis Powell from Jenny—like, she was heartbroken. I hope it was worth it—"

"Davis?" I cut her off. "I talked to him at putt-putt *once*."

She ignores me. "And then Austin Scott from Lily."

"Lily?"

"Lily. D2. Don't play dumb. They were super tight until you sabotaged her."

"I didn't sabotage anything," I insist. "Austin asked *me* out. I was totally shocked."

She sneers. "Uh-huh. They might think they like someone, but ... they could be wrong."

"*Mean Girls*?"

"I mean, you're trying to be the Regina George of Mayberry," she says. "Leo, Chase, Davis, Austin. Quite the ladder climb." She tilts her head with malice. "Who will you steal next? Levi?"

My stomach rolls. Is that why the G3-ers haven't invited me anywhere in weeks? Why Izzy doesn't sit by me? Why Jenny replies with one-word texts?

And whoever thinks I stole Leo from her. I guess my floor is next to hate me. Zoe's already on her way.

"It's not like that," I mumble.

The words barely leave my mouth before the memory hits—last semester, when I was mocking Kit. *Not impressed, Levi. Try harder*. My eyes fill at that memory in a new light. *It's not like that*, she whispered. I was so jealous I couldn't see straight. So convinced she lived a charmed life.

How long have I been doing this—assuming I get people, rewriting their stories around mine?

Kit said the same thing I just did. *It's not like that.* I didn't believe her either.

"I hope you understand," Izzy says, the picture of diplomacy. "I just can't be around you. It's too much drama. Boundaries, you know?" And she disappears around the corner.

At lunch the next day, I channel my own wrecking-ball energy—a benevolent version—all the way to the A2-G3 tables.

Found him. "Davis."

He quirks a crooked smile. "Sophie Appel, as I live and breathe."

"Mind if we talk, uh, over there?"

His table goes quiet.

"Just have a quick favor to ask!" I singsong. "Carry on!"

He follows.

I spin around at a quiet-ish area of Saga. And ... what now? I have no plan. I just want to fix things. *Need* to fix things. "You know Jenny?" I start.

"Sure," he says, amused.

"She's adorable, right?"

He lifts his brows. "Is that a trick question?"

I gasp. "She is! She totally is."

"Girls never want you to compliment someone else. Just trying to stay out of trouble over here."

"Oh. Right. Okay. I was just thinking that you're really great, and ..."

He squints. "You still with Scott?"

"Huh?"

"Are you still with Scott?"

"Yeah."

"Then what are ya doin'?"

"What? No. I just—"

"You're gonna get me in trouble talking all shady like this."

"Oh. Sorry."

"See you around?"

"Yeah."

"'Kay."

After classes, I search G3 for Jenny and find a brick wall.

"I had no idea you really liked Davis Powell," I say. "And I never went out with him for real, I promise. It was just that one night we hung out with the group."

"Okay." She doodles in the corner of her notebook.

"I just want to make sure we're good."

"Yep."

"And the party that time, it was—"

"We're good, Sophie." But her cold, sad gaze sends a chill into the room.

The loss sits like a well-worn ache in my chest. Not much different than what I was raised on—keep it light, keep it together, and you'll never get trapped. But this?

Feels more like a trapdoor than anything I've been dodging.

CHAPTER THIRTY-NINE

Austin

Levi throws his signature leather backpack over his shoulders as we head across campus for lunch. He's here to escort me like a prisoner in transit. Apparently lunch today is not optional.

He's a good buddy. Thanks for him.

"How are you, man?" he asks.

"Well, all my favors are dried up, the guys on the floor borderline resent me—"

He winces. "Been there."

"—And every part of my life that isn't Sophie is hanging by a thread."

I convinced twenty-four college dudes to hang twinkly curtain lights down our hallways—because mood lighting is essential—and blow up a billion silver and gold balloons for a masquerade party. It was a hard sell after we did all that work for the Super Bowl just a week ago. And Catamelon is this week, so they've been putting final touches on the Flooders watermelon catapult. Thirteen Flooders were swayed by assurances that the whole glorious floor of G1 would come ready to mingle. I'm sure the fact that Levi and I won over the two best girls on campus gave them hope that they could land a similar outcome. Convincing the next seven felt like lobbying in DC. All I can say is I'm glad I'm not going into politics. Levi convinced the last ten because he's Levi and the dude is just a real one.

"You're going to blow her mind," Levi says. "You have me wondering whether I'm off my game or you're off your rocker."

"It's definitely the latter. I'm surviving on coffee, protein powder, and that time Sophie said she loves me."

His eyebrows shoot up.

"Oh. Yeah. I pulled out the L-word when we were in Dallas."

"That's big, man. Congrats. Wow."

"You gonna tell Kit?" I eye him and go for it. "Hundred percent she loves you back."

He adjusts his backpack. "I almost did. That's what the Rose Garden date was for. But I suckered out. Maybe I'm overcorrecting after pushing her so much at the beginning." But the line between his eyebrows says there's a lot more to it.

"Whatever you think, buddy. You're a stud though. No worries that she'll reciprocate."

"Thanks for that." And he's back to joking. "But you're killing me, Samwise. Weekly grand gestures? Plus The Game? How are the rest of us supposed to keep up?"

"Dude, Kit's so into you that people shield their eyes when she looks in your direction."

He laughs.

"Besides, she hates attention and when you spend money, right? Which is all this kind of stuff." Yeah, he was joking, but I'm not leaving this alone. I'm not having the king of the school second-guessing himself on my watch. "And a dance studio is fifteen or twenty of my gestures. You're still very much the one to beat."

"Thanks, buddy, but I'm more checking in on your sanity."

"I do worry about the sustainability of all of this." I rub my neck. "Someday she's gonna be like 'Remember what you used to do in college?'"

Levi twists toward me, brows high. "Someday? Like ... you want to marry her?"

I nod sheepishly.

"Now who's the sap?"

"Whoa, whoa. That's definitely still you, Jeeves."

"Yeah, I don't know. Sounds like you're trying to beat me out for that title too."

I whack him on the chest, and he whacks me back.

"Have you talked to her about UT yet?"

"I'm not going. I told Coach." But not Dad. A brick drops into my gut at the mere thought.

"You prayed about it?"

"Course. What gives, dude?"

"Nothing. But tell Sophie."

"Yeah. I will."

Eventually. She's gonna lose it when she finds out I shrugged off the experience of a lifetime. And I have a bad feeling she'll spiral. It screams commitment, and we haven't really talked about that.

She might even call the whole thing off.

We push through the Saga doors, and there they are—our girls, on either side of the G1 table, leaning forward, deep in discussion. Levi and I exchange a look. I shrug.

Sophie

"Kit, I've been the absolute worst. I'm so sorry."

She reaches across the table for my hand. "What? Have not."

"No, I have been. You don't assume the worst about me. You

never gossip. You never give up on me. You don't even shut your door. You deserve every good thing you have ..."

She shakes her head, all wide eyes and protest.

"... And I just want you to know I see it now. And I'm going to be a better friend from now on, okay?"

She squeezes my hand. "Where is this coming from?"

"Tell you later. And I need your advice. But look who's here."

The moment she sees him, her face lights up—like God just created the sun and lit the solar system.

I launch into "You Got It Bad"—and a case of déjà vu.

"Don't even with me," she says, eyes still locked across the room. "You are just as far gone."

We watch as they stroll over, trays in hand. Then they exchange a look and turn back to us in unison—Levi's brow raised, Austin smirking.

I roll my eyes. "Yeah, okay," I call to them. "Sit down, will you?" I mutter to Kit, "We're not helping their male egos one bit."

"No kidding," she says, sly. "They'll be intolerable soon."

AUSTIN

Song of the day

"BEAUTIFUL AS YOU" by Forrest Frank

Austin

"Are you real?" she asks.

"Define 'real.' I don't file taxes yet," I joke.

Sophie runs a finger around my palm, tracing down my fingers.

I can't kiss her here. I shouldn't. I brought out a blanket to look at the stars with her. It's fine—midnight picnics happen on a college campus. There's a steady stream of people walking by, so it should be safe. And she's acting a little off—leaning back on her hands, craning toward the sky instead of lying down like usual.

We just came from the masquerade thing. She lit up the whole room, and it was worth every shred of effort. Trouble is, I'm fixing to pass out, and I still owe the guys a full cleanup of the lounge and hallway. It was my idea, after all.

I curl up on my side, resting my head on my arm.

She bends over and squeezes my hand. "Austin ... Tonight was ..." She swallows hard. "It's like you undo all the times I was forgotten. You know me and still *want* me—" Her voice breaks.

My jaw's tight, but words scrape out. "Of course I want you." A verse slips out in a mumble. One of Janie's favorites. "Clothed with strength and dignity. Laugh without fear of the future." It's Sophie. More every day. I press a kiss to her palm. Her tiny bracelet slides down with the motion. I run my thumb over it. "What's the story here?"

"I bought it after I got baptized last year. To remember." She twists it. "No clasp. They welded it on."

Something floods my chest. A yes. I want my whole life welded to hers. To grow old with her. Laugh-wrinkle old.

She's The One.

She is, right? I've made a real mess if not.

But ...

"I have to give up The Game," I blurt. "Is that okay?"

She glances over. "Of course. What do you mean 'give it up'?"

"Let the floor have it."

"Let them. It was incredible." A playful smile tugs at her lips as she looks down at me. "I want a kiss. Taxpayer or not."

My heart pounds unhelpfully. "When I drop you off, 'kay?"

"Am I going to get another guerrilla kiss? Or gorilla kiss?" She swings her arms like an ape. "Not sure what that is, but I'd like to try it. Maybe for the next truth-or-dare game."

I chuckle. “Gorillas.”

“Austin.”

My droopy gaze snaps up.

“Why do you push me away?”

“What? I don’t.”

“You never let me kiss you. And when you do, you stop me with a Conclusion Kiss.”

“Oh.” I nestle into my arm again. “Cause my thoughts scare me.”

“What thoughts?”

“I start thinking about the back of your Jeep,” I slur. “And what you’d say yes to. And how I could justify it. Oh, Soph. I gotta tell you something.”

She rubs my shoulder, my neck. Feels so good. I let my eyes close.

“What is it?”

“Y’know how I played in that league with Dontrell Wayne?”

“Yeah.”

“I did it ’cause my high school coach pushed for it. And my dad’s been paying for legit game tape for me to send to UT.”

“Okay …”

“I’m really back. Coach thinks he could get me a connection. A walk-on spot.”

Her hands go still.

“A maybe spot. Just a chance to prove myself.”

She shakes me gently. “Hey. What were you saying?”

I rub my eyes. “Didn’t wanna tell you. Jeeves said I had to.”

“Austin. Are you transferring?”

“Never. I’m not leaving you.”

Her voice sounds miles away. “Do you want me to go with you? I’ll go with you if you want.”

“No more football.” I feel myself drifting. “Practice all the time. I’d never see you.”

I must have fallen asleep. No idea how much time has passed.

"Soph. Did I freak you out?" Is my voice romantically quiet or half-asleep? "Are you gonna break my heart?"

But I don't hear the answer.

I don't get her song of the day sent, but I remember first thing in the morning.

Song of the day

"Make You Cry" by Walker Hayes

CHAPTER FORTY

Sophie

Last night did a number on me. Gave me a striking clarity I didn't think I'd find. Now I'm snuggled into Austin's giant bear body, head on his chest, legs stretched out on his perfect rust-colored couch. I never knew closeness and comfort could be this thrilling. Cue Lizzie McGuire in "This Is What Dreams Are Made Of." Images of prairie bonnets and churned butter lurk, but I won't let Austin go.

I finally understand why people are willing to compromise so much to be with the one they love. It's not because I'm investing in my future—I have no idea what my future looks like. It's because I'm desperate for Austin to be happy. I crave what he craves. I long for his dreams to come true. I know it sounds crazy, but if it pushes him an inch toward those dreams, I will absolutely pack up my things and move to Austin, Texas.

Maybe even in all the ways.

Besides, the Texas capital is a thrill, right? Everybody says so.

So we'd both be getting what we want, at least while I'm in school. Now I just need to figure out how to convince him to reconsider giving up his dreams.

Mom would have an aneurysm, call this humiliating. Antifeminist. But what has worst-casing ever bought for her? What has selfishness ever bought? I want Austin to be as happy as he makes me. I need that.

Teach me to be as good to him as he is to me, as good for him as he is for me.

Austin's charged hands toy with my fingers, sending sparks up my arm. He's lazy and content—feet on the floor, legs in sweats, back slouched into the corner of the couch. His faded-blue Cowboys hat hides his curls today and, often, my eyes when he leans in to kiss my head.

Austin's big surprise this week was throwing an insanely dreamy Valentine's Day party for me and my floor on Wednesday. And last weekend our crew went camping—Austin's best s'mores included. Even Levi had the best time. So we have a rare slow Saturday afternoon on campus. I told Austin I wanted to watch his game with him, and now my man is practically purring as we watch the Mavericks together. The lounges are packed—one with another basketball game, one with some group gaming session—so Austin's laptop is propped up on big math books on his desk chair. He tells me about his favorite players, how the team hasn't been the same since they traded their best player. Explains things, but only if I ask. I'm humming "Simple" by FGL. I keep wanting to bring up UT at each commercial break, but it hasn't worked out yet.

It's long past time we did a day like this. We're always out doing what I want. He deserves a girlfriend who shows up for his stuff too. WWJD if J were me? Honestly, I think he might be right here, watching Austin's game.

I don't like his Westerns, and I could go my whole life without chewing through beef jerky again, but bonfires? Flannel? Hiking? County fairs? I'm so in for his faves. It's all the opposite of

Pasadena-life, but that might be exactly why I love it. It makes me think maybe I could figure this thing out long term. That we could avoid ending up like my parents.

At halftime, Austin mutes the laptop. We're alone in here, but probably not for long. Flooders noises float in from the hall. Guys pop in now and then to talk to Austin, and I expect Levi and Kit will be back soon. Maybe it's the right time to broach the UT subject, so I lean my head back to look at him upside down—but I'm immediately distracted by my favorite mischievous smile. The one that almost always precedes a kiss.

Wait for it.

Fingers graze my ear, my jaw. His hat covers my face in a dark cocoon, and he tilts the bill so it doesn't hit me. Fingertips land at my neck. He kisses me twice, upside down, Tobey McGuire Spider-Man–style. Then a final kiss—a Conclusion Kiss—before he fixes his hat and drops back against the couch.

My heart races, as if it heard the starting gun at a track meet.

Sorry, heart. I know this guy. The one kiss is all we're getting.

"Well, it's official, Sparky. I have a big head now."

"Oh no. I've been afraid of this."

"The most beautiful girl in the world is on my couch watching basketball with me. I have arrived."

"Do I have to stop complimenting you?"

"I'm not sure—please elaborate. With examples."

I reach to tickle his side, but he catches me easily. "Nice try."

He sets my hand on my stomach, then trails both hands up my arms, across my shoulders, into my hair. My eyes roll back in my head.

"Tell me more about when you met Jesus?" he asks.

I smile, lazy and safe under his touch. He doesn't have to bribe me. I'd tell him anything.

But a thought slinks in. A troll. "*Why did he keep UT a secret?*"

But I shoo it away. Austin's the most selfless guy on the planet. That's why.

"You said you were volunteering?" he says.

I start talking, his fingers twisting through my hair. "Yeah. I needed volunteer hours for school. We were picking up trash in this random neighborhood. Another volunteer I met said chasing freedom never worked for her. Drinking, sex, sneaking around—it all sounded like freedom but ended up just trapping her more." I give a little shrug. "That really landed. Partying had felt that way to me. So when she said she had looked up all the verses that say 'freedom' in the Bible, I went home and did the same. I just... knew it was true. So I tried talking to the air." I gesture around us. "Told Jesus I needed that free life I'd never been able to find."

He's silent, fully locked in.

"I don't think Jesus just gives freedom. I think he *is* freedom ... Because the rules in the Bible aren't prison bars. His way is like a fence around a playground—boundaries that keep us free."

I hear myself say it like I mean it, like I get it. Still, something itches. Like maybe I haven't really stopped chasing freedom, just gotten sneakier about it. But before I can scratch at that thought, his hands are back in my hair. I chuckle. He's not done listening.

"Church still gives me the ick, but Praise and Prayer has been game changing. The simplicity. The hymns. And 'More Like Falling in Love'—that song helped everything click." Saying the title out loud feels oddly vulnerable, but I push through. "The one by Jason Gray? It's Jesus Life in a song. Anyway, I'm still kind of shocked I ended up at Mayberry. I thought Christians were wacko. Kit was super intense. I felt so out of place in August. Still do sometimes."

"What? No." He brushes a thumb along my jaw. The path he touched must be glowing now. "Soph, this place needs you. I need you. You just ... get it. Jesus isn't a ... a hobby for you. He's the whole point. The whole enchilada."

"I do love enchiladas."

He plants a lingering, cocooning kiss on my forehead, like that's the best way to say what he means. "I love you."

A thoughtful pause rests between us, and then his hands

resume their languid path through my hair. "You said 'Jesus Life in a song.' So how should the Jesus Life look?"

I swallow. *Should I tell him?*

Weaving my fingers together, I dive further in. "Falling in love with you actually helped me figure it out. The second I met you, I wanted to see you again, talk more, know more. And the more I knew you, the more I felt seen and known and happy. So ... that's what Jesus is offering. Falling in love with him. But so much more. Better. To an extreme, you know?"

His eyes glisten. He nods.

I roll onto my side to face him. "It's super hard because you're right here, inviting me to come over. Jesus is always there, waiting. It should be easier that way, right? But it's so hard for me to tune out everything, to put it all away and just hang out with him. Hearing from him is so different from hearing from you. But when I start to coast, to give up on listening, this"—I gesture between us—"reminds me. I fall more in love with you every week, every day. And Jesus is just so much better than you." We share a grin. "So if I'm not falling more in love with him, it's 'cause I'm not making enough space for him."

Oversharing makes me twitchy, but he deserves it. He's earned it. And maybe it's not oversharing with Austin. Maybe it's just ... vulnerability.

"Dang, Soph. Never felt the urge to propose before."

I laugh—until I see he's only half-smiling.

"Can I ask you one more question?" he asks.

"Yeah." I swallow. "Of course."

"You said you're shocked you're at Mayberry. How'd you end up here?"

I trace a pattern on my knee. "I just ... knew. I was supposed to be here. I couldn't explain it, didn't want to listen. I was supposed to go to USC like my dad. Got in somehow. But one night, I was spiraling and Googled Christian colleges. Something about Mayberry's pictures—just the trees, the space, I don't know—made me feel like I could finally breathe. Turning USC down felt crazy, especially that late. Mom still hates paying for this place. But I knew. So I came."

His eyes catch fire—blue flames flickering, growing. "He got you here."

Tenderly, urgently, Austin pulls me onto his lap, cradles my face. I search his eyes. He's said no to this before, and an alarm flashes in the back of my head. But when his nose brushes mine, I fall silent. After everything I shared, I ache to be near him, close in a way words can't reach. Even with Austin, in the safest hands, letting someone see this much of me stings with risk. I need this. To soothe. To reassure. To prove I'm safe.

But just before his lips meet mine, his eyes snap to the door.

He sets me back down—too gently. And just like that, the moment cracks.

Guilt floods his face. He won't meet my eyes. Rolls a shoulder. Clears his throat.

Mine tightens as I follow his gaze.

CHAPTER FORTY-ONE

Sophie

Levi and Kit walk through the doorway. Hesitating, she motions toward the hallway. I shake my head—it's Levi's room too. They don't need to leave.

Austin presses a kiss to my hand. I squeeze back, but an unwanted truth settles. Even Austin has a limit. He can't hold it all for me.

Because that's your job?

"What's going on in here?" Levi teases. His eyes lock on me, almost accusatory.

"You looked so serene," Kit says in a ridiculous voice.

I laugh at the *She's the Man* quote. "I made breakfast, darling!"

"Mavs game. Halftime," Austin answers Levi. He relaxes back into the couch. "Playing with her hair convinced her to tell me things. Works like a charm, dude, if your telepathy ever fails you with this one."

I turn to send him a silent message, and his smile tightens to a grimace. He didn't mean to reference the dark period of their relationship.

But no concern from the lovebirds.

"My telepathy often fails me with this one," Levi says.

Kit's Disney eyes flick to Levi with a sly, flirty look. Whoa. That's a new side of Perfect Little Kit. Bold and dangerous?

Austin suddenly pushes up and steps to Levi. "What's up, dude?" His quiet voice perks my ears. "You're not telling me something." He shakes his head, impatient. "Not that. Something else."

Levi silently opens his closet door and turns around with a sweater and dress pants in his hands. Fancy, even for him. Must be a Valentine's date. He holds them out to Austin in some kind of wordless bro-coded message.

Austin studies him. Levi flicks a glance at Kit—then at Austin again, like he's waiting for something.

Austin stares at the sweater. "Oh."

Levi scratches the back of his neck. Message sent. Message received. They've always had this unspoken thing, but this feels heavier. Almost like a warning.

"Sophs," Kit says, too bright. "Levi's taking me to a tapas place in Portside. It's all authentic and fancy, and we could pretend we're in Spain. You'd love it."

Levi drops his head. Like the secret's out.

There's more to this. Kit's big eyes practically plead. Not sure why yet, but she's right—after that description, I'm dying to go.

All three of us look to Austin.

"Feel like tapas, Soph?" That voice. The one I heard before bowling, in Dallas, and more all the time. Resigned. Weary.

I turn to Levi. "Do you even have a reservation for four?"

He nods—guiltily—at Austin.

Valentine's dinner for four. So he'd wanted us there. Maybe not anymore.

Kit's restless eyes flick to the window again. She stiffens.

That's what's off. The forecast says rain. So why not another night? If she'd even blinked, Levi would've canceled. But she's not blinking.

"Can we watch the rest of his game before we decide?" I ask.

Levi's eyebrows lift in approval, and he checks his watch. "Sure."

"I'm headed back to change," Kit says. But she doesn't move.

I tilt my head. "Just in case, can you bring me some things?"

"Yes!"

"I'd need my heeled boots and makeup bag. Oh, and this place is fancy, you said? Pick some earrings—I trust you. And a dress that goes with yours."

"The black one," Austin pipes up.

I break into a grin. Too bad I can't actually wear that workout dress he loves.

"And ..." Kit falters. "Can I make your boyfriend ride shotgun?"

I glance out the window. Could this mean something to Levi? Is she pushing past her anxiety for him?

Something stirs in my belly, and I step close. "Hey, KitKat? What if you drive? Maybe you'd be okay in the driver's seat."

She frowns, flicks a glance at Levi.

"KitKat, huh?" Levi teases Austin.

"Apparently," Austin says, quirking a smile.

"You can take the Jeep." My gut tugs, but I buckle down. "Whether we join or not."

She chews on her lip. Finally gives a tiny nod.

When we're alone again, Austin returns to his spot with me. I love this couch, but it's a thousand times better when he's on it.

I turn his face to mine. "We don't have to go tonight. You seem really tired."

"Are you five nine?"

I blink at his non-response. "Five eight. Why?"

He breaks into the tune of "5 Foot 9." "God makes five foot eight, brown eyes in a tennis dress."

I clap and grin. Another lyric swap just for me.

"Loves dinner out and small-town music ..." He putters out with a quiet chuckle. "Wait, how does it go?" He bends forward to search for the Tyler Hubbard lyrics on his laptop. "Ain't no way that me and this school made her fall in love. Saga makes good pizza, but God makes the good stuff."

I curl into him, laughing. "You're so clever. And funny. And sweet. And sacrificial."

"Whoa, whoa. Big head, remember?"

Meeting his gaze, I turn serious. "I mean it. You should get to pick too."

"I pick you. I want you to get to go." His eyes smile, but that weary voice says otherwise.

"I'll make you a deal. We go tonight, but no crazy date next weekend. I'm ordering in. Lots of meat. You're going to accept it, and you're going to like it."

"Ah—"

But I duck under his hat to plant a kiss on his lips, silencing his protest. A kiss that lingers, that bares my closeness and trust and need.

"I love you too, Soph," he whispers against my lips.

My gut clenches painfully. See the world or drink sweet tea. I knew this would happen. But we can make this work. I'm not giving him up. I can make this work.

Please.

AUSTIN

Song of the day

"Like No One Does" by Jake Scott

CHAPTER FORTY-TWO

Sophie

It's Tuesday hang time, but I have an idea to help Austin lighten his load—a cocktail of multitasking and endorphins.

Run together today?

AUSTIN

Love it. Will you slow down for me?

Funny. He could run laps around me with his strong legs and crazy endurance. Wait, unless his knee is bugging him.

What's wrong old man? Your knee acting up again?

Ha ha. Knee's fine

So now we're jogging out Mayberry's front entrance, toward

the quiet neighborhood nearby. Austin's grinning in an old T-shirt with the sleeves ripped off, and I'm wondering why we haven't done this every Tuesday. He's in his element—the man-bear has extra energy to burn, even when he's running on fumes.

"Still praying during your runs?" he asks, keeping our pace slow enough to talk comfortably.

"Yeah, I really like it. It helps me focus and not think a thousand things at once."

He runs a hand down my ponytail. "Let's pray now."

"Now? But you're here."

"You don't miss a thing," he teases.

"You mean pray out loud?"

"Yeah. Try with me?"

Nerves flutter in my chest. "Okay."

Here goes. I squeeze my fists as my arms pump, suddenly hyperaware of everything—his steady breath, the rhythmic pounding of our feet, my own heartbeat picking up speed. What if I say something stupid?

"Hi, Jesus. I usually pray for Austin, but he's right here, so this is super weird. You don't mind, right?" I force myself to keep my eyes forward. If I glance at Austin, it'll feel too much like I'm talking to him instead. "Please take care of him. Show him how much you love him and give him all the things he needs. Everything we need to get better at, make sure we do. Interrupt him in the way you do and teach him the things you have for him, things that will bring him closer to you than ever. Change us and make us more like you, Jesus."

I brave a glance over. His turn.

His jaw tightens, and his Adam's apple bobs. "You pray for me? Like that?"

I frown. "Hey."

"No. Soph. I'm so thankful."

Are his eyes wet? "Oh. Yeah, I do. I mean, the end wasn't really me, if that makes sense."

"Wow. The Spirit told you what to pray?"

Silence settles. Even running, I can't sit in this a moment longer. "Your turn, mister."

A long pause. "Hi, God. You are holy. Worthy. Good. You deserve all my attention and choices and hours. Guide me and help me to hear your voice loud and clear so I can do what you want. Help me to know what's for you and what's extra. Be close to Sophie as she seeks you with all her heart. Every day I see you clothing her with strength and dignity. Every day she laughs with less fear of the future. Keep teaching her to see herself how you see her. Cross out any lies in her head. Keep showing her what to pray. Keep giving her messages to deliver to the people around her."

I suck in a breath. Me?

"Show Sophie and me how to honor you in everything we do. Show us how to do this better. Amen."

I reach for his hand and squeeze it. "Thank you." Like Praise and Prayer, except with my favorite person. "New Tuesday tradition?"

"Definitely. I loved that, Soph. Thanks for being vulnerable with me." He scratches my arm. The "I'm here" scratch.

"Now see if you can't pick up those elderly legs," I say. "I'm kicking up the pace here."

He pretends to struggle to keep up. "You're an amazing personal trainer. Highly motivating."

"Oh yeah?"

"Then again, if I slack off I get to watch you run away."

I smack his arm. "If you keep up, I'll give you a kiss at the end."

"Now, Sophie," he says faux seriously, "affection isn't earned."

Laughing, I push harder. Arms pumping, air rushing past. My lungs burn just enough to remind me I'm alive.

"Wait—yes, I want my kiss!" he calls, fake panting.

His footfalls thunder behind me, closer, closer. I try to stay out of reach, but I'm laughing too hard.

Being chased by a bear is so underrated.

AUSTIN

Song of the day

"Inside and Out" by Tyler Hubbard

CHAPTER FORTY-THREE

Austin

"Nah," I tell Levi. "I'm not gonna let you bail me out of something else. It's my floor too, and you have election prep to think about."

Our group just finished playing cards, and we're already packing up to head out of MSC. I lost every game. I'm pitifully tired, and my friends watch me in a way I don't appreciate.

"It's student body president, not US Congress," Levi says. "And it's my fault the prank is happening now. We pushed it back because of the dance studio, remember?"

Of course I remember. It was a whole drama on the floor. A drama I will not repeat. "We rescheduled it because we need so many of us at once to pull it off," I correct. And because he needed our prep space. But still.

He shakes his head. "You're so stubborn. You don't know when to quit."

"And you do?" I press my fingers into my eyes, willing myself to let something go. “Soccer. Y’all will be fine without me. What if I just take a few weeks off?”

“Good. No more soccer this season. I’ll tell the guys.” And he heads off with Kit.

“A couple weeks,” I call. “And I’ll tell them.”

What I don’t want to tell them is it’s time I get a job instead. With me, Sophie will have everything, and I’m running low on funds. I’m sure a few of my parents’ neighbors could use some hourly labor. Somebody to repair the fence or haul brush. Without soccer I’ll have two nights a week.

A memory flashes to mind—that time I stole Sophie away for a cookie cake run, when she was trying to convince me to say no more often. I wonder if she sees that it’s working, just not in the way she thought. I love her so much, I’m learning to say no. No to football, which means no to Coach and, worse, no to Dad. No to intramurals is a no to the Flooders. I didn’t even cheer on my floor’s entry at the annual campus Cardboard Boat Race last week. I’ve been saying no to tutoring sometimes. And I can only manage all this because if they didn’t get my no, Sophie would. I don’t just like when she’s happy—I need it. I need that beautiful smile on her face, whether I can see it or not. I need her to have everything she wants. Whatever it takes.

“Austin,” Sophie whispers, as if she heard my thoughts.

A chill runs up my spine as her arms curl around me from behind.

I twist around to her and brush waves from her face, curl a hand around her waist. She’s all play, no pity. I could kiss her for that alone. Her latte eyes are sparking with adventure.

“What d’ya have in mind, Soph?”

It’s nine o’clock on a Friday night, and my eyes are giving me away with slow blinks. I rub them and try to pep up.

“I won’t keep you out too late. Come on.” She grabs my hand, impatiently breaking into a jog toward Albert Hall.

My smile grows as I follow. I’d go anywhere with this woman. Up the west stairwell, into my room, she slides open my closet door. Then she digs through my drawers until she finds a swimsuit crammed in the back of the bottom drawer.

As she hands it to me, her grin droops. "Don't worry. We're just going to the pond. It's plenty public."

I stand motionless, my swimsuit still dangling from her hand. I used to have game. I used to be chill. Not anymore.

My mind darts around, trying not to remember how good she looks in a bikini. Electromagnetics. Grandmaría and Grandpa. Baby platypuses. Nothing's helping.

"Please, Austin?" her warm voice coaxes. Hands land on my stomach, so I won't be getting out of this. "It won't be shady. Just a little adventure to get your mind off things. And then early bedtimes for both of us. I promise."

I run fingers from the back of her neck to her collarbones. Her eyes widen.

"That yellow swimsuit you wore to the creek," I murmur.

"You remember that?"

"I wanna see you in it again." My fingertips lift and trail where the straps pulled around her back, where they sat on her hips. "Tell me no, Soph."

She swallows and nods. "No bikini. Mayberry approved." A salute. "Can we still go?"

She's right—the pond's a fixture on campus. We throw guys in there when they get engaged. Several floors have traditions there. No doubt someone will be up to their antics.

"I'm in."

When she claps and bounces, I reflexively loosen, accepting my swimsuit from her hand.

"Meet me at the bench by my door? I'll go change too."

A snake or two live in that water, but they're harmless. Should I warn her?

Too late. With a smacking kiss on my cheek, she's jogging down the hallway.

We were wrong. The pond is vacant. Voices drift from the soccer field nearby, but pines block the view. Swimming lasts all of three minutes before something brushes Sophie's leg and she bolts out, laughing her head off. So now we're curled up in blankets I brought, shivering as pond water drips from our suits.

A running top and skirt. It helps.

I run a hand through my hair. It's not her fault that she's perfect. Thinking about her respectfully is on me. Touching her respectfully is on me. But oh man, it's so hard to keep my hands off her. It's so hard to keep my mind in bounds.

But she heard me. I really can trust her wholeheartedly, even with this kind of thing.

She snuggles against my chest, blankets between us, and twists to look up at me. "Talk to me."

"Hola," I say, going for deep and suave. "¿Cómo estás?"

With a giggle, she shakes her head. "You never lose at cards like that, Zorro. 'Fess up."

I could dodge this and blame Mia, the resident card shark. But Sophie knows better.

"I'm cooked, Soph. I dunno. I'm just kind of sucking right now."

Her face contorts, like I couldn't have said anything stupider. It would be cruel if we were talking about anything else.

"You don't suck at anything, mister. Except maybe taking care of yourself."

"Eh."

Hands on my jaw, she jerks my face to hers. "Don't *eh* me."

My heart rate rises at her bossy look. "Feisty."

"Why do you keep saying yes if you want to say no?"

"'Cause I don't wanna say no."

"Austin."

"I don't. I want you to have everything. With me, you'll always have everything."

Her eyes fill. "I'm the problem."

"What? No, Soph."

"I knew this would happen. You deserve your sweet tea, and I'm always dragging you away from your porch."

Sweet tea. Like what she said on the water tower? "I'm the one screwing it up. Not you. You're not responsible for me."

"I want to be. I don't know how though. You have to teach me." Concern etches into her face. "Except you don't know how either, do you?"

When I meet her eyes again, they knock the breath out of me. Full of longing, love, *admiration*. But ... it couldn't be. Not tonight.

"What?" she asks.

"You look ... happy with me."

She pushes my arm. "Duh. You're the best. My favorite person in the world."

My head spins. But ... we just addressed that I'm sucking right now, wrecking my life. I'm doing it all so wrong I don't even know which parts to fix. She brushes fingers down my jaw, all affection. I did nothing to deserve this. I pull away from her hand.

"Why wouldn't I be happy with you?" she asks softly, almost hurt.

"I'm a mess. I didn't do anything good all day."

"Austin, stop it. You said affection isn't earned."

Her words hit me like a bullet to the chest. A raw, gaping wound is left in their wake. I see my inconsistency, but I don't have the brain power to puzzle it out. I just know it hurts to think about.

She straightens, like she knows exactly the play to call. "Jesus, help him. Teach him to say no when he should. Change things around for him so he gets the rest he needs. Shake him if he—and we—should chase down that spot at UT. Like you did for me coming here." Her eyes flick to the side in thought. "Make him see how good he is, how loved. Make him see that he's more than enough. Help us do this better." She bobs her head once, pleased with her solution.

And with that, she infiltrates the only remaining fraction of my heart. I am irrevocably hers. She's a dream. Impossibly good. I love her. I pull in a breath, but it comes out shaking.

Hold up. Am I crying?

My face is all wet, and I honestly can't tell if it's pond water or tears. Her hands return to my face as she searches my eyes. Must be tears. Great. This is next-level embarrassing.

"Austin," she whispers.

A comfort. No horror, no awkwardness, no pity. Just belief. Just love.

"It's okay to be overwhelmed. We're gonna figure it out. We'll figure it out together."

I can't speak, so I just squeeze her hand and wipe my face with the blanket.

Every night before bed, I sit at my desk and pick the perfect song for her. My mind doesn't work like Sophie's, constantly nailing the perfect song on the fly. I don't remember every word to every song like she does. It takes a minute to look around, check lyrics, confirm the song gives just the right message. But tonight? I already know. The artist is one of Mama's favorites, a voice I grew up on. It's practically hardwired. I hope Sophie hears what I can't put into words.

She softens to a smile, like I'm looking better.

I know what I need—what Jesus told me when I was asking him how to rest. I squeeze fists into my blanket to gather the courage to ask.

"Hey, Soph? I know you were going to order in for us tomorrow, but ... I wonder if—I mean I think it might be nice—Maybe you could ..." I trail off.

She finds my fingers and interlaces them with hers. "It's just me. What is it?"

And again I need a song as a crutch. It's the only way I'm gonna get this out. I rack my brain for something that will make her understand. She waits me out through the silence until I finally break it, singing the chorus of "Kinfolks" by Sam Hunt. The pines. My people. The home that made me.

She doesn't hesitate—just picks up where the lyrics leave off.

"Yeah," I say. "All of that."

"I'm in."

Far from jumping and clapping, her dampened expression is a blow. It's ... resignation. Willingness. Worse—a favor.

I was right to think she wouldn't want to go. It hurts at a gut level. But I need this. I need to see my people. To breathe. To be still and pray.

This will be the best kind of favor—the kind that won't feel like one for long.

Sophie

The worst kind of favor—the kind I have to say yes to. A gutting, soul-twisting favor.

After slogging to my dark, empty room, I peel off the skirt clinging to my skin. I want to crawl out of my skin too.

His house? His family? I've been dreading this since Portside.

I grab clean pajamas, then pause—I'll need those tomorrow night. Instead, I toss them onto my desk and dig through drawers for something old and oversized. Close enough. I rinse with mouthwash like that makes up for skipping the rest, then sink into bed.

I'm trying to learn how to do this—how to be for him what he is for me. But I can't convince his perfect little family I know how to take care of their beloved son. I haven't even convinced myself.

Turn my pillow to the cool side. Flop back down.

Dread courses through my veins and congeals into panic. What if this is it? The moment he sees—I'm not that girl.

His family will ... I can't sew. I can't feed chickens. I can't make biscuits and gravy. Just thinking about it makes me crave a gas pedal.

A whisper. **I want you close.**

But I rip the blankets off. I can't actually go to bed this early. Of all the nights to let myself overthink.

His parents and sister are going to ask about my family. Austin calls them—individually—every single week. Of course they'll ask. And what will I say? That I literally haven't spoken to my parents since Christmas break? Not once. It's nearly March.

I'm not calling my dad. We barely even have a relationship. But I can call Mom. Then I can say I called her today. She's awake. She finishes work in front of *Suits* most nights, and it's two hours earlier there.

Help. I hate this.

I tap her name before I can talk myself out of it.

"Sophie? Are you in trouble?"

I mute the phone to let out a burst of frustration.

Please help me to be kind.

"Nope, just calling to see how you are."

"Oh." A pause. "I'm fine. Work is busy. I don't have long."

"I know. Any fun projects?"

Another pause. "Shouldn't you be worrying about your schoolwork? You'd better not waste all the money I'm spending sending you to that asinine private school."

I squeeze my eyes shut.

She's always been distracted, but she didn't used to be this harsh. The divorce made things so much worse.

"I have A's, mom."

Typing in the background.

Just tell her. She's my mom. Maybe she'll care. "I have a boyfriend."

"Okay."

I pick at my nails. What do I even say? "It's ... serious."

She exhales sharply. "Always so dramatic. You're nineteen, Sophie."

"I'm going to meet his family tomorrow."

National Charity League flashes to my mind. I was Viola

demolishing wings in *She's the Man*—too loud, too restless, too goofy. A complete and utter disappointment.

"What good could possibly come from that?" she asks.

I scrape at my nail. "It's important to him."

"They're just popping into Nowhere, Texas?"

"No, they live around here."

"Oh, wow." So casual, so dismissive.

With every flippant response, the vice around my chest tightens.

"I love him." This is stupid. Asking for it. She couldn't possibly understand. But I'm desperate. I need her to see. I need her to care.

"There is nothing but grief on the other side of this. You'll see."

I know. I already know.

I don't speak for fear she'll hear the tears clogging my throat. She doesn't do crying.

"Are you finished with the Jesus-freak phase yet?"

With a hard blink, I try to compose myself. "No, Mom. It's not a phase."

"Right. I need to get some things done before bed."

Without a goodbye, I hang up and pull my blanket over my shoulders. I should've known better. I did know better.

Before I plug my phone in for the night, a text comes through. My song.

AUSTIN

Song of the day

"My One Safe Place" by Andrew Peterson

I press Play, bury my face in my pillow, and sob.

CHAPTER FORTY-FOUR

Austin

"Are they expecting someone … like me?" Sophie asks.

"They don't have a checklist, Soph. They're just excited to meet the girl I won't shut up about."

She gives a sigh that's more like a whimper. "So what's going to happen?"

"I dunno. We'll show you around, sit on the couch and chat probably. Dinner eventually, play a game, take a walk in there somewhere."

She turns with wide eyes. "Your parents are going to sit there and stare at me?"

I frown. "Uh, yeah. Some of the time. They don't ignore their company."

"So I'm basically getting interviewed?"

"No? We're just gonna hang out. What were you expecting?"

"I've literally only seen a meet-the-parents thing on TV."

Spiraling? Why?

"They're not gonna give you a hard time. Don't worry. It'll be better than you think."

I try not to be disappointed that she doesn't want to meet my people. I try to remember that her mom is a piece of work, that her home was strained, not somewhere she'd want to bring me. I try.

Sophie slows the Jeep at the mailbox I point out. The gate's open for us. I motion for her to drive down the gravel road. My shoulders relax involuntarily—even as Sophie tenses up beside me. Eighty beautiful acres. The pond to our right, our cows at the electric fence, trees towering.

The clock on the dash reads 1:52. Time for their treat. Mama's probably waiting to let Sophie try it out.

A couple dead trees. Might could help Dad pull them down while I'm here. My old pickup—now Janie's ride—is parked in its spot. Can't wait to introduce my two favorite girls.

I work up the courage to glance at Sophie again.

Horrified eyes dart around. "Is that a giant ... garden?" Like she's never seen such a thing.

"Yep. There might be some carrots or something ready to eat. Mama'll know."

I realize I've been waiting for Faith to come running. My old collie died over a year ago. Somehow I still expect her every time I drive up.

"Oh, here's Janie." A few notes of "Ode to Joy" play inside the house at the gate's motion sensor.

Sophie parks the car. Her breath is fast and shallow, like she might have a panic attack.

"You okay?" I brush back her hair, scratch her back.

She nods too quickly, says nothing. Another bad sign. What could possibly have her this rattled? Carrots? She was perfectly normal yesterday—bouncing, encouraging, adventurous.

I wanted to have some time to talk to you, to rest.

Is that not going to happen? I'm so tired.

"Hey, let's take a minute." I angle toward her. "Can you tell me what's wrong?"

But she slinks from the car, avoiding my hands and eyes.

I grab my backpack and Sophie's whole suitcase from the rear cargo.

My sister is hovering on the driveway, trying not to be a creep.

"Janie, get over here," I call.

"Austin!" She takes off in a run and tackles me in a hug—the biggest one after Sophie's—and I introduce her to the reigning hug champion.

"Soph, my sister, Janie. Janie, this is Sophie, in the flesh."

"Hi," Sophie mumbles, raising a hand in a weak wave, like it will suffice as a greeting. No smile. No bounce. No thousand-word monologue. Nothing Sophie adjacent.

Janie had already stepped forward for a hug but stops abruptly, picking up on Sophie's body language.

Seriously? This is my baby sister.

I frown at Sophie to communicate.

She rolls her eyes.

On her worst day she doesn't roll her eyes at me. I guess this'll be a short trip.

I glance at Janie. "We'll meet you inside, 'kay?"

Picking up on my cue—at least someone does—Janie heads inside. She looks taller. How is she taller in a month and a half?

I drop our things on the gravel and step toward Sophie. Her arms are crossed tight, her expression locked down and guarded.

"Hugs are a thing here." No time. Gotta cut to the chase. "I know you don't love hugging strangers, but maybe just meet her halfway. A pat-pat-not-hug works. And you can shake my dad's hand if that's better. Even a smile. But a wave?"

"Come on," she says. "So sensitive."

My jaw tightens. "Spill, Sophie. What's going on?"

No reply.

"Sophie."

Nothing.

How is this happening today? We just had an intense heart-to-heart at the pond last night. None of this was there then.

"Listen. I love my family more than my own life, and I will not subject them to a temper tantrum." I'm really overdoing it here, but I'm exhausted and protective and it's just coming out. "Why don't you head back to school? I'll catch a ride to campus tomorrow." I slide her suitcase back in but leave the door open.

She gapes.

Should've come alone.

Did I foul this up?

"Eventually my family will accept you as one of their own and love you, whatever's going on in your head. But it's a lot to ask for you to be like this when you meet them for the first time. I've told them how I feel about you. They're expecting a lot."

"Be like this?" She spits. "Expecting a lot?"

I wince. I was way too harsh. I'm tanking this.

"Maybe a different weekend would be better." I needed a nap on the couch. A home-cooked meal. I'd be happy to help Sophie acclimate, but I don't have the energy for this craziness. I've spent it all on her the last month and a half. I wanted to. I'll do it again. But it really seems like she should be able to manage a few kind greetings in return.

"A different weekend?"

"I'm going inside. Come in or don't."

I plod to the house, gravel crunching comfortingly under my boots. Onto the cement driveway. Through the garage, toward the kitchen door.

"Austin?" Sophie's voice catches. "Just a minute?"

I bury a sigh.

I'm wiped, but I don't want to take it out on her. I don't have the patience for this, but I want to. She did for me last night. I'm sorry. Make me like you, Jesus. Help me take care of her.

I stop beside the closed door, eyes shut tight, waiting to see if God will bestow instant patience upon me.

Guess not. I'm still a class-A grump.

"Yep."

She sets her suitcase down primly. Lifts her chin. "Any other rules I should know before we go in? Hugs are compulsory. No cursing? What do I call your parents?"

I squint. "You never swear."

I don't feel like it, but I walk the four steps to her and wrap her in a hug. She clings to me, squeezing hard, and my shoulders drop. Her hair smells like mint today, and it grounds me, reminds me what matters. I love Sophie. Even when she's flipping out for no known reason. Even when I'm exhausted and useless. Always.

My head rests against hers. "Wanna talk about it now or later?"

"Later."

"'Kay. Mr. and Mrs. Scott. Mama'll pretend you should call her Tracy, but you'll do better not to. Ready?"

She nods unconvincingly and grips my offered hand with Red Rover intensity.

When I open the door, that feeling crashes over me.

Home.

CHAPTER FORTY-FIVE

Sophie

I must be a sociopath.

I panicked. Alienated Austin's beloved sister. Picked a fight with him.

Two feet into this place, and I lost it. I was already lightheaded, but then his perfect sister came frolicking out, too excited to see him to wait three minutes for us to get inside. Something snapped.

And now I have to go inside and pretend I know how to be … what? "Part of That World" pops in my head, but I couldn't sing if I wanted to.

Devoted family aside, this place is nothing like I pictured. No wheat. No bonnets to speak of. But cows. A two-story house. Red brick, ivy crawling up the walls, a chimney that belongs in a book of nursery rhymes. And the yard—can you even call it a yard? There's so much land around the house that this place couldn't exist in Pasadena. Not even A-listers have this kind of lot. It's the kind of place a painter would escape to for a year, trying to capture its aura. Like van Gogh did in France.

And the cows. Mooing.

I don't belong here. It's as foreign to me as, I don't know, Bangladesh.

Pine and cedar trees as far as the eye can see, as if they're weeds instead of thirty-foot trees. Enough tropical plants bordering the house to impress this SoCal native. And *Austin* everywhere. A firepit. A fishing pond. We passed his favorite creek and rope swing on the way here. Mabel's Dance Hall is just down the road. So many things I've grown to love, but suddenly they don't feel like my memories to claim. They're his. They're theirs. I'm an intruder, an impostor.

It won't all fit—I can't seem to cram it into my brain at once. It's all so Austin, so beautiful, and yet I desperately need to get out of here.

The world goes fuzzy.

Austin steps inside, dragging me behind him.

Please help me. I don't want to screw it up. I don't know why I'm falling apart right now.

The smell hits me. Not just cornbread. Imagine if cornbread were baked with twenty years of laughter and board games and inside jokes, mixed with dad washing the dishes while Mom helps with homework. Must taste different too.

Bangladesh. Like a figment of my imagination. Too good to be true.

Mom pops to mind. What would she think? She'd smooth her skirt and slide back in the car to protect her Celine boots. She'd distrust it—too wild, too unpredictable. Like me, yet ...

"Sweetheart! Please come in! I'm Tracy!" Austin's mom leans in for a hug when I'm barely two steps inside, and I pull myself together enough to hug her back, trying to maintain a tiny bit of personal space. I'm so much taller than her that I crunch against her hairspray. And I have to pat-pat the back of her floral dress to keep my side of this century-long hug from seeming like a rejection. These people are so affectionate to strangers. Only Austin gets hugs this long from me. Period.

She finally pulls back, and I stifle a relieved sigh.

"Aren't you just as purty as a pitcher!"

I try to thank her, but she's already saying, "Clint! Sophie's here!"

"I see that, my dear."

No time to brace before I'm hugged again. No luck on the handshake plan. He gives me plenty of space, but his Austin-sized hand pats my shoulder like he has time—like I'm worth pausing for. Unwelcome tears threaten. I step back and see he's even taller and darker than Austin. Blue-collar strong—I thought he was an engineer?—and still trim. His eyes are kind, like Austin's. His smile easy, like he's never needed to prove anything to anyone. My dad would eat this guy alive. In a courtroom and otherwise.

Janie stands near the edge of the room, assessing. Gorgeous without a touch of makeup. Wet, curly brown hair stuffed into a clip. If you uploaded a picture of Kit and Austin to one of those weird photo generators online, Janie would be the result.

With a fortifying breath, I open my arms to Janie and shrug. I don't need to incite World War III with the Cleaver family over a rejected greeting. She brightens and gives me a no-nonsense hug—quick but sincere. The smell of coconut and effortless perfection drifts off her.

I can picture it—Austin, someday, with a little girl on his shoulders who's the spitting image of Bella's daughter in *Twilight*. The child, not the creepy baby. Obviously.

Austin makes it through his round of intense greetings. He was just here a few weeks ago, but they both get a hug as big as I ever do. "Mama. Pops." An additional arm squeeze for Janie. "Munchkin." He ambles to the stove, cuts cornbread from the pan, tilts his head back to catch the square in his mouth. Crumbs everywhere.

So happy here.

Mrs. Scott marches over and swats his hand. *Smack.*

I jump.

"Out of my kitchen. You know better." The sheer happiness in her eyes ... My parents never swatted my hand or spanked me a single time. Around here you get a swat when your parents are thrilled with you?

I glance past Janie to the living room. We're in the sticks, and I realize I'd expected an old trailer, or at least some peeling wallpaper or grease stains. Not here. It's tasteful. Homey. This house isn't just lived in, it's loved. A pretty staircase. A loft. Somewhere upstairs, a chime gongs, marking the hour.

"Austin," Mrs. Scott says.

I jerk again. No idea why. But I drop my half-twirled hair and awkwardly clasp my hands together.

"Give Sophie a tour, would you? And then you can feed the cows their treat."

"Yes, ma'am."

Feed the cows? Feed them? I neutralize my face. "Sure! Sounds good!"

Austin flinches. He knows me too well.

When I meet Mrs. Scott's cheery, expectant gaze, it dims somewhat. She doesn't like something she sees.

He grabs our bags and tilts his head toward the stairs, kicking off his shoes before stepping on the carpet. I follow suit. These stairs feel off. Shorter, maybe. Like I should be taking them two at a time.

At the top, he points at a large room painted a grayish blue—like his eyes.

"That was my room," he says, turning left.

"Wait, can I see it?"

"'Kay."

I take in every inch. Cabinets line the right wall beneath enormous windows overlooking the field. Pond. Cows. The cabinet tops form a window seat—perfect for curling up with pillows. A partial wall backs the bed, hiding a tucked-away desk and bookshelf. A random sink and mirror in the corner.

"It's not really what it looked like. I took everything off the walls when I moved out. Boxed up my stuff." He shrugs, almost shy. "I thought my parents would want it as a guest room."

He would.

I find his arm. A touch isn't enough, so I wrap mine around his like it's a life preserver.

He kisses my head.

Through the window, geese float beside a white gazebo. Like a postcard.

"Did you ever sit here?"

"Yeah, this became my morning spot. I'd prop a pillow here and read my Bible and pray. The sun rises over the pond." He points casually, like it's a minor detail and not a devastatingly beautiful addition to his incomparable childhood. Like the earth isn't shifting under my feet.

Of course he'd want to drink sweet tea on the porch. Why would he want to escape from this level of perfection? People escape *to* this kind of place.

"Ready to move on?"

"Not yet."

"Wanna talk?"

"Not yet."

I don't know what I'd say. I still don't know what's wrong with me. *Try to name what you're feeling*, Dr. Shannon would say. *Start wherever you can.*

He watches me, kind but slow blinking, like he's fighting to stay vertical.

"You did mention you have cows."

"Yep." As if that's the most normal thing in the world.

"Do they have names? Do you eat them?"

He chuckles softly. "They have names, yeah. We don't eat them. My parents keep them for the agricultural tax exemption. Sometimes we do have to sell one to market though. That's the worst. Our cows are more like pets."

"Pets." My dad would never. Efficiency alone.

"And they're hungry, so we'd better wrap up the tour."

"They're hungry."

"Soph," he says. "You're repeating words like you're shell shocked. You're safe here. This isn't a war zone." He brushes my arm, and I almost believe him.

Move my feet.

Cows.

The upstairs is open to the living room below, and the loft upstairs holds an older sectional couch and a TV. We stop between two bedrooms—Janie's and the office, Austin tells me. His parents' room is downstairs.

It's just a house.

Not a mansion. Not a Mediterranean villa. I have plenty of friends with nicer houses, nicer things. But here... it feels different. Like affection has been painted onto the walls, like the carpet fibers harbor peace and harmony. I'm indescribably ... sad. And freaked out.

Names for my feelings.

Thank you for that.

We walk downstairs, and I pull my sneakers back on. Austin calls out that we're going to get the bread, and I follow dumbly as he leads us through the garage. He slides into a pair of filthy work boots and offers his tiny mom's. I decline them. We step outside along a brick path neatly pressed into the ground. My clean sneakers shuffle along after him.

"Your cows don't eat, like, hay?"

"They eat plenty of hay and grass, yeah. But Mama also gives them an afternoon treat. Feed bread and old snack cakes and things she gets from H-E-B. These are not grass-fed cows." His deep chuckle—my heart warms a degree on impact. "It's all expired. Since the store can't sell them to people anymore, they're dirt cheap. But the cows are pleased." He pushes up his sleeves, and it grounds me even more. It's just normal Austin. Talking about his cows.

"The cows are pleased." Oops, I'm repeating again. "Do you milk them?"

"Nope."

We reach a barn on the other side of the house, away from the paved road. He raises a hand at the door. "Hold up." After disappearing inside, he waves me in. "Come on in. Snakes get in here sometimes."

I shudder and watch where I step.

Brightening, he says, "Check this out." His voice is suddenly light, like a little kid. "Honey Buns for days."

"What's a Honey Bun?"

"What's a Honey Bun?" If he weren't laughing, I'd think I offended him. "Only the greatest processed pastry in the world." He rifles through a grocery bag. "Ooh, this one's only a month expired. Try it?"

Oh, he's serious.

"It's expired."

"Eh, it's fine." He rips open the plastic as we walk toward the back of the house. His arm juts out in front of me, a half-open Honey Bun in his hand. "Electric fence."

He angles the yellow handle expertly, lifting the wire for me to pass under before stepping through himself.

Bangladesh.

And now we're in a cow pen? There are the cows. The actual cows. Enormous actual cows.

Austin hands me the Honey Bun, and I take a tentative bite. A stale donut. I get the idea.

I hate how lame I am right now.

"Hold it out in an open palm and they'll come pig out."

I position the stale Honey Bun on my hand, stiff and still, as cows approach.

Austin admirably holds back a laugh at my grimace. "Don't worry, Soph. These girls are sweethearts. That's Roxanne there, and this is Eileen. Named after songs."

A smile starts in my cheeks. "Aw."

Roxanne sticks her giant tongue out and swipes the Honey Bun out of my palm. I squeal. Austin chuckles and brushes the back of my head.

I gape as Eileen nuzzles into his side.

"Hey, girl." That voice. So soft. He scratches under her chin. "Missed you."

She's precious. Gentle. Trusting.

We're supposed to feed them the whole bag and half the loaf, and I actually get the hang of it. Warmth and goodness radiate off these cows, like they're a microcosm of this place. Named, loved, wanted—is it weird to say they're the animal version of Austin? He wasn't just raised in peace. He ushers it in. I thought I knew him, but he's ... more.

Eileen inhales another pastry, and my heart warms another degree.

"This is a weird kind of therapy," I say.

"Hundred percent."

Somehow I find myself singing to them—quiet and tender, their namesake songs. And Austin relaxes fully for the first time in days.

CHAPTER FORTY-SIX

Sophie

After Eileen and Roxanne are finished with their snack, Austin stashes the leftover bread in the barn and walks me back along the brick path. The Red Brick Road.

"I assume you still want your run?" he asks, already pulling out his phone to send me a pin—a huge park nearby. Taking care of me, even when I'm a mess.

When I return, he's passed out on the sectional upstairs, curled around the corner. Poor guy. Stretched so thin he's practically transparent.

A sinister voice flickers. *"Because of you."*

It's true. He was never like this before we were together.

A rush of grief and affection tightens my throat. Last night at the pond was awful—like watching my own hands crush spun glass. The blood, the pieces splintering apart under pressure I never meant to put there. The horror that I could break someone so good. And yet, somehow, I still had hope. It's my fault—I know it is—but I had started to think we could figure this thing out together. Because it's too good not to. It's just too good to be temporary.

Now? I don't know.

Leaning on the doorway, I watch him sleep. His overwhelm last night makes perfect sense. He's like these beloved cows, known and kept and nurtured. But I'm a barn snake, trying to sneak into their utopia, trying to consume the goodness they've created here.

For the first time since I met Austin, I want to belong here. I want to snuggle next to him at that fire pit outside. I want to joke with his old friends at Mabel's. I want to fish with him in his pond. I want to be the kind of person who can help him make all of this again, for another generation.

But I don't belong here. I can't stay, and we all know. His family will set him straight.

I cling to the doorframe to stay upright. I miss my rose-colored glasses. I miss my ignorance. I wish I didn't know how much I want to be this for him. But I'm not apple pie and rural charm. I'm not rest and peace. I'm the opposite. I had to be. To survive my opposite life.

When Austin groans in his sleep, I instinctively step forward, aching to curl up beside him. But I stop myself. I shouldn't. And I'm sure that's not allowed here.

I hate that I'm disappointing him. I wish I could have just bounded in all sunshine and laughter, like he must have expected. So he could be glad he brought me home. Proud of me. My throat tightens. I find a blanket and drape it over him. Slowly, carefully. Then I settle on the floor and pray—for God to give him what he needs. Who he needs. The best possible gifts. That he'd stop at nothing to give Austin his best.

By the time I push up from the floor, I'm trembling.

I shower. Try to look nice. Try not to embarrass him. Try to paste on a smile, be good company. But there's no hope of that. Not for lack of caring—I just have no idea how to behave here. I did some improv in high school, and I tell myself I'm on set with a pretend family. The prompt? Don't offend them. Don't say the wrong thing. Don't let their cheery smiles turn to polite, horrified frowns.

We eat chili and cornbread at the dining room table. Austin's mom keeps insisting I lather more butter on my cornbread, more cheese on my chili. Austin watches with an amused mini-smile. I eat just to keep my hands busy. Spoons clank against bowls as everyone scrapes the last bit out before getting seconds. Austin chats with his family about everyday things because they already know everything about his life—there's nothing to fill them in about. They know about me, about the things we do. They know Levi and Haymitch.

This whole family looks like they stepped off a magazine cover, all matching with dark hair and blue eyes. The subtitle would scream *How to Win the Genetic Lottery!* They tease. They praise. They're at ease. Bangladesh.

First order of business: avoid making a face that screams *help*. Secondary goal: act more human, less startled owl.

"Sophie, sweetheart, how are you liking college?"

Channel Ignorant Sophie. I can do this. "College. Um. I love it."

"What's your major?" Janie asks.

"Oh, I don't know yet."

"She's good at everything, so it's hard to pick. Right, Soph?" I could swear his accent is growing stronger with every minute.

"Aw, bless your heart," Mrs. Scott says.

Austin frowns.

"Austin says you're from California," Mr. Scott says, transitioning. "Whereabouts?"

"Pasadena."

Janie leans forward. "Where the Rose Parade is, right?"

I could tell them how the floats take months to build. How

they line up on New Year's Eve, just down the street from my place. I could tell them I helped build a few. Rode on one.

But I don't. I don't have the words today. Or the energy. All I have is ... loss.

I nod.

"What's your family like?" Mrs. Scott asks.

The very last thing I want to talk about.

"Nothing special," I hedge. "I'm an only child."

"Sophie's a beautiful singer," Austin interjects, seeing I can't hold my own at this table.

"Is that so?" she asks politely, and she blows on a spoonful.

I'm not impressing her. At all. Austin overpromised and underdelivered.

"This chili is incredible," I try.

"Oh, thank you." But she settles in her chair, like she's finished with the attempt at chatting.

I scramble for something as Mr. Scott watches. "I love your cows' names."

Her polite expression loosens into a chuckle. "Thanks, honey."

Something else. Something. "What kind of music do you like, Mrs. Scott?"

"The cow names are oldies, but mostly for lack of something better. I'm open to new cow names should I need another. Bless their hearts, they can't live forever. Anyhow, I've got some favorites across the genres. I was raised on country, of course. I like pop in moderation. I had a punk rock phase when I was young. Ever heard of Relient K?"

"'Be My Escape' is them, right?"

"Yes! I loved them. Used to drive to Dallas for concerts whenever I could. Switchfoot too. And I mostly listen to contemporary Christian now."

Keeping up this pleasant expression drains everything I've got. I'd pay them each a thousand bucks if I could escape this dinner—

this whole night—without judgment. Without consequences. Just disappear.

Austin chats with his dad about sports news as Janie smiles at me.

"She's not like other moms," she says. "She's a cool mom."

"So fetch," I say, but my voice doesn't sound like mine. Too quiet. Timid. Lifeless.

Her eyes light up all the same. "Mama says 'contemporary Christian', but her music is mostly ancient. It's actually pretty good though. Do you know Rich Mullins?"

I shake my head.

"Steven Curtis Chapman?"

"I love 'The Great Adventure.' It was on that camp movie on Netflix, right?"

"Yeah, that movie was decent," Janie says. "SCC is a fixture around here. He has decades of good music."

"I didn't know. I'm pretty new to Christian music." Shouldn't have spilled that.

Janie bends forward. "That settles it. We're gonna make you a playlist—the best from Mama's dinosaur days and the current essentials."

She taps Austin's phone in his pocket, and he pulls it out for her.

"You're only allowed to skip one out of every ten songs," she says. "Choose wisely."

Her fingers type away, then she hands it back and taps on her own phone.

Ding.

This is Janie Scott.

"This playlist's a living, morphing thing, so don't judge it till the next update." She meets my eyes and grins.

Everything in me wants to distance myself from these weird,

beautiful Stepford people, but Janie's so ... real. Opinionated. Fun. Normal Sophie would love her.

"Your contributions are nonnegotiable, 'kay? Don't leave me hangin'."

I agree to her terms. "Know Forrest Frank?"

"Duh. But add your faves."

"Hulvey?"

"Genre?"

"Rap."

Mrs. Scott cringes.

"Doesn't ring a bell. Teach me your ways."

"Tauren Wells?" I ask.

"Absolutely. Especially that one he sings with the guy from Rascal Flatts. What's it called?"

"'Until Grace.'" I almost smile, but my face can't accept any more instructions right now.

Austin bends forward, meets my eyes in concern. I flit away.

"Rascal Flatts stands the test of time," Janie says. As if she has the same thought I do, she straightens and recites, "'Your standing films will time and test themselves.'"

Some part of me almost claps, like life wants to bloom inside me again. But it doesn't. "*Win a Date with Tad Hamilton*," I manage. "Such a classic."

She nods in approval. I drink it in.

"Is that the one where Topher Grace fails at farm chores?" Austin asks.

"You're just mad because she picks the scrawny guy," Janie challenges.

He elbows her. "I only care who Sophie picks." His gaze slides to me and turns flirty. "Don't pick the scrawny guy, 'kay?"

A full smile crawls across my face for the first time all day.

"I'd pick the scrawny guy if he noticed my six smiles," Janie says. "That speech should be in the Smithsonian."

Austin's jaw ticks. When Janie does find her smile guy, her giant brother's going to lose his mind.

Over banana pudding—yes, seriously—I learn that Mrs. Scott doesn't have a job so that she can do things around "the property" all day. Must be a lot to do. Mr. Scott works from home and sometimes drives into Dallas. He doesn't talk much but seems content to listen.

"Before I forget, please be ready to leave by eight-thirty tomorrow," Mrs. Scott says. "I need to help with some tables before service."

"We're not going to church tomorrow, Mama."

"Of course you are."

"I'll come to church next visit." I feel the exertion of his pushback from here. He hates this. "I'm not gonna make Sophie do the meet-and-greet thing this weekend."

I almost gasp. He's saying no to his mother for me? I meet his gaze and send a thousand wordless thank-yous.

"You can sleep in till eight," Mrs. Scott says. It's final.

"He's an adult, Tracy," Mr. Scott says. "And he's more than earned our trust." Locking eyes with Austin, honor passes between them. Love.

Something cracks in my chest. I drop my quivering spoon into the bowl and squeeze my hands in my lap. I try to imagine my dad and me in their seats, and whatever cracked shatters completely.

CHAPTER FORTY-SEVEN

Sophie

"Up for a walk?" Austin hands me the last two spoons to drop into the dishwasher.

I nod so hard my neck tweaks.

He steps toward the living room like he might call out to his family, but his eyes flick to me, and he thinks better of it. Without a word, he heads for the garage, shrugs off his button-up, and hooks it by the coats. His fingers wrap around mine as he searches my face for something I don't know how to give.

Down the driveway, through the grass, past tractors and ant piles the size of volcanoes. Finally, we reach a trail cut through the dense brush and trees.

Letting out a breath, my iron grip on his hand loosens.

Austin navigates the trail with ease—yet another new side of him—until we arrive at an open iron gate. If he told me it had been there two hundred years, I'd believe it.

"This is the back forty," he says.

I marvel. Back forty—just like that Jordan Davis song we argued about at B-Dubs. At the very beginning.

His sly smile. "No need to phone a friend next time."

The thick tangle of trees and wild bushes taper off into a huge field. I point at a coyote running on the far side.

A nod of his head and a tilt toward an open treehouse, wrapping up two enormous trees. Can that be real?

His eyes shine. "C'mon." Such an accent it could've been Haymitch. And then he takes off running, a little boy in grown-up skin.

My heart squeezes, and I take off after him. But he jolts to a stop at the bottom of the treehouse steps, hand reaching to grab mine. A staircase to the first level. A ladder to the second. At the top, he steps behind me, one arm around me, the other pointing up. "Stars are startin' to come out."

I follow his finger. A few faint specks overhead. Barely visible in the darkening blue sky. Is this what taught him to love the stars?

A tear trails down my cheek.

No. What? I paw it away.

Help me, Jesus. I don't know what's happening to me.

I twist from the sky. To him—this guy who's deeper, more complex, more beautiful than I even realized. I can't see the stars, but I can see him. The weight of it buckles me, and my forehead sinks into his chest. I don't have the words to ask him all the things I want to know.

"Austin?" I blink up at him. I've officially gone full owl—perched in a treehouse, no less.

"Hey," he says softly, drying my cheek with his thumb. "Trying to make me feel better after yesterday?"

I chuckle through my thick throat. Lifting his hand, I kiss the back, his palm, his fingers.

He brushes hair from my face.

"I can't believe you grew up here." A sob threatens in my throat, but I press it down. "It's so ... it's so ... good."

He squints and nods. He squeezes me into a hug, and I beat the sob down with every ounce of strength I have left.

Austin

What a fiasco.

If the palpable awkwardness and personality transplant came from anyone else, I'd be twitching hard. But it's Sophie, so today has been excruciating. Nothing I do helps.

Please, just give me a clue.

It's just home. It's peace and rest and family and amazing food. Not for her, clearly. She helped me through my meltdown yesterday, and I thanked her by dragging her to some unknown torture.

Is this on me? Should I have known better?

I have no idea what I'm doing.

"Wanna head back?" I ask into her hair.

She shakes her head violently.

"Okay, we'll stay."

Desperate to cheer her up, I seat her next to me and point past the fence of our property. "Grandmaría and Grandpa—the OG Austin Scott—live ten minutes that way. And Caleb's family lives twenty minutes back there. Mama wanted to invite them all tonight, but I talked her out of it. Thought it'd be overwhelming." And good thing. They wouldn't have met the real Sophie, just this sad, detached shell of her.

Her eyes widen in horror. I'd ask why, but she hasn't answered a single question today. She's horrified by all things non-horrific.

No sign of improvement, but I charge ahead. "They're all fussy at me. But they can wait till next time to meet you."

Her eyes widen more. "They know about me?"

"Of course they know about you." My brows press together. "I told them about you months ago. I love you." What planet is she from? Has she not told her family about us? My family knew how I felt about her before she did. I squeeze her knee, and she leans forward for a kiss. I don't know if it's a good idea to kiss her when she's so wonky, but I shouldn't withhold affection either. When she presses her lips to mine, all thoughts evaporate. She scoots closer for another. So cute. I wrap a hand behind her head, through that beautiful hair, and melt into her. And—

Salt water.

Tears are streaming down her cheeks. What?

I pull back, try to read her face. I've never seen Sophie like this. Not even on her rare sad days. Not by a long shot.

"Austin, I'm sorry," she whispers.

"What? No."

"I want to do this right. I don't know how. I'm so sorry." She tugs on my shirt, sucks in a shaky breath. "I was supposed to make them like me. I was supposed to show them I can take care of you." Her trickling tears turn to sobs. "I don't know how to do any of this."

My favorite person in the world is boo-hoo crying on my tree-house, and I might fall apart again.

Help me help her.

I grip her jaw and get right in her face. "Soph. I just want you. More than anything. I just want you here with me."

"Not like this. I swear I was trying."

"I know. I know you are."

"What can I do? What do you want me to do?"

"I just wanna fix it for you," I say. "I wanna make you happy."

"No. Your family. What should I do?"

"Talk to them. Like you did. You tried, and that's enough."

Sharp head shake. "Austin. Stop."

I scramble for something. "I dunno. Dad likes dominoes. And watch Mom's show later? They'd like that. Is that what you mean?"

She bobs a nod.

I wipe her face dry and kiss her forehead. "I love you, Soph. We're gonna do this together, right? Like you said?"

She swallows thickly. "Okay."

Music. Something to bring her back. I stand and tug her hand. "Up you go."

When "Y'all Life" bursts from my phone speaker, she actually cracks a smile. I humble myself and serve up my most ridiculous dance moves.

There it is. A full, bright Sophie laugh. It pulls me in like gravity. A grin spreads across my face. She's back.

She sways to the music, more seductively than she means to. Without warning, she grabs my shirt and yanks me close, crashing her lips against mine with such force that I see sparks. My heartbeat stumbles, then takes off at a full gallop. Kisses on my cheek, my jaw, my ear.

"Thank you," she says.

When she pulls back to meet my gaze, her steaming latte eyes warm my cold insides. I need my lips on hers, and not just once or twice. I'm about to push her up against this tree and kiss her like I've always wanted to. Like she's asking me to.

Just in time, my feet edge back and save me from myself. I tug at my hair. I'm sick of being good all the time. I wish I could just do what I want for one day, one hour.

She runs a thumb across my lip, and I squeeze my eyes shut.

"I didn't bring a flashlight," I mumble. "We could use our phones and risk a dicey walk back, or we can go with this last light."

She deflates. "Right. We can head back."

And just like that, she's gone again.

Sophie

We walk back through a symphony of crickets, snapping twigs, and the whir of wind through bare branches. Austin has a hiking trail in his backyard. Like everything else here, beautiful and bizarre.

A round of chicken foot and an episode of *The Great British Baking Show* are my earnest attempt before the group collectively heads to bed.

"Thank you for being here today!" Janie calls.

In a freak moment of Normal Sophie, I give a royal wave like Julie Andrews in *Princess Diaries*.

Austin and I help his mom make up the pullout in the loft, and then he informs me I'll be sleeping in his bed. I try to argue—because that feels like the responsible thing to do—but I'm deeply relieved when he shuts it down. His room feels safer, as if his essence is captured inside.

I'm a good little Cleaver and collapse at ten. But when I hear Austin's hushed voice downstairs, I throw off the covers and silently crack the door open.

"Son, I'm concerned about you getting serious when you could be transferring in a matter of weeks."

"I'm not going. I'm sorry, Dad."

I flinch.

Mr. Scott clears his throat, like he's hesitating. "You weren't sure. You were gonna submit the game tape and see what happens, see how God leads."

"I told Coach. Called it off. I know, I'm sorry. Look, I just know I can't have Sophie *and* football."

Softer now. "She asked you to stay?"

"No, she offered to come."

"I see."

Silence.

"Is this what God wants?"

"I don't know, Dad." He sounds about to collapse. "How does anyone know? But I won't be able to live with myself if I give her up."

"You're sure you're ready to throw away your lifelong dream? Your one-in-a-million talent?"

The implication screams loudest. For *her*?

CHAPTER FORTY-EIGHT

Sophie

The first sound I hear is birds singing outside my window. I cringe. It doesn't fit.

I lie still, blinking at the ceiling, my limbs too heavy to lift. I should get up. I should want to get up. But I don't. A pit has dug deeper into my stomach. Leaving this bed feels impossible, like pushing out of wet cement.

Eventually I force myself upright. The blankets are wadded at my feet. Maybe I fought something in my sleep. I drag myself to the door. The house is silent, the pullout already folded away. Maybe I should be relieved, but all I feel is tired.

I paw for my phone and see my song link still came last night. His gesture means even more since I earned a red Sharpie F for my girlfriend performance yesterday.

AUSTIN

Song of the day

"Start Nowhere" by Sam Hunt

The track starts as I curl around my pillow on the bare bed. A yellow tractor maneuvers around trees on the other side of the pond. More Bangladesh.

I send Austin a text.

What happens now?

Be there in five

Teeth brushed, I skip the rest. Crazy hair, bare face—it doesn't matter. And yet ... it does. Because somehow I can fall back into bed as I am. He loves me like this. However I look, even as I fail him. I squeeze the pillow—his pillow—like it will keep me afloat.

This bear den is a refuge, even without any of his stuff on the walls. Out there, Bangladesh is terrifying. I don't know how I'll manage when his family returns from church. I need my grizzly in here with me.

Downstairs, the door clicks open and shut. The clunk of boots against the floor. Four steps up the stairs. And there he is, pulling off his hat, running a hand through those wild brown curls, scenting the room with Austin and a twist of cedar and hard work. The motion shows off the underside of his arms, the vulnerable part of the bear I like so much. His neck and forehead shine with sweat. The graphic on the front of his thinned white T-shirt is faded beyond recognition and smeared with dirt. Holes line the seams. Jeans as old as that shirt wrap around his strong legs. Farmer Austin. Absolutely the most irresistible I've ever seen him. I lift to my elbows. My lips part, but no words.

He stops at my side of the bed, a questioning smile curling his lips. His eyes skitter down my shorts pajama set like I'm a work of art. A scary work of art. "I was working on a dead tree."

"Oh." No idea what that means, but I want to watch him do it. I yank the front of his grungy shirt so he's leaning over me.

His eyes flash with fear. "We can't. I can't."

It only fuels my need to kiss him.

"Just for a minute," I beg.

My greedy lips take in his. His jaw, his neck. His skin is a balm, a buoy, the sweetest comfort. His hands brace on either side of my shoulders, but his foot stays planted on the floor. He moans. Something in the back of my mind screams to pull back the reins, to slow down. I weave fingers into his hair.

Sophie, this isn't freedom.

"I love you, Austin," I whisper between kisses.

His lips crush into mine uninhibited, like I always want and never get. Intoxicating, transcendent, a tornado of pleasure and want—

He bolts out of the room. Not a word. Gone.

I lurch up and watch the door, knee bouncing.

Sophie.

No. I need this.

Two minutes later his footsteps return, slow this time. He stands in the doorway. Eyes down, jaw tight, hands in his pockets. "My parents won't be home for another hour at least. C'mon, we'll get some breakfast."

His lips are a dark red, and his chest rises and falls too fast. I did that. His gaze flits to his hat on the floor, but he doesn't move.

"You're so far away." I reach toward him. "Come back?"

"Sophie." So stern. So serious. "I can't kiss you on my bed with zero accountability."

No. I love him. I'm scared. I need him close. I crawl closer to his warmth and safety. He doesn't budge, so I slide off the bed and plant myself against him. My body and heart are in crooked alignment, conspiring against my mind. I need this. My hands slide up his chest. I know better, oh I know better, but my mouth goes to his ear and the words tumble out, just a whisper. "Austin, please."

"I can't," he chokes out. But he trails a kiss down my neck.

His feet hit the floor, and he stares at his hands for what feels like an hour. When I graze his arm, he flinches. He hides his eyes and escapes. The bathroom door closes. Opens. Four steps down the stairs like as many claps of thunder.

What have I done? My bracelet crawls down my wrist.

I try pulling my knees in, as if I could shield against my guilt, but I can't stay in this bed another minute.

Clothes. Suitcase. Thank-you note on a scrap of paper. I think I saw that on a movie once. I center it on the island as if a perfect ninety-degree angle will make up for what I've taken.

The gravel road crunches beneath my tires. Hands shaking on the wheel. Even my Jeep is hollow without him. It knows.

There he is.

Pushing over a dead tree with work-gloved hands. That tree must be forty feet tall. And the tractor—that's his?

An ember of hope lights at the sight of him. Hope that I can make amends, that our closeness just twenty minutes ago will argue on my behalf, that maybe the newly desperate longing swirling through me is reciprocated or okay somehow. I throw the Jeep in park and unbuckle. But when he catches sight of me, the whole tractor jerks. I recoil like I was slapped. His gaze snaps to the steering wheel, and his head shakes once, hard. Maybe in communication. Maybe in disgust.

Something heavy and dark fills my chest, suffocating the pathetic hope. Something worse than dread.

CHAPTER FORTY-NINE

Austin

I'm missing three classes and a quiz today. I can afford to miss a chapel. I tear down ten dead trees, but my insides boil and spew and spark. Not like yesterday. Nothing like that.

I broke the secret promises I made to her. I broke Dad's trust. I broke my belief in myself. I chose Sophie over my Creator ...

I think I broke me.

I've been killing myself to keep Sophie safe. From me. From what I crave but isn't good for her. Killing myself to give her everything. And I still didn't have what it took—

Breathe. Just focus on the job. The chainsaw rattles to life, shaking my bones with a cathartic jolt. I sever each branch from the trunk and hurl them into the trailer. Cut. Toss. Cut. Toss.

I'm Samson. The maniac who thought he could toe the line and walk away clean. The one set apart to stand firm but who gave himself away piece by piece. The guy who was supposed to be strong but let everyone down. I didn't wait for anyone to cut my hair in my sleep. I wanted her more than I wanted to obey. All she had to do was ask, and I passed the scissors myself.

I slam the side gate shut, and the whole trailer shudders.

My phone buzzes. Levi.

LEVI

Send me the address. I'm on my way.

Not a good idea.

I'm driving to Graham. I'll sit in the supermarket parking lot all day if I must.

I stare at the message, willing it to answer itself.

My girlfriend tells me I'm impossible. Sound about right?

I send the address and cram my phone back in my pocket.

After parking the ancient yellow workhorse, I drop off my supplies and plod toward the house. Mama eyes me as she shakes off some spinach from the garden. She can make whatever assumptions she wants. She told me so, and I deserve any shame she levels at me.

"Mind if Levi comes for dinner?" I sound like the zombie I am.

She bursts up. "Levi?"

"Thanks."

"I was planning on chicken and dumplings tonight. You think he'll like that okay?"

"Sure."

Maybe after my shower she'll give me something to chop.

At dinner I hardly say a word. I pretend we're in a sci-fi movie where someone's memory is erased. If only. Janie tries to ask, but I silence her with a desperate look. I'll figure out how to tell her something another day. A day when my voice won't shake. Levi makes use of his born-politician skills to carry the conversation, steering it away as needed.

I grip my spoon and stare into my bowl.

God ...

I'm so sorry ...

I know you didn't ...

But I can't finish.

I try not to look up at my bedroom door. Try not to think about Sophie's melodic voice or soothing touch or bouncing hair or perfect freckles. I can't want what I only destroy. Not if I want to survive. By the end of dinner I've strapped silence around me. It's the only armor I've got left.

As Levi drives me back to campus in the dark, an urge to punch a hole through the window bubbles up. Better not. I'm sure even the windows cost more in a Range Rover.

"I'm here if you want to talk, buddy."

I grunt.

Silence.

"It might help to say it out loud, whatever it is."

"Sophie and I ..." How do I say any of this? "We ..."

He flits a glance to me.

My mouth opens, closes.

"Start with something else," he says. "Something easier."

Okay. "She cried a lot. Said almost zero words for an entire day, apart from repeating what I said."

"Zero words from Sophie?"

"Dude. Not you too."

He swallows a laugh. "No repeating. Got it."

"She started crying while she was kissing me once." My gut pulls. "And then when she woke up Sunday morning, something was different. My family was at church. She started kissing all over me. It was ... you get the idea. I said I couldn't, but she pulled me onto my bed with her. I've never let it get like that before." My fists harden. "I'm careful. It's near impossible, but I'm so careful …"

Levi hesitates.

I hate telling him all this. He doesn't get to kiss Kit at all. I suck as a friend. I rub a hand over my face. But he needs to know if he's going to understand. "She was in her pajamas."

Levi's loaded look says he gets it.

"Yeah." I suck in a controlled breath. I can say this out loud one time. "I ran out of there like the place was on fire, so ticked at her for making me have that much self-control. I don't have enough for that, for her. She's—" No. Get to the point.

Levi's stuck in a permanent flinch.

That look on her face … No! I will not remember a single detail with pleasure. I will not. I rip my hat off and wring it in my hands. "But these things happen. She's really into me, and that's … yeah. So I went back—"

"You went back?"

There it is.

He knows. Of course he does. My head pounds. My teeth are gonna grind themselves away. I'll be wearing dentures at thirty. I dread his reaction. He's the most disciplined guy I know. He never would have caved. He has his act together like nobody else, and this is who I decide to spill my guts to. I finally risk a glance at him, bracing for judgment in his eyes.

None, but it's worse. Like I ran over him with a truck.

"Speak," I demand.

"Nothing. I haven't told Kit."

"Told her …"

"I dated Genevieve before I knew Jesus. I didn't have a reason to say no."

"Oh."

The air sits heavy. The trees fly by.

He shifts his jaw and resets. "So, everything?"

I force a nod.

"Is there a chance she's—"

"No."

"Alright. Have you talked since?"

"No."

"Are you—"

"I'm ending it. Obviously."

The steering wheel jerks.

I shift in this stupid leather seat in this box speeding me closer to her by the minute. I need to get out of here.

Levi speaks in a soothing voice, as if anything could calm me down right now. "This isn't just any girl. This is Sophie. Think about what this means for her. She just—"

"I know!"

"You two have to talk. Are you this angry at *her*?"

I stare out the window. She'll think so. But I can't help that. It's the only way.

"What if it was as much an accident for her as it was for you? What if she didn't mean—"

"So what if it was?" I yell. I still couldn't say no.

His jaw shifts, and it becomes clear—he's going to be a problem.

"This wasn't one no," he says. "A hundred decisions came after walking back into that room."

I know. Of course I know. I can't stand another word like this.

"You both made decisions. A lot of decisions. I mean, you dressed like Zorro, dude, and dragged her into the hottest pitch-dark dinner I've ever heard of. If Abu had given you an hour in there, you'd have taken it. Who knows what would've happened."

Waves of loss pummel me, nearly drowning my resolve. Sophie dragging me by the hand. Freckles stretched in her perfect grin. Calculating eyes planning adventures. Soft vulnerability as she trusted me with her secrets. The larger-than-life, Technicolor world she weaves around her. I bat it away, fighting to keep my head above water. I can't go back.

But I need to know what to prepare for. Whether Caleb's experience is the standard one.

I suck in a breath. "How bad was it for you? Breaking up after ..."

He meets my gaze. Pauses too long. "It doesn't have to be like that for you. What if you never break up? You marry her? In five years tops that will all be in bounds. Encouraged, even. This will be a timing screwup and not a permanent scar."

"Foregone conclusion," I snap. "Let it go."

He doesn't have to answer my question. I met him months after his breakup, and he was still a mess. He didn't even love Genevieve—nothing like I love Sophie.

When we're almost at school, he breaks the silence. "You praying about this?"

How could I? I turn back to my window. It was my job to protect her. And when it counted most, I didn't. A lump grows in my throat that I will not address.

First thing the next morning, I find Sophie on her way to class and plant myself in front of her. The memory of the last time I surprised her like this grates like nails on a chalkboard.

I feel her eyes, but I don't dare meet them. They might cool me down, and I don't trust myself anymore. I never should have.

Even without looking at her, she pulls like the strongest magnet. My body begs to step closer. My heart reminds me I won't find this again. My skin tingles at the proximity. My mind screams to get out of here.

"I can't do this. It's over." My voice shreds in my throat. "And please ... just let me have Flooders."

"Austin. Wait. Austin?"

CHAPTER FIFTY

Sophie

On the lounge sofa, Kit brushes my hair back as I blubber in her lap. I did this for her once when she thought she'd lost Levi. I told her to go get him back.

She can't tell me that.

Admitting the truth is humiliating. Dizzying. Debilitating. I can't for the life of me understand why I behaved like I did all weekend.

I'm sorry, Jesus. I'm so sorry.

"Do you think I"—my throat snags—"wrecked it permanently?"

"I don't know ... But you didn't wreck things with God."

"Didn't you?" that sinister voice demands. A troll, taking my thoughts hostage.

I send up a wordless prayer—and cringe, like I shouldn't.

You are my handiwork, created in Christ Jesus to do good works, which I prepared in advance for you to do.

My breath shudders.

Handiwork. What a word for me today.

But the troll is silenced.

I run a finger around my bracelet.

"It might be rough for a while," Kit says. "Maybe for a long time."

Lifting my aching body, I slump into the rigid corner of this awful couch. "I figured I'd ruin it eventually." I knew I'd never deserve him. No one could, but least of all me. And now I have the proof. I wipe my face again with the blanket I'm strangling. "Sometimes it lasts. But usually it just hurts."

Her eyes widen in alarm. "You basically just spoke Adele lyrics without even trying to sing them."

I shrug.

She stares out the window. "You need to understand something."

I inch further away, old defenses threatening. "What?"

"You called me Perfect Little Kit when you were upset about Leo."

And basically every day in my head. "Yeah?"

"It's not true."

"Okay ..." What does this have to do with anything?

"I screw up all the time. My screwups are just more hidden. I fight God internally." She presses a hand to her chest. "But you're so good at that part. Do you see?"

"I literally have no idea what you're talking about."

"When God moves, you respond. You wanted to try church again, and you've been to Praise and Prayer almost every week. I hear you singing those hymns all day, every day. You pretend you don't like it, but they're trying to get you to sing on stage." She huffs a laugh. "You thought you should read your Bible more, and now our lounge walls are covered in verses in your pretty cursive. You decided to pray while you run, and now your runs are twice as long."

I'm a lot. I know this. "I still don't get what that has to do with"—I can't seem to say his name—"what happened."

"And Dr. Shannon!" She points behind her, eyes widening. "Months ago. You delivered a message for me when you were brand new at hearing his voice. Remember? You don't second-guess and overthink when it comes to what God wants from you. You go and do. And you do big." She flings her arms wide.

I did big all right. I wad the blanket in my lap.

"I live next to you, so I have a front-row seat. You're the Elle Woods of faith. The Kat Stratford. No, the Katniss Everdeen."

I suck in a breath.

"All gas, no brakes. God teaches you something, and you go do it. I admire you so much."

"Katniss would never have done what I did."

"What? Katniss was supposed to shoot Snow!" She holds her hands straight beside her face, as if to direct my attention, but then she slumps. "I wish I were more like you. I wish I were brave and big like you. I make myself so small."

"You're not small. Except in a height sort of way. You're Kit Talbot, for crying out loud."

She half-smiles, pulls her knees in. "You're doing it again, see? Listen, I messed up so much last semester trying to be the mastermind of my own life, my own protector. And still, God made something beautiful out of it. The mistake you guys made isn't worse than mine. It's real—it hurt Austin, and it hurt you. You'll both have to live with it. But it's not unforgivable. From where I'm sitting, it seems like you made a really bad choice in a really hard moment. But I spent months making the same choice over and over again." Her hands knot together. "Maybe what happened with you will have a bigger fallout, but you're not resisting God's work in your life."

"You've been through a lot, Kit."

"So have you. Feeling invisible in your own house? Your parents quitting on each other? You don't give yourself enough credit."

I bite my lips and consider that. "I expected a lot more judginess from you."

"Nope. After the last year, I think life with God is a lot more about surrender and love and trust. If we can just do those for him, he changes us so we can obey in all the other ways."

Could that actually be true?

She bends forward. "Pray hard about this, okay?"

But I bombed it. What could you want with me now?

I have created you anew.

"He wants me close," I mumble.

"He wants you close. And ..." She winces. "We can talk about this more later, but ..."

I eye her, fists clenching in preparation.

"God gave me a project I still haven't gone and done."

My fingers relax. "A project?"

"I think he wants me to give dance lessons. In my studio."

I almost smile. "You're telling me so I'll make you follow through?"

"Guilty."

A couple of days ago, I would've jumped at the chance. Something new. Something fun. Something to focus on, to make me feel okay for five minutes. But I don't trust myself anymore. What if I make an even bigger mess trying to feel free?

What do you say?

She is my handiwork, created in Christ Jesus to do good works, which I prepared in advance for her to do.

"This is a good thing he planned for you to do, KitKat. Maybe for us to do. I'm in."

She squeezes my arm in her way. "Thank you."

"But in exchange, I'm gonna need you to teach me the dances in *Work It*."

She drops her head back with a hearty Kit laugh.

"You have seen it, right?" I prop my chin on my wadded blanket. "It has John Ambrose from *To All the Boys*, except he's ..."

"Jake Taylor," she says. "Who's actually Jordan Fisher. Oh, I've seen it."

A smile almost forms but never lands. I wonder if it ever will again.

Her voice lowers. "Did you ask for forgiveness?"

"He won't talk to me."

"No, from God."

"Oh. Yes."

"Then it's done. Your sins are as far as the east is from the west. Believe it."

My throat closes with emotion.

At a *ding*, I scramble for my phone. My heart stops when I see *Scott* on the text, but it's not Austin. It's Janie. Can that be right?

No words, just the link to a playlist. Ten songs. I squeeze my phone, as if it will communicate back with her. She sent me songs.

Maybe she doesn't know yet. But maybe she does and she's sending them anyway.

CHAPTER FIFTY-ONE

Austin

I try to do my homework, but I stare at the page. I try to eat, but I forget to chew. I try to gather my laundry, but my hands are useless.

I collapse onto my couch.

The lights are on, but the world is dark. People need things from me—I know they do—but I have nothing to give. I curl into a ball, lost.

She's gone.

And so am I.

Because so is he.

I used to be God's guy—the hands and feet, the one people could count on. I thought that's who I was. But now, I can't even stand. What good is a broken tool? Or worse ... a warped one. Not just useless, but dangerous.

CHAPTER FIFTY-TWO

Sophie

Two weeks and I haven't left campus. Before, I would've field tripped with G3, gone out with Jenny, filled every second with noise. But I can't. They barely look my way now—like God cut the ropes before I could tie myself to the wrong lifelines. Even the invitations from classmates have dried up. I haven't had the energy to fake it enough for the people who don't really know me. They don't know what I had, what I lost.

Despite what a terrible friend I've been to Kit, she's fully here. Even Mia's pared down her schedule to be around more. I don't have to chase them down. And somehow that's enough. More than enough. Being with them doesn't distract me. It heals me.

Today, Kit dragged us outside again to paint our nails on a picnic blanket in the grass. The sun thaws me, inch by inch. The wind cools my face, somehow better than any freeway in my Jeep. Kit must have seen the Dark and Twisty Daily To-Do list I wrote on a Post-it, because she's been silently assuring I check them off.

Memorize a verse
Touch grass
Sing something
Go for a run
Tell God about it

It helps.

Thank you for them. For not giving up on me. For giving me a place to belong.

Psalm 139:16—"You saw me before I was born. Every day of my life was recorded in your book. Every moment was laid out before a single day had passed."

We've been memorizing Psalm 139 together, bits at a time. I just hand-lettered that verse to add to the lounge walls. They're barely visible now, covered in psalms I've written and taped up. It's the strangest thing—he keeps whispering. I thought I'd have to earn it back, prove I was on the straight and narrow. But he took me back on day one. No hoops to jump through, no radio silence. He never left. It's like ... he wants me close.

"I miss Haymitch," I blurt, painting my pinkie toe. "And this is the brightest color of purple I've ever seen. I'm officially overcompensating."

"So don't," Mia says. "Miss Haymitch. 'Cause I do too. I can plan a thing tonight."

"I mean ... sure." Dread and desperation coexist at the thought of seeing ... him ... again. No, recovery is not going well. I still can't say his name without going fetal.

Kit screws on the lid of her nail polish. "If you're ready."

"It's a win-win," Mia says. "If Austin shows, he's forced to remember how gone he's always been for Sophie. If he doesn't, just awkward-free time with the crew."

I try to smile.

"Walk tonight?" Mia asks. "Or field trip?"

"Your favorite hike?" Kit suggests. "The lake?"

I miss the trees. The crunch of gravel. That forest feeling that everything will be okay. But how could I walk through a forest without thinking of Austin every second? I swallow hard and shove the thought away. "Maybe just a movie?"

"I'll come up with some options," Mia says.

"I'll text Levi," Kit says.

For hours I decide what to say if he shows.

He doesn't.

As I finish an afternoon run, Austin materializes halfway across campus. Must be on his way to an absurdly early dinner, one of many strategies he employs to avoid me at all costs. Phone number blocked, Flooders claimed, routine rearranged, paths to class adjusted. I once saw him at the library. One step toward him and he zipped his backpack and slinked away without a trace.

Can I talk to him? Can I make him listen? I just want to tell him I'm sorry. He doesn't even know I'm sorry.

I've been praying and praying, and I just know I'm supposed to wait for Austin to reach out. My hands pulse into fists at my sides. I'm not a sit-and-wait kind of girl, and it's absolutely murdering me trying to leave him alone, trying to let him heal and come around.

I could shower and put on that black workout dress.

I could cut in front of him so he has to watch me run.

I could try a guerrilla kiss.

I shake my head to convince myself. No to all. No tempting. That's what did this in the first place.

Write him a letter? He'll burn it.

Resurrect the hangman game? No idea who was doing the socials.

Convince Levi to get us stuck in an elevator? He'd sooner buy Crocs than betray Austin.

I'm still running, passing student after student until I'm a mere thirty seconds away. He loves these workout shorts, and he won't think I put them on for him. Maybe just an apologetic-looking hi? A sad smile that invites a conversation?

Psalm 73:25—"Whom have I in heaven but you? I desire you more than anything on earth."

I drop my head and slow to a walk. The psalm I hand-lettered just before this.

I mean, yes. But I miss him like an amputated limb. How am I supposed to do my whole life without him?

Do you desire me more than anything on earth?

Austin's ten feet ahead. That curly hair and broad back. Hoodie sleeves pushed up his forearms. I want to wrap my arms around him. I want his eyes on mine. I want him to stand up straight again. I want him to know how sorry I am, how much I love him, how it'll be different now.

But I want you more.

Or, I'm trying to.

There's a multiple-choice option flashing ahead that could fix everything in a moment. Every muscle itches to sprint those last ten feet.

But I'm choosing you. You can't heal what I won't hand over.

Time for "Need to Not." I switch the song and scroll down the lyrics to click on the chorus. *Convince me, Jordan Davis.*

I lift straight hands next to my face like horse blinders and about-face—almost barreling into someone—to sprint back to my suite. Before I make an even bigger mess of my life.

I'm a maniac. Keep me in line. I only need you.

Austin

Dysfunctional maybe, but the self-inflicted pain of the gym is becoming a drug. Downside? The off-ness of my workouts are now a constant reminder. I used to talk to God between every rep, often about her, pushing the exhaustion into prayers.

Not anymore. How could I? I defied orders, went AWOL.

I want to snap out of it, be me again, but I don't know how. 'Cause it's all gone. Sophie. My drive. My peace. Football. Her protection. My ability to look in the mirror. I used to be someone. I showed up. I mattered. I took care of Sophie. I looked out for my friends. Now? I just exist. I plod to Saga, to class, to the gym. And there's nothing else to me. The rest of me bled through the cracks that day.

A blond ponytail sways across the gym, but I lock my eyes on the machine in front of me. It's not Sophie. I make sure of that. But my peripheral vision betrays me—she's walking with a short brunette. I turn on impulse.

It's her.

My stomach twists like after those spinning rides at the county fair.

She doesn't know I'm here. I could watch her walk if I wanted. I can't want, but I still watch. My heart beats *I love her. I love her. I love her.* It won't go away. Won't even lessen. But that doesn't change anything. My stupid heart knows nothing. It doesn't get a say anymore.

I've only seen her once in two weeks, and this is why. I avoid her with precision for survival, yes, but for her too. I don't want this gnawing ache for her. I want her to heal, move on, find what she needs. The less she's reminded of what we had before, the better.

She looks content. A little nervous, picking at her nails. No bouncing, no singing, but Kit's talking to her like she's a person and not a charity case. Better than my friends can say for me. The vice of dread around my chest eases. She's okay.

They continue down the hallway with the multipurpose rooms, toward Kit's dance studio. The joggers she runs in. A high ponytail I would have tugged on. All I can think is, *Clothed with strength and dignity.* I squeeze my eyes shut, like that'll stop the image from burning in.

I need God. I know that. But prayer seems impossible. Like, "Hey, I know you gave me everything I could ever want, but I still took more. Broke everything. Crashed through all your expectations—because I wanted it. Because I could. Anyway, we good?" I shake my head numbly.

My thumbs move before my brain stops them, texting Levi like I've learned nothing.

Is Kit teaching Sophie ballet?

LEVI

They've been planning a class. Why?

Saw them at the gym

Sorry man.

"Yo, can I work in?"

I glance up. "Oh, sorry." I was hogging the machine. "Yeah, for sure."

My mutinous eyes pan for Sophie. I wanna follow her, but I know they'll close the door. What is wrong with me?

"You know them?" That same guy—T1 I think. Doesn't play intramurals or I'd know him. He nods toward Kit and Sophie.

"Uh, yeah."

"Know if the blonde is single?"

I don't answer. Just stare at him.

One look at me, and he jerks back, hands lifted. "Sorry. Got it. Didn't know."

I rub a towel aggressively down my face. Like that'll help.

Just bench press. Then I'm done here.

Sophie

For my Post-it homework, Kit and I sang "Jesus Paid It All" on the way to her studio. I drop it to a hum as we pass through the gym. There's something about hymns—antique theme songs, handed down like heirlooms. By Jesus lovers, for Jesus lovers. They're not flashy, not churchy in a weird way. They just feel real, and singing them is a reminder that I've been adopted into their family. Jesus's family.

Another chance at family. Teach me what that even looks like.

At the familiar smell of metal and lemon, I realize in a flash—Austin could be here in the gym. Odds are decent actually. My nerves go on alert, preparing for a painful zap. I still jerk to scan the weight room.

Bam.

There he is, in all his weight-lifting glory, bench-pressing a million pounds.

I flinch. Not two hours later, and here we are again.

And now he's in one of his ratty tees, sleeves crudely torn off, hems fraying.

Help! Help me obey.

It takes everything in me to twist back around, keep my eyes on the door, wait for Kit to unlock it. I frantically tap my nails together as Kit digs for her key. He avoids me on purpose. If he caved and wrapped his arms around me, he'd hate me even more in the long term. I'd lose any remaining chance of him coming back for good.

"Never. Not after what you did. After what you took."

I am God's handiwork, created in Christ Jesus to do good works, which God prepared in advance for me to do. And whatever those good things are, they're my good works, and they're not with Austin. Not right now. I roll my shoulders. Like Kit's class. We almost have the first one planned out. Just focus on the class.

But as we step through the doorway, the troll tries again.

"You're pathetic. He doesn't hate you. He doesn't even miss you. He's just over it. You're not good enough, and that's it."

Kit steps out of her shoes and unlocks her phone.

How precious are your thoughts about me, Oh God, I recite under my breath. *They cannot be numbered. I can't even count them; they outnumber the grains of sand.*

It doesn't fix anything. Doesn't even distract me. I kick the door closed—harder than I mean to—and wince, whipping toward Kit. But nothing. Not one flinch. Just tap-tapping on her phone, connecting to the Bluetooth speakers.

I gape. Since when? Has God been healing her right in front of me?

But maybe healing doesn't make a scene. Maybe it just sneaks in and takes root.

The troll slithers closer. *"Austin thinks he's too good for you, but all of this is his fault. He's acting like you did this alone, but he was there. You're here because of him."*

Bitterness burns up my throat. If he's so mad about it, he should've made different choices. He should've said no.

But the Taylor Swift song plays in my head, and my anger ebbs. Cheat on me? Never. Austin's no villain.

Kicking off my sneakers, I catch my reflection in the wall of mirrors: the ponytail he used to tug, the lanky frame he helped me make peace with. He'd whisper that I looked like a faerie, brush the freckles on my cheeks, wrap his arms around my waist. He called me feisty and brilliant and alive. Perfect.

My lungs struggle to inflate. Remembering hurts. But where is Mom's voice? Where is her grimace? Austin helped cross it out. His voice counted more. Somehow, it still does, even if he refuses to breathe the same air as me. I meet my eyes in the reflection. Maybe this was the gift all along. I thought it was Austin, but maybe it was seeing myself differently.

A text lights up my phone—a new playlist from Janie. The title sends a shock through me: *Hymns—Old and New.*

How could she know?

I skim down the list. Dozens. Forrest Frank's I recognize. Kings Kaleidoscope. And so many more.

"Kit…?"

"Yeah?"

"You don't ever talk to Janie, do you?"

"Austin's sister? No, I've never met her. Why?"

So it's you. You told her to do that?

Thank you.

CHAPTER FIFTY-THREE

Sophie

A week later I plop onto the suite couch, then immediately abandon it to sit on a throw pillow on the floor. New rule: no more suite moping. My circumstances aren't changing, so my behavior has to. Kit tosses me a pillow, queues up the chips, and nukes my queso like it's second nature. No questions, no explanations.

"Thanks, girl. So, rebounds are bad, right? That's a thing?"

She bites her lip and tries to control her horrified facial expression. "Rebounds?"

"Davis Powell kind of reappeared today. Like, out of nowhere. And I know it's only been three weeks and I'm a wreck. I'm not even pretending this would fix anything. It's just … I can't sit on my hands another day. I need something else to focus on besides fixing the mess Austin refuses to allow me to fix. I'm not trying to move on. I'm just trying to move."

Speechless, she busies herself, carrying chips and the hot jar to the coffee table, tidying the lounge.

I dunk a chip and lose a drip to the table while the pines sway outside. That last morning with Austin, the trees were perfectly still. Like they knew. The pillow won't cooperate, so I readjust and drop the chip.

"Besides, I sort of owe him. I blew him off before." I send her a look. I'm not blaming her, but ... Fine, maybe I am a little. It's hard not to think I could have picked the fun, low-stakes college thing with Davis. Instead of being buried under rubble.

Kit steels her shoulders. "I want what's best for you. And I still believe that's Austin."

My eyes trace the lines on the pillow. "You know that's not a multiple-choice option. He'd have to ever speak to me again, let alone forgive and forget."

She lets out a sigh and studies the corner. "I know. I'm so mad at him. But that aside, Austin wasn't the only reason I panicked about Davis."

"Okay ..."

"So what do you want to do this weekend? Movie marathon again, or we could venture out?"

Sudden change of subject. "Nice try."

Austin was always saying that. It stings every time. Like playing Operation as a kid—the way the buzzer would go off when someone touched the wrong spot. Except now, the wrong spots are everywhere. Every time someone pushes up their sleeves. Says "you" with an accent. Goes back for seconds. Sends a flirty smile. It's not getting better. It's getting worse. And it scares me as much as it hurts.

"Spill, KitKat. I need to hear your other reasons."

When she doesn't, I motion for her to start talking.

"First," she starts, "can I ask you, are you angry? At Austin?"

I let out a breath. "Sometimes I think I should be angrier. I mean, it's not okay that he never even talked to me—just dumped me cold. So not being mad ... that feels like shame, somehow. Like after Leo broke up with me because I wasn't treating him right, it felt messed up to be happy. And after that party ..." I trail off, spinning a chip between my fingers. "I was living under my mom's cringing disapproval. But Austin helped me escape that. I didn't know anyone could see me like he did. And, maybe it sounds weird, but he made it easier to believe God when he said he wanted me close."

She watches me, still and quiet. Like she's holding it with me.

"And, I've been thinking about my Dark and Twisty days, and the long stretches of it ... That fog. Everything feels off, but even the awful stuff happening doesn't quite explain why. Like the volume's turned down on your whole life, and even the stuff you used to love just ... sits there. I've wondered if that fog is where Austin is right now. I hate that for him. I want it gone, for his sake. And I can't really be angry at him—not if he's stuck in that. When you're there, it's not about pushing people away. You can't even reach for them."

"Sophs? Is that how it is for you right now?"

I squeeze my pillow. "Some parts, but it's not like before. During my parents' divorce, it was awful. I couldn't function. That was drowning—no air, no fight, no desire to get better."

"What's different now?"

"Well, Jesus is different. The weight is there. The darkness, the ache. But this time I'm not alone in it. I'm pretty sure I'd be drowning without him. He's like ... my snorkel."

She nods like she gets it.

"But also, depression is unpredictable. I had a really bad day a few months ago, and I had Jesus then. I just don't know. To be honest, I feel guilty that I'm not worse. Like, how heartless am I to not be comatose after losing Austin? It's not like I'm okay at all, but ..."

"That's the Enemy. Tell him to get lost." Kit stares me down, more than serious. "Any amount of okay-ness we have is a gift from God. We just cannot even imagine how much evil he holds back for us every day. If you have good days, if you're not comatose, that's a gift, not a reason for guilt. You can say thank you and move forward."

Silence spreads, threatens.

The chip finally cracks between my fingers. "Well, story time's over. Time to tell me why I shouldn't go out with Davis."

"Our snorkel," she says reverently. "Jesus. How could either of us have survived the last year without him? But Davis won't get that."

I narrow my eyes. "You're one of those people who thinks you have to agree on everything before you go on a single date with someone?"

"Seriously? I called Levi an alien for a reason. We're on opposite sides of the political spectrum. He's creepily rich, and I can't afford a trip to IHOP. He's about to win student body president by a landslide, and I have like five friends. We have vastly different hobbies and almost no similar childhood memories."

I blink. She's not wrong.

"But at the end of the day, that man wants to make Jesus happy more than anything. And if he's in the wrong, he wants to hear the truth. Somehow it's working between us. Despite the million reasons for us to misunderstand each other, we're learning how to be each other's person."

"What if Davis respects where I'm coming from?"

"But how could he? If he doesn't know the Snorkel?"

I send her side-eye. She means well, but I'm not in the mood for the Sunday school version of dating advice.

"So go on a date with him," she concedes. "Try to prove me wrong. But ask hard questions and pray the whole time, okay? And please meet him somewhere. In public."

I pull out my phone, out of defiance or desperate optimism, I don't know. Either way, I hit Send.

CHAPTER FIFTY-FOUR

Sophie

I settle into the sleek velvet booth, a low-hanging light glowing overhead, dim and moody. It's a guilty relief to be out in the world on a Saturday night. Nigel from *Devil Wears Prada* would say I'm a "sad little person," but still—a person.

Thank you for that.

And yes, I still think about Austin every three seconds, but I want to try one date. Just give me this.

"Tell me about the super-cool tutoring thing I've heard about," I start.

Davis grins. "You're making me blush."

"Come on, spill."

So he does. How he built it from the ground up, how he connected smart students at Mayberry with local kids who needed help—for free.

"There's nothing like helping somebody out with no ulterior motive, you know? It just feels good," he says.

I hesitate. Isn't feeling good an ulterior motive? "You're an entrepreneur."

His smile tilts. "Not making a penny, so I'm pretty sure a real entrepreneur would say I'm a failure."

"Nope. You're using your strategizing to make a difference rather than to profit from it."

"'Preciate that."

I swallow. That *Operation* buzzer again.

Kit said to go deep. Here goes. "So what's your secret? Plenty of people want to help but don't do anything about it." Oh, and I'm supposed to be praying.

Sorry. I'm listening. I trust you if you say this is a no. A no now or a no always. Whatever you say.

"A deep question. I love that. It's no secret, but I wanna be proud of my life, ya know? I don't wanna look back and think 'I did nothing in college. I only partied or got good grades or went out with pretty girls.'" He winks across the table. "It's not enough to make me content with myself."

Content with himself. So relatable. And yet ...

I shift in the booth. "So what do you have planned for after college? Or is that too Daterview?"

He shakes his head. Energy radiates from his side of the table. Enthusiasm. He's fully in the moment. Like the old Sophie. "I like that you care about this stuff. I'm so jacked you agreed to go out with me tonight."

I half smile.

"I know—I'm setting myself up for a major rebound situation. But I've been kicking myself seeing you everywhere with ... Anyway, I should've just asked you out at Goodwill."

"Hello, random stranger holding a rare velvet artifact," I imitate. "You seem like a winner."

He slides forward till his middle hits the table. "If I had just asked your name, I would've learned everything I needed to know. The G3-ers had already told me all about you, remember?"

This guy just says how he feels. No waiting till he knows I'll reciprocate. No hedging his bets. He just goes for it.

"But I said no when you did ask," I tease. "What makes you so sure it would have been different mid-costume-shopping?"

"I'm not. But it would have been better than yelling over the madness of Saga. And at least I would've had a few days to shoot my shot."

He seems great. Right? Is there a catch?

I rest my arms on the edge of the table and blindly trace the chip in my nail polish. I like Davis. I'm a 0 on the emotionally available scale, but he knows that.

"Oh. I got derailed again. You're just so pretty I can't seem to stay focused." He nudges my hand. "What was the question again?"

A smile twitches. "I asked what happens after college. With your tutoring stuff or anything."

The server in crisp black glides over and sets down water in beautiful glasses. I could almost be in Pasadena. Then she asks what we'd like to drink, and her voice pulls me straight back to Pinecrest. "Be back for y'all's order in a jiffy, mkay?"

"Yes, ma'am," he says. "Thank you."

They're so much alike, he and Austin. Raised just miles apart with the same country manners, the same rhythm to their speech, a similar warmth.

He turns back to me, waving his wrapped silverware, as if he's composing a tiny orchestra. "I wanna leave a mark. I dunno how that'll look yet. I'm international business, so it could go a lot of directions." He chuckles. "Literally. But I mean, I wanna be more than some blue dot bobbing around the map."

He wants to make a difference. You love that, right? And maybe you have a plan for him to find you later.

An actual smile settles on my face. "Have you always been like that?"

"Kinda, yeah. Life is just ... unfulfilling if you don't do something about it, you know?"

I really do. But also, the sentiment is incomplete. I flick my hair behind my shoulders and study him, as if focusing better will give me a miraculous vision into my own future. Is he in it? Do I care? "International business ... So you're not going to stay in East Texas?"

"Nah, it ain't in me. 'Specially now that my parents are divorced."

I let a breath out. "That sucks."

His smile drops, but he shakes his head, as if to dispel the feeling. "I'll come back to visit my folks, of course, but I'm gonna live somewhere ... louder. Travel as much as humanly possible. I'm gonna try it all." His grin returns. "You like my answers? You're looking happier with me."

I chuckle. "You're a cool guy."

"You're a cool lady. You're also different from before. Are you super bummed?"

I nod honestly.

"Shoot. I'm sorry." He plops back against the booth. "And I'm going off about my own stuff. You should just tell me to shut up. Want me to take you back?"

"No, I'm good. And I want to hear. But ... that's the thing though. I'm not sure if I'm going to get better." I meet his eyes vulnerably. "I might just ... be this way now."

"Sophie Appel, I have a major crush on you. I'll take whatever you wanna give."

The lightness in his posture tells me that he hasn't had his heart broken. Or nuked his own heart, like in my case. He's been dragged through a family divorce, but he couldn't know what he's offering here.

"So what about you?" he asks. "What are you and your beautiful intensity gonna accomplish?"

This guy knows how to use his words, and my chest is a vacuum, sucking them in.

But I'm listening. You get to pick.

Be honest.

I can do that.

"Whatever Jesus says."

He squints, waiting for the rest.

"I don't know my major yet, but I'm coming to terms with that. I have no plans, and I kind of think it's for the best. I just want to do what he says, even if I don't hear very many steps in advance."

"Okay ... but how can you be sure what a hypothetical formless being says?"

I shrug. "I get where you're coming from. I was there last year. But he's not hypothetical anymore. He's talked to me over and over. And he loves me. I just know."

A skeptical glance. A muted readjustment. "Sorry. Shouldn't've gotten all heavy with religion talk. Let's just have fun. I don't wanna wreck this so early on."

"I don't want to start something where I have to walk on eggshells."

His eyes widen. "Start something? You're gonna give me a chance?"

I stop short.

"Sorry, derailed again." He unwraps his napkin and sets it across his lap, rocks his fork on the table. Upside down, right-side up. "Can I ask you something ... personal?"

"Yep."

"Did you ask God about starting up that relationship with Scott?"

A knot twists sharp in my chest. "Um. I should have. But he still gave me an answer." When I was spiraling. Because I knew it would destroy me when it ended. I rub my breastbone, like that will help. No more trip down memory lane. Not here. Not now.

He studies me. "Mind me asking what you *heard*?"

Something in my gut says this matters, so I pull in a steadying breath. "He said it was a gift."

"A gift," he mutters.

I'm dying to bolt to a safer topic, but I hold my ground and wave him forward. "Go ahead."

"I guess ... I don't get it. Trust me, my life would be a lot easier at Mayberry if I'd drink the Kool-Aid. It sucks being the odd one out. But this is exactly why I'm not on board anymore. You did everything right, and it still blew up in your face. It really ticks me off. I mean, either you heard wrong or God's not really there ... Or he's cruel, right?"

I shake my head, but how do I explain? I remember looking at the world like that, hiding behind my independence. It's terrifying to be on your own with all the weight, all the responsibility. Every good result is earned, and every bad result is unfair. It warps your vision. You hit a high and just want another, but you know it'll never last. The world is scary, unpredictable, *cruel*. I hate that for Davis.

What do you want me to say?

I bite my cheek. "I hear you. If you want facts, there are smarter people that can talk philosophy and archaeology and all of that. But I can tell you that I pray and hear back. I read the Bible and it changes me. I ask and he helps—" My voice catches. "But I brought this on myself. You can't blame God for it."

"Because you ended it? I mean, I'm assuming. Who would leave you? And Scott was so far gone."

"I really don't want to get into it."

"Sorry, yeah, of course. Ugh, I'm blowing this. Everybody knows you don't ask about breakups on a first date."

"No, you're good. But Jesus isn't some platitude for me. I'm not going back to how I used to do things. Chasing freedom, adjusting the rules as I wanted. It didn't work."

His eyes flicker with interest. "What was that? Chasing?"

"Chasing freedom? My friend used to call it that."

He hums low. "You don't want freedom anymore?"

"It's not that. It's just, doing what I want, avoiding the hard stuff? That wasn't freedom. It was panic in a leather jacket. I need more than that."

"More than that."

Tell him.

"Mind if I tell you more?"

"Go ahead."

So I tell him. About rules as a playground fence. About my Snorkel. And he tells me about when he gave up on God—when his parents gave up on each other, on their family. And I tell him about mine.

The food is plated to perfection. I try to eat, but my appetite is still hiding somewhere, and I have the rest boxed for Kit and Mia.

Before we part ways, he turns to me. "Hang out with me tomorrow?" That crooked smile. "I know the movies say I'm supposed to wait three days, but I'm not doing anything the right way anyway."

CHAPTER FIFTY-FIVE

Sophie

Kit rockets my direction when I return to the suite. "You're back safe."

Levi must have just left.

"Have you been pacing?"

"Maybe a little."

I chuckle.

Thank you for her.

"Let's get Mia." Three weeks and my voice still doesn't sound like mine. Too low, too slow. Davis reminded me how far I've drifted from the old Sophie. But Austin isn't coming back, so I have to figure out how to do things without him. Kit follows me to my room. "It's time I get back to the lake. Come with me?"

"Absolutely. I'm never out past ten anymore."

I echo her sad smile. "And I'm buying you a Blizzard on the way." I point at her. "And you're not going to be weird about it."

"I'll try. Can I at least have a spoiler?"

I fire off a text to Mia and drop my phone on the desk. "Davis is great. Fun, kind, heart-on-his-sleeve, cute." Ditching the skirt, I opt for sweatpants and a hoodie. Tug on my sneakers. "We're actually really similar. And he kept saying these sweet little things, almost by accident. He seems to really like me."

We land back in our lounge, and I plop onto the floor.

Kit lowers gravely beside me. "Okay."

"He had all the right answers. Mostly. We want the same things. Mostly. And our families ... We're actually compatible. Mostly."

"That's a lot of mostlys."

I pick at a pillow, trace the outline of the *Hang in There* cat. The pines outside sway with the breeze.

"And?" she prods.

I pick at my nails. "The troll didn't speak up once."

Her brows knit. "The troll?"

I swallow. "That voice that says I'm too much. That I was never good enough for Austin. That I was bound to ruin everything."

Kit recoils. "No one should ever make you feel that way. Austin did that?" she demands.

I rub my hands down my thighs. "No. I mean, he stopped me from kissing him a billion times, but he never said that." His devoted eyes peering from under his hat. His hand that always found mine. Reorienting his life around me. He loved me. My stomach lurches. I push to my feet. "He never said that." But my voice wavers. "Before."

Ding.

MIA

Meet you at the Jeep.

I barrel to the door. The world will feel better out there.

Kit scurries after me, pausing to slide into her flats. "Then he still feels that way, Sophs. One choice doesn't change a person's entire view. Did Austin say something to you?"

"Kit," I clip. "He hasn't and he won't. I know how he feels *because* he won't speak to me. I'm just saying with Davis ... the troll was quiet for a minute. To Davis I'm still a good person. He wouldn't care at all what I did. He'd be—" I slow to a stop in the hallway. "He'd be jealous. He doesn't live in the Christian world of rules and expectations. Austin will never speak to me again because of something that would make Davis ecstatic." I steady myself against the wall.

"Are you okay?" she asks softly. "Are you sure you want to go out?"

"Yes." I push off and tear down the hallway, out the lobby doors toward the parking lot.

She jogs to catch up. "Rules and expectations. Is that how you see Mayberry?"

I pick up my speed. "I mean, yeah. Jesus is freedom, but churchiness isn't. The people around here are way too obsessed with regulations and red tape. But Davis isn't. That's what I'm saying. He goes out and does good things instead of being all proud of himself for following a million rules—rules that may or may not even be in the Bible."

Kit accidentally halts like she does when she's thinking. I turn impatiently.

"That's a valid concern," she says.

I shove my hands into my hoodie pocket. "I like him, Kit. Maybe I'll wait a few weeks, but I should just be with him. It would be so much easier. He's a good guy, and he likes me, and maybe he'll help me silence the troll. We're actually compatible. Similar. If it ever did border-hop rebound territory, I'd actually be setting myself up for success." My throat constricts. "And what could I ever possibly do that would make him as angry as Austin is?"

A mutinous tear rolls down my cheek. More threaten to join it.

A memory plants itself in my consciousness, refusing to

budge. Austin on his couch, fire in his eyes, asking how I fell in love with Jesus, loving me *for* my faith. It was everything.

I try to imagine Davis there instead. Maybe in a month, maybe in ten years. I tell him what I've been praying about—he cringes. I show him the verses I meticulously hand-letter—his face says *there, there*. I talk about my Snorkel—he changes the subject.

We could be anywhere ... the Eiffel Tower, the Maldives, on a pair of Jet Skis. The great wide open, not a tether in sight. It wouldn't lessen the blow when he doesn't care about what I care about most.

Would it ever be enough?

More unwelcome memories. Austin against the chain-link fence, squeezing my hand as he spoke Bible verses over me. The way his voice caught when he talked about making Jesus proud. Insisting on being interruptible like him. How earnestly he prayed for me on our run.

Davis *does* have a motive for helping—he wants to feel good. He wants to be content with himself.

Austin gives so hard it crushes him.

They're almost ... opposites.

"Sophs, you're not buying what you're selling. Are you?"

I drag my gaze to her. "You know the guy who hates me with the fire of a thousand suns?"

Kit cycles through seventeen facial expressions. "Perfect *10 Things* line. But the truth of it is so awful. But the fact that you're quoting movies is a good sign. But I'm so mad at Austin. But maybe there's hope. And despite his deplorable behavior right now, I'm still rooting for him."

"Deplorable? You use really big words, KitKat."

She pulls my arm so I'll face her. "Sophs. What were you going to say about Austin?"

The knot in my chest aches. I can't. My legs need to move.

"Don't give up on him," she says. "He's just Wreck-It Ralph right now."

I shake her off. "No. I can't keep doing this to myself. Let's go."

Austin

Shuffling back from the gym on Thursday, I spot Ethan with a girl. D2 maybe. She looks ready to fake a phone call.

"Finn." My voice sounds like a growl, so I clear my throat. "Walk with me."

He gawks at me, like *Kinda busy here.*

"Can't wait. C'mon."

He jogs to catch up. "What was that?"

"I should ask you the same thing."

"I was in the middle of asking Chloe out." He glances at me. "What? We're friends."

"What were her hands doing, bro?"

"Uh. Holding each other? I dunno."

"And her feet?"

"Kinda crossed-standing-up?"

"And her face?"

He slumps. "Nervous 'cause she likes me back?"

I shake my head.

"I'm a creep."

"Not yet."

"Fine. What do I do?"

I eye him and suck in a breath. "Give her a week to recover, and then tread lightly. Gotta watch the nonverbals, my man."

"Could you talk to her for me?"

I scowl. "What is this, middle school? No."

"At least tell me if I have a shot."

"You're a stud. You have a shot with any girl."

He grins, but it dims. "So ... uh ... Abu wants to restart The Game this week."

Once Flooders gets ahold of it, I give it a week before the whole school knows Ethan's the guy behind hangman. Attention's weird—looks fun until it's not.

I meet his eyes. "Your thing, buddy. Your call." I hold out a fist bump.

He tries to hide another smile, and I almost have one of my own.

Back in my room after a shower, I plop into my desk chair and flip open Electromagnetics to start my eight thousand problems of the night. A knock hits my wide-open door. Kit. Right—it's Thursday.

"Jeeves is at his council meeting. Got moved this week." I keep working.

"I know."

"Then what are you doing here?" Not my most polite, but that look in her eye worries me.

"Sophie's with Davis Powell now."

I already heard, but the words are still a punch to the ribs, knocking the air out of me. Hearing them from her is too real—like watching the door lock from the outside.

"Not my business." My pencil goes rogue, scribbling nonsense.

She lets out a breath. "It's time you get over yourself and fix this."

I spin around slowly. "You're sticking your nose where you don't belong, Kit. It's 'time' you get going."

"You did this for me once, and I needed it."

"Is Sophie confused? Am I sending mixed signals?" I turn back to my work. "Nice try."

"You're not fooling me. You are not this angry about one mistake. That's not you. Especially when you made plenty of your own. And when she was a mess? No. You love her so much. It must have gutted you to watch her like that. So what's this really about?"

I flinch harder with every word. How could she know that?

Levi doesn't even seem to know. Desperation churns in my gut. I have to get her out of here. "You don't know what you're talking about. Please leave me alone."

"No," she fires back. "Sophie's running around with some popular, charming guy who's not a believer, and it's your fault. Who knows what could happen to her?" Her volume rises. "You have to fix it. Now."

I clench my jaw so hard my teeth rattle, read the same problem again and again.

"I tried talking sense," she says. "I really thought she'd go on one date Saturday and see he wasn't you. But now she's seen him every day since. I don't like it. She won't listen to me. Just waves me off and says he's a good guy."

I've never heard Kit like this. She's not going to leave without some words, so I push some out, as respectfully as I can without facing her. "He is. Known him since Little League. Christian his whole life. He's just ... figuring stuff out. He won't hurt her. Now go."

The image of Sophie with Powell beats my insides to a pulp. *Don't think about it. This is how it is. It has to be.*

Can't breathe.

Moving on is good. I don't want her to be alone. This is—

"Please." Her voice drops. "I don't trust him. I don't like how he looks at her. You have to protect her. This is your job. God gave her to *you*."

My stomach rolls. I should have protected her. It was my job. But I didn't.

"You know Sophie." She's urgent now. "I'm afraid she'll do anything to stop thinking about you, about what happened."

Unbearable images flash. The pencil lead snaps, and I manically click the end.

"You're the only one who can—"

"Get out," I roar.

When I turn around, she's gone.

Oh no. She's been so much better lately, I forgot about her

triggers. But I can't chase her down—wouldn't that make it worse? I rip out my phone.

Answer

Kit needs you

And then I jab the Call button. "C'mon, Jeeves. Answer."

Thirty seconds. Then I'm tracking him down. No clue where they meet.

"Samwise?" he answers. "Where is she? What happened?"

"To her room, maybe. I yelled at her, and—"

"You what?" he spits.

"I'm really sorry. Lemme know if she's not there and I'll—"

But he's gone too.

CHAPTER FIFTY-SIX

Sophie

A foreign beanbag chair greets me in the suite lounge—bright purple, with a squish so deeply satisfying. Like a Willy Wonka x Sophie collab. I stare at it, willing it to answer my questions.

Kit doesn't have the funds. Levi would perish at the sight of it. Does Mia have a secret admirer? Has Ayumi returned from the dead? Has a benevolent soul taken pity on our suffering? Davis … Couldn't be, could it?

It fits snug in the corner of the room, molding to me as I burrow in with my Bible and pens. But as I try to read, my brain keeps sliding back to Graham. The two most confusing days of my life. I shudder, shove it away, and fiddle with a pen.

Sophie, I want you close.

I huff. Isn't that why I'm sitting here?

A nudge. Something like, **Look at it. Face it.**

So I do what any spiritually mature person would do—dig deeper into my pen pouch and pretend I didn't hear it.

But the silence is loud.

Lately I've been having this nightmare where Austin's standing right there but can't hear anything I say. In his kitchen. With the cows. I ramble on and on, and he carries on with his task, completely unaware. It's awful.

What happened? Why was I so crazy?

Unable to shrug it off, a reel runs in my head. Driving through the gate, gripping the wheel. Mom's voice: *Only grief is on the other side.* Austin's hug-fest with his Brunette Stepford family. That look with his dad. My words evaporated. I couldn't function. Everything was heavy. A blur.

The pen stills in my hand. I hang my head.

I was Dark and Twisty?

It's a key that decodes.

Knowing doesn't fix anything, but it helps. Back in the Hundred Acre Wood, I couldn't keep my hands off Austin. I wanted him to lighten the weight. And for a second, he did. Just a second. But then I wanted more. Craved it, like an addict chasing a fix he wouldn't give me. That morning in his room was—

My legs jolt me upright. I can't.

Sophie

I smack my Bible onto the table and collapse back into the beanbag.

Fine.

I let the memories rush in, and I'm nearly crushed under their weight.

I asked you for forgiveness for what we did. Why isn't it over?

"What you did?" the troll answers. *"No. Who you are."*

I flinch.

This isn't helping. I feel so much worse.

I love you. I want you close.

Then, it's like I can see Jesus's eyes on me. Fiery but gentle. Watching me crumpled on this beanbag, waiting for me to look back.

He loves me. Fully.

Maybe ... I've been waiting for him to leave too. To give up on me.

I reach for my Bible, flip back to Psalms.

I'm here. I'm staying. I need you close. You forgive me.

My finger skims, then stills. This one. The one Mia mentioned.

"He does not punish us for all our sins; he does not deal harshly with us, as we deserve. For his unfailing love toward those who fear him is as great as the height of the heavens above the earth. He has removed our sins as far from us as the east is from the west."

My ribs unlock. Something under them fuses back together. And the troll falls silent.

On Friday I cut out of the stairwell early—onto A2. My nerves hum. Maybe this thing with Davis isn't a long-term fix, but the pain management is undeniable. The flirting, the joking, the texting. Shallow, but tremendously distracting.

We've hung out a little every day—MSC, a Taco Bell run. Some of the G3-ers are even easing up on me, mostly for his sake, making room at their tables. Hanging out with him is fun, no pressure, easy. He's so eager. So straightforward.

I stop the first A2-er I pass. "Hey, which room is Davis Powell's?"

The guy stiffens. "Hey."

I huff. Even the A2-ers are loyal to Austin?

"... Is he around?" I press.

"Uh, yeah. West Lounge." He points to the one that would be called the Dark Lounge one floor up. "His room is after that."

"Cool. Thanks."

I stop in the doorway of the lounge. The guys are launching Styrofoam balls across the room. I recognize a few from lunch earlier.

"Sophie Appel," Davis calls across the room. "Who are you looking for?" He grins.

Every eye swings my way.

"Mm. Dontrell Wayne?" I tease, citing one of A2's most campus-famous names. "Have you seen him?" I pretend to look around.

Davis's face falls, hardens. "Nope."

"Ohh," Davis's friends call, smacking him on the arm and throwing pillows.

Yikes. He's mad?

I've never seen Austin self-conscious. Not once. If he hadn't mentioned his freshman year, I'd assume he didn't understand the concept. To think I always took that for granted.

The guys are still watching us like a tennis match.

"Just kidding. I'll be in your room."

"Bro," someone says as I leave. "Isn't that Samwise's girl?"

I hate how much I love that question.

"Not anymore," Davis says.

Not anymore.

More *ohs* and *bros* and dude noises.

"You're brave. He's like twice your weight, dude."

"Yeah, Samwise is jacked."

"And off his face for her."

"I thought you and Samwise were buddies."

"I heard she dumped him hard. Zero warning."

"Savage."

With a whimper-sigh, I lean on the doorframe of the room next door. A guy I assume is Davis's roommate is studying at his desk.

"Hi, I'm Sophie. I'm waiting for Davis." I point back to the lounge.

"Uh-huh." And he's back to his work.

"What happens when he comes back for her?" I hear.

"Bro gets pummeled. That's what happens."

"What is this, 1805?" Davis says. "No one's fighting over a girl. She gets to pick."

He saunters over, his near-constant smile returning. My tension eases in an instant. Look at that. His quick forgiveness earns him a hundred points. And that cologne earns him another five.

"I can get rid of my roommate," he whispers in my ear.

"Eh, I'm not really into assassins."

He chuckles and grabs my hand, intertwining our fingers.

This is new. I want to like it.

"C'mon." Davis steps through the doorway. "Hey, bro, think we could have the room for a bit? I'll owe you one."

I drop his hand, pretending to fix my hair.

His roommate looks between us and rolls his eyes. "Yeah, fine." He drags his books with him and shuts the door on his way out.

I blink at the closed door. That's strictly against Mayberry rules.

Davis turns the lock, as casual as can be, crosses the room to plop down on his cushy blue couch.

I should go unlock it, open the door back. But my legs don't move. My brain doesn't move. Everything's stuck. I just barely stop myself from twirling the piece of hair I grabbed. Maybe just some more information first. "Um. Random question. What are your thoughts on beanbag chairs?"

Not even a flicker of recognition. "I'm firmly pro-beanbag."

"And how was your test?" I stall.

"Better than I thought. C'mon." He pats the cushion next to him.

I wish he'd quit saying that. He says it just like Austin.

When I lower to the sofa, I run my hands over the cushion, expecting the same worn fabric as a certain rust-colored one a floor up. But no.

"Want a shoulder rub?"

"Really?"

He points in front of him. "Have a seat, pretty lady."

I drop to the carpet and move my hair over a shoulder. A back rub. That's so nice.

When his hands move into my hair, I feel like a cheater. But I'm not. I glance at the ceiling as if I have X-ray vision. The one who did this first doesn't want me anymore. I lean back and smile at Davis upside down. He smiles back ...

And leans in for a kiss.

I slump down to miss his lips.

"Oh. Wow. Did I misread that?"

"Um. It's just ... We're—" I motion around his room and between us.

"The RA just left. We're good for a bit."

"Good for what?" I blurt.

"Whatever you want." A line appears between his brows. "Hey, sorry. I thought—Well, you offered to come over here, and then you said you'd be in my room. I kinda thought you wanted to mess around."

My face burns. Did I give him the wrong impression? I flash back to Zoe in the hallway. Is that why Davis's mood improved so quickly? I shift to the sofa next to him, plenty of space between us. "I'm not ... That's not me."

"Isn't it?" the troll replies. My vision darkens.

"Got it. Should we, uh ..." He motions at the door.

"Yeah. Yes."

He opens it, rubbing the back of his neck.

"Hey, Davis?"

"Yeah."

I wave him back to his spot.

He sits, his expression softer.

"Do you have, um, boundaries? Like, physical boundaries?"

He shifts. "Sure."

"And what happens if yours aren't the same as the girl you're with?"

The line between his brows deepens. "I wait till she's ready. Obviously."

"And if she's waiting till marriage?"

He eyes me. "This isn't hypothetical, is it?"

I falter. Because I didn't. But I am again.

"But you didn't," the troll insists. *"You aren't."*

He exhales. "Thing is, around here everybody says they're waiting. Few people mean it."

I gape.

"It's up to each person to decide what's right for them. Sometimes opinions change over time."

My heart hammers. One floor up and one door down, Austin pushed me away over and over again. He loved me, chose me, wanted more—but he kept stopping me.

What happens when you date someone with stronger boundaries than yours? You wait for them to change their mind.

I jerk up from the sofa.

"Sophie? I'm saying it's okay if you're not ready."

What happens if you date someone with fewer boundaries than you? They wait around for you to change your mind. They hope for a change of heart. They "take whatever you're willing to give." That's what Davis said on our date, right?

"This isn't going to work," I announce.

He stands. "All this 'cause I was gonna kiss you? How is that bad?"

Every brain cell begs to find a distraction and never think about this again. To run. It's too tangled up with Austin and what I did and everything I can't think about for one more second.

Please, not this.

But I can't ghost Davis like Austin did to me. I can't withhold an explanation like I did to Leo. He deserves an answer. As I spin around, I draw the courage to meet his gaze.

Give me the words.

"I really like you, but you'd never understand my reasons. I'd always feel like I was letting you down." I can't imagine being the Austin in a relationship. What torture to say no again and again.

I'm dying to rush out before this can drag on, but I hold my ground. Wait for a response. *Come on, Sophie. Be mature.*

He shakes his head, mystified. "What if I promise not to push you?"

"But do you want that? I mean ... everything?"

He softens and steps closer. "Have you looked in a mirror lately? You can't blame a guy for wanting something. But I was raised right. Promise." Hopeful eyes trained on me. Another step.

We could keep it sweet. Innocent. Fun and light. So distracting. Healing, maybe.

He's offering exactly what I want. On my terms. His scent drifts closer.

Gentle fingers brush my side, play with my belt loop. Another inch closer. "Can I take you out? We can talk there if you want. You like sushi?"

Sushi.

His mouth curls into a vulnerable almost smile, and I nearly close the gap. It would be so easy to lean in. To blur the lines and call it clarity. Can I afford to let this opportunity go?

My gaze drops to his lips again, and they break into that crooked smile.

Nope, nope, nope.

"Sorry, I can't." I jerk past him and bolt out.

Jogging down the hall, I expect regret over Davis. Or relief. Something. But there's nothing. No ache, no loss.

Only the bandage tearing off. Air stinging the raw wound beneath. A wound that refuses to be ignored.

CHAPTER FIFTY-SEVEN

Sophie

When I step off A2, the door slams behind me, echoing up and down the cinder-block stairwell. Austin's right there. One floor up, first door on the left. Probably sprawled across his perfect couch. Or buried in homework. I should keep walking. Instead, my feet inch toward the stairs to Flooders.

I need to tell him I'm sorry. Not just for that morning in his room, but for all of it. For pushing him, for pouting, when he was trying so desperately to obey Jesus. I take a step up. I need to tell him.

Help. Like my spirit prayed it for me.

He said to wait till Austin's ready. I have to run—not up those stairs, but away from the urge to storm Flooders, to crash through his doorway. Maybe this is the kind of running I'm actually supposed to do.

Austin, running from his room that morning.

Austin, making me talk instead of kissing it better.

Austin, fighting our chemistry with Conclusion Kisses, fire extinguisher in hand.

He ran.

The door rattles above me. Mateo speeds down the first half flight, then slows when he sees me. "Hey."

I freeze. Caught. He knows why I'm never on Flooders anymore. Maybe he doesn't know-know.

"Been a while." He brushes dark hair from his face. "You okay?"

My feet shift backward. Away. I'm supposed to wait. My body carries me down the stairs with Mateo, like muscle memory. Like I did a thousand times before, except with Austin's giant hand wrapped around mine, grinning like a fool.

"Yeah," I lie. "How is ..."

Mateo eyes me. "You did a number on him."

I swallow.

"An A2-er now, huh?"

"Uh, no. It's over."

"Good. Give Samwise another chance."

I stutter. The Flooders don't even know that he dumped me? And this from *Mateo*?

"Why do you care?"

"You were good for him. And he deserves to be happy. Unlike some people, Samwise works himself to the bone to earn what he has. Had. You included."

I meet his gaze, speechless.

Outside, he aims toward the gym. "See you around."

"See ya," I mumble.

Kit meets me halfway across the field. "Sophs! Are—hey, what's wrong?"

I stare at her as I speed walk. Should I tell her what happened with Davis? Maybe she'd understand.

The troll scoffs. *"She told you not to go out with him."*

She's my handiwork. And so are you.

"Did you find Davis?"

I decode Kit's facial expression. Now she's feigning nonchalance? Girl's been weird all day.

"Yeah." My words tumble out. "It was dumb to assume he'd be like Leo and Austin. It's not like this school is Hogwarts and only accepts magical dudes."

"Davis is a Muggle ... What did he do?"

"He tried to kiss me. And ..." With a flip of my hand, I continue my motor-memory march.

She scurries to catch up. "Are you okay? Was it scary?"

Shoot—forgot to be sensitive about this subject. I jerk back to her. "I'm sorry. No. I'm fine. He's very respectful ... in his way. The thing is, I thought Austin and Leo were opposites, but they're mostly not. Just in these, like, minor ways. But they're so similar in the ways that actually matter."

Leo. I'm so sorry. He was so good, so gentle. And how did I thank him? I dragged him around and wanted someone else and never appreciated him for a second.

Give him someone who deserves him. Someone good and sweet and devoted to you, like he is.

Kit tries to form words. "You're reconsidering Leo? 'Cause—"

"Huh? No."

"Want me to come with you? Where are you going?"

"No. You go visit your man." I swivel back to her, step closer. "I bet he never gives you a hard time about not kissing, huh?"

She blinks. "No. He doesn't. Why?"

"Why is Levi cool with waiting to kiss? That's sort of extreme, right? And he wasn't exactly raised like that."

Kit bites her lip, but her bright eyes drill into mine with intention—so different from last semester. "Honestly, I wonder sometimes. I guess he just wants to be with me. He doesn't want to push me away."

"He knows you won't change your mind, right?"

"I sure hope so." Her brows raise. "Do you think otherwise?"

I nod like a bobblehead on the dash—then switch to the

Hawaiian dancer when I realize what she actually asked. "No. He fully respects your faith and your choices. If I had to guess, it's that he won't bet against you—he just assumes you're probably right." A breeze kicks up, blowing my hair in my face. I bat it away. "Yeah. Soon it'll be his rule too."

I've rendered her speechless.

I can't believe I bombed what I had with Austin. So obnoxiously happy and I didn't even know how good I had it. Didn't know the half of it.

My feet carry me toward Griffin, but I stop, spinning back to Kit. "What are the odds that Leo and Austin would both be so ... good? And Levi too?"

"They all love Jesus enough to make radical choices." She flicks a glare toward Albert. "Usually."

I nod slowly. "There's always an ulterior motive for being good."

"Yeah. I guess there is."

"What if Levi were doing the no-kissing thing with you instead of for you?"

Her Disney eyes fill. "That would take a lot of pressure off."

How I wish I would have done that for Austin. "Go ask him. Maybe he already is." I shoo her toward Flooders. "He's a radically good dude." He and his roommate both.

I don't realize I'm running until I burst into my room. I barely shut the door before my knees hit the floor and a sob rips through me.

"Sophs, you in here?"

Mia barges in and nearly plows me over. Without missing a beat, she lifts me by the shoulders and steers me to bed. Unties my shoes, tosses my socks aside, finds a scrunchie on the bedside table, pulls my hair into a bun. Tucks me in, like she's done this before. "Tea," she announces.

I stare at the table. She already returned Savannah's mugs for me.

When she returns, she sets a mug on a stack of old papers and leans against her bed with her own. The one whose own blood tries to kill her is the steady one. "Sad is expected, but this seems like more than sad. Is it time to call your counselor?"

Mashing my pillow into the corner, I curl up with my tea. Hibiscus. "Yeah, maybe. And thank you. This is perfect."

"Always." She takes a careful sip, well before it's finished steeping. "The Davis thing isn't helping, is it?"

"It's over."

She exhales. "You barely avoided my come-to-Jesus on that one."

I trace the rim of the mug. "Have you talked to Austin?"

"Have you?"

"He's never going to speak to me again."

"No one else believes that." She rubs her forehead. "I went over there earlier, half planning to punch him in the teeth."

A chuckle squeaks past my throat. She's such a firecracker.

"I won't try to decide for him if he should have dumped you or not," she says, "but forgiveness isn't optional for Jesus followers. It's part of the deal."

My smile dies. "I don't deserve it."

"No, you don't," the troll says.

"That's the thing about forgiveness. It doesn't matter." She tilts her head. "But you do deserve it. You loved him and took care of him the best you knew how."

I squeeze the mug against my chest. It burns my skin, but I need the warmth. "You know what I did. That was not my best."

"I meant the rest of the time." Her voice softens. "You're right, that moment wasn't okay. For either of you. But it doesn't define your entire relationship. None of us knows what we're doing, Sophs. All we can do is ask Jesus for help and grow along the way."

I stare into my cup.

"I'm worried he's on a pedestal. To the point that you think his behavior represents God's. It doesn't. He's just a dude."

There is now no condemnation for those who are in Christ Jesus.

"He wants me close ..."

"He wants you close."

"What did ... Austin say?"

"Ran into Levi outside Albert before I could get there. He was having none of my tough-love plan. Insisted Austin wasn't ready." Mia glances at the door. "I shouldn't tell you this, but Austin still lies on his couch all day. It's been three weeks, and he isn't even showing for soccer practices. He skipped Donut Thursday. Dude couldn't rally to step outside and receive a free donut?"

My stomach churns.

"Levi confirmed—silently, of course—that Austin isn't helping anyone or planning pranks. He grunts more than speaks." She watches me. "You know how much he must hate himself to deteriorate from Thor, protector of the universe, to a stain on his couch? Sophie."

"Please stop." My voice is barely a whisper.

I did that. I brought that shame on him. *I'm sorry. I'm so sorry.* I squeeze my eyes shut, as if it will all go away.

"Working out. Refusing donuts," she mumbles. "He can't even do Fat Thor right."

"Mia."

"Fine."

I shift to stare out the window. "Does it have to be a counselor?"

Her voice softens. "I don't know. Kit needed that."

"Yeah."

Well? Dr. Shannon wouldn't get it. Not anymore. I don't think you're her Snorkel. And if she hates Levi ... she'll just see this like Mom would. But I don't want to be stupid about it. What do I do?

With a heavy swallow, I straighten. I think I know my next

step. It's too late for someone to whisper what's true into my ear every night, but it's not too late to find out what those things were. I don't know how to do any of this. How to be real-free. The way God intended. But maybe I can learn.

I turn back to Mia. "What are you doing for spring break?"

Time to subject myself to another home sweet home.

CHAPTER FIFTY-EIGHT

Austin

"Is Kit okay?" I ask Levi.

I called her last night to apologize, but she could've lied to make me feel better. She would.

"She's fine," he says.

"I'm sorry I snapped like that."

"She pushed you too far. But don't you dare yell at her again."

"I won't."

I thought he was fixing to leave for chapel, but he's still hovering by the door, antsy.

"What's with you?" I ask.

He sets his phone down on his desk. "Sophie asked to meet after chapel."

I break his intense gaze. "Oh perfect. I'll come along, and we can all hold hands while we kumbaya and process our feelings." I drop my elbow over my face as I lie on my couch. Like a blob of uselessness.

The click of Levi's Tic Tac box says he's still standing there.

"There's no use, bro," I say. "May as well bail and avoid that awkward conversation."

"There's no use because you're never taking her back?"

As if it would go like that. As if she should even want that.

I peek at him. He's staring me down—completely over it. Fair enough.

This is gonna suck. But if I don't nail the we're-done monologue, he'll never let it go. If I can just sell the lie, he'll stop trying to push us back together. He'll want better than that for his friend. I just have to sound bitter enough. Final enough. Lock it in like there's no coming back. I curl into a ball in preparation. He and Kit deserve each other.

"We were in the best part," I start.

Levi lowers to his desk chair, forearms on his knees like he does. "The best part?"

"Falling in love and all the feels. If we can burn it to the ground during the best part, imagine during a hard part—"

He interrupts, squinting. "You were a lovesick puppy, barely dog-paddling enough to keep your head above water."

"Nice."

"And you said Sophie was crying the whole weekend. It was clearly a hard part for her too. I mean, The Farm is a whole thing."

"Do what now?"

He leans back in his chair with a sigh. "We're drawn to what we know, what feels familiar, even if it's dysfunctional. Your house freaked me out the first time too. I can't even imagine meeting your parents as their Golden Boy's girlfriend."

The word *golden* slaps me in the face. I rub my eyes and scooch to a seated position. "But my family loves you. And you didn't act weird."

"You know I'm good at faking it."

Am I really so oblivious?

"It's so ... peaceful there," he says. "Like it's pretend. An alternate reality or something. And your parents—dude, they're obsessed with you. I didn't want to know what I never had."

"Peaceful? It's just a house. Janie picks fights. Mama controls everything. There's poison ivy."

"Oh come *on*."

"What?" I spit. He never talks to me like that. "You grew up in a castle. How are we having this conversation right now?"

"Money doesn't buy peace. Listen, you had an idyllic upbringing. Like a banana split. So sweet, but overwhelming for breakfast."

I study him. "A banana split for breakfast." Is that why she kept talking about the cows? But I don't ask—no more of this. I slide onto my back and hide under my arm. Must finish the speech. "It's water under the bridge. We learn and we move on. It's over."

"I'd be livid too to have my physical vulnerability trampled on. But you are not innocent."

My shoulders hunch in. Nothing could be more obvious. She was a breeze, and I blew it into a hurricane. Innocence I should have protected. But I didn't.

"Your relationship isn't irredeemable, Samwise. She loves you. She looks really sorry. To my knowledge, this is the first time she's ever broken your trust after months of building it. You're both Jesus's disciples and growing all the time."

Every word is a punch to the gut. I hold my arm over my eyes as a shield. "I don't want anything with her anymore. I don't."

"I see." He pauses. "I'm going to talk to her anyway."

I cut a glance at him. How dare he not believe my performance. I endured all that for nothing?

"Remember when I panicked and thought Kit was going to be Genevieve: The Sequel? I had washed my hands of the whole thing, and you got her to the lobby. You tricked me into seeing her again."

I pull up on an elbow. "She complimented your watch, bro. This isn't that."

"M-hm." He folds his arms.

"Hey!" I'm on my feet. I don't know what I'm going to do. I won't punch him, but I might push him.

He stands too, with humility. He'd let me hit him, I can tell. "I love you, buddy. And talking to Sophie is what's best for you."

I glare at him. "Fine!" I'm sick of being the nice guy. But I'm sick of being a jerk too. Lying to my closest buddy. Yelling at Kit. I'm a monster.

"Let's head out. You've already skipped your three chapels this semester. You won't want to write another paper because you couldn't go sit in a chair for an hour."

My scowl deepens. I have nothing clever.

"If we leave now, we can sit in our spot. You can refuse to look Sophie's direction the whole time. That'll show her."

I do hate writing papers.

"Fine."

But I still can't bear Sophie in my line of sight. I'll have to sit in the front with the rebels and loners.

CHAPTER FIFTY-NINE

Sophie

"I'll get to the point," I start. "I need another chance with Austin. What would convince him to talk to me?" I shift in my café chair, on a rocket shooting from vulnerable to humiliated.

Levi drops his arms to his knees and examines the coffee-shop carpet.

What was I thinking meeting at MSC? The vibe is all wrong. The sounds—students laughing and chatting and calling across the cavernous atrium. I have ten minutes before I have to leave for class, and this is my only hope.

"Hello?"

He lifts his head to frown at me.

"He was praying," Kit says.

"Oh. Sorry."

"I want that too," he finally says. "But I think you're asking the wrong question."

"He's so mad."

Levi lets out a slow breath. "No."

I give a nod ... until the word clicks in my brain—"No? Of course he is. Besides, he avoids me with impressive commitment."

"I don't think he's angry at you at all."

Kit nods, and everything goes fuzzy.

The puzzle pieces fall apart, and I don't know how they fit back together. "Then ... what?"

Levi's eyes meet Kit's.

"If he's not ready to talk," Levi says, "it's not my place to speak for him."

"Is he okay?"

He hesitates. "Yes?"

My eyes start to fill. "Do you know what happened?"

"I know his side."

Squeezing my knees beneath the table, I press the tears away. "I was kind of ... broken, a total mess. That whole time I was there. I screwed up. Bad. I think I thought ... I dunno." Why did I think this was a good idea? And with Kit here? But I need his help. I kick the rest of the words out. "I think I thought it was the only thing that could make me feel better."

Sadness fills his eyes. No judgment though. "The first time at The Farm was hard for me too."

"Wait, really?"

He studies me. Heavy on the eye contact today. I flit to Kit to tone down the intensity. No idea how she stares in those eyes all the time.

"His life is weird," he says. "In a good way."

"So weird."

Kit ping-pongs between us, baffled.

He half-smiles at her. "Kit's house is probably the same way. Without the cows."

I bite together, pained. "For sure."

She tilts her head but doesn't interrupt.

"We fed them Honey Buns," I explain to Levi.

He nods slowly. "I think this goes without saying, but you're not going to find another guy like Samwise. He's at his very worst right now, but he's still, without a doubt, the best dude out there."

I take a shaky breath and squeeze the arms of my chair. "Weird question. Do you know if Austin's family knows we broke up?"

His expression hardens behind a poker face.

I reach a hand out, like *Don't worry*. "I won't do anything stupid. I just need to know if Janie knows. Surely they do, right? It would be so out of character—"

"Yes, they all know."

Janie knows and she's still updating her playlist every few days with new songs, responding to my additions like the playlist is a living thing. "Did he—"

"No more questions about that."

I agree quickly.

His jaw shifts in the silence. I don't interrupt this time. "He's kind of in a cast right now—resetting, so he can grow back healthier, I hope. If you want him back, you will have to earn his trust again—I don't know how—but I'm not convinced that's the main obstacle here. Before you even get to the trust part, you need to consider something." More eye contact. "He needs someone to take care of him. You were on the right track when you whisked him away for wings and football. I know you did a lot of things for him, but he's nearly incapable of self-care."

That day in Dallas. His lips had curled into a sweet smile while he chewed, watching me. A lump comes to my throat. I love him. I miss him so much. But I was the problem. Should I even be trying to get him back?

"Dude's a superhero," Levi continues. "He'll spend his whole life taking care of people to his own detriment. Everyone else in his life will take, take, take. He needs someone to show him that he's already enough, someone to be a rejuvenating place for him ..."

The troll laughs, sharp and cruel. Rejuvenating? Not even

close. I'm exhausting. Too much. Loud. Dramatic. *Calm down*, people say. *Chill out. Take a seat.*

"... Someone to deeply appreciate him for the lunatic he is."

A half laugh slips through my tight throat.

He squints, waiting.

"Maybe ..." A swallow scrapes down. "Maybe I should let him go. I want him to be so happy. I've always known I'm not ..." A breath, a blink—still not composed. Kit rubs my back, which only draws the tears closer to the surface. "I'm not as good as him, as selfless. I'm a lot. I'm loud and ... and restless. I'm new at being a Christian, and I have no idea what I'm doing most of the time."

They're both frowning. The silence begs to be filled.

"Before, I didn't even think we could be together long term because we didn't want the same things. But the cows showed me they're not the problem. I can't believe I'm saying this, but I love those cows. And the cornbread."

Kit and Levi watch me, trying to follow along.

"What I'm saying is ... I don't want to pick my life based on bonnets or no bonnets. And even if I did, the dancing and the creek and the fishing—those are all part of it. All part of Austin. Why would I be mad about the things that made him who he is? The things I actually love too?" Trying to slow down, I pick at my sleeves. "I used to think that I wouldn't make it two weeks in a small town, but who cares where I am if I'm not with him? Anything else sounds stupid. Hollow. Pointless. I'd live anywhere with Austin. Anywhere." My nose runs, and I dig in my pocket for a tissue, like an old man with a hanky. A rambling old man.

What do I do? Please help. Please.

Their frowns have morphed to matching little smiles.

"You two." I roll my eyes. They're so much alike. And yet ... they're not. Like she said.

"A verse popped in my head," Kit says. "Can I share it?"

"Shoot."

"'But he said to me, "My grace is sufficient for you, for my power is made perfect in weakness." Therefore I will boast all the more gladly of my weaknesses, so that the power of Christ may rest upon me.'"

We fall silent as the verse shoots through my veins.

I glance up—and can't help but tease, "Levi, you're fully drooling."

He snaps his mouth shut and drags his eyes away from an oblivious Kit. "What? It's like Prince Caspian and Hermione Granger had a daughter."

Her eyes sparkle. He intertwines their fingers, and I have to look away. A group of girls walks by, eyeing them and whispering. Someone skips from the other direction, laughing as she drags her smiling dude by the hand.

It's like Levi knows what I'm thinking, because his voice lowers. "If Samwise comes around, I know you'll treat him well, sacrifice for him in return, be worthy of his trust." His protective gaze penetrates my soul. "I wouldn't trust him with anyone else."

My jaw drops.

"But I honestly don't know if you two will get another chance at this. And, in my experience, God's not in the business of Band-Aids." Levi gestures between he and Kit. "We tried with Samwise and got nowhere."

Kit jerks her gaze to her shoes. Levi taps her knee, and she gives a tight head shake. What's that about?

I straighten in my seat, reset. Must process later. "Next subject. I have some big favors to ask."

Levi turns wary. "Go on."

"Kit, how would your family feel about the six of us visiting for spring break?"

Her eyes light up like blue flying saucers. "Really? Levi already bought me a flight home. I've been begging him to come with me." She squeezes his leg. "I'm dying for him to meet my family."

He softens, kisses her hand.

"It would be so fun to have everybody. Please come."

"But your parents," I remind her.

"Oh, I'll ask, but they'd love it. Sometimes fifteen teenage boys sleep in the basement. We'd be tame in comparison."

Levi turns back to me, poker faced. "How are you getting Samwise there?"

"I'll buy us all flights. Oh, you mean, how will I convince him to go on a trip with me? You'd have to do that."

Levi's jaw works on overdrive. "Alright. And Haymitch is going home."

"Oh. Bummer. Makes sense though."

Kit bends toward me. "I love this idea so much, but what's the strategy? I thought we decided only God can do the work."

"Right. I've been thinking, and Austin can get a real rest if your house has the vibe his does, maybe more since he won't feel the need to pull down trees and stuff. I asked way too much of him while we were together, and whether he comes around or not, I really want to do what I can to reverse that."

Levi smiles.

"But it's also for me, for a related reason," I admit. "I need to take lessons. From your mom."

"Wait. Lessons?" Kit asks.

"Lessons. I've heard enough to know she knows what she's doing. I need to talk to her about snorkeling. And the whispers." How to explain it? "I need her to teach me how to avoid repeating my mistakes. And what I'm missing. How she does Jesus Life."

Levi's eyes speak, but I can't translate that language. "Your idea is brilliant, Sophie. I need lessons too."

"Wait, what?" Kit says. "You guys don't need lessons."

"Yeah, yeah." I wave her off. "I didn't grow up with a model for this stuff. And I don't know what I don't know until I've already blown it up. For nineteen years you've watched your functional parents do life, so you just naturally know what to do next."

"She is talking to me, right?" she says. "I don't know what I'm doing. Everyone was ready to strangle me last semester."

"She's right," Levi says to her. "You and Samwise have a leg up on us. We have a lot to learn."

"They'd be thrilled to talk to you both, but they're just regular people."

"I know," we say in unison.

"Your mom's gonna judge me so hard," I say. "But that'll have to be okay."

She squeezes my arm. "Actually, she'll understand. You'll see."

Levi rises. He must have a class next too. "I'll work on my part. For both our sakes, I hope he can be convinced. But don't buy plane tickets."

"It's less than two weeks away. For spring break. To Denver. It'll cost a fortune and more every day." I'll be getting a scathing text from Mom about this. I shudder. Still worth it.

"I'll cover any increase. Don't buy tickets."

I let out my breath, defeated.

Leo's profile catches my eye from a distance. He's leaning against a wall, more confident than I've ever seen him, grinning ear to ear. Pushing to my feet, I crane my neck to see around the tables between us. Who is he smiling at like that?

"What?" Kit asks me.

Ayumi.

Dainty, shy, surrounded by grinning G2-ers.

I meet Kit's gaze. She gives a small nod—hesitant, knowing. I can't explain it, but happy tears come to my eyes. God is so much better at this than I am.

CHAPTER SIXTY

Austin

"Finn. How is she today?" I shoulder his door closed behind me for privacy. Like my arm couldn't handle it.

He launches a ball toward the basket on his wall, and I catch the rebound by reflex.

"Seems okay. Less groggy-looking lately. No singing yet."

I release a breath and underhand him the ball. "Kit's still looking out for her?"

"They're practically attached at the hip."

"Good. What else does she need?"

"Between Kit and Mia, I can't imagine anything. Got that tea delivered, so their floor is stocked for a while."

I send a smile. "'Preciate that, buddy." I go to open the door.

"So"—his shoulder twitches—"Davis Powell ..."

I suppress a shudder. "I don't want details."

A quick nod. "Should I keep this up?"

“Yeah. If you don’t mind. I’m gonna order some markers for you to smuggle into her lounge.”

“Got it.”

“And, Finn? Really. Thank you.”

“Dude, stop. Pretty sure I owe you, like, my firstborn by now.”

I step to clap his shoulder and then escape to the hallway.

Back in my room, Levi’s waiting for me at his desk. “You’ll never guess what Sophie had to say.”

I groan. “Not this again.” Exhausted from my last conversation, I fall back on the couch in loser position. But this is my last day of moping. Tomorrow, I’m picking a fight with the crusty old boxing bag in the gym. That’s gotta be more productive than lying here like roadkill. Or punching my nosy roommate, who still won’t quit. “She’s with Powell now, so—”

He drops a brick of a book on the desk. “No, you idiot. That’s already over.”

I smother the relief like a house fire and risk a glance up. He’s rarely this harsh.

“She said she wants us to take you to Colorado for spring break. Never knew we already bought tickets, remember? She wants you to have a ‘real rest.’” Air quotes. “She’s still trying to take care of you.”

A hysterical laugh bubbles out as I dig in my pocket for my phone. “I can’t believe I forgot. I owe you for those blasted tickets. I might could pay you now since …” I trail off and tap my bank app.

“Put that away.” Confident as a senator.

I send him a glare, like *Don’t boss me around*.

“You’re not paying me back. But I do need you to get on that plane.”

“Is *she* going?”

“Yes.”

He cannot be serious. “I’d sooner go to Mars with no return flight. Grow potatoes like Matt Damon.”

"Funny. After we get back, you can quit the fam for good if you need to. No grief from me. But I need to speak with Kit's father, and I'd rather not meet him solo."

"I thought this was about—"

"Please, buddy? I hate asking when you're in a bad spot."

Wait … "Jeeves. Are you gonna ask her dad *the* question?"

"I don't know yet."

I wanna be happy for him. I really do. Hands dragging down my face, I let out a breath-long grunt and run out of air. I'd hate myself for letting him down, but I'm not that guy anymore. The selfless guy. The good friend.

I close my eyes to pray, but … what? Where do I even start?

Levi's voice drops. "Listen, I need backup. Sophie's meet-the-parents …"

I peek through my fingers. I've never seen him feeling this small.

"Okay. I'll go."

Oddly, agreeing to help finally moves the dial—like something inside me shifts back into place.

"Thanks, bro." He's audibly relieved. "I really appreciate you having my back."

I lift myself to standing and plod down the hall. "Haymitch."

He's hunched over his brightly lit desk, but one look at me and he snaps his books shut. "Samwise." A good-friend move.

I plunk down onto his sofa. "Jeeves still wants us to go to Colorado for spring break. Meet the parents and all that."

His brow lifts.

"Yeah, traveling with her sounds about as fun as a root canal."

No one is amused with my dramatics.

"It's a big deal for Jeeves, so I need to suck it up and make it happen. I think I can survive if I can stay in a little box." I motion with my hands. A whole week … "The thing is, I'm crazy right now, and I need someone to shield me in my box as much as to shield everyone else from me." Last year's Haymitch would've ducked out of the drama. Now he's up for it. I know he is.

"Wish I could help. Wasn't gonna wait till May to get back to Mobile, so Jeeves never bought me a ticket."

"Who's gonna keep me in check if I'm being a punk? Who's gonna make sure Jeeves and everybody get what they need?"

He studies me. "You mean, who's gonna be you?"

I frown. Is that what I do?

What I did maybe.

"I'm sorry, Samwise. You know all of us will love you no matter what. All of us."

I pretend not to follow his meaning. "You're good, buddy. Can't miss a chance to see your woman." I clap him on the shoulder on my way out.

Better quit my moping early and hit that boxing corner. Time to figure out how to punch stuff.

Sophie

At a *ding* I whip my wrist up to read the text on my watch. It's just Levi. You'd think after almost three weeks I would quit doing that.

LEVI

I bought us five plane tickets.

Austin said yes. Levi is a miracle worker.

Wait, no. You are. Thank you.

Send me a request on Venmo

I'll cover flights and the SUV. You could take care of groceries for Kit's family and our agenda?

Well, that's generous of him.

Super nice of you. How did you convince Austin to come? Is there hope?

No more or less than before. He's coming because this trip is important to me.

I deflate. Of course. Austin is the best of friends, even with smoke shooting from his ears. Or whatever's going on over there.

I guess I'm about to find out soon.

CHAPTER SIXTY-ONE

Austin

Levi said the crew is rewatching *Now You See Me* tonight. At nine I drag my coward butt to MSC, banking on mid-movie focus. But the second I plop down—as far as possible from Sophie—everyone hops to attention, like *We're super normal and welcoming!* Pats on the back, all of that. I'm shocked I haven't been roasted yet. This bunch usually pounces on anything remotely off, so I either look pitiful or scary. Toss-up which is worse. But then ... silence—the opposite of normal.

I pass Haymitch a bag of snacks. He digs inside like a four-year-old spotting sprinkles and comes up with the box of Cheez-Its I bought for him. Hands the carrot sticks and hummus to Levi, our resident weirdo. Then the tortilla chips and nuked white queso go down the row.

What? Everybody likes queso.

I yank the bill of my hat down. The less peripheral vision I have, the better. Doesn't help though—her gaze burns a hole through my hoodie. I absolutely cannot let myself look that direction.

If this is trip prep, it's already backfiring. I'll be out of here well before the credits.

Sophie

I can't sit still. Austin slumps in his seat and shoves his sleeves past his elbows, like he forgot he doesn't wear his uniform anymore. Too bad he looks just as good in sweats.

Is he okay? What does the queso mean? We're all wondering, because no one's talking at Dave Franco or the guy who played Mark Zuckerberg in that other movie. No "Haymitch" cracks about Woody Harrelson. No banter, no teasing. Nobody wants to scare off the stray cat who's finally licking up the milk left out for him. Except he's not a kitten. He's a saber-toothed tiger, and this sighting is as rare as it is dangerous. Not for them, but for me. I cram a chip into my mouth and sit on my hands before they do something stupid.

We're in the same smallish space for the first time since that morning at his house. My resolve crumbles with every glance, but he hasn't turned his head once. I may as well be invisible. Like at home with my parents. Like in those dreams. The worst feeling in the world.

My usual solution for invisibility is looking my best. My parents care about that. They're proud of me when I look nice. The girls in high school squealed over new skirts and boots and makeup. But here, a few seats from Austin, it's obvious: trying for pretty makes no difference where it actually counts. Cute clothes and hairstyles will get me nowhere with him. The beauty he saw in me wasn't a prize. It was a responsibility that pressed on his chest. A risk more than a reward.

Somehow it all works in reverse. The time he was most tempted, I looked my worst—wild hair piled on my head, no makeup, pajamas. My gut twists at the memory. His eyes danced around me like I was a work of art.

Why do we girls try so hard? Maybe it earns us some short-lived attention, but it wedges into our friendships. We scramble to win beauty like it's a competition, but guys just like who they like.

Austin liked me. He fell in love with me. He could have won over nearly anyone, and he chose me.

But I turned beauty into leverage. And burned the rest to the ground.

Tension coils in me—the impulse to plant myself in front of him, spill every apology, promise I'll never do it again. But I know better. It won't help. Instead I jerk out my phone and jab at Janie's playlists. Reciting the songs in my head loosens my grip.

"Closer" by Sanctus Real—saying yes to whatever grows my love for Jesus.

"Clear the Stage" by Jimmy Needham, especially the bridge—destroying any idol I've made out of Austin.

"Cloud and Fire" by Josiah Queen—a love song for my Guide in the wilderness.

I know them by heart. Shuffled with my favorite hymns, I've had them on repeat like a lifeline. Or rather, as a rope to the Lifeline. To the Snorkel. A reset of my perspective. A reminder of who he is and who he says I am. That I can choose to keep him close. That he wants that as much as ever. I bury my head in my knees and pray-sing silently. Austin won't even look at me, but Jesus is using his sister to throw me that rope. His sense of humor maybe.

Firmer in my resolve, I text Kit and Mia. I'm not watching this movie anyway.

Make it stop

MIA

Think his chair will be singed when he gets up?

Prob. He is Hades from Hercules right now

MIA

100 percent

KIT

But that's a love fire, not a hate fire.

Don't

KIT

Ok. I'm sorry.

You think so?

KIT

Yeah, I do. But that doesn't mean he'll drop the villain era act.

MIA

What Kit said.

Spring break should be interesting

When I laugh at Kit's exaggerated grimace, I feel it—his gaze. I whip around, but too late. Just the quick jerk of his head. He looked.

Austin

The movie pauses. Huh?

Mia prances to the door, remote in hand, chin held high. This cannot be good.

"I'm interrupting our scheduled programming because we're going to love on he who wishes not to be named."

I leap from my chair and beeline to the door, but she's already standing guard. I'm incarcerated.

"I want everyone—except she who may as well be named—to

say one thing you admire about Austin. Unless you want in, Sophs."

My head jerks forward. Admire? About me? "Have you lost your mind? I'm trying to lay low here."

No one listens. They argue about who's first.

Mia claps her hands. "We'll start here closest to me. Haymitch? One thing for now."

Everyone watches him stand like he's giving a toast. I spin, wishing a magician's exit would appear—smoke bomb, trapdoor, whatever.

"Samwise, my friend. If I can only pick one thing, I'll say your faith is inspirin'. How you pray at the gym is the coolest thing I've ever seen. Or heard, I guess."

Shoot. Didn't realize those prayers were audible.

"I never thought to use my gym time for the Lord. You're killin' it, bro."

Except, not anymore. Didn't think it was possible, but my heart breaks further. "Thanks, buddy," I mutter.

Levi rises. "Samwise, you're the most sacrificial person I've ever met, always putting yourself last, never wanting recognition or rewards. You're so much like Jesus."

Not anymore. But something inside says I could be again. Unwelcome tears threaten, and I force them down. "Thank you," I manage.

Kit's next, smiling big. "Austin, I see how you take care of Levi and Haymitch and all the Flooders. You know what they need before they do. I want to be more like you."

That one sticks. Fills in a crack in my heart. I can't speak. Just a thankful nod.

"That's my seat." Mia oozes with authority. "I admire that you're a humble leader. Everyone likes you, but you never let it go to your head."

Another crack fills. I try to smile my thanks.

You're still taking care of me? The way I've been?

Levi raises a hand, teasing. "Excuse me, that was two compliments. It was a challenge to limit to one, and you cheated."

Mia lifts a brow. "May the well-liked portion be expunged from the record, Mr. Secretary."

"Thank you," he says, with one of his single nods.

I shake my head. These crazies. They're the best around.

But Sophie stands, and I panic.

I shoot a silent, pitiful plead to Mia. She lets me through. The door doesn't close behind me.

"We're doing Sophie next," Mia announces.

I could hug her for loving on Sophie, but my legs burst into a jog. Out of the building. I just ... can't.

We leave tomorrow. Mia's stunt yesterday proved it—my hideout clock's expired. I've been parked on top of my desk for twenty minutes—phone in hand, text drafted, back of my head beating the window—trying to work up the guts to send it to Sophie.

I need to pray. I know I do. But it feels like whispering through a locked door. The desk creaks as I shift. *C'mon, Scott, just do it. This isn't about you.*

Hand through my hair, grip my neck. Sneak a glance at the ceiling.

Um. Hey.

So, Levi needs this. Help him? And help me be there for him?

Deep breath. Closed-eye tap: Send.

> This trip is important to Jeeves. I don't want to foul it up with awkwardness.

Phone clunks down. I shove it under some papers—

And jump at a *ding*.

SOPHIE

> How can I help?

What?!

My insides twist. I dig my palms into my eyes like I can hold myself together.

How can she help? ... How?

She could wear an invisibility cloak. Promise not to sing. Hate me. But she'd still be Sophie. And I'd still be ... this. Not who I thought I was. Not what she needs.

I squeeze my phone, try to crush it all down. Why did I text her again? Worst idea I've ever had.

Can we meet up?

Can't do that

Can we eat dinner at the same time?

No

My nos are flying. Bizarre.

I squirm on the desk, thumbs typing.

Just pretend I'm not there. Do your normal thing

You don't need to get quiet just cause I'm in the room

K. I'm so sorry Austin. I made a terrible mistake and I'm so sorry.

Also

You're being awful. We both messed up and you should've talked to me before disappearing.

Last thing. You've undone so much of my mom's influence. Even if you quit me forever I can't regret knowing you. You helped me see myself like God does, to believe what he says, and what it means to give up anything to be like him.

Tears crowd my vision. My thumbs hover, begging to spill my guts. To beg for forgiveness, to lavish the praise she deserves. But if I reply—even a fraction—she'll read between the lines. She might even try to fix it. Might not keep the buffer we need, especially this week, in the same house. If she knew how much I love her, how much I long for her, would she try? Would she corner me, make me look her in the eyes? I couldn't control it. Couldn't take care of her. Couldn't make sure she gets what she needs. I'd drag her back to me and my mess. And we'd end up here all over again. Or worse, she'd end up stuck with this broken disaster. Someone who can't even take care of himself. Someone who can't be trusted.

Desperation slams through me. To see her again. To beg for another shot. One more minute, then I'd let go.

So I chuck my phone across the room—straight into Levi's trash can. As if that could undo the other thing I trashed.

Didn't help.

I hop down, fish it out, power it off, drop it back in. There.

Levi clears his throat from the couch. "Halfback pass? Good aim, iffy form." His eyes are heavy, but his mouth quirks.

I send him a head shake. "Receivers. Always divas. Do I get a carry-on tomorrow, or is this one of those backpack-only airlines?"

"Yes, carry-on. But I'm pretty sure you have enough baggage, buddy."

I almost smile.

Headphones. Shoes. Run it off, then pack later.

"Can I borrow your phone for an hour while I run? I'm not turning that thing back on."

He hands it over without hesitation. What a friend.

CHAPTER SIXTY-TWO

Austin

Kit's house sits on a street where the trees still hold their ground against the houses. Basketballs echo. Families pass on the sidewalk with their dogs and strollers. Like a neighborhood you'd see on TV, but Colorado-flavored. The Talbots are great. I twitch every time they insist we call them Chelsea and Archie, but it's cool how they treat us like adults. Kit's brothers, Mav and Grey, are hilarious, and we've already adopted them as Junior Flooders. They'd fit right in at Mayberry—true pranksters.

It's nearly midnight now, and I'm still staring at the ceiling. Levi is passed out next to me. I have this feeling that I should talk to Archie one-on-one, but I don't know if it's the Holy Spirit's leading. Or if he even does that for me anymore. Either way I might get brave here soon. Archie said he'd love to chat if we ever want to bug him during his workday—just look for his office door open. Extremely cool of him.

The first day has been better than expected. I try not to avoid

Sophie unless she's alone. But that means I have to see her constantly—in the airport, down the hall, at breakfast. It's like stepping into the ring with my hands tied behind my back. Every minute near her lands sharp and deep, rattling something loose inside me. I tell myself it's all part of the healing process. Inoculation, one day at a time. But catching her washing the dishes when no one was looking? I didn't need to see that. And curled up in an armchair, eyes closed, cradling her Bible? That one dropped me to the mat.

She hasn't been wearing makeup, golden hair swept back and forgotten in a clip. She's never needed the extra effort, but what does it mean? That she's moving on? If only it helped. My mutinous heart won't surrender. It claws for the helm, barking orders I refuse to follow.

I hate that she can see me like this—nothing like who I was. I hate that she knows. But I shouldn't. This will force her to move on. And that's good.

Outside this guest room is Kit's basement living room, complete with a fantastic sectional sofa. When we got home from tubing this afternoon, I napped hard, but now I'm wired. And hungry. Finally giving up on sleep, I sneak upstairs to see if I can find a snack. A light is on in the office.

"Oh, hey, Mr. Talbot—ah—Archie."

"Austin, hey. You're still up?"

Out of nowhere, a verse surfaces. One Dad's said a couple times. *Listen to advice and accept discipline, and at the end you will be counted among the wise.*

"Yeah, hey, I know now probably isn't the right time," I hedge, "but maybe while I'm here I can talk to you about something?"

He smiles like Kit. "Now's a great time. Get your coat and hat and I'll make a fire. You like s'mores? Hungry enough for a hot dog?"

"Yes, sir. Thank you. I could eat three if you can spare them."

He laughs. "Absolutely. Meet you out there."

It's midnight, and I'm gonna hang out with my friend's dad on the back deck.

Is this you?

Doubt nags. Haven't I wrecked any chance of that?

Archie builds a fire like he's done it a thousand times, and soon it's roaring. The heat pushes me out of my coat. I skewer all three hot dogs at once. He hands me a bottle of hot sauce, and we shoot the breeze about Mayberry and basketball while my second dinner blisters perfectly. I talk up Levi, not that he'll need it, then drag the hot dogs into a bun. The smell alone says I'm gonna sleep like a rock after this. When Archie passes the tub of s'mores supplies, I wish I could mow his lawn for a year. This is a beautiful night.

"It seems like you're going through it right now," he says.

I let out a breath and twist the skewer. "Yes, sir. A ... brutal breakup."

He grimaces, like he's reliving a painful memory.

"It's Sophie."

"The Sophie who's—" He points upstairs.

"Yes, sir."

"Oh. Ouch."

Whatever he's thinking, it's worse.

Silence drifts in, and the fire simmers.

A few minutes later, he speaks up. "Mind if I tell you about my own brutal breakup?"

"Sure." I guide two marshmallows to the glowing embers.

"Chelsea and I broke up for a year."

I glance up. No way. Them?

"It was, without a doubt, the worst year of my life. We'd only been dating a few months, but I was out of my mind in love with her, acting like a crazy person. Even in that short time, we found maintaining our boundaries to be excruciatingly difficult."

I almost drop the skewer. My heart races, like it instinctively knows something important is happening. But I kind of don't want it.

If this is you, help me stay and hear it.

Archie settles into his patio chair, steady and unbothered, like this is the most normal topic in the world. "What's meant to be an antidote in marriage is poison too soon. Part of our problem was that I wasn't pulling my weight, but a good portion of it is what Chelsea started calling the Snowball Effect."

"The Snowball Effect?" I stack my double s'more—they have Reese's instead of Hershey's, a stroke of genius—and sink into it.

"A snowball at the top of a hill is inclined to roll down it. As it does, it collects more and more snow. It's just physics. Same with kissing. Enough said?"

I finish my bite quick. "Yes, sir. But you got back together?"

"We did. We committed to keeping Jesus above our relationship always, God blessed our efforts, and I got to marry that woman." He holds his hands out toward his home, still astounded after twenty some years. "All these blessings." Archie is straight up dropping teardrops. "God be praised."

What a man. "If you don't mind me asking, how did you combat the Snowball Effect the second time around?"

"We quit playing the game."

"Sir?"

"When we talked over the fresh relationship we were creating after the year apart, we decided to quit kissing until we were engaged. Even that was tricky, but then we had a short and specific time to wait."

And just like that, Kit and Levi's no-kissing rule clicks.

"It's uncanny," I say. "The beginning is so much like me and Sophie."

He hums softly. "Maybe that's why God has us talking." His gaze meets mine. "I know we just met—it's up to you how much you want to share."

I slap the back of my hand and suck it up. "I'll try to keep it short." Talking about her hurts bad, but somehow it helps too. I spit it all out, even the Graham weekend. CliffsNotes, but he gets it. I finish with my humiliating blob-like state.

"I'm really sorry you're going through that." He sits silent, heavy. I hope he's praying. "How are you and Jesus in the middle of this?"

I hesitate. "Not great, sir."

He watches.

"I haven't really prayed in weeks."

"Why is that?"

"I'm not sure."

I guess you know?

"It's like I don't know how anymore." I rub my aching eyes.

"It's different now?"

"Well, of course." I readjust. "I mean, it couldn't be the same now."

He bends forward.

"The way it was before ... it's not really in the cards anymore. With God, I mean."

"How so?"

I hate this. I don't wanna talk about it. But I also don't want to leave Archie hanging, so I fumble for an explanation he'll understand. "Do you manage anybody, sir? Like, employees?"

"I do, yes."

"What would happen if one of them stole stuff and broke things? And then they didn't show up to work for a month? What then?"

"I'd fire them."

I give a slow nod. "I'm not saying I lose my salvation or anything. But I'm kind of ... grandfathered in."

"What if it was one of my kids?" he presses. "Ask me what would happen if Grey did those things."

Something stabs my insides, but I risk a glance up. "What would happen?"

"He'd still be my son, and no less than before."

I suppress a head shake.

"Grey's learning about cars, and I love it when he changes the oil for me. But it's a bonus. A cherry on top. I just want him to be with me, love me back. He could take my car out without asking and total it, and yeah, I'd be ticked. There would be consequences. But I'd still want him here with me. Do you see? It's very dangerous to look at God like your employer, Austin. It's a completely different role—for him and for you. Jesus taught us to pray 'Our Father who is in heaven.'"

I'm silenced by emotion. The fire blurs. A long moment sits between us.

"God, you're so good to us," he prays. "We love you. Show this fine young man how you love him, how it is to be your son. Honor him with his own Chelsea to care for. Guide him into a beautiful life of simplicity. A life with you."

CHAPTER SIXTY-THREE

Austin

"Well dude, safe to say, if you marry Kit, you'll have the coolest father-in-law in history. I feel bad that I cut you in line, but he and I had a sick fireside chat last night." I check Levi for irritation. Only curiosity. Of course he's chill about it.

"You're kidding. Tell me."

"I couldn't sleep. He fed me hot dogs and s'mores and talked to me about Sophie. I think God set it up. It was cool."

"Come to any conclusions?"

"Not going there," I say, eyeing him.

"Alright. God's got this. God's got you."

I clear my throat. "I laid some groundwork for you. When do you get to hang with him?"

"Thanks, buddy. I owe you big. Tomorrow. I was planning to take him out for Mexican."

I pull a face. "Mexican? In Colorado?"

"Kit says it's his favorite."

"I can't imagine Mexican being good this far north. Might as well eat lobster in Kansas."

He chuckles. "Can't rule it out. Maybe somebody's Grandmaría runs that kitchen."

"Great. Now I want her tamales."

"If only. Anyway, your camping-vibe success has me thinking we should do something more low key. I wonder if it's too muddy for a hike."

"I say pray about it, bro. Can't outplan the Big Guy." I blink. It just came out. Like the old me.

He notices. "Great call."

Sophie

"Here, would you line these socks up from smallest to biggest?" Chelsea ties her auburn hair into a knot—exactly like Kit's knots, except at her neck instead of on her head. Wading through the mountain of laundry she poured on the living room rug, she throws socks to me one at a time.

"You know, being a new Christian is a gift. You have what David called the 'joy of your salvation.' And you aren't bogged down by knowing how the church does everything. You can look at the Bible with fresh eyes. So please speak up when church people act like there's one way to do something and it's not what you're reading in your Bible. We need you. Like this"—she motions between us—"I'm just so impressed by what you're doing, Sophie. Owning your background and weaknesses and pursuing growth is exactly what we should be doing as Jesus followers."

"Oh." My chest warms, but my mind slaps a warning label on it. "Thank you."

"Yep. Another thing—thank you for telling Kit about your counselor. Do you mind if I ask if you still see her?"

"Not really anymore."

She nods, lowering to the rug. "Studies have shown that talking to a trusted friend can be as beneficial as counseling, but my experience is that some issues really call for a counselor's experience and guidance. Maybe Dr. Shannon, or maybe someone new, but please be praying about whether you should be seeing someone, okay?"

I agree.

"Now, talk to me. What are you looking for in our chats?"

Austin and Mia are throwing a football at the park, so I can speak freely. The furnace fills the house with a comforting hum. Kit and Levi are canoodling somewhere, probably gazing into each other's eyes as she shows him around her picture-perfect childhood.

I let out a sigh. "Honestly, I think you'd know better than me. I just want to know what makes a relationship good. To stay together, but also to like it."

"The *like* on top of the *love*. It's rare."

I'm only nineteen, but I've noticed.

She shakes out a pair of jeans and folds them in quarters. "God, we love you," she prays aloud. "Give me whatever words Sophie needs. Keep me from saying anything else. May your Spirit speak to her and comfort her and grow her. Honor her desire to honor you."

Yes, Jesus.

Another pair of jeans.

"This is *so* much laundry," I mutter.

"Yeah, and I don't even have Kit's anymore. But it's not too bad if you know what matters to your people and streamline the rest."

"What matters?"

"Like ... Mav likes his button-ups hung right away so he

doesn't have to iron. Grey likes his socks in his shoe basket so he doesn't have to run back upstairs. That kind of thing."

"What does Archie like?"

"He's a remarkable man, but he's kind of a slob." She laughs. "Like those genius types. He doesn't put his clothes away, and if I do it for him, they just get thrown around again as he digs in the drawers. But then because of that, he can never find what he needs because it's in a dirty pile on the floor."

I eye her.

She shrugs. "So I don't fold his clothes. I'm happy to wash his stuff more often than I wash my own because it takes no time at all to throw it in a basket for him." She gathers several of his workout shirts and illustrates with a toss. "That's not how I was taught to do laundry, but who cares, right? He doesn't care if it's folded. And it's these little things that can either be small acts of love or small steps toward bitterness. No way am I sacrificing an ounce of what we have because of some extra laundry." A wadded pair of jeans and three unmatched socks ... straight into his basket.

"You don't mind catering to everyone's preferences?"

"Really good question." She smooths out a pair of smaller jeans. "It requires a lot of self-awareness. I think selflessness needs to build gradually or it can actually be toxic. Is it Jesus making you more like himself? Or are you trying to earn belonging or love? Or is it some bitter-undertoned obligation nonsense? With my personality, I don't have a hard time telling them 'Your preferences are obnoxious. Do it yourself.' So God has had to soften my heart so that I can see that this is a little gift I can offer the people I love. But for a nicer person than me, they'd have different laundry soul-searching."

Sock after sock, I line them up as I digest. "But ... how can you be sure it's all fair?"

"Ah, yes ... 'fair.' It doesn't feel fair. Ever. 'Fairness' has been the theme of some of my biggest fights with Archie."

"You fight?" I blurt.

She raises a cool brow. "Of course we fight. We had a huge blowup just last week."

Bizarre. Austin and I never fought.

"But the longer we're married, the shorter they get. And less frequent." A smile quirks. "And kinder."

"Okay. So, fairness?"

Her head tilts like Kit's. "We're both hard workers, and we both tend to be convinced that we're doing the lion's share. I'm learning to aim for 'reasonable' instead of 'fair.' Not *How much is he doing so I can do the exact same*, but *Is it reasonable for me to do even more?* That's been working for me. Right now I have plenty of time, and I want to make my boys happy. It's reasonable for me to do their laundry. I would never sit around relaxing while they're working hard. That wouldn't be reasonable. And Archie does a million things every day for me. Sometimes I have a crazy week and I ask them to handle their laundry. It's a fine line, but when I think of Jesus washing his disciples' nasty, sweaty man feet"—she shoots me a Kit-grimace like she just smelled it—"this is nothing."

I grin.

"How did you see the 'fair' thing play out in your relationship?"

So I tell her about Austin and how weird and wonderful he is. How he gives until it hurts. How I wonder if we never fought because he didn't tell me his side—his "preferences." Chelsea doesn't just nod politely, she leans in, like she cares about the details. The soft "hmms" coax me on, and before I know it I'm spilling things I don't usually say out loud. But I'm interrupted.

The front door opens, and Mia's presence dials up the house volume five notches. Austin follows behind her, quiet but dragging less, even than yesterday.

Chelsea turns to me. "Are you a hugger?"

Finally someone asks. My clip slips loose with an emphatic shake no.

"Got it." She gives my arm a quick squeeze. When she meets

my gaze, it's Kit's blue but with a different spark. "Jesus loves you. He has beautiful plans for your life. And also"—her eyes smile—"I really like you. Now. Let's get these last washcloths folded, and I'll finish the rest tomorrow."

I do as she says, already plotting a floor shirt for her: Mrs. Miyagi.

The awareness of eyes lifts my head toward Austin. But he's already striding into the kitchen.

CHAPTER SIXTY-FOUR

Austin

Back at Kit's house in the early morning, I bend over the driveway, hands on my knees, gasping for breath. Longest run I've done in months. No gym here. No weights, no bag to pound. My throat burned something awful in the cold, but I couldn't wait for the sun to take the edge off. Ever since Sophie's text, my insides have twisted, begging me to be the guy she thinks I am. The guy my friends think I am. I just don't know how.

Ready to head inside, I rip my headphones out—and slam into a sound like a brick wall.

That voice.

Her voice.

Singing.

My body locks. In a split second I'm drowning. Captivated. Gutted. She must be on the porch. Can't see around the big spruce, but I don't need to. Archie and Chelsea keep heaters and chairs out there. Kit said they sit out every night and talk. It's no wonder they give off flirty best-friend vibes. They're living my dream, the one I fight tooth and nail to forget. But Sophie's in Chelsea's seat, and it yanks me further under the wave.

I don't trust my feet to move the right direction, so I hover like a creep, pressing back into the garage door to stay upright.

She sings—haunting, hypnotic. "Hold You Tight" by Dan Bremnes. A love song from her creator. A lullaby for the dark.

The song wraps around me, filling in holes and splitting others open.

It's everything.

I lurch for the far gate, bolt to the back door. Let them think I'm breaking in. I can't walk past her without telling her the truth.

That afternoon I change clothes again. Lately the only time I feel halfway normal is on a run.

My hands still, shirt halfway on. Halfway normal. Dark and Twisty. My breaths turn short and shallow. What Sophie used to talk about. Suffocating. Hollow. Unwinnable. My gut tightens. My throat tightens.

With trembling hands, I yank my shirt down and shoes on. Jog upstairs.

"Oh good." Mia, deadpan from the sofa, typing on her laptop. "I've been worried you weren't getting enough exercise."

I grunt in response.

"*Heart* disease is a killer," she calls.

Ignoring her, I round the corner, pass Archie's closed office, almost reach the front door—

And stop cold.

Sophie starts down the stairs, dressed for a run. Favorite joggers, wavy ponytail, oversized cropped hoodie pulled over her hands. The hem rides up, baring a sliver of skin. She moves slower now, like I do. Less bounce. Less humming. Scrolling and jabbing on her phone, she doesn't notice me. No doubt making a playlist.

The sight knocks the air out of me, sharp and familiar. Sophie.

I take a half step toward her. Then another.

I almost reach for her hand. Almost brush the hair from her face. Almost ask if she's sleeping okay. Almost beg at her feet.

To forgive me. To take me back.

But I can't. I shouldn't.

She hits the last stair and freezes. I wrench my eyes away just in time, stagger back. The door creaks before I get to it. Kit blows past me, tears streaming, up the stairs. Levi steps in a beat later, pale. Like he's just been punched in the gut.

"Kit?" Sophie calls. Her concerned voice washes over me.

Levi barely meets my eyes, then slips back out, clicks the door shut, and collapses in Chelsea's chair. I follow him out to Archie's.

After a long silence, the words break loose. "We walked to her elementary school down the road. She's been so happy. Skipping and teasing. I slipped on the ice like an idiot and landed in a snowdrift. She was laughing so hard and ... straddled me. Just a hug, I think, but—" He squeezes his eyes shut. "I wanted more. Badly. So I yanked her off. Too fast. Too rough. It scared her. Hurt her feelings. So then I was trying to fix it, and somehow I let out that once you've done something, it's a thousand times harder to say no." He presses fingers to his temples.

"There's a cheery tidbit," I mumble.

"She started asking all these questions at the worst possible time." His head drops into his hands. "So many questions, and I just—" His voice breaks. "What if I lose her over this?"

I turn away, giving him privacy, and nearly lose my own composure.

Is the whole thing rigged? Do any of us stand a chance?

"She'll come around, buddy," I lie. "She's not going anywhere."

A few minutes later, Kit walks out the front door and meets my eyes.

I stand to head down the walk.

She lowers to the ottoman at his seat, right in his space.

"I'm so sorry, Kit," Levi says brokenly. "I'm so sorry."

"Hey," she says gently. "I forgive you."

I'm not even to the driveway when I hear her voice again.

"Levi? I love you."

I stumble to a stop. Now? She says it now?

Silence.

I almost run back and whack him upside the head. *Say it back.* But I hear his deep murmur and drop my guard.

Thank you.

Take my yoke upon you, and learn from me, for I am gentle and lowly in heart, and you will find rest for your soul.

Goose bumps line my arms.

But how?

Go up on the mountain and pray.

Back from my second run, the coast is clear on the porch, so I push through the front door and aim for Archie's now-open office doors. "Excuse me, sir?"

Archie turns, shifting his over-ear headphones to one ear. "Austin, hey."

"Is now a bad time?"

"I need to drop off for a few minutes," he says in a business voice, then drops his headphones to his neck.

"Oh. I didn't mean for you to—"

He interrupts with a firm shake of the head. "What's on your mind?"

My mouth opens. Shuts. "Does it seem to you like God sets us up for failure? With the ... dating boundaries stuff?"

He hums low, studying the corner of the room.

I shift on my feet, sweat cooling on my forehead and neck.

"You know, the prioritizing"—he holds up a thumb to start counting—"obedience, strategies for temptation, self-control ... Those are all vital to learn before the stakes are so much higher in marriage." He turns to his bookshelf, scans the spines, and hands one to me. "I love this one. *Celebration of Discipline*. It's spiritual weight lifting. Strength training for life with God."

I wait for more, but he just watches me.

"Ah, strength training, sir?"

"Like fasting, for example. Practicing saying no to food has been game changing for me in obeying and sacrificing in other areas of my life. It's indirect. And somehow that helps." He points at the book in my hand. "All these practices were modeled for us by Jesus himself. Maybe pray about whether he has one for you to add into your routine."

I stare blankly at the cover. White, hardcover, red letters. Weight lifting.

"Thank you, sir." I turn to go.

"And Austin? Those exercises are to be done *with* God. Not just *for* him. Remember—you can't out-weight-lift the Pharisees."

My gut shifts, and my heart clicks into place.

With, not just *for*.

CHAPTER SIXTY-FIVE

Austin

"Hey, dude," Mav calls from the basement door. "Mind if I join?"

"Get down here." I mute the TV.

"Where's the rest of the crew?"

"Ice skating, mostly."

"You refuse to ice skate?" He jumps over the back of the sectional and stretches out. "What a waste of potential."

I chuckle. "I'm trying to ... rest. March Madness fits the bill."

Something pangs in my gut. **Go up on the mountain and pray.**

"Rest?" He watches me rather than the game.

"Feels lame to bail on the group, but I think this is what I need right now."

Not what I said.

I roll my shoulders.

"Cool. Ooh, did Dad give you these snacks?"

"Sure did."

He reaches for a box of Cap'n Crunch. "Mom's always trying to get us to eat broccoli and hummus or something. She makes Dad hide his contraband stash so maybe we'll forget about it. Who's on?" He points with his chin.

I catch him up on the game.

"So, you like Mayberry?"

"It's the coolest, looniest place ever. If you can go, you should."

"Loony, huh?"

"Pranks, traditions, floor pride to a hilarious extent. Lots of really quality people. I talk to my cousin and high school buddies about their time at college, and I just have no doubt I'm in the right spot."

"Sounds prime."

"High schoolers come shadow a bunch. You're welcome on my couch anytime if you wanna check it out."

"Thanks, bro. I'm there. Hey, question." Sitting up and planting his feet, he stares me down like we just transitioned to a formal interrogation.

I outweigh this kid by at least eighty pounds. Can't help but crack a smile. "Go for it."

"Levi. Is he cool enough for Kit?"

I confirm. "Zero reservations. Kit's got it made in the shade with him." I should clarify. "And I don't mean about the money. He takes amazing care of her."

"And how does he feel about Jesus? Like, love, fan, what?"

It hits like a pass to the chest. Mav gets it.

Do I still?

"He's obsessed," I tell him. "Number one priority."

My throat tightens, but I push past it.

Mav lets out a breath as he relaxes back into his confident recline. "You have a sister?"

"Yeah, she's your year."

"You been in this spot yet?"

"No, and it better be a decade down the road." Luckily,

Janie's focused, has big plans. She hasn't even been tempted to date in high school. And let's just say I've made bothering my sister very unappealing to the guys back home.

He raises his brow. "How does she feel about that?"

I let it slide. "What would you have done if I told you Levi was a loser?"

"Good old-fashioned duel. *Hamilton*-style." He drops a handful of cereal in his mouth and talks around it. "Why, need to change your answer? Not sure if I'm a good shot, but my rapping is pretty good."

I huff a laugh. "You're a good brother. Gotta protect your sister as best you can."

He nods in another flash of earnestness.

"Kit getting all serious must be weird."

"Super weird," he says. "But also not. She'd love to get married young. I mean, so would I."

A chip stabs on the way down. "Why's that?"

"Our parents kinda trained us to lock it down when we find the right one, that a first love should never be wasted because of bad timing—"

I'm saved by a clutch three from the top of the key.

Mav smacks the sofa, grabs the remote to unmute the game. "What a beautiful shot! You care who wins this one?"

"No, I—Give him the ball!" I shout at the forward. "Another one!"

"Oh! My bracket's a dumpster fire already," he says with delight. "If they pull this off, I'm ruined."

A stampede of steps rattles the ceiling, followed by shouts for Mav.

"Down here!" he hollers, eyes stuck on the screen.

Grey skids to a stop at the top of the stairs, out of breath. "Mav. They're here. Only a couple hours to lock this down."

More guys fill in behind him, arms loaded with half-opened Amazon packages and faded sport coats.

Mav springs up like he heard *The Avengers* theme. "Roger,

Broseph." To me, "Destiny calls. Secret Service detail waits for no man."

A prank? A smile slips out, but I hesitate. "Set up down here? I'll help out."

"Dude, it would be a pleasure. Nay, an honor."

High schoolers flood the stairs. One clutches a scuffed briefcase that has never contained nuclear codes.

"Ayo!" he calls to them. "Basement'll be HQ. This is Austin, Kit's friend." To me, "Suits, ties, aviators, and maximum educational disruption."

I send a nod of approval as I stand, holding out fist bumps over the couch. "What's up."

"You a Flooder?" Mav asks. "Kit tells me they're the Spartans of pranking."

I grin. They're gonna love that title. "Sure am."

"Well? Impart your wisdom, sir!"

More high schoolers trail in, adding to the chaos. One plugs in an iron and rests it on the Ping-Pong table. Another hangs suit coats on curtain rods and doorknobs.

I plop back on the couch, considering. "Earpieces? To really sell it?"

Mav throws his arms out. "What?! Yes!"

"How are we gonna make that happen?" someone asks.

"I doubt there's overnight shipping for that, and we're already over budget," another says.

All eyes shift to me.

I push off the couch, nod toward the Ping-Pong table. "We're gonna need an ironing board so your mom doesn't kill us. For earpieces, we'll need old earbuds or cords it's okay to cut up. And a hot glue gun."

"On it!" Grey calls.

"Y'all are good on ironing?" I point at the guys across the room. "Cool. I need someone to coordinate jacket try-ons. You can assign one to each of you so you're not scrambling tomorrow. If you'll bring the cords and hot glue gun in here, we can watch the game while we work. Just twist it in a coil and run a line of hot glue. Boom, comms."

One high schooler shoves my shoulder and another whoops.

Grey chucks a tangled mess of cords across the room. "Heads up!"

I start separating it into piles. "Anyone without a job can start untangling."

"Uh, wanna show me how this iron works?" a guy calls.

I clap Mav on the shoulder and head that way. He has no idea how much I needed this.

Thank you.

My steps slow.

Show me how to do this with *you?*

The house has been eerily quiet since Mav and company left. Helping them left me filled, not drained. I can't figure out the mechanics, but for the first time I have hope. Maybe I still have something to offer the world. Maybe I can still participate in God's plan, even in a small way.

"Samwise." Levi interrupts my thoughts, sweeping down the basement stairs.

I pause the game. "Jeeves, buddy!"

He hands me a fork and a giant burrito in a takeout box. "We stopped at Costa Vida on the way back. I got you sweet pork. Eat that and try to tell me their Mexican food is no good."

I wrap an arm around his shoulder and jostle him. "This looks amazing. Thank you. Now sit down and spill."

He chuckles, reading my face. "Well, you were right. Archie's wicked cool. So intimidating though."

I didn't get intimidating. Then again, I'm not dating his daughter.

"Most of his impression of me was already made by what you

and Kit said. We had a good talk." His leg bounces faster than normal.

"Did you ask him?"

"No. I need to make sure he knows I'm not unhinged first ..."

I snort. I've been the unhinged one. Levi's as solid as a boulder.

"Then take lessons and then ask for their blessing, in that order. The last part will have to wait."

"Then what'd you talk about?"

"He asked about my routines, my relationship with Jesus. He did a lot of nodding. Prayed with me. I snuck in a lesson too—asked him about Chelsea and how things work for them." He's talking so fast, leg about to break the sound barrier.

"You're never nervous, dude."

"He's the gatekeeper for marrying Kit. She'd never go through with it without his blessing ..."

And Mav's. And Chelsea's. And Grey's. I flash back to Sophie meeting my people. Like a deer in headlights, Mama grilling her on the worst possible subjects. Regret coils tight in my chest. *I'm sorry I put you through that, Soph.*

"There's nothing more nerve-racking than that," he finishes.

I try to smile, but it lands wrong on my face.

"Sorry," he says. "Which game are you watching?"

It's a great game—the underdog's mounting a comeback for a major upset—but that's not what he needs right now. I silence my phone so no one can text me spoilers.

"What'd you learn in your secret lesson?"

He settles into the couch. "Basically, everything goes better because they actually like each other. He called it 'the like on top of the love.' They like each other, so they hang out a lot, and that makes them like each other more."

"Oddly revolutionary."

My parents are fully committed, and I'm grateful for that. But I don't think "like" is the right word between them. It's wild to imagine that sticking around for decades. They're more ...

accustomed? Tolerant? Partners, not gushy. But even "partners" feels off. They don't lean on each other—just handle their own parts. Stay in their lanes. Dad takes care of his side. Mama expects him to. It's not unkind, just practical. But it's not the same as having someone with you, not just beside you. Someone who carries the weight too. Who wants to. Your best friend. Someone like—

My jaw clenches. Can't go there.

"And if they find they aren't liking each other or hanging out a lot," Levi continues, "then that's an emergency to problem-solve, not just a fact of life. His perspective is so different."

"How's the lesson thing gonna go moving forward? Seems tricky to get real advice from someone you're still trying to impress."

"Tell me about it. But they're the ones with the marriage I want. It has to be Archie."

"I get that. They're old and still all over each other."

Yesterday I spotted Archie tugging Chelsea into his office. She's a mom, and she straight up giggled.

A wave of nausea pummels me. It's them. It's her. Maybe I just need real food. I pop the lid and start shoveling.

He chuckles. "Yes, exactly. So I'll just have to be painfully real with him. God's sense of humor."

Yeah.

Like how I avoided Sophie with near-spy skills for a month and now you've got me stuck in a house with her and accidentally talking about her at every turn?

My prayer trails off, and I look to the ceiling. Is that kind of talk still allowed?

To Levi, "What's your timeline like? When do you think you'd pop the question to Kit?"

But now I can't swallow. Or breathe. This topic is going to demolish me, but I signed up for this week of torture for him.

He squints, reading my mind.

"Timeline," I press.

"You know I'm there already. But I haven't brought it up with her. I'm still trying not to freak her out."

"But she looooves you," I taunt.

He jerks up. "You heard?"

"Yeah. Sorry for eavesdropping. She just blurted it out when I was still close."

His head shakes slowly. "Can you believe that?"

I open my mouth, but everything I've locked behind a wall is about to burst out.

Dizzy, I snap the lid shut over my burrito. "I'm amped for y'all," I get out. "Mav said she'd be down to get married young. They see it like a good thing around here."

"You've been playing wingman again?" He reaches to whack my arm. "Thanks for the intel, buddy."

"But you've been together like two minutes. You're not afraid you're gonna go the way of me and Sophie?"

His eyes turn piercing. "When you know, you know."

My stomach tightens harder. I really think I might hurl. The Cheetos aren't helping.

"I wonder if not kissing makes you in more of a hurry or less," I wonder aloud.

Should not have vocalized that thought. Breathe. In through the nose, out through the mouth.

"I'd guess less. Not sure this is the best subject right now."

I'm doing all I can not to open the kissing album that's waiting in my brain. Pictures are spilling out. Push it away. Don't. Open. It.

Sophie, blissed out against the brick of the math building. Her lazy smile, upside down on my couch. Velvety latte eyes as she wove fingers through my hair.

"Game time." He grabs for the remote.

I hold it out of reach. "So Kit's been hyped to show you all her home stuff?" I avoid the lovestruck look sure to be on his face.

"Yes."

"Has it been better here than when you went to my house the first time?"

"Yes."

He's withholding for my sake. I finally turn to him, but only so I can glare. I don't want his pity. "Jeeves."

"Samwise."

"I'm fine." Kind of. My gut is squeezing miserably, and my throat is tight.

He throws a pillow at me and snatches the remote away as I reflexively catch it.

Well played.

CHAPTER SIXTY-SIX

Austin

We've been watching basketball for an hour when the sub who runs out on the court reminds me of Powell. I almost growl. I still don't know what happened with that. Haven't had the guts to ask.

Levi turns serious, twirls the remote. Suspicious.

Maybe it's time I try to move on, like Sophie did. I've been so laser focused on her that I don't even remember what else is out there. Nothing serious—just someone nice enough. Someone to help me leave Sophie alone. But where do you even start when everything you want is the one thing you gave up?

I need to pray.

How do I start?

Memories crash down like hail. The hollow look in Sophie's eyes at my house. Her shell-shocked personality transplant. Tears on my treehouse. Desperation in her voice as she begged me to kiss her.

Like the day against the chain-link fence. Like *me* the last month, curled up on my couch.

Dark and Twisty. Depression.

Sophie. My eyes fill, my breath quivers. I almost lose it. *Oh, Sophie, I'm so sorry. I didn't know.* My body trembles. *I should have known. I should have protected you.*

Proof. More proof I wasn't what she needed. She deserved so much better. Still does.

The room goes quiet—game paused.

I flinch, yanked out of my thoughts.

"I know you don't want to talk about Sophie," he starts. "I won't try to talk you into anything. But give me five minutes and then I'll try to leave you to your dysfunction."

"Fine," I grumble.

"Together, you and Sophie are a force. You really could be a Chelsea-and-Archie couple. But I saw something dangerous happening, and I should have spoken up. I think you started loving Sophie more than you loved Jesus."

I cut a sharp eye over.

"I only know because I started down the same path, and he had to wake me up."

"That is not fair. I was still putting in the time. I was still getting up to read my Bible every day, even when I'd barely slept."

"Absolutely. You were doing, doing, doing."

For some reason, that makes me cringe.

"But you needed to go home to rest, right? To pray and be with him? Like Jesus ran off all the time—that's what you said. But then you dragged Sophie with you. How were you supposed to rest during a meet-the-parents weekend?"

She taught me to say no, to check that impulse to please everybody and choose what matters most. But I never could check it with her. Not really. Was it because she was what mattered most to me?

I stare at the ceiling.

"You prioritized her over yourself every day and every night—

you have a lot to teach the rest of us—but when you took her to Graham, I worried you were prioritizing her over Jesus too."

My shoulders droop. My chest caves in.

God let me take care of his most beautiful creation, and how did I thank him? I worshiped her instead. I curl over to cradle my head in my hands.

Is this punishment? Or did I just get what I chose?

"Samwise?" Levi's gentle voice hits a nerve.

"I gave you your five minutes," I bite out. "We have a deal."

"Got it," he says, subdued.

As my breath returns, I send a glance his way. "You're a good dude. Are we okay?"

He holds out a fist. "Ride or die, buddy."

I knock it with mine.

Sophie will be back soon, and I can't be around when she does. I can't trust myself to keep my distance right now. I tap my phone to check the time.

A missed call. A voicemail. Three texts.

"Ahh ... Gotta make a call."

Levi squints. "Call right here if you want."

I tap the missed call, clear my throat. With a "yes, sir" and an "absolutely, sir," the ground shifts under my feet. "Yes, sir, Coach. Thank you, sir. Hook 'em." My phone drops to my lap.

"Hook 'em?" Levi asks.

"UT's running backs coach." Almost in slow motion, I twist to him. "I'm in. I got that preferred walk-on spot." I stare at my phone. "How is that possible?" In a daze I pick it up, read the texts, heave a sigh. "Dad suspected that Sophie dumped me that weekend I was home. He talked Coach into sending in the tape."

"You're kidding."

I grip my phone. If I could make amends for her. If I could fix it. If I could just ...

But I can't.

"I'll need to head down there the day after we get back." I rake both hands through my hair. "Oh man, this is exactly what I need." The best way to let her go.

This has to be you. Things like this don't just happen.

"I need to hit the gym. I gotta—" I launch off the couch. "Where's Archie? Is he around?"

"Yeah, I think—"

But I'm out of there, taking the stairs two at a time. My knee flares up.

"Samwise," Levi calls, painfully smooth, "what happened to 'just a tragic backup plan'?"

I pretend not to hear.

Sophie

On Saturday skiers weave between towering pines while I float up the mountain on a chairlift for the first time. Skiing is wild. A bucket-list event. A distraction I relish. The sky feels bluer up here. Bigger. The air's thin and crisp, and I gulp down deep, greedy breaths.

We spent most of the day learning on the packed bunny hill, and now it's finally time to try the wide green run called Molly Mayfield. I didn't realize how exhausting skiing would be. Or how much I'd love it. It's the perfect mix of nature and adrenaline and full-body effort. Kit didn't even seem to mind crawling along at our pace, teaching us all day.

Now she sits next to me on the lift, fidgeting with her poles. "I told Levi I love him on Thursday," she says suddenly. "Because of you."

My breath snags.

"After that ... walk," she says.

"The walk-walk? When you came in crying? Why because of me?"

"Yeah, that one. Because ..." She rests her poles on her legs.

"You love—and forgive—so fiercely. Even without understanding why Austin's keeping you apart, you still believe in him. You remember who he is, in the middle of the mess. That's huge. If you can admire him there, then I can trust Levi too. I can love and forgive like you do. Because they've both shown us they're the kind of guys worth sticking our necks out for."

I let the tears roll down my cheeks. "Being loved does that, huh? Makes us brave."

She nods. "And if Levi loving me back can make me brave, how much braver should I be if I'm loved by the creator of the universe?" A pause. Then, quietly, "I think he was going to say it on Valentine's night. Remember that tapas dinner? He was so nervous. Wanted you guys there but tried to bail."

"But we did come. And Levi didn't say it then, did he?"

Kit exhales. "The walk-walk topic? I think that's why he was so hesitant."

Silenced by shame. But she spoke straight to it.

I can't speak, so I tap her pole with mine.

Austin whacks Levi three chairlifts ahead. And somehow, at this moment, I'm sure.

I've lost him for good.

It's the way he moves now. I've seen him on campus, traced his path toward the gym from my window. For weeks he looked as bad as I felt—dragging, bent. Like he was carrying something too big even for him.

But this week the weight has lifted. The droop in his posture has sloughed off, replaced by something closer to his usual easygoing stance. He's cracking jokes ahead of me—I can tell just by his body language. And when he laughs, my heart flies into a tailspin of enamored, relieved agony. I miss his teasing. I miss the banter. I miss his giant hand pushing hair out of my face. I miss the adventure in his eyes.

I wanted him to rest, and I've succeeded, but at the expense of my last thread of hope. He managed to shake me off in four weeks. I, on the other hand, am barely holding myself together with exaggerated smiles and a peppy voice.

CHAPTER SIXTY-SEVEN

Sophie

We finally make it to the top, and I wipe out trying to slide off the chairlift. Then Mia crashes into me, and we both dissolve into laughter, a tangle of limbs and skis. I let myself stay in it—I'm not ignoring the hard stuff. This is just true too. Sometimes God doesn't shows up in quiet moments and deep thoughts. Sometimes he belly-laughs with me in the snow.

When I finally push back up and glide around the corner … The view. A mountaintop experience in all the ways. God knew I'd need this. Like standing at the edge of the ocean, it's near impossible to feel entitled or bitter with all this glory stretching wide in front of you. Our Creator is just so big. Powerful. Creative. Beautiful. And he promises that with faith we can *move* mountains. Bizarre.

Easing down the mountain, snowplowing like my life depends on it, I launch into a full-volume, yell-singing version of "Come

Thou Fount." Kit and Mia join in, and soon we're waving our ski poles to the beat like madwomen.

One green run is more work than it could possibly sound like, so we call it a day and sprawl across a patio table outside the lodge, peeling off layers under the sun.

"Gotta go study that ten-dollar grilled cheese so I can imitate it back at the house." Mia smacks a kiss on the top of my head and calls behind her, "Be back in a minute."

"And get more water," Kit chides. "Remember, we're at twelve thousand feet—the land of dehydration—and clots are strictly forbidden."

Mia chuckles. "Sí, jefa."

When Kit looks out at the ski hill, her drool-y stare gives it away—the guys are nearby. I spot them halfway down the hill. Austin and Levi skied many times growing up, which worked out just fine for the Sophie-avoidance plan Austin has doubled down on the past two days.

Kit lets out a dreamy sigh, and jealousy rears its ugly head, just in a new way. I've been doing so much better at seeing Kit as God's handiwork, but now it's her beautiful relationship that stings. A reminder of what I had. What I lost.

"What you shot out of the sky," the troll hisses. *"She would never."*

I freeze. Is it the troll? Or ... is it Mom's voice? The thought hits like a slap.

"She's God's handiwork. And so am I. Now get lost," I tell it. Her? Them?

Turning to Kit, I sing to the beat of Walker Hayes's "U Gurl" —"Girls like Kit like boys that look like Le-vi."

Whirling around, she laughs, light and admission in her eyes. Every time. But her laugh putters out as the worst look of pity fills those Disney eyes.

Ughhh. "Nope! Don't need that!" With all my fake cheer.

Bobbing her head, her expression morphs to resolve and then

to sadness. "Sophs? I ... I owe you a big apology. I've been putting it off."

My stomach drops at her tone.

"It's just ... something doesn't line up between how Austin acts and what he wants us to believe." She sneaks a glance my way, tucking hair behind her ear. "I really thought it would help to make him say it out loud, you know? And you were with Davis, and I sort of ... panicked. I didn't trust you, and I should've."

"What happened, Kit?"

"I went to Flooders while Levi was out. To make Austin talk. I was scared. About Davis. Of him being another Aiden. But I made Austin so mad, and then he never came around like I was convinced he would. I ... I think I made it worse, pushed him further down his dark hole. I've been blaming myself ever since. I know it was stupid, but when I talked to him alone before, like way before, he told me the truth."

"Way before?"

"Back in October. He called me out for confusing Levi, and I got him to confess that he liked you. Said you were end game."

My mouth falls open.

"I'm sorry I couldn't tell you. You were already with Leo, and he wasn't ready yet. I swore I wouldn't spill his secret."

I rest my head on her shoulder. "You're the best."

"Wait. What?"

"Very Gus to my Shawn. Except, you deserve good things too. And I don't steal your money."

She huffs a laugh. "I get to be Gus?" she asks thickly.

"Can you tap dance?"

"A little. Not really."

"So yes."

"I took tap in like fourth grade," she hedges.

"'I can't do this with you right now,'" I quote.

Her giggle bounces my head.

I sit up to meet her eyes. "You said you make yourself small, but you've only ever gone big when you're looking out for me.

Don't worry about the Austin thing, okay? He's got a stubborn streak in there. Like a Gobstopper." My hands mime ball shrinking with each layer. "Muscles, marshmallow, stubbornness." I bump her shoulder. "Hey, when's your first dance class? Feels like you're stalling."

She bites her lip but lets me change the subject. "I've been praying about that this week."

"Yeah?"

"Yeah. Bravery is complicated for me. But knowing I'm loved changes the flavor of it. That made no sense. The feel of it, I mean."

"'I've heard it both ways,'" I quote.

She chuckles.

I almost sound like the old Sophie. I miss her. But also, I don't. The old Sophie couldn't have been a real friend just now. She couldn't have fully understood. She would have been thinking about Mom and how she—I—never measured up. She would have been too wrapped up in herself to even hear clearly. But in some ways ignorance was bliss.

An arm squeeze from Kit pulls me back. "God loves you so much. How does that change the feel ... the flavor ... of what you're going through?"

She leaves me to consider as families stream in and out of the lodge.

"I've been thinking about God's gifts like Skittles," I tell her. "You're Skittles. Mia's Skittles. Mayberry—it's all Skittles. And being with Austin was like a giant handful of my favorite red ones. I wrecked it. Dropped—or, really—knocked them out of my own hand. And God could've scooped them up and handed them back. He could've caught them midair. But he didn't. He doesn't have to." I breathe deep. "And that's okay. Because they were always his Skittles. He's given me so many good things, but I keep finding that the Skittle giver is so much better than the Skittles themselves. They're just a cherry on top. So he can rain them down or take them all away, and that's his call. He doesn't owe me a single Skittle. And I don't need them to have enough."

Kit gives a slow, thoughtful nod, like I really am Shawn and just solved a big case.

"But the crazy thing is, he keeps giving them anyway. And I see him doing that for you too." I nudge her. "So yeah. If I have to let go of the Austin Skittles, I will. Maybe the Skittles he wants to give me aren't the guy I want. Maybe it's the best job ever. Or friends I get to keep for life. Or adventures that make my heart explode. Or maybe none at all. I trust him to hand them to me when he thinks it's a good idea."

A smile tugs at Kit's lips. She nods, eyes glassy, but she doesn't crowd me.

She finally speaks. "Might splurge for some hot chocolate. Want some?"

Releasing me before I hit emotional burnout? I'm all for it. "Is that even a question?"

My gaze drifts back to our boys—nope, *the* boys. They're closer now, dropping their gear in a pile by a tree. It's so warm that they've ditched their coats. Austin pulls off his helmet and runs a hand through his hair. Probably gearing up for one last run.

Austin's compression shirt is so proud, wrapped around every muscle, over the dip where his shoulders meet his biceps. I'd give anything for a hug from those arms. To hear his affectionate voice. Just for a minute. Just for me. Murmuring something good and true and steady. If I could just run my hands through those wild and sweaty curls as that pre-kiss mischief grows on his face. He's so close and yet so far. I'm growing lightheaded, making myself sick, but I don't look away. One more day and then I cut ties. One more day and I let those Skittles go for good.

Several girls our age call over to Levi and Austin as they pull with their ski poles back to the lift. My stomach drops in dread. I know what's coming.

Like a swarm. I can't hear what they say, but the high pitch of their flirty voices drifts all the way to me. A couple are brazen enough to lean forward with bold, lingering touches. Levi plants his poles and pushes himself back. Austin stays, smiling and chatting. He cranes his head back to say something to Levi, who escapes. I count seven girls. They press out of their skis, so they can stick out their hips and rip off their beanies and shake out their hair. It's back to this. I hated watching Austin share his smile with all those girls. I loathed it. It's infinitely worse now.

Everything in me wants to bound out of here. To find Kit and Mia and sing a song and make a joke and pretend. I don't want to cry. I know better than to avoid my feelings, but I can't anymore. It's too much.

I'm stuck. In quicksand.

The girls wave over friends to join them. Of course Austin's pulling girls to him like a giant magnet. Look at him. Nothing more attractive has ever been spotted on a ski hill. But they couldn't know the half of it. I long for him to search for me like he used to. He'd pull me closer in a crowded room. I was enough for him. He never needed another pair of eyes on him. He never needed all that attention. He loved me so fully. My teeth chatter with suppressed tears.

I can't bear to watch this anymore. I force myself to stand, to clunk around the table. The awful urge gnaws at me—one last glance. Just one. But when I give in, Austin's bent lower, his arms around two sets of giggling shoulders. And for the first time in a month, he's looking straight at me.

CHAPTER SIXTY-EIGHT

Austin

Her face almost knocks me to the ground, but this will be worth it. She'll see. *This is for you, Soph. Anything for you.*

Sophie

I spin on my heel, but the sounds of cooing and laughter follow, slicing through the air like a taunt as I clomp down the stairs, as fast as ski boots allow. Which is to say, torturously slow. The worst getaway method in the world.

Finally.

I collapse into the snow and lean back against the cold brick wall. The moment I'm out of sight, the sobs break free.

Is this his revenge? He knows I'm still desperate to have him back? It had to be intentional—the perfect way to push me away for good. He knew how much it crushed me when he dated all those other girls. I told him. I was so vulnerable. And now he's using it to sever the last thread between us. *Fine, Austin. I get it. It's over.*

Jesus, why? I'm trying. I'm trying to stay close to you, obey you, leave it to you. Why this? I could have been sitting anywhere else.

This is my answer. The line in the sand. The don't-miss-it message.

Loud and clear. Just ... Help me move on. Help me stop wanting what I can't have. Help.

When I run out of tears, I wipe my face, pick myself up, and wander to the restrooms. The line stretches around the hall, so I text Kit and Mia.

Crazy bathroom line. Be back after.

We fly back to Texas tomorrow afternoon. I'll recover from this, from him. I'll cut ties. I'll swear Kit to secrecy so he won't even hear about me third-hand. And I will be okay.

With you, I'll be okay.

MIA

I have your stuff. We'll leave at 4.

Not sure how the guys are going to be ready in an hour since Austin is standing around flirting his heart out, but whatever.

The bathroom line takes as long as I guessed, and I don't rush to finish at the mirror as I make myself presentable again. Surely the regression to chronic flirting will no longer be on display after twenty minutes.

Meet back at the table?

KIT

No. Sorry, we need a few minutes. Meet up soon.

Why so cagey? I plod back to my pitiful spot with my back to the building and slink down.

A FaceTime call buzzes on my watch—Davis.

I stare ... and manage to unzip my pocket and answer on my phone before it's too late.

"Scarlett!" A hoodie over his beanie, and his nose is red. Where is he?

"Bruce," I eke out. My voice is hoarse.

He shakes his head with a smirk. "Sometimes I forget how beautiful you are. It just hit me all over again."

I roll my eyes, but the world around me brightens. The snow is whiter. Happy chattering noises reach me from the other side of the lodge.

"You'll never guess what I found out today," he says.

"That you're a shameless sweet talker?"

He grins. "That's not news."

"True. What then?"

"The universe wants us to be together."

A spark lights in my frozen chest. "Oh does it?"

"No, it does. Listen to this. I'm in Colorado too. Twenty minutes from you. The guys I came up here with are skiing another day, but I was ready for something different. I tried out snowshoeing this morning, and then I was gonna rent a snowmobile. Found some guys who invited me to join their group—stop laughing at me—so I'm killing time while they get my waiver ready, and I saw your reel." Those warm brown eyes smile into mine. A bell dings as he opens a door. "I'll be back in an hour or something," he calls to someone. "Sorry about that!" Snow fills the screen behind him. He skips down outdoor stairs. "How long are you up here? What are your thoughts on snowmobiling? I wonder, is it dangerous to snowmobile when it's getting darker? I bet I could find someone to rent us one with a light on it or something, right? These people seemed cool."

His attention is a hit of something—exactly what I was needing. Relief and thrill course through my veins. All I can do is laugh.

"You're not saying anything, Sophie Appel. I'm not mad about it though. Your laugh is everything." He steps into an SUV. "Hold up. Don't go anywhere." His video shows the Pause button, but I can hear him talking to himself as he types on his phone. "Cooper. Leadville. Yep. Twenty minutes away. That's insane. Thanks, Fate." He's back. "I was trying to be chill about it, but now that I'm looking at you, I'm just heading your way. I'll be there in twenty. Is that cool with you?"

My jaw goes slack. "What about your snowmobiling group?"

"Are you kidding? Why would I go with those random dudes when *the* Sophie Appel might come with me? Will you? Will you please go snowmobiling with me?"

Is this you? Is this your mercy? Your kindness? Are you showing me that I'm still lovable? Is this a gift? You know me so perfectly, and you know this is exactly what I want. It's what I need.

But it sits in my chest like an ill-fitting puzzle piece.

Davis's seat belt shrinks back into the wall as he waits for my reply.

"That sounds like exactly what I need today." I'm sure I can find a way back to Kit's house. Uber or something. I try to cram the puzzle piece in my head.

He pumps a fist. But my stomach slides into my throat.

And I know.

I absolutely know.

But this is so perfect. Isn't every perfect gift from you? Please. Please let me have this.

But I know.

With a breath, I open my free hand on my lap. My shoulders slump, head drops back to the brick wall. A sob threatens in my throat. But I choose the Truth.

You. I pick you. This won't work. He can't fix me. He can't fix this. Not for long. I need you. Even if it hurts. I pick you. I'll sit in this if that's what you want.

Peace floods my distraught, lonely heart.

I love you. You are my handiwork.

"It doesn't have to be a date." Davis's voice breaks through. Serious, like he knows too. "We can be adventure-junkie friends." A vulnerable half smile. "I'll take whatever you want to give."

My head swivels side to side, almost involuntary. "I can't. I'm sorry. You deserve better."

"The 'Jesus told me' card." The camera droops as he drags open the SUV's door. "You know how many times I've heard that?"

I pull in a breath. "He didn't tell me anything. I'm telling *him* something. I like you, but it's not enough. Have so much fun." And I punch the red button. As I lower my phone, the enormity of my aloneness settles around me. And yet I'm okay. Digging under my sleeve, I find my bracelet.

With you, I'm okay.

My phone dings, and I brace for a text from Davis. But it's Kit.

KIT

Meet us at the beginning of the parking lot, please.

Um, okay.

I stand, adjust my shirt, and steel myself. Two hours in a car with the human embodiment of "We Are Never Getting Back Together." Should be a blast.

I need you close. Get me through this too.

CHAPTER SIXTY-NINE

Austin

Here she comes. It's time.

My heart hammers. My mouth dries. I don't know what I'm doing except giving her another multiple-choice option, as she would say. No more second-guessing.

I nod to the choir behind me—my new friends willing to spend an hour practicing a song they barely know for a girl they've never met. Leader Girl counts us in—"One, two, three, four"—and I bravely launch into "Life with You" by Walker Hayes. The same song Sophie picked the first time she gave me a chance at this.

My soloist's killing it back there, looping the hook like she was born for the stage.

Sophie's jaw is on the ground. She's eerily still. Not smiling.

By the time I finish the chorus, I'm about to call Kit and Mia down to revive her. The only part of her moving is the wisps of hair the wind pulls around her face.

I'd planned a strategy for when we were back on campus, but the wait was murdering me. I thought the coincidence of meeting an entire choir was God doing me a solid. It's been near impossible to stay away from her the last two days, but I have plenty of practice waiting for the right time. And I've made such a mess—perfect timing is a must.

Unlike water tower night, I'm not here to convince her. Whatever she says, I'll accept it. But I'm dying for her forgiveness. And another chance to be the one to hold her, to care for her, to make her smile? I just want to be *with* her. I had to at least ask. Maybe it's not too late.

I step forward, reach for her—shouldn't do that—yank my hand back. "Soph? Say something?"

The choir's background "oohs" while I sang to Sophie ... I thought she would like it.

After my talk with Levi on Thursday, I found Archie. He said he'd take me to his gym, but a few questions later I was shuffling around the block instead, praying, hearing that nudge again to go away and pray. So Friday I drove Chelsea's SUV up to the mountains with Archie's Bible on the seat beside me.

Up there, on the hiking trail he'd recommended, in the clear air and pine trees and the silence, I felt God *with* me. That day was magic. Just me and the Boss, who insists I call him Dad. Not because I've done enough. Not because I have it all together. Just because I'm his.

Ten minutes into my hike, I was falling to my knees in the slushy snow, re-surrendering to him. I can't explain it except to say he welcomed me back with open arms. Like a father running out to his prodigal. And he spent the day whispering to me. **Austin. My son.**

When I finally dropped the armor I'd been scrambling to hold up, I got real honest. About the fact that Sophie's going to end up with a sinner no matter what. About the fact that she's not perfect either, and I can't worship her, no matter how special she is.

I can't ache for her for one more day without telling her the truth. I want her all the time, no matter what. That kind of love—it's this vivid, electric picture of how God feels about me. But I've been forcing it into a box it was never meant to sit in.

I'll never forget the gravity of my choices that day—worshipping her beauty, myself, what I wanted. And yet, if the God of the universe can take me back and call me his anyway ... maybe Sophie could too. Maybe she could learn to love the new me. The less impressive but also less breakable me.

I still don't want her to compromise. I still want her to have everything. But how ridiculous was it to think I could be the one to give her everything? That's her Savior's job. Still ... what if I could be his hands and feet? The one to remind her how precious she is. How treasured. How alive and golden and wanted.

It didn't take more than an hour to get back to the truth, but I stayed out there all day, talking to him out loud. Just me and God and snow-crunching silence. We talked about what football meant to me and how it's time to let it go. We talked about Dad. About who I am when I'm not earning it all. And my soul ... breathed again.

As I warmed up in Archie's car, I read the story of the woman who anointed Jesus's feet. This part sent a zap through me—"Therefore, I tell you, her many sins have been forgiven—as her great love has shown. But whoever has been forgiven little loves little."

I took Jesus for granted. I thought I was on top of things, that I had it under control on my own. I thought I had to handle it, that I needed to earn my place. But now that I've fully bombed my life, I can see what a mess I am. How needy and broken I've always been. I have so much to be forgiven for, and I love him so much more for taking me back. I'm overcome with hope for his plans for me.

But right now? Sophie's standing in front of me, gaping in horror. Almost like when I asked her out the first time. Then again ...

"What's happening?" she finally asks, eyes firmly on the girls behind me.

I planned every word of this, but my mind goes blank. "I love you, Sophie. I'm sorry. I needed"—my voice catches—"I needed you to have everything."

I press the bridge of my nose. I'm not making sense.

Please give me the words.

"You must know this now—I'm not who I was before. Who I thought I was. I couldn't make it work. I wanted so badly to convince you, to captivate you, to be enough. But I'm not. I can't do it all. So I tried to let you go. I wanted you to have better than me. I tried so hard to give you space to move on. But you deserve to know how loved you are. How admired. How missed. How dark the world is without you. I shouldn't have hidden it from you. I shouldn't have decided for you. There's so much I don't know, Soph. But I'm sure about this—you're it for me. My all or none."

She still won't look at me. Studies the packed snow between us instead.

"If you gave me another chance, I'd love you the best I could. I'm learning, and I ... I'm so sorry." I drag a hand through my hair. "Whatever you need, that's what I want. Even if that's not me. But you deserve to know the truth. You should get to decide for yourself. I'm sorry I let you think I was angry at you. We made a mess, but we did it together, and I've only ever loved you."

She gestures to the girls behind me. "But ..."

"Oh." I hold out a weak arm. "This is a choir I met. From Lincoln, Nebraska, right?"

They cheer in dramatic high-pitched voices.

I send them a smile that costs me. "Thanks so much, ladies. Y'all sounded great."

More cheering.

Sophie's lips purse. Another bad sign.

Someone pipes up behind me. "Say yes! Take him back!"

"If you don't, I will. That boy is fire."

Sophie scoffs.

I rub my eyes. Not helping.

The choir girls laugh and jabber a mile a minute.

Sophie moves her weight from boot to boot. Her brows bend down in suspicion. She won't look my direction. "We need to talk, but ..."

Finally. Words. But her voice is too neutral. Not the lilting voice of happy Sophie. She turns to the girls behind me for the millionth time. *Look at me, Soph. Let me see your eyes.*

"Yeah?" I can barely hear myself with the racket behind me. I tilt forward, desperate for a better reply than I'm expecting, a better reply than I deserve.

But she's yours. Not mine. I can trust you with her. You'll take care of her. You'll give her everything she needs.

Furrowed brow, she stares at my middle, my boots, my hands. She opens her mouth, like the words won't come out. Her sweet, perfect mouth that I kissed and treasured. The mouth that told me a thousand stories and laughed with me and comforted me and trusted me with her secrets. I step forward again—close enough to feel the warmth I'm missing, close enough to see the way her lashes flutter like she might cry. I'm dying to close the gap, to erase the space with my hands, with my lips. But I stop myself, muscle my hands back to my sides. *Let her choose. Let God choose.*

She's so special, so wonderful, so alive, so beautiful. Love for her explodes out of my heart like a volcano.

But the lava burns on impact.

A slow head shake. Her eyes fill, and my gut fills at equal pace with desperation. My legs go limp.

I did this.

Austin. My son.

A sob hovers in my throat. I fight to stay upright.

You'll make this okay. You'll make me okay. Whatever she needs. Whatever you pick.

I drag my gaze away.

She's yours. I trust you with her.
Yours.

CHAPTER SEVENTY

Sophie

Austin Scott, in the flesh. Singing to me, staring at me, talking to me ... pleading with me. But it's one sentence playing on repeat in my head. The one that reframes everything else—*I tried so hard to give you space to move on.*

It's so Austin it hurts. He was too Austin to function.

Everything clicks. The absolute avoidance. The grief in his posture. How Kit and Levi were convinced his hangup wasn't anger.

The lifetime supply of hibiscus tea Savannah thanked me for buying—I didn't. But Austin knew that's what I drink when I'm sad. The Super Tips markers I found in the lounge—they weren't Kit's. But he knows those are the kind I hand-letter with. The beanbag chair. The trail mix that appeared in our cabinet. What else was him?

Thrill. Longing. Hope. Fear. Anger. Joy. Vulnerability. A hundred emotions in one body.

What is this? What do I do? What if we try again and I'm crushed a second time?

So if you sinful people know how to give good gifts to your children, how much more will your heavenly Father give good gifts to those who ask him?

The gift.

I thought seeing myself in a new light was a gift. And it is. But what if the gift that night really was Austin? The Us I've wanted back so badly.

I can't explain it, but I just know—I can trust Austin with my heart again. Even if memories from home scream not to touch that fire twice. Words need to be said first, but Levi's right—he's the best guy out there.

So I hold my head high. I risk the heart we both broke. And I accept the gift.

Austin

"Okay," Sophie says. "Yes."

I jolt upright, like I've just been yanked from a nightmare.

Cheering explodes behind me.

"A second chance?" I call over the noise.

She nods.

Jerking forward, I yank her in, squeeze her close. She's thinner now. Did she lose her appetite like I did? Has she been just as sad? My heart breaks all over again. More late-night pancakes. More fancy dinners. I'll start picking up desserts with Levi. Cookie cake. Definitely cookie cake.

Sophie. She's here. I breathe her in. Vanilla today.

Before I realize what I'm doing, I'm lifting her and spinning. A real Sophie laugh rings out. The best sound in the world. Her hands land on my shoulders, and every knot in me unravels. Then reality slams in. I shouldn't have hugged her without asking. I set her down gently.

"Soph, I'm so sorry. Will you forgive me? Please forgive me. For failing you when you needed me. For not protecting you. For not talking to you about it. For ghosting and hiding and ... decomposing for a month."

Soft brown eyes meet mine—I suck in a sudden breath. Soothing, latte-brown. Warm when I'm cold. Cool when I'm hot. I went without them for weeks. I will never hide from them again.

She nods, tears on her cheeks. Can I wipe them away? I don't know if it's okay to touch her face. I don't know if it's okay that I spun her around. I've lost all right to touch her, to be close to her, to know everything about her. Do I really get to earn it back?

"I messed up first," she says. "I betrayed your trust. Will you forgive me—"

"Yes, I forgive you," I cut in. "Yes."

Sophie

Whiplash. Those girls fawning over Austin and then commanding me to take him back. Whiplash. Releasing him for good just minutes before twirling around in his arms. Whiplash. My friends' looks of pity this afternoon and the fascinated, exultant glances in the rental car now.

I insisted he ride shotgun next to Mia, climbed in the backseat, yanked Kit's willing arm with me. I'm a coward.

Her Rapunzel eyes shine, assessing me for visible insanity.

I turn to watch the mountains and snow and endless pine trees, morphing into a new perfect scene with every twist of the road. "I'm scared."

"Keep talking?"

"I can't be sure if we'll be like your parents or mine."

A soft noise. "We get no guarantees. But you can pray and obey and keep showing up. That's the best anyone can do. And

…" She flits a glance to the front. "I really think you're in good hands."

I let out a slow breath. God knew I'd need all of this. Friends who forgive, not flake. To face shame and stop running—except in temptation, where running's the power move. To see Austin for who he is: imperfect, breakable. Like me. Like everyone. But also profoundly good. And stubbornly determined to obey his Creator.

You've been busy.

I drop my head. Humbled. Grateful.

"Go on," Kit interrupts, pointing to the empty seat in front of me. "Talk to him."

I shake back to the present. "Here? No way."

"Sophs, it's okay. Do it scared."

"All of you are here!" I hiss. "I literally haven't talked to him since that morning in his—"

Levi twitches in front of me.

Shoot. Quieter. Quieter!

She squeezes my hand. "Okay. We'll find a place for you to be alone." To Levi, "Babe."

He twists around with the cockiest grin I've ever seen. "Yeah?"

"You call him *babe*?"

She laughs. "Are we still going to Beau Jo's?"

"Whatever you want," he says.

I make gagging noises.

"Yeah, right," Kit points at me. "You're the one getting spun around like you're Disney on Ice."

Levi chuckles at her. Dude's so whipped he should come with a nutrition label.

"You two can get your own table," Kit says. "Far away from ours."

"No. Too much pressure."

"Okay. Dinner at home and we'll do Beau Jo's later? Or pickup order?"

Bending forward, Levi reaches to receive something from the

front. Austin catches my eye and sends a tentative smile. The air in the car shifts.

Levi hands me a note written on the car rental agreement in Austin's handwriting. I unfold it slowly, like it might detonate.

> go on a walk with me when we get back?
> ps - i missed you so much

And he signed his name with a scraggly little heart—pure boy, pure him. So sweet my chest aches.

He's still craning around to see my reaction. I meet his gentle gaze and nod.

Kit tap-taps my leg. "Can I read it?" She tucks her hands under her chin like a prayer.

I hand it over.

She squees with delight, and more of my armor flakes off.

But what if he leaves again?

Tears fill Kit's eyes and turn them an otherworldly blue. "I'm taking partial credit for this," she teases, raising an imperial brow. "I've been praying for you two every day since you broke up. This is my yes."

Up front, Austin cranks up "Goldest," and Mia's look speaks volumes. This music is not her jam, but Austin's too happy to shut down. Levi reaches around his seat for Kit's hand, and their fingers lock, a wordless agreement. I feel myself nodding.

What they have is worth all the risk.

CHAPTER SEVENTY-ONE

Sophie

Austin and I try to sneak out of the house after pizza at the Talbots', but our covert op is anything but. Kit's brothers toss catcalls at Austin. Then Mia dares a loud "hand check!"—so wildly over the line that everyone freezes ... before bursting into laughter. Like Mia didn't just cannonball into the trauma pool. Honestly? It's kind of perfect. The energy is infectious, the forgiveness is real. But also, I'm still catching up.

Safely out the front door, we wander down the sidewalk in Kit's neighborhood. It's magical out here. The setting sun casts a golden glow. Spruce branches bow under piles of snow. A crisp breeze dances through bare trees. I get it now—why Kit loves home so much, even apart from her bizarrely happy family.

Austin's giant bear paw hangs loose at his side. Would it feel the same as before? I bet it's still warm in the chill. Rough and gentle and more comforting than ever. I run through it all again—

relationships are never perfectly safe, and I never liked safe anyway. I believe him. I really think I can trust him. Apparently needing no further reassurance, my hand lurches out for his. His engulfs mine instantly, greedy and confident. Joy leaches into my bloodstream.

"We have a lot to talk through, Sparky."

I break into a grin at my long-lost nickname.

Please help. Make sure I say what needs to be said. Nothing more, nothing less.

"I'll start," I say.

"Okay, hit me."

I almost smack his arm, but it's too soon for play hits. Too much still unsaid.

"You have a weary voice. Tons of voices, actually, but the weary one hurt to hear."

"Voices?"

"Playful is your default. Used to be." I send a sad smile. "There's also pensive. Affectionate-slash-sultry—big fan of that one. Football voice. Stern voice." I pause to chuckle at his reaction.

He just stares, like I've recited his shoe size and he's never checked the label.

"Happy-at-home voice. And the weary voice—that one was my fault. I see that, and I have a plan."

"That you were paying attention like that? My head is getting dangerously big again. But Soph, the weary voice wasn't your fault."

"It's still my turn, mister."

"Yes, ma'am."

"I'm ready to make sacrifices to be with you," I continue. "We're so different, but we can compromise. So I can get the new I want and you can get the rest you need. I love you too much to let you sacrifice everything for me again. It's a no for me, and it's how we can keep the weary voice away."

"I love you too." He squeezes my hand—a long, anchoring squeeze that says a hundred things at once. Then he blows out a breath. "I wanna push back on that compromise word, but you're not wrong about part of it—we are different. But the weary voice was all me. Trying to please everyone, burning the candle at both ends, not letting God pick what mattered most. I can't be the one deciding how I spend my time anymore. That's what blew up in my face. And it makes sense. I was over here acting like I needed less rest and quiet than *Jesus.*" A wry smile. "He'll have to be the one to give you everything. And I'll be praying hard he does. But whenever I get to be the one he uses, I'm so there. Every time."

I melt into the sidewalk creases. Who is this man?

You didn't just give me back Austin—you gave me a stronger, self-aware Austin?

Impulse tells me to wrap him up in a hug and call it, but I don't. More needs to be said. Still, a *Mario Kart ding* sounds—we made it through the first lap.

"Listen," I start. "I'm going to say some things to you, but then I don't want to hear about them again. Understand?"

He eyes me. "Not really, but go ahead."

"That time Lily showed up in your room, you practically teleported to my door. And I know you called Kit out when she confused Levi half to death. You fuss at me when I criticize myself. All of that proves that you're capable of confrontation when it matters." I wait for his nod. "But too many times, you refused to use your words." A Chelsea phrase. "Like tapas night. You should have said no. And then at your house and after you dumped me—"

"I didn't dump you," he interrupts, horrified.

"Uh. That was a pretty textbook dumping."

"I could never *dump* you. I pushed you away. For your own good."

"Let's press pause on the fatalistic worldview subject."

He clamps his mouth shut, frown still present.

"It's not okay that you ghosted me." My voice grows smaller. "I can't handle that kind of fighting. At home, the loud fights were awful, but the silence meant it was over forever." Brokenly, I try to make him see. "Austin. I can't do that again." I brace myself. If he can't hear this, what are we even doing here?

But he's pale, eyes wrecked. "You're right. About all of it. Soph, I ..." He swallows. "I know I'll still make mistakes. But I promise I'll talk things out with you. I won't choose for you again. I see how wrong and unfair that was now. I'm so sorry."

I let out a breath. "Now. I forgive you. For all of it. Okay?"

His eyes shift.

Ah yes. Accepting forgiveness—the hard part for him.

"Anything else before we put it to rest forever?" When he avoids my gaze, I tug his hand. "I will not have you groveling about it anymore."

The tiniest smile plays at his cheeks. "I love it when you're feisty." It fades. "I more than learned my lesson. I hate that I hurt you. I hate that I didn't protect you, especially if you were Dark and Twisty that day. I just want you to know how desperate I am to be better. That I'm praying about it all the time."

I catch his gaze and clasp my hands together. "I'm blowing it up now." And I fling them apart with a ridiculous explosion noise.

His eyes fill. "Thank you," he whispers.

He grows an inch. The sweetest, tenderest smile.

But then with a big breath and sidelong glance, he dials the mood back to Ultra Serious. "You have a lot of power over me, Soph."

Help me with this. Show him how sorry I am.

I open my mouth for my apology monologue—but he keeps talking.

"I'm putting myself back in your hands because I trust you," he says.

I jerk back to him. Just like that? "You did everything for me,"

I argue. "You sent me the 'You Are My One Safe Place' song, and I nuked it."

Those eyes. So vulnerable they could destroy me. "I trust you. Will you be my one safe place again?"

I can't speak, so I give a nod.

"Anything else before I explode this one too? I don't want it hanging over you for another minute."

"I'm so sorry." My voice trembles. "Never again."

"I know." His voice is thick. "It's going away now." And he imitates my explosion.

And just like that … it's gone.

"Can I?" I reach for him.

"Please." He yanks me over, squeezes me tight against his hoodie. A man-bear hug. I bury my face in his neck and breathe him in. That perfect cocktail of musky firewood and fresh air and goodness.

He lifts a hand but stops. "Can I touch your face?"

I bob my head.

His giant paw encases my cheek, my jaw, my head. "I missed you so much." His thumb brushes my temple, trails into my hair. "I was an embarrassment to humanity."

My eyes roll back in my head. I'm Belle, leaning into Beast's giant hand. "Mia called you a stain on your couch."

He huffs a laugh.

"It wasn't just that though," I say. "We rubbed against the grain of the universe."

"Yeah. Nasty splinters."

His other hand rises, and I fall somewhere south of coherent.

"But … somehow … he used the sin," he says. "I can't believe I'm saying this, but I needed the last month—the soul-crushing fallout of losing you. I needed to see. To break down. Start over. So I don't make the same mistakes again." He presses a kiss to my forehead, lingering. "No earning, God," he prays, voice barely holding. "Just *with* you. And … God, please …"

You brought him back to me.
Better than ever.

AUSTIN

Song of the day

"Hell on the Heart" by Eric Church

CHAPTER SEVENTY-TWO

Austin

The final March Madness game of the day ends, but no complaints here, because Sophie is curled against my side on the Talbots' worn-in sectional. My deep, contented sigh is halted by warm lips on my neck.

"I've missed this," Sophie whispers.

My pulse doubles.

Sophie was nowhere. Now she's everywhere—leaning on me, touching me, draping her legs everywhere. I've lost my tolerance. Every touch is a new zing. A life-giving, threatening zing.

I'm doing this with you, right? How do you want it to go?

Levi calls a good night and leaves with a confident nod. He thinks we've got this.

"Hey, Soph?" I say into her hair. "Can we talk about boundaries stuff?"

She sits up. Her eyes flit to mine. This subject is dangerous.

I find her hand. "Before, I was being insanely careful—I

mean, I thought I was—and things were already getting really intense."

"Yeah."

"And we still have a long way to go." I squeeze her hand between mine. "You're too beautiful for your own good. It makes this a billion times harder."

"Ohhh-kay."

"Hey," I clip. "Don't argue with me on that topic."

Her lips quirk.

"So we need a better plan. White-knuckling this stuff isn't going to last. Especially not anymore."

She agrees, pushing her hair behind her pretty shoulders. "What helps with other temptations?"

I straighten, trying to focus. "Habits keep me from skipping the gym."

"Yeah, habits. And *need* helps me. I need my runs. I need my Jesus time."

I tug her back to me, kiss her head, squeeze her close. "Better than a dream. I'm so lucky."

She grins, chin on my chest. "I love you. Oh. Mia's mom's donut thing."

I chuckle. "What?"

"Mia's mom loves donuts, so she won't even walk through the bakery part of the grocery store, much less go through the Krispy Kreme line. I thought it was so random when Mia told me that." Her eyes grow big, like she's having an epiphany.

"The donuts are too tempting, so she has to stop a step back. Saying no at the store is easier than resisting one sitting on her counter." Oh no. I beat my head against the sofa. The nos halfway down the hill are already rolling too fast. The nos at the top? Not easy, but doable.

"The Snowball Effect," we say at once.

I jolt.

"I talked to Chelsea. But I'll tell you about that later."

"'Kay ..."

What does it mean?

I let out a breath that's more like a whimper.

You're the Boss.

And my Dad. You want what's good for me. It's your call.

Her voice pulls me back. "What if ... we copy Kit and Levi? Quit kissing. At least for now."

My jaw falls open. She's the one to suggest it?

"I know..." She falls dramatically against the couch. "I want to throw that idea in the air and shoot it with a shotgun."

A strangled laugh escapes me.

"Something funny?" she asks.

"No, no."

How do we do this? Help.

She falls serious. "I want to obey as much as you do. Things are going to be different this time around. I'm doing this *with* you."

I edge forward. *With.*

"Okay?" she asks.

I nod, but she's more irresistible with every word.

"We need a couple days to pray hard about it," I say. "It won't last if we're not a hundred percent sure that's what he wants from us."

She agrees, pressing kisses to my hand. So affectionate. After everything.

I reach to run fingers up her arm, over her shoulder, through her hair. If only we could skip this part. I just want to do our life together now—tangled-up naps, sneaking up on her in the kitchen, camping in the treehouse, breakfast tacos in bed.

"When can I marry you?" I blurt.

She bursts into a laugh, closes the distance until she's wrapped around my arm. "Not right now, mister. We have to figure this out."

I grunt. "Fine."

Hand still in her hair, I flash back to Friend Phase. I was so anxious to blast past it, but those months were good. Simple. We learned so much about each other but without all the complication, the temptation. I wouldn't go backward—not on your life—but I wish I hadn't been such a bulldozer with the timing.

You're on it, right?

With a deep breath, I steel myself to sit in this part. Having her back is so good. I wanna soak in all this goodness before we have bills and jobs and real life—that is, if she'll have me.

"I'm gonna ask you that for real someday." I drag a thumb down her jaw. "And I hope you'll have a different answer."

As her eyes grow with fiery affection, a slow shiver rolls down my spine.

Her eyes drop to my lips, and she bites her own—

Until she bolts off the couch and up the stairs. "Good night!"

I slump against the sofa—equal parts gratitude and longing.

Back on campus, I sit at my desk, humbled at the chance to take care of my favorite business. Pitch dark out the window in front of me, but my eyes aren't drooping shut. And I can meet my reflection without flinching. Just got off the phone with Dad, and now it's time to text Sophie a song link. Like I used to. Like I will again. Tonight? A song from Dad's favorite band.

Song of the day

"All In" by Lifehouse

Next, I write her a note. It takes me three drafts and a brief handwriting crisis, but I finally get it perfect. I try to tear it out ... and the page rips in half.

"Come *on* ..."

Levi tosses over a roll of tape, laugh barely suppressed.

"Save it," I mutter. "And thanks."

sophie,
you have 5 smiles.

1. faking it
2. medium happy
3. excited (often with clapping)
4. when someone sings along with you or goes along with your crazy idea (even more clapping)
5. in my arms

love,
austin

After class the next day, I'm walking in and tossing my backpack on the floor when Sophie texts.

Your note, mister...

She found it. I snuck it in her notebook yesterday. Adrenaline already buzzing, I smack my palm.

Did I nail it?

Not fair. You're not even scrawny.

A grin splits my face.

I'm a puddle.

Levi and Haymitch stride in. Power stance from one.

Disappointed head shake from the other. My face falls. This can't be good.

"Phone," Levi demands, hand out.

"It's better if you don't resist, Samwise," Haymitch says, all fake sympathy. "'Fraid you brought this on yourself."

And I know.

A pack of Flooders barrels in behind them, tackling me on the couch, grabbing me by the wrists and ankles.

"I know where y'all sleep!" I holler over a laugh, ripping free before they dogpile me on the floor.

Mateo swaggers in, crosses his arms. "Took you long enough."

Next stop: the communal showers. And then I'm airborne—limbs flailing, dignity optional—into a fully clothed, ice-cold, sopping-wet fresh start.

CHAPTER SEVENTY-THREE

Sophie

Tuesday run time. Austin bumps my hip again, all innocence and fake surprise.

I can't run very fast laughing like this. "If you keep doing that, I'll jump on your back and you'll have to run for both of us."

"Mmm. Promise?"

I shove his arm.

"Ready for Gotcha Week?" he asks.

The annual Mayberry-wide game of last student standing—Nerf-style. My girls and I raided Target yesterday for our blasters.

"My gun's bigger than your gun," I sing-song.

He laughs, poking my side. "Maybe so, but mine's built for stealth."

"Oh, stealth, huh?" I jab him back. "My strategy is to hide behind my ripped human neon sign of a boyfriend until the last minute. And then I'll jump out and dazzle everyone with my speed and accuracy."

"Dazzling is your middle name." And then he gasps. "Soph. Please wear that stretchy black dress thing."

"Which one?" I tease.

"You know which one. The one that makes you look like a panther."

"The Black Panther?"

He grins. "Not exactly. Ooh. Do I get to fire off rounds to protect you? Like we're in an action movie?"

"Too swoony," I whine. "You'd have a movie deal within the week."

"C'mon, I'd feel so manly. And it'd be great practice for that zombie apocalypse."

"Okay, fine. You can be Gale if I can be Katniss."

He eyes me. "Are we changing the ending?"

I clap and grin. "Absolutely. And I love that you know the ending. I have Janie to thank, I assume? When can we get her to campus?"

At that, his face softens in pure gratitude. Food and family—his constants.

"The second you offer, she'll come screaming around the corner in the pickup," he says.

"Ayumi's extra mattress! Sleepover in the lounge! What if I convince her to bring your mom's cooking?"

"Sophie," he murmurs.

His eyes blaze, and The Farm shifts in my mind—not just the place we fell apart, but maybe the place I can make it right.

I'm composing a text to Janie in my head when crisp white poster boards steal my attention. Two rows of them stretch across the windows of Albert Hall, a giant *2* already filling one of the spaces.

He eyes me with mischief, quirks a smile. "What?"

"Austin."

"Wonder what it says."

"I have to wait like everyone else? You have to tell me!"

"Sure about that? Might be for you."

I groan, nearly bursting. "Fiiine. I'll wait."

"Good. Time to pray?" he asks.

"Yeah."

Maybe I should be nervous to open up again. Two days back together isn't much. But this—us—already feels different. The spark is still there, buzzing and zapping, but now it's laced with peace. With this quiet knowing that wasn't there before. And under it all, the kind of freedom only Jesus could pull off. I don't have to hold my breath anymore. I don't have to prepare for the worst. Because if it comes, he'll be there.

Thank you. All the thank-yous.

"Hi, God. I'm so—I'm so thankful," he starts, voice deep and husky.

I watch the buildings we pass to give him privacy.

"You gave me a second chance with Sophie. You keep chasing after me, giving me good things I don't deserve. You took me back, and I just love you so much for it. Help us do this thing. Show us how to do it better."

My wide eyes slide to his and meet the same startled expression.

"Right? Dangerous prayer," he agrees, then sobers. "Keep working with me, teaching me. I need it. I need you. Keep helping Sophie, and open her mom's heart to love you and to love her better. Amen."

I squeeze his lightly pumping arm in thanks.

Silence and a mini-smile signal my turn.

"Hi, Jesus. I'm thinking about Mom a lot too. She seems more open now. Please plan everything just right—show me when to call and what to say and when to hang up. Give me a chance to tell her more about you when she's ready. Please work in every part of her life so that she can hear the truth and believe it. Just like you did for me. And ... I've been thinking about Jenny a lot. Is that you? Should I track her down? Take care of Austin. Show me how I can be there for him. Show him how to keep from getting so tired again. I want to be a ..." My throat tightens without warning. "A rejuvenating place for him. Teach me how."

"Soph. You are." He halts mid-step and yanks me into a hug so tight I squeak. Angles to kiss me—and jerks back like he touched a stove. "Sorry."

The ache of almost twists, but we promised to wait. To pray about it.

"Old habits. It's okay. You can trust me."

He squeezes my hand. Pointing his head, he begins again at our previous pace. "So ... I think God answered me while you were praying. But I don't wanna boss you around. You can pray about whether it's for you too."

"Austin, you never boss me around. Spill."

"I think God wants me to insist on a full twenty-four hours of rest and worship. It sounds impossible with my schedule, but my Archie book makes me think it would change everything. Like Mia's mom's donut thing—pulling the line back because I know this is a problem for me."

"Austin making boundaries?" I drag my eyes over him and give a theatrical shiver. But it's not all an act—my heart's about to melt through my ribs.

He falters mid-step, gaze gone molten. Fingers skim my arm—so tender my chest aches. "Uh. Where was I?" He rakes his curls, dazed.

I push his chest. "Running. And Sabbath."

"Right." He clears his throat, picks up the pace. "So, I know your idea of rest is different from mine, and I don't want to—"

"I know. You don't want to boss me around. I want to try it with you, okay?"

Mia's "force multiplier" line flickers through my head—how rare, two people chasing Jesus better together than alone.

Look what you made.

"Which twenty-four hours?" I ask.

Quiet. Rest. I feel my old defenses building an escape hatch, but I double down. It's a safe place, sitting with Jesus.

"Sunday morning to Monday morning. That way I can finish all my homework in advance. And since I'm quitting football, except for intramurals—"

My stomach drops. "Wait. Rewind."

He tells me about his offer from UT. That he turned it down on the drive from the mountain. That it was God's call, not mine to shoulder.

I loosen my arms, as if I can fling off the memory of his dad's horrified voice.

It's your call. I just want to be the right kind of help.

"I feel good about it, Soph. It was too much to take on Dad's dream. High school football was amazing—state championship, scouts, all of it. I loved it." He's so ... at peace. "But I'm ready for new dreams." He meets my gaze with meaning.

"Okay. But ..."

He tickles my side until I agree. Then he tells me he'd really like to coach G1's last few games.

I'm on a tilt-a-whirl.

A *ding* on my watch. And with it, the feeling Jesus has another adventure for me.

JENNY

You free later?

Thank you.

"So I'd better take Friday afternoons and Saturday mornings for homework," Austin says. "I ... have a lot to do with these classes." A guilty grimace. "And more all the time."

"Austin, stop it. I want you to have time to get your work done without feeling bad."

"Good, 'cause there's more."

"Okay, shoot."

"I can do easy homework with you, but I'll have to hide in my room for the rest."

"Why?"

"Well …" He flashes me a look so loaded it spikes my body temperature.

"Oh. Really?"

"Really. You're just gorgeous, Soph."

"Hm."

"Pretty sure I've told you that once or twice," he teases. "I can't concentrate on much else when you're around."

"Whatever you need."

"I'll have it all done by Saturday afternoon—our weekly adventures aren't going anywhere."

"Really? Are you sure?"

"Yeah, I'm sure. But they might not always be …"

"As extra as a Disney firework finale? I love you already, you know."

He tugs my ponytail. "You deserve extra."

"You're my favorite kind of extra, mister." Then a thought. "I used to plan everything. Remember?"

"Course."

"I liked it. What if I help? Take that off your plate?"

He nods slowly. "Okay. But only sometimes. And not this Saturday."

"What happens Saturday?"

"It's a surprise. Duh."

I squeal and clap. "More surprises! You're the best. So how else can I help?"

"You can keep me in line if I don't follow through. I need you to be feisty, okay?"

I salute, then break into "Start of Something New."

He grabs my hand, kisses it. Warmth sinks deep. "Just, thank you for another chance, Soph. I missed you something awful." And then, with a sly grin, he speeds up and veers across the street.

With him? Anywhere.

AUSTIN

Song of the day

"Made" by Spencer Crandall

And that hangman message?

TO 2ND
CHANCES

EPILOGUE

Fourteen Months Later

Sophie

Azores sand between my toes, wind cooling my face. Seabirds cawing and waves crashing. Snorkeling this morning was incredible. As I push up to my elbows, my bear-man stands up out of the ocean. Dripping swimsuit and a feral grin. Unreal.

Now he's running this way, about to soak me with a sopping bear hug. I pretend to wave him off, but I'm not moving. No way. He pretends to fall on top of me—landing strategically on his right knee—and brackets my shoulders with his forearms. Then he slings water from his thick, soggy curls, and I laugh so hard I can barely breathe. He distracts me from wriggling away with a kiss on my neck, on my cheek, on my nose.

Wait for it. I always have to wait.

Finally, his lips meet mine, and I melt into the sand. Heat, comfort, thrill—they shoot together, like fireworks under my skin. The first kisses are gentle, soft, like we have nothing but time. And we do. He's all mine. I get to kiss his juicy lips as much as I want. He never pulls away.

I glance back at the house. He's not missing another meal on my watch.

"Austin," I whisper.

Oh. I know better.

His kisses shift from sweet to fiery. Reckless and safe. White-hot and soothing.

I squeeze out the rest of my sentence. "You need food."

"Later," he murmurs.

"You must be starving," I get out between kisses.

Pausing, he reads my face. His smile grows mischievous as his body curls around mine, tucking close like two sides of a puzzle.

Later, his hand finds mine as we slosh to the dry sand from our dip in the ocean. Austin planned this magnificent island surprise for our honeymoon, and Levi's friends loaned us their beach house. Kit made me promise not to be weird about it. The only payback allowed is to visit them in Colorado after graduation. I mean, duh. Until then, we'll live in a cute little closet of an apartment while we save nearly all of Austin's paychecks for a plot of land of our own.

Oh, and Austin's proposal? Buckle up. A hangman game that spelled:

MARRY
ME
SOPHIE

I knew the message day two, but he played dumb! Carried

that ring box around in his pocket for days, all smug and sly. At the end of that week, he told me to dress up but blindsided me and my glittery dress with a field trip to a campsite in the forest, grinning the whole way in a fancy suit. Kit and Levi were already there and just as overdressed as we were. He asked me under a sky full of stars, next to a campfire, while being mercilessly pelted with unsolicited commentary from our best friends. Somehow, he convinced a Michelin-starred restaurant in Dallas to let him take food to go, and we even toasted with something bubbly. It couldn't have been a better blend of everything I love—fancy dresses and firewood, fine dining and s'mores. And the friends who stuck like glue.

I squeeze his giant hand, still slick from the ocean as we shuffle through sand and grass up to the house. This life. This man. It's more than I could have dreamed up for myself. I want him happy, with his people nearby, a home to grow into, and work for his hands when his mind gets loud. And I think a couple of those good things God planned for me involve helping to make that happen. So, after months of convincing, Austin's finally come around to what I think is the perfect compromise—country living where land is cheap, plus traveling and adventuring with all the money we save. We'll be minutes from his family and two hours from an amazing international airport. But I don't need a boarding pass—or even a Jeep—to keep me free. Not when I have a God who writes wild stories and made me his.

And ... okay, I'll admit it. I've fallen hard for Graham. They don't make plans two weeks out and then bail to watch Netflix. It's casserole potlucks all day and lake bonfires all night. Aprons, sure, but no bonnets. And the boating, two-stepping, four-wheeling, and cliff-jumping. What's not to like? I even learned to drive a tractor last summer. Farmer Austin might even top Beach Austin.

He landed an engineering job close enough to home and flexible enough for travel. Kit and I found new counselors who love the Snorkel as much as we do, but Chelsea's been the real second-mom game-changer. And Archie? Forever Austin's man-crush.

Austin twists the hose spigot at the house and sends a spray at my face. I squeal, but he pulls me back with a laugh and washes the sand off my feet. Some things never change. But some do.

Like this: I transferred out of Mayberry. Shocking, I know. But God's plotting was flawless—send Sophie to Texas and surprise her with Austin, found family, and hymns. Then God dropped the perfect degree in my head—event planning. New friends, a thousand things to juggle, all the fun. Planning my wedding sealed it. I'm obsessed. Austin couldn't be happier that, as he says, "life of the party" really is a degree. And I couldn't be happier that the Praise and Prayer spirit is alive and well at my new school—me, a friend with her drum, and whoever God sends through the door.

Another shock: I got married at twenty, and both of my parents actually came for the thing. Low bar, maybe, but it's real progress. Austin negotiated with Mom by signing a pre-nup. I still want to be mad at him for agreeing to that, but how could I? My dad couldn't even sit down with Austin before the proposal. Just sent me a wire, like paying for the wedding was his contribution. But then he showed. With his new wife. Our vows alone were a gospel message, and I'm praying harder than ever it sinks in. That they see who they are to their Creator. I have this picture in my head—praising Jesus in Heaven. All three of us. Whole. I'm clinging to this as our future together.

Inside the beach house, Austin cocoons me in a towel with a kiss on my head. When he pulls meat out of the fridge, I secure the towel around my waist and try to push him out of the kitchen.

He doesn't budge an inch. "Nope. Making burritos for my woman."

"You can do that for dinner. I'm making lunch so you can take a nap."

His sweet little smile. "Are you trying to take care of me, Sparky?"

"Trying. Now gooo." I push on his stomach.

But he wraps me in his arms like he's the burrito. "Okay. Thank you. But later I'm taking you on that volcano hike."

"Only if there's time," I argue, tugging on his waistband. A no-no for so long.

I'm rewarded with the most delectable smirk. And a thorough kiss.

My eyelids drag in a slow blink as I return to reality, and off he goes to plop onto the couch.

Austin

I curl up at the corner of the sectional and peek at Sophie humming "My Wish." Can't believe I'm the guy who gets to hear her hymns echoing off the walls. God's the one taking care of her —I just get to tag along and play assistant. An eager, clumsy son helping his Dad with a favorite project. In that way, she's mine— to have and to hold, to chase and to follow Jesus with. I can't believe God granted my biggest wish. The rest? Can't wait, but it's just gravy.

Song of the day

"Over And Over" by Ben Rector

The End.

BEFORE YOU GO

You've reached the end of *Anywhere*. Thank you so much for spending time with Sophie and Austin! It would mean the world if you left a quick **star rating on Amazon**. Even better? A short (or long!) review. Every single one helps Amazon suggest this book to someone who'd love it.

Up next: a **sneak peek** of the next Mayberry book—*Anytime: A Rom-Com for Jesus Freaks*. It stars two familiar faces from *Anywhere* and so much chaos, banter, and fun.

Want early (and sometimes unhinged) updates on my upcoming books? My **newsletter** fam gets the best of me. Sign up at www.kristinawelchauthor.com. And come hang out on Instagram @_kristinawelch for story-inspired graphics and other fun extras.

After the sneak peek, don't miss my **Author's Notes**. I've included the exact Scriptures that found their way into each chapter of *Anywhere*. And find my profile on Spotify for **playlists** based on my books.

I've been praying for you—that God meets you in a personal way through these pages and reminds you how wildly He loves you. How close He longs to be. How you can take another step toward Him.

Warmly,

Kristina

SNEAK PEEK: CHAPTER ONE OF ANYTIME

Janie

"You guys know the drill, but if you're feeling wordy, feel free to gush." Next to me, some guy plops his backpack in the aisle seat and rustles through it. "Words like charming, hilarious, and manly earn you bonus points."

"Broseph!" Sophie cheers beside me. Odd, since she's brotherless—an only child who just married my only brother, Austin.

"What's up, Sophie?" Two crumpled bright-orange socks materialize from the chaos of this guy's backpack. When he meets my gaze, a new expression flickers. Surprise? But it's gone just as fast, covered by a dimpled grin—that he throws like a weapon.

Why does he look so familiar? He wasn't at Sophie and Austin's wedding. I would remember this guy.

"Charming, hilarious, and manly," I repeat. "You must have forgotten overconfident."

Sophie cackles.

His blue eyes spark, still straight on me.

"Hand them over, Mav," Kit calls from the other side of Sophie as Sophie sends her a silent best-friend look.

Mav? I blink as the name snaps in like a puzzle piece. Last

year, back when Sophie and Austin were still dating, she and Kit were at my house most Sunday nights. I heard plenty about Kit's "reckless goofball" brother—pranks and nonsense, but also stories that took hard left turns into sainthood, like him praying for a stranger in a grocery store parking lot.

He mimes a hoop with his arms. Kit plays along, imitating his motion, and he throws the sock wad like a basketball and fakes a swish noise.

Kit taps her lip. "I'm thinking rambunctious, loud, and pestersome."

"Come on, Sis, you're making me look bad in front of your pretty friend." His eyes find mine again—mischief and a jolt in one hit.

Am I flattered, annoyed, amused, or insulted? Somehow ... yes.

"Sharpies?" she calls, holding out a hand across Sophie.

"Oh right." He digs a black Sharpie from the front pocket of his dark-wash jeans. Tiny pink flamingos cover his navy short-sleeved button-down. And then another marker from a zipper pocket in his backpack.

"Permission to sit on your ex-floor's row while I wait?" he asks.

"Permission denied," Kit says, all sunshine. She hands a Sharpie and a sock to the G1-er sitting on the other side of her, then points at Mav.

The other girl's mouth quirks up, a little dazed. Yep. She's clocking his glinting blue eyes.

When I finally risk another glance, he's already sprawled over the aisle seat like he'll be there a while. He has Kit's eyes—but dangerous, like deeper water. He's broader. Sharper jaw. That smirk. Same shiny brown hair but in a sharp cut. I almost hear Gru saying "up to no good."

I sit straighter in my seat. I fully ignored the cowboy types in Graham, and absolutely nothing's changed. I'm at Mayberry for momentum. For focus. For my future.

When girls from my floor file past us, we scooch our knees to let them by. I wave and don my best friendly smile when I see three of them are my roommate and suitemates. I still hardly know them. And had no idea they were meeting up to come to chapel together.

"Bro," someone says to Kit's brother from the aisle, whacking his arm. "Flooders sit back there." A bright orange lanyard hangs from his pocket. I know from Austin that no one wears a lick of that color on this campus unless they're a Flooder. It'd be like wearing maroon to a UT game.

"Got it, Hiccup," Kit's brother says.

The guy shrugs and walks off. Sophie twitches next to me.

"What?" I ask her.

Before she can answer, Kit's brother nudges me with his elbow, like a dog who wants his belly scratched.

"Oh, are you still here?" I tease.

His ready smile deepens to that striking grin.

I forcibly remove my gaze—my journal has exactly zero bullet points for charming dimples. Or eyes with an undertow. Plenty else to look at as hundreds of students file into the auditorium for our first chapel of the year, each to the rows unofficially assigned to their dorm floors.

"Kit doesn't live on G1 anymore," he says, "but you must. Wanna kick me off your row?" That playful challenge in his voice, dripping with confidence. He rests his head on the back of the seat. Then his eyes float closed, on his way to a nap. "'Now the full number of those who believed were of one heart and soul, and no one said that any of the things that belonged to him was his own, but they had everything in common.'" He nestles further down. "As you decide, remember that sharing with your brother in Christ is biblical."

A laugh bursts from my mouth, unladylike.

"What?" A smug smile, eyes still closed. "I had to memorize a lot of Bible verses as a kid."

"He's such a ham," Sophie says to Kit.

"Genetic defect," Kit says.

"Do you normally leverage Bible verses as lines to use on girls?" I ask.

"Hey. It wasn't a line." He swivels to me. "Why? Wanna get a coffee after this?"

Something zaps in my chest, as foreign as it is unwelcome. "No thanks."

"Another time then."

Concern flickers across Kit's face. "Is he gonna flip?" she whispers to Sophie.

"You can't imagine," Sophie says, unbothered. The smell of Sharpie drifts to me as she writes in cursive on one of Mav's socks. *For my brother-in-law from another mother-in-law.*

Then the sock hits his face. He chuckles.

Sophie passes me the Sharpie.

"What's the sock about?" I ask her.

"Flooders tradition," Mav interjects. "A competition to see which freshman can get the most G1-ers to sign a pair of these bad boys. And former G1-ers should count." He motions to Kit and Sophie. "I've added a wager this year to make things more interesting."

"Then why did Winston sign it?" I hold up the top.

"That's its name. The other one's Dwight."

"Ah. Favorite TV characters." I dig my snack out of the backpack at my feet.

"Impressive."

When I tear open my plastic bag of mixed nuts, half of them leap for freedom. Mav shoots to his feet—fear in his eyes, scanning the floor like it's a minefield.

"Oh, yikes." Kit hops up and shuffles to brush them off his chair with her forearm. "Mav is crazy allergic to cashews."

I slap a hand over my mouth.

"You tried to kill me." That dimple betrays him, but he's still eyeing the floor like one wrong move could take him out.

What a mess. Mama would be horrified—probably just laid a

dainty hand over her chest, somehow aware of my crimes from twenty miles away. I flail at the nuts with my shoe, trying to kick them away from him before I'm charged with manslaughter. "I'm so sorry. I didn't know."

He gingerly sits, avoiding the contaminated armrests. "Bad news, Kit's Pretty Friend. Now you'll have to keep those cashew hands to yourself."

I swallow a laugh.

"No flirty arm touches, no accidental knee grazes."

Reference to *The Holiday*? "*That* won't be a problem." I lace my fingers together to plead. "But please forgive me for the cashew missiles."

"Forgiveness granted," he says. "'Be kind to one another, tenderhearted, forgiving one another, as God in Christ forgave you.'"

"What a relief you're already putting your verses to better use."

He inches closer. "You like a man undergoing sanctification?"

I press my lips together, barely suppressing another laugh. "Still want me to sign your sock? I'll try not to touch it."

"If that's the only way to learn your name. 'Kit's Pretty Friend' is a mouthful." He stretches the sock between his hands so I can sign it in the air.

As I dot the i in Janie, his arms sag.

"Janie? As in Austin Scott's sister?" Bending to see around me, he levels an accusatory glare at his sister. Then at Sophie.

"Maaaay-be," Kit says.

Sophie bursts out laughing.

"You know my brother?"

He faces the stage with a slump, points with his thumb. "These clowns and their friends stayed at my house for spring break a long time ago. He offered his couch and showed me around campus. Convinced me to come to school here and live on Flooders."

Austin would help anyone, but convince someone to live on

his beloved floor? Only for the very best. I study him—and jerk away before a heart-eyes moment.

He turns back to Kit. "You know how he is. And you let me go on like that?"

"The man crush is real," Kit says. But then her mouth twists. Regret?

"I'll allow it," Sophie says, passing his other sock from G1-ers behind her. "It's the only rational response to the man."

"What should be done about this one?" I point at Mav, playing along.

Kit turns serious. "Now you know, Mav. Leave her alone or I'll tattle on you myself."

He crams the socks into his bag and sends me side-eye.

"You can't blame the guy," Sophie says to Kit. And then she starts singing "Whatever It Is" by Zac Brown Band, loud enough for the row to get the idea. A song about indescribable attraction. Super.

I try staring at the stage, feigning sudden deafness, willing someone to come up and start speaking. Mav half-stands, twisting toward the Flooders' rows. They must be full, because he drops back into his seat with a thud. Her song goes on. He squirms. Finally, the speaker starts up, blessedly interrupting Sophie's unprovoked karaoke.

Kit's gaze flits between me and her brother. She'll find nothing warranting Sophie's song in her perusal. This morning, like every other one, I squashed my crazy curls into a clip and threw on whatever T-shirt was clean. I have many goals, but datable is not one of them. Speaking of goals, what do I need to check off this week? I unzip the section of my backpack reserved for my journal, then hesitate. But it's no secret. I slide it out.

"Planning your life to the minute?" Sophie asks.

With a shrug, I flick it open to the bookmark. Before I can find my tasks by week, she snags it and plops it into her own lap, wriggles the pen out of its holder on the cover, and fans the pages to a future date. In luxurious, beautiful cursive she writes,

"Journal Takeover. Special Guest: Jesus." And then she crosses out "Journal" and writes "Life." On random days, she adds tasks like "Be spontaneous—call Sophie for assistance" and "Prepare for a surprise." Then she dusts her hands like her work is done and hands it back without another word.

"You're like a fortune cookie," I whisper.

"Mm. Pad Thai," she murmurs.

I stare back at the words. Can't say *surprise* is a word I'd willingly write in my journal. Back to this week. My first monthly goal begging for a checkmark?

August Task: Join a Pre-Law or Speech & Debate Club

Closing my eyes, I pull air through my nose. This is only the beginning. I can't screw this up. Maybe I'll ask Sophie on the way out of here. If those clubs exist on campus, she'll have heard about them. It's just one task, and faithfulness starts now. I flick a glance at the ceiling.

Then my attention is pulled not to the stage but to Mav next to me, hunched over a ragged book with the cover folded around the back. Very Jess Mariano, but why does he think he's too good for chapel? I edge to read the title. *Crazy Love* by Francis Chan ... He's ignoring the chapel speaker for one of the most convicting books I've ever read?

His shoulders tense, enough to make me freeze mid-lean.

"Some space, please?" he snaps.

I glare. "Happily."

Good—another reason to avoid this guy. Like I needed any more.

AUTHOR'S NOTES

Sophie's and Austin's experiences with God stem from my own. I've hidden in shame. I've tried to earn love by performing—more employee than daughter. I've logged prayer and Bible hours while missing what he was practically shouting. I've also been lit up by Scripture, convinced God speaks there. I doubt I'm alone.

My prayer—for me and for you—is that we cannonball into Scripture like Sophie. The real people of the Bible come alive when we meet their stories with hope and hunger. They're relatable and cringey, audacious and bizarre—created, loved, chosen, wanted. Just like us. And when God's correction lands, may we—like Austin—hit our knees and change.

Below is an index of **every Scripture quoted or referenced in the story**. Unless noted, verses are from the New Living Translation (NLT); other versions are tagged (NIV). I only attribute "nudges" or words from God where I believe there's strong biblical precedent, and I've paired those moments with similar events in Scripture. First, the two passages that surface most often; then every reference, organized by chapter.

Sophie's favorite handiwork verse is found in chapters 23, 32, 34, 50, 52, 57, 67, and 68. Ephesians 2:10 (NIV)—"For we are

God's handiwork, created in Christ Jesus to do good works, which God prepared in advance for us to do."

God also whispers and sends a message through Sophie's friends that I need to hear constantly: "**He wants you close.**" (Chapters 12, 32, 43, 50, 56, 57) Here are some related verses:

- John 15:4–5—"Remain in me, and I will remain in you. For a branch cannot produce fruit if it is severed from the vine, and you cannot be fruitful unless you remain in me. Yes, I am the vine; you are the branches. Those who remain in me, and I in them, will produce much fruit. For apart from me you can do nothing."
- Psalm 73:28—"But as for me, how good it is to be near God! I have made the Sovereign Lord my shelter, and I will tell everyone about the wonderful things you do."
- Hebrews 10:22—"Let us go right into the presence of God with sincere hearts fully trusting him. For our guilty consciences have been sprinkled with Christ's blood to make us clean, and our bodies have been washed with pure water."
- Isaiah 40:11—"He will feed his flock like a shepherd. He will carry the lambs in his arms, holding them close to his heart. He will gently lead the mother sheep with their young."
- James 4:8—"Come close to God, and God will come close to you. Wash your hands, you sinners; purify your hearts, for your loyalty is divided between God and the world."

Chapter 14:

Mia refers to Paul's comments about singleness in 1 Corinthians 7.

Chapter 15:

"A whisper of a thought that isn't mine" is something I've experienced, but it also aligns with John 10:27—"My sheep listen to my voice; I know them, and they follow me."

Chapter 19:
Sophie references the book of Esther.

Chapter 21:
A nudge like "not him" was verbalized to Samuel in 1 Samuel 16:6–7—"When they arrived, Samuel took one look at Eliab and thought, 'Surely this is the Lord's anointed!' But the Lord said to Samuel, 'Don't judge by his appearance or height, for I have rejected him. The Lord doesn't see things the way you see them. People judge by outward appearance, but the Lord looks at the heart.'"

Chapter 24:
Matthew 7:11—"So if you sinful people know how to give good gifts to your children, how much more will your heavenly Father give good gifts to those who ask him?"

Chapter 29:
Philippians 1:9 (NIV)—"And this is my prayer: that your love may abound more and more in knowledge and depth of insight."

Chapter 32:
The idea of slowing down to talk to God is found here: Isaiah 30:15—"This is what the Sovereign Lord, the Holy One of Israel, says—'Only in returning to me and resting in me will you be saved. In quietness and confidence is your strength.' But you would have none of it."

Proverbs 3:5-6 (NIV)—"Trust in the Lord with all your heart and lean not on your own understanding; in all your ways submit to him, and he will make your paths straight."

Chapter 35:

Austin mentions Jesus resting and "disappointing people" because he was obeying his Father rather than the crowds: Mark 1:35–37—"Before daybreak the next morning, Jesus got up and went out to an isolated place to pray. Later Simon and the others went out to find him. When they found him, they said, 'Everyone is looking for you.'" Luke 5:15–16—"... Vast crowds came to hear [Jesus] preach and to be healed of their diseases. But Jesus often withdrew to the wilderness for prayer."

Chapter 39:

Proverbs 31:25—"She is clothed with strength and dignity, and she laughs without fear of the future."

Chapter 42:

Proverbs 31:25— "She is clothed with strength and dignity, and she laughs without fear of the future."

Austin's prayer for Sophie references Spirit-led messages for those around her. Here are related verses: 1 Corinthians 14:3, 29-31, Acts 13:1–3, Acts 21:10–11, 1 Thessalonians 5:19–21, Romans 12:6

Chapter 50:

Kit references Psalm 103:12—"He has removed our sins as far from us as the east is from the west."

Chapter 52:

Psalm 139:16—"You saw me before I was born. Every day of my life was recorded in your book. Every moment was laid out before a single day had passed."

Psalm 73:25—"Whom have I in heaven but you? I desire you more than anything on earth."

Proverbs 31:25— "She is clothed with strength and dignity, and she laughs without fear of the future."

Chapter 54:

The idea of God lovingly pulling us to honesty in his presence (Spoken "Look at it. Face it." in the story) is shown here: 2 Corinthians 7:10, Hebrews 4:13, James 5:16, Psalm 32:5.

Psalm 103:10-12—"He does not punish us for all our sins; he does not deal harshly with us, as we deserve. For his unfailing love toward those who fear him is as great as the height of the heavens above the earth. He has removed our sins as far from us as the east is from the west."

Chapter 57:

2 Corinthians 12:9 (NIV)—"But he said to me, 'My grace is sufficient for you, for my power is made perfect in weakness.' Therefore I will boast all the more gladly of my weaknesses, so that the power of Christ may rest upon me."

Chapter 62:

Matthew 6:9—"Pray like this: Our Father in heaven, may your name be kept holy."

Proverbs 19:20 (NIV)—"Listen to advice and accept discipline, and at the end you will be counted among the wise."

Chapter 63:

Psalm 51:12—"Restore to me the joy of your salvation, and make me willing to obey you."

Chapter 64:

Matthew 11:29 (NIV)—"Take my yoke upon you and learn from me, for I am gentle and humble in heart, and you will find rest for your souls."

Examples of Jesus going up on the mountain to pray: Luke 6:12, Matthew 14:23, Mark 1:35

Chapter 65:

Examples of Jesus going up on the mountain to pray: Luke 6:12, Matthew 14:23, Mark 1:35

Chapter 69:

Here is the Parable of the Prodigal Son passage, precedent for God treating repentant sinners as his very sons: Luke 15:20—"So he returned home to his father. And while he was still a long way off, his father saw him coming. Filled with love and compassion, he ran to his son, embraced him, and kissed him."

Luke 7:47 (NIV)—"Therefore, I tell you, her many sins have been forgiven—as her great love has shown. But whoever has been forgiven little loves little."

Chapter 70:

Matthew 7:11—"So if you sinful people know how to give good gifts to your children, how much more will your heavenly Father give good gifts to those who ask him?"

DISCUSSION QUESTIONS

1. Which scene hit you hardest? Which was the swooniest?
2. If Netflix called, which scene would you demand they keep? Casting advice?
3. Who surprised you most by the end? Did you see their growth coming, or did it sneak up on you?
4. What do Sophie's choices and inner thoughts reveal about the truths she was raised with? How does that compare to Austin's background—and your own?
5. The troll in Sophie's head grows loud. Have you ever dealt with an inner critic like that? What shuts it down—or fuels it?
6. Why do you think Sophie started dating Davis after the breakup? What do you think of the way she compared him to Austin?
7. Did you like Austin for Sophie? How did his qualities impact her relationship with God?
8. From Mia and Kit to Jenny and Izzy, what green flags do you see in Sophie's stronger friendships? What what was missing in the others?
9. Sophie and Austin crossed lines they'd set. Were their choices realistic? What makes boundaries stick in dating relationships?
10. What did you think of Austin's spiritual shift away from busyness? How did Sophie impact his decisions? How do you know if your life is too full?
11. What signs of depression did you notice in Sophie? Would you have caught them in a friend? How do you love someone well through a fog like that?
12. What consequences of her parents' divorce is Sophie still carrying? If you've been the child of divorce, how does that life experience impact one's identity as a child of God?
13. Which part of the story stuck with you in a way you didn't expect, and what does that show you about yourself?

ACKNOWLEDGMENTS

Jesus

You know I plead with you for guidance, for your perfect and intricate involvement in my writing ... and then I'm wildly confused by your interventions. I know it must be an answer to those prayers. Thank you for your care and patience. What a thrill that you allowed me to be part of this project. Thank you. May you be glorified in every sentence of this story and in every heart that reads it. Thank you for precisely the right people, events, and nudges in my life. I'm your daughter. Your handiwork. And I'm lost without you.

Brit

You're the blueprint—what it looks like when a guy's head-down, heart-in, locked in on Jesus first, and then one woman. Lucky me! Still pinching myself fourteen years later that I married someone so intent on making me happy, so in tune to my roller-coaster internal life. Your input as I read this story aloud to you was gold as ever. Utterly essential. Also, I love to join you at B-Dubs, on hikes, and around any campfire. But running? Don't let this story fool you. Still a hard no.

My kiddos

For all the hugs, questions, congratulations, and peeks at my illustrations. You're the most encouraging crew around. Right now I have an athlete, a ballerina, and a magnet tile extraordinaire, but whatever projects you take on, may they be with and for Jesus, every step of the way.

@reading_rosy and @lululobbesreads

I'm so thankful for your influence in the reading sphere. For encouraging us not to settle for what the world recommends but to seek out the excellent clean reads. And also, God used you to send so many readers my way. Thank you for giving my books a chance!

My ARC readers

You said yes before the book was even finished. Thank you for being early cheerleaders and faithful launchers. I don't take it lightly.

Mom

For being my "Lorelai Gilmore—level mom." The one who really listens, who always helped my friends too. What a wild difference those early voices make in our lives. Thank you for whispering beautifully encouraging things in my ear my whole life.

ABOUT THE AUTHOR

When Kristina Welch isn't adventuring around the world with her husband and three little blondies, she's home near Denver, Colorado. She thrives on date nights, forest hikes, and peanut butter cookies. Her days include half-homeschooling her kids, thrifting for treasures, regretting DIY home projects, and soaking in the beauty of the mountains—and their Creator—from her favorite writing spot.

Let's Stay Connected

Did this story make you smile, cry, or yell at a fictional character? I'd love to hear your thoughts! These are my imaginary friends, after all. Email and links below. Also, inspired by Bob Goff's bold move in *Love Does*, I'm putting my number in the back of my book: (720) 224-2648. Feel free to text me about the story or Jesus—my very favorite subject. Just mention the book in your first text.

Want more Sophie and Austin? Check out the Pinterest board and Spotify soundtrack I made for their story—perfect for all the feels after you finish the book. Find them on the Extras page of my website. And don't forget to subscribe to the newsletter on my website for freebies and updates on upcoming books. Links on the next page.

—Kristina

Website: kristinawelchauthor.com
Email: kristinawelchauthor@gmail.com

amazon.com/author/kristinawelch
goodreads.com/kristinawelchauthor
instagram.com/_kristinawelch
pinterest.com/kristinawelchauthor

www.ingramcontent.com/pod-product-compliance
Lightning Source LLC
Chambersburg PA
CBHW060758310726
48980CB00002B/146